THE
STONY
PATH

Rita Bradshaw

HEADLINE

First published in 2000
by HEADLINE BOOK PUBLISHING

10 9 8 7 6 5 4 3 2

British Library Cataloguing in Publication Data

Bradshaw, Rita
The stony path
1. Domestic fiction
I. Title
823.9'14 [F]

ISBN 0 7472 7370 7

Typeset by Palimpsest Book Production Limited,
Polmont, Stirlingshire
Printed and bound in Great Britain by
Mackays of Chatham PLC, Chatham, Kent

HEADLINE BOOK PUBLISHING
A division of Hodder Headline
338 Euston Road
LONDON NW1 3BH
www.headline.co.ut
www.hodderheadline.com

To my lovely family; we've trod our own share of stony paths, but always shoulder to shoulder and loving each other. You're all more precious than words can say, and I count myself the most fortunate wife and mother in the world.

What plan of life is this,
the stony path so oft times tread?
An endless path when youth is sweet
and nature's hand is beckoning.
A path of yearning and vain lament,
of heart demise and sorrow.
And yet my love walks the stony path
and I will see him . . . in my dreams.

Anon

Prologue

The July evening was mellow after the fierce heat of the day, and dying shafts of sunlight spangled the dusty floor of the old barn, slanting softly through the half-open door.

Outside the barn there was the occasional low mooing of cattle settling down for the night, and the odd squawk from indignant hens as the resident cock marshalled his harem into their crees.

Inside the wooden structure the only sound came from the sweet-smelling hayloft set far above the floor and reached by a ladder propped against the platform. The low murmur of voices was punctured by a gurgling laugh, followed by a girl's voice saying, 'I always feel so happy when we're together like this, Henry. In fact I think it's the only time I *am* truly happy. Do you know what I mean?'

'Of course I do. You know I feel the same, lass.'

'Then how can you even think of marryin' Hilda? She set her cap at you from way back, you know it, same as you know you only love me. You *can't* marry her, Henry.'

'Don't start that again.' Henry Farrow was of slender build, his finely boned body and delicate, almost pretty face giving the impression of someone much younger than his twenty years. In direct contrast, the girl lying beside him in the fragrant hay was hefty, her broad frame and voluptuous curves reminiscent of a full-blown Rembrandt beauty.

She propped herself on one elbow now, stroking the side of Henry's face as she said softly, her voice still holding an echo of laughter, 'I will start it, I have every right to. I love you; I won't give you up to that milksop who doesn't know her backside from her elbow. She will never make you happy.'

Henry stared up into the deep sea-green eyes looking down at him, and his voice reflected the turmoil within as he murmured, 'Happy doesn't come into it, lass. You know that. We've got to finish this, kill it stone dead, and if it means me being wed then so be it.'

'But you love *me*.' Eva tossed her mane of thick brown hair back from her shoulders as she continued looking down into his face. It

1

was beautiful, it was so beautiful. She couldn't remember a time when she hadn't thought how beautiful Henry was, or loved him. He was everything she would ever want in a man, in a husband.

Aye, he loved her. Henry felt his body harden as she stroked his face again, her fingers light and teasing. He had avoided being alone with Eva these last months since he'd asked for Hilda Craggs, knowing his weakness if she touched him, but still she had managed to waylay him several times and the result had always been the same. He burned for her, that was the trouble. She only had to look at him in a certain way, slanting those green eyes of hers, and his body responded. That was why he had thought marriage would dampen down the fire. And tomorrow was his wedding day, and likely even now his mam and da were on their way home from visiting Stone Farm, Hilda's home, where the jollifications for the morrow were to take place.

'Tell me you love me, Henry.' Her hand had moved to his unbuttoned shirt, and as her warm fingers began to wander over the slight dusting of body hair on his narrow chest, he felt his breath catch in his throat. 'Say it. I tell you often enough.'

She was right, she did. Right from a bairn it had been Eva, just a year older than him, who had played with him and mopped up his tears and taken care of him when his mam had been too busy with being a farmer's wife. He had been just fourteen when she had brought him up to this very spot and shown him how her love had ripened and diverted, and then, like now, he had been unable to resist the allure of her rounded curves and the utter abandonment with which she had given herself to him. The feeling she had for him was unconditional, and though she might consume him on occasion, wear him out with her constant need of him, he knew he felt the same. They were a pair. How often had she said that? But she was right.

Something of his thoughts must have shown in his face because now Eva lay fully beside him again, pressing her lips to his ear and throat in little burning kisses before she whispered, 'You can't marry anyone, Henry, you can't. I've got somethin' to tell you—'

And then her voice was cut off as he turned to her, covering her lips with his own as the desire she had been invoking rose hot and strong, and soon they were oblivious to anything but their need of each other . . .

It was their names being screamed that tore them apart as if by a giant hand; Henry to curl almost double as he attempted to hide the state of his dishevelment from the horrified gaze of the woman perched on the ladder against the platform, and Eva to kneel up in the hay, her hair tumbling about her shoulders as she fumbled with her gaping blouse.

'You . . . you . . .' That Alice Farrow couldn't believe what she was seeing was evident from her stunned face. One hand was pressed

2

against the starched white collar of her blue serge dress – her Sunday frock; she couldn't have them at Stone Farm thinking the Farrows were paupers, even if they only employed two men and a lad to Weatherburn's seven or eight men and inside help – whilst the other maintained a precarious hold on the ladder.

'Mam.' Henry gulped and spluttered as he straightened his clothing. 'I can explain, Mam. Listen to me for a minute.'

'*Listen* to you?' His mother's voice cracked and she wet her thin lips with her tongue before she said again, 'Listen to you, you say? Do you know what you were about? But of course you do, aye, an' that's the truth! An' with your own sister! Listen to him, he says! It's Sodom an' Gomorrah on me own doorstep!'

The force of the last invective almost caused the ladder to fall as Alice's body twisted in her anguish and was only saved by Henry's dive at it. He held it fast as he said, 'Mam, please, I'm askin' you to listen a minute.'

'I've no need to listen.' Alice scrambled into the hayloft, there to confront her daughter, who was now standing and endeavouring to smooth her tangled hair. 'I blame you for this, girl. Aye, I do. You're dirty through an' through an' you've bin that way since the day you was born.'

'You'd like to think that, Mam, wouldn't you?' Eva had regained something of her composure now the initial shock of being discovered had faded a little, and as she faced her mother the angry colour was hot in her cheeks. 'Right from a wee babby you've never had any time for me, have you, an' you've let me know it. The only person who's ever loved me is Henry.'

'That's not love.'

'Oh aye, it is, an' you can't bear it! You've made sure me da's never liked me but you couldn't turn Henry agen me an' that's always stuck in your craw. Well he's not marryin' that dried-up stick tomorrow, he's not. I won't let him!'

Eva's face was dark with resentment and hatred, and like two combatants the women faced each other; Alice's small wiry frame bristling with self-righteous fury and her daughter's big stocky body straining against the rough material of her working clothes.

When her mother's hand caught Eva full across the face it was not a surprise. Alice had often boxed Eva's ears from as far back as her daughter could remember and Eva hadn't been expecting anything less, but what did surprise her was her own response to the blow. She seemed to hover over the smaller woman like an enraged giantess and then her hands shot out in a violent push which sent her mother hurtling backwards to land with a thud against the far wall of the hayloft.

She wasn't aware her father had entered the fray until she heard Henry shout, 'No, Da, no!' and then she felt as though her hair was

3

being torn out by its roots as she was pulled backwards with enough force to take her off her feet.

'Get down there, the pair of you.' Her father had left Eva sprawled in the hay as he went to help his wife, and now his big face was crimson as he raised Alice's thin shoulders under one mighty forearm before turning to his children and growling again, 'Into the house if you know what's good for you.'

'Henry? Oh, Henry.'

When Eva reached the bottom of the ladder she swayed for a moment, her eyes fastening on a collection of old farm implements in the far corner of the barn, and then her brother, who had followed her down the ladder, took her arm, saying roughly, 'You knocked her out. What on earth were you thinkin' of to push Mam like that?'

'Me?' It stung Eva into life, a touch of her old defiance returning as she said, 'I'm sick of her skelpin' me, that's why,' but by the time she had followed Henry out of the barn, past the row of cow byres and the stable and into the yard, she was shaking with fear at what was in store.

The farmhouse was small but clean – a large scrubbing brush and hard bar of carbolic soap saw to that, along with the scouring of the stone slabs on the floor once a week when the range was blackleaded and the brass fender polished to gold – but now, as Eva came to a halt in the kitchen, she gazed round the familiar surroundings almost vacantly.

A couple of hours ago she had stood in this room, after watching her mam and da depart in the horse and cart for Stone Farm, and she'd known exactly what she was going to do. She would tell Henry he had to call off the wedding. She'd told him the same thing several times a day without fail for the last five months, since her brother had asked Hilda Craggs to marry him, but this evening he was going to be informed of a certain fact which made it imperative he didn't get wed.

Eva walked further into the kitchen, her feet dragging, before she sank down on to a hardbacked chair in front of the table covered with an oilcloth on which were piled several soot-smeared pans and a heap of dirty dishes. Her mother had left these for her daughter's attention before she'd gone to visit the prospective in-laws.

A fire was burning in the hearth despite the warmth of the muggy summer night, and a massive black kale-pot containing the family's supper of thick rabbit stew was hanging from a chain joined to a cross-bar below the chimney opening. The smell rose up in Eva's nostrils and she swallowed hard, her stomach heaving as she told herself she couldn't be sick. Not now. Not right now.

'He'll kill me. When Mam tells him he'll kill me.'

Henry voiced what Eva was thinking, and she brought her eyes to

4

the slight, thin figure of her brother standing in front of the fire and to one side of the range oven. 'He won't.' It carried a shred of bitterness. 'It'll be me that gets it. The sun shines out of your backside with the pair of 'em an' you know it.'

She wanted to ask him if he was going to stand with her in this; brave the wrath of their parents and maintain a united front, but she didn't dare. She was too frightened of the answer or the look on his face when he lied to her.

And then her father burst into the room, his face demented, and all hell broke loose.

'By all that's holy, Walter, you could have killed her.' Alice's thin face was even more pinched than normal, her voice nothing but a whisper.

'You given her the laudanum?'

'Aye, I've given her it, but she's in a state, Walter. She is that.'

'She'll survive; the devil looks after his own.' It was savage.

'She needs a doctor—'

'Don't talk daft, woman. You get a doctor to her an' what's the result? Our business spread across half of Sunderland. She's a slut, you know it an' I know it, but are you tellin' me you want it spread abroad, eh? Put plenty of goose fat on her an' she'll do.'

'The buckle's marked her—' Alice's voice was cut off abruptly as her husband slammed his fist down on the kitchen table with enough force to make the pots and pans jump.

'She's to be kept away from him until he's wed an' off on the fancy honeymoon Hilda's brother's paid for, you understand me? She's no bit lass, not Eva, an' you know it. By . . .' Walter ground his teeth, his jaw working fiercely. 'When I think about it me guts turn to water.'

'I know, I know.' Alice stared at her husband's bent head for a moment or two, before reaching for the big brown teapot and measuring two spoonfuls of tea from the caddy into its cavernous depths. After lifting the kettle from the hob she filled the teapot to half full, mashing the tea and letting it draw a minute or two before she said tentatively, 'Shall . . . shall I take him a sup?'

'What?'

'Henry. Shall I take him a sup the night?'

Walter's head had been bent over the kitchen table but now he raised it slowly, looking into his wife's eyes as he said, 'Aye. Aye, take him a sup, lass.'

Alice motioned with her head but she didn't speak again before leaving the room with a big mug of black tea, and Walter continued staring after his wife as the sound of her footsteps echoed on the bare wooden stairs leading to the upper storey of the house. He heard the door to Henry's bedroom open and close, and when his

5

wife's tread didn't sound again assumed she had remained with their son.

By, this was beyond his understanding. He dragged his hand across his face, which was still sweating as a result of the beating he had given Eva. His own flesh and blood behaving worse than any harlot. Even the worst of the whores down on the dock sides in the East End and Monkwearmouth kept it out of their own backyards. And it was her, not him. Oh aye, it was Eva all right, he was with Alice on this. She was bad right through, tainted.

Walter reached out for his own mug, which Alice had passed to him before she'd poured Henry's tea, but as he raised it to his lips the nausea he'd experienced in the barn when Alice had come round sufficiently to acquaint him with the full facts overcame him again, and he put it down without tasting it.

And him up there getting wed the morrow! On this thought he turned from the table and rose, walking to the kitchen door, which was open. Outside, he stood looking up into the darkening sky, and as if in answer to something which had just been voiced he reiterated out loud, 'Aye, it's that trollop all right. Look at 'em; she's twice the size he is an' as brazen as they come, the lad wouldn't have stood a chance.'

Well, she'd remain where she was, bound and gagged like the dangerous animal she'd shown herself to be, until the lad was safely away. Henry had to marry Hilda. Walter flexed his great hands, letting his chin fall into his neck before he again raised his head to the charcoal sky, in which the first stars were beginning to appear. It was a good match, a marvellous match – his lad marrying Weatherburn's stepsister. The Weatherburn farm's fields adjoined theirs, and the farm was doing well – more than well – unlike theirs. Blood was thicker than water in these situations, and an ally like Weatherburn wasn't to be sneezed at.

Walter turned abruptly, stepping back into the dark kitchen now lit only by the glow of the fire, and walking across to the heavy stone mantelpiece running the length of the range. He reached for the clay pipe lying at one end and, picking out a thin coil of tobacco from a small earthenware jar next to where the pipe had been, retraced his footsteps outside.

Why had he only had one son and him as slight and small as his mother, whereas his daughter took after the Farrow side? The thought of Eva brought Walter's blackened teeth grinding together, and he walked across to a roughly made bench set against the wall of the farmhouse and sat down, working the twist of tobacco between his fingers until it was sufficiently shredded to fill the pipe.

Once he was puffing he rose again, walking across the yard and out in the opposite direction to the cow byres. Five minutes brought him to the crest of a slight hill, beyond which stretched sheer blackness, but as though he could see the Weatherburn farm – situated east of South Farrington with its fields adjoining Silksworth – and on beyond into the expanding suburbs of the rapidly growing town of Bishopswearmouth, his eyes continued to roam back and forth.

How often had he complained about the four-mile drive into the heart of Sunderland? he asked himself. Plenty, especially when the weather was bad and the horse and cart got bogged down in snow drifts that had him digging out the wheels every ten yards or so. But he was thankful for it now, by, he was that. In the villages and the towns you only had to sneeze for it to be common knowledge. The chill inside him deepened. He'd kill Eva, aye, with his bare hands before he'd let a word of this lot get out. They might not have two farthings to rub together but he'd always been able to hold his head high; he'd be damned if the Farrow name would be brought low by his own kith and kin.

Henry would do what he was told. The certainty of his son's malleability brought Walter no joy, only the nagging sense of irritation he always felt when he thought of his younger child. And then he shrugged the feeling off with a physical movement of his massive shoulders. He needed Henry and his new wife living and working on the farm; pray God Hilda was fruitful and would give him a quiver of grandsons to bring fresh life to the place. Big, robust grandsons, lads who would turn the ailing fortunes of the Farrows around and continue the blood line.

He turned slowly, pulling his cap further on his head as he began to retrace his steps to the farmhouse below. Another month or two and he was going to have to face letting old Amos and his son go, possibly Wilf too, after hay-making. Their four shillings a week wages along with their perks and their cottages wasn't much compared to what Weatherburn paid his men, but nevertheless he couldn't stretch to it. But how was he going to manage without them? By, he didn't know which way to turn, and that without this latest trouble his slut of a daughter had brought upon him. He'd wring her neck for her . . .

'It's done then.' It was the evening of the following day and Henry was married. Alice and Walter hadn't spoken a word during the ten-minute drive home from Stone Farm in the horse and cart, but once in the yard and before she climbed down from her seat Alice had turned to her husband and voiced what was in both their minds.

'Aye, as you say, it's done.' Walter could see Amos in the far field through the rapidly deepening twilight, and his voice was preoccupied when he said, 'I'd better go an' check they've done all I wanted afore they turn in. I'll send the lad' – Walter always referred to Amos's youngest son as the lad despite the fact he was eighteen years of age and did a man's work – 'to see to Bess an' the cart. You go in, lass.'

Alice clambered down from the cart mindful of her Sunday frock, and stood watching the tall, broad figure of her husband as he walked briskly out of the farmyard to the lane beyond. She continued to watch him as he opened the large wooden gate set in the dry-stone wall bordering the field, and, after fastening it again, walk across the field through the herd of grazing bovines to the approaching Amos.

You go in, lass. What Walter had really meant was for her to go in and see to Eva. The thought brought her brow into a frown. He'd made it very clear over the last twenty-four hours that their daughter was her responsibility, emphasising that nothing must be done or said to upset Henry's new wife when the couple returned from their few days at the Grand Hotel in Bishopswearmouth. Which was all very well, but he knew Eva's strength of will and blind stubbornness – he should do, she got it from him.

Alice shut her eyes, screwing them tight as though in pain, and when she opened them again her mouth had set into a hard line and she didn't look towards her husband and his farm hand but turned and entered the kitchen.

The fire was all but dead in the range. Alice glanced at the faintly glowing embers, which was all that remained of the fire she had so carefully banked early that morning with slack and damp tea leaves. She'd better get that going before she did anything else; Walter would want his sup of tea and shive of lardy cake before he went to bed. He was a great one for his supper, was Walter.

She drew her stiff hessian apron off the peg behind the kitchen door, well aware that she should go and change her dress before she touched the fire. The shadow of what she had to face when she climbed those stairs had been with her all day, clouding the wedding service at the parish church in Silksworth and the jollifications at Stone Farm afterwards, and even now she was putting off the moment.

She placed some kindling on the embers and blew it with the bellows until the fire sparked and sent flickering flames licking at the tinder-dry scraps of wood, muttering the while, 'She won't keep her mouth shut when the other un's here, not Eva, an' then there'll be murder done. Aye, there will right enough. Murder.'

When the fire was blazing and the kettle was on the hob Alice forced herself to leave the kitchen, lighting the oil lamp before she left and placing it in the middle of the scrubbed table, and taking a tallow candle to guide her way upstairs.

She walked first into the room she had shared with Walter for the last twenty-two years, placing the tin candlestick holder in the small grate the room contained and then quickly stripping off her Sunday frock and small straw bonnet, which she placed on top of the chest of drawers the room contained. This item of furniture, along with a small double bed with a straw mattress and an ancient narrow wardrobe, made up the entire contents of the room, and the floorboards were bare, without even a clippy mat for cold winter mornings. Not that she minded about bare floors; it had been the straw-filled mattresses and pillows at the farm which had caused her several sleepless nights when she'd first come here, Alice reflected, pulling on her coarse print dress and the calico apron before slipping her feet into her working clogs. Even at the workhouse where she'd lived the first fourteen years of her life, before coming to work for Walter's ailing mother, they'd had flock mattresses. It had taken her weeks to get used to the straw piercing her face and pricking her body through her calico nightdress.

They would have flock-filled mattresses at Stone Farm, she'd be bound; Hilda was going to have to get used to plenty once the newly-weds were back, same as Alice herself had when she'd first come here. She nodded to the thought, not without some satisfaction. She didn't like her son's new wife and the airs and graces Hilda adopted.

Stone Farm might be a grand place compared to this, but when all was said and done, Hilda had no real claim to it. Her stepbrother's mother had died in childbirth with Frederick, her first child, and when Frederick Weatherburn's father had married Hilda's mother, some eight years later, the woman had been a widow and Hilda a little lassie of three or thereabouts. So Hilda was barely related to Frederick in truth.

Alice found this thought comforting and it was not the first time she had dwelt on it, but now, as she heard her husband in the kitchen below, she was galvanised into action.

Eva's small room was the last of the three bedrooms the farmstead boasted, and like her parents' and brother's rooms was devoid of comfort and merely provided a narrow iron bed with a straw mattress, and a row of pegs on one wall for her clothes.

Alice opened the door quickly and stepped inside, shutting it behind her and walking over to the bed, which was set under the window and directly facing the door. She felt very tired and had a sick sensation in the pit of her stomach, but it was less to do with the rich food the wedding feast had provided than the catastrophe her children had brought upon them all.

There was a feeling of revulsion in her as she stared down at the dim shape of her daughter on the bed, but it was threaded through with a certain amount of reluctant pity. Walter had all but ripped the clothes from Eva's back when she had fought him, but big as her daughter was, Walter was bigger. By the time Eva had reached the end of herself and her clothes were hanging in strips, her father had still possessed the strength to use his belt on her. He would have killed her if she and Henry hadn't finally managed to drag him away. Alice ran the back of her hand over her dry lips. Numerous times they'd tried but Walter had shaken them off like an enraged bull and gone back to the squirming figure on the floor.

The memory mellowed Alice's voice as she said, 'You awake, lass?' It was probably the softest tone she had ever used to her daughter, but then, as she lowered the flickering candle to the trussed form on the bed and the small flame illuminated the enmity blazing forth from the green eyes, it surprised her into taking a hasty step backwards.

Alice's face was a touch paler and the hand holding the candle was trembling when she again stepped close to the bed, but her voice carried its old strident note when she said, 'Don't you dare look at me like that, girl, not after what you've done. You should be cryin' an' beggin' the Almighty to forgive you – aye, an' your da an' me an' all. When I think of the shame of it, an' to entice Henry to fall so low! Wicked you are, wicked.' She stared at Eva and the green eyes stared back at her above the gag Walter had ordered must remain in place while they were out, and then Alice emphasised her words again as she repeated, 'Wicked, through an' through.'

But bad as she was, Eva was still a human being; they couldn't keep her tied up like this forever. She'd been twenty-four hours now without food or drink, and those weals on her back and legs needed more goose fat.

Alice put the candle holder on the floor by the bed, saying as she did so, her voice deep and flat, 'I'm goin' to take the gag off, an' if you know what's good for you you'll keep quiet, girl. Your da's downstairs an' he'll not take any nonsense, you understand me?'

Eva's hair was caught in the strip of cloth Alice had tied so hastily that morning. Her daughter had been dozy from the excessive dose of laudanum Alice had forced down her minutes before, but even so Eva had wrestled against Walter's grip as he'd held her down for Alice to reapply the gag, and it had been an uphill struggle to get it in place.

As soon as her mouth was free, Eva's voice came in a croak, saying, 'He's married?'

Not a word of remorse. Henry, it was always Henry. Alice straightened, her voice rising again as she cried, 'Aye, he is, all legal an' proper like, so that's that an' there's nothin' you can do about it, girl. An' this marriage was Henry's idea, don't forget that. Biggest gliff of me life I got the day he told us he was walkin' out with Hilda Craggs, Weatherburn's stepsister, an' her as plain as a pikestaff an' with a tongue on her an' all. We might not sit at a fancy table of an evenin' an' have a cook an' kitchen maid to wait on us, but to my mind Henry could've done better than Hilda Craggs.'

Alice's voice had lowered on the last words; Walter had a pair of cuddy-lugs that could hear the grass grow, and she knew he'd hear no word against the match. The farm was all that mattered to him, it always had been, and he was looking at Frederick Weatherburn's stepsister as a means to an end.

'I'm havin' a bairn, Mam.'

Alice had been about to tackle the ropes biting into her daughter's wrists and ankles, but now she froze, one hand going to her throat and the other clutching the material of the apron at her waist, and her voice was a whimper when she murmured, 'No, please God, no. No, Eva. Tell me you're lyin'.'

'I'm not lyin'.'

It was the underlying note of fear beneath the flatness which convinced Alice her daughter was indeed speaking the truth. Her mouth opened and shut twice before she was able to say, 'Does . . . does he know? Henry?'

'No.' Eva shut her eyes tightly, and when she opened them again Alice saw – for the first time in everything which had happened, including the beating her father had inflicted – tears glistening in the green eyes. 'I was goin' to tell him when you found us, but . . . but I didn't think he'd go through with it anyway – marryin' her – not when it came down to it.'

'How far gone are you?'

'Not far. Two months.'

There was silence in the room for some seconds, and then, as Alice bent and began to slowly work at the knots in the rope at her daughter's wrists, she said, 'He'll kill you. You know that, don't you? He'll kill you, girl.' And Eva didn't need to be told to whom her mother was referring.

Walter did not kill his daughter, but once Eva had washed herself in the tin bath in the scullery that, together with the dairy on one side and the kitchen on the other, made up the sum total of the downstairs of the farmhouse, he told his wife to take the girl to her room. He didn't look at Eva as he spoke, neither did he acknowledge her presence, but once Alice had smoothed more goose fat on her daughter's seared flesh and settled Eva in the remade bed with a glass of milk and a thick chunk of bread and dripping, Walter came to the threshold of the bedroom.

Eva stopped eating the moment he appeared, and although there was no trace of the cocksure daughter he knew in the quiet, white-faced girl who stared at him, her father noticed that the green gaze was steady and burning with some dark emotion. Well, that was all right, likely she'd need a remnant of her old spirit if what he had in mind came to pass. The thought was totally devoid of pity. 'Your mam's told you you stay put until I've made up me mind what's to happen?'

Eva nodded once.

11

'See you do, else you'll be out of here in just the clothes you stand up in an' it'll be the workhouse. Do I make meself plain?'

Again the brown head nodded, but Walter noticed with some satisfaction that the white face had turned a shade paler. Alice had fed the bairns stories about her beginnings along with her milk, and both his son and his daughter had a healthy fear of the hell on earth that was the workhouse.

'Da—'

Eva's tentative voice came to an abrupt halt as Walter held up his hand, his palm towards her. 'I'm not about to soil meself by havin' a conversation with you.' There was a moment of utter silence. 'You're nowt to me, dead an' buried like the muck from the privy, but I care about me good name an' you'll not take that down with you while I've breath in me body.'

When the door was shut it was closed softly, which terrified the girl in the bed more than any show of temper could have done.

Eva sat hunched awkwardly on the old straw mattress, the blue and red weals and wounds inflicted by Walter's buckled leather belt causing her whole body to feel as though it was on fire, but it was fear of what had been evident in her father's face which was making her breath come in short, painful gasps. He meant to do for her. She stared across the room, the grotesque shadows from the flickering candle providing no comfort. Her mam wouldn't let him do that, would she? Not in cold blood?

Suddenly she wasn't hungry any more, and after finishing the milk she slowly placed the tin plate holding the bread and dripping on the floor and blew out the candle, sliding carefully under the thin grey blankets. Cautious though her movements were, they were enough to crack the worst of the congealed lesions criss-crossing her back, buttocks and legs, and she groaned out loud, holding herself stiff for a few minutes as her heart pumped like a piston and red-hot pokers prodded her body.

Henry was married, *married*. She stared wide-eyed into the darkness as the tears rained down her face. And he had left her at the mercy of their da, knowing what he could be like. All her dreams of living and working on the farm with Henry until her mam and da were gone, and the two of them were alone, were over. Henry had killed them at the altar that morning. Why couldn't she hate him? She wanted to, so why couldn't she? And what did the future hold for her now?

Eva found out what the future held two days later.

She had stayed in her room the whole time except for a visit to the privvy once it was dark to empty the pot under her bed, when she had taken the opportunity to sluice her head under the pump in the yard. The ends of her hair had been thick with the fat her mother had

12

smeared over her back, and she had rubbed at them with a piece of the coarse hard soap from the scullery over and over again until they were clean.

The next morning she had stayed put as she'd been told, but after her mother had brought her a shive of bread and butter and a mug of hot tea, Eva had refused the offer of more goose fat on her wounds. Once she was alone again, and after eating her breakfast, she had eased off her calico nightdress, grimacing silently when the material stuck to dried blood in places.

Pulling on her flannel drawers, shift, dress and coarse white apron had been a painful and slow affair, but she had felt better once she was dressed. She had spent over an hour working the tangles out of her long thick hair, but in concentrating on her toilet she found she was able to keep her thoughts from the pictures that had been torturing her mind since the night of Henry's wedding day. Mental images of Henry and Hilda. Intimate, earthy depictions that made her want to shout and scream and do herself harm. But she couldn't do that, she mustn't, because if she succumbed to what she was feeling her father would make sure all avenues to Henry were cut off, either by the workhouse or a mental asylum. That he was quite capable of incarcerating her in either place she had no doubt.

The long, hot day crept by with all the normal farm sounds outside her window, but inside her room Eva waited. She had seen her father drive off in the horse and cart mid-morning, and she felt in her bones that the business he was about concerned her.

Her mother brought her a bowl of bacon broth and a wedge of stottie cake at noon, expressing no surprise at seeing her daughter dressed, and remaining mute and tight-lipped as she left the room again without a word.

Eva forced herself to eat the broth, spooning the lentils, carrots, turnips, onions, potatoes and other vegetables into her mouth and swallowing them quickly before the ever-present nausea she was feeling overcame her. The two small dumplings she left in the bowl. The stottie cake was easier to get down; her mother always cooked the bread until it was firm and lightly brown, and its distinctive texture suited her queasy stomach.

The meal eaten, Eva resumed her waiting. It was just as the evening sun reached the far wall of her bedroom, mellowing the old lime mortar and stone with its golden touch, that she heard the steady clip-clop of Bess's hooves.

She didn't go to the window but she heard her father calling for Dick, Amos's son, to see to the horse and cart, and then the sound of her mother's voice from the direction of the hen crees, where she must have been gathering eggs. Eva had risen from her sitting position on the side of the narrow iron bed, and she continued standing for some minutes before she realised her father wasn't coming straight up. Her straining ears caught the low murmur of voices from the kitchen below, but she couldn't distinguish individual words. She had no sooner sunk down on the bed again when footsteps heralded her father's approach.

Eva was staring fixedly at the door when Walter entered the room without knocking, and she was again standing, her hands tight fists at her side as she fought for composure.

'It's sorted.' Walter's keen blue eyes took in Eva's stance and also the fact that she was dressed and apparently suffering little effect from the thrashing he'd given her. 'You'll be wed within the month.'

'Wed?' The fear she had been experiencing was swallowed by sheer amazement; whatever she'd expected, it wasn't this.

'Aye, wed.' Walter shut the door behind him and came fully into the room, standing a couple of feet away from his daughter as he whispered harshly, 'I've bin into the town to see someone, a bloke I heard about last market day. Appears his wife died an' left him with two young uns. Accordin' to his sister-in-law, a customer of mine, he was lookin' for someone to cook an' clean an' mind the bairns when he's down the pit, but no one would work for the pittance he could pay.'

'A pit yakker?' It was a faint whisper, and then, as her voice came stronger, saying, '*A pit yakker?*' her father took a threatening step towards her, causing Eva to stumble backwards and sit down suddenly on the bed.

'Aye, he's a miner all right, an' to my mind Nathaniel Blackett is too decent a man to be dealt scum like you, but needs must.'

'But a miner livin' in the town . . . I can't, I can't live in the town, Da, you know I can't. I'm like you, you know how I feel about bein' outside; times you've said I do a man's job in the fields—'

In her distress Eva had reached up to implore, and now she felt her hand smacked down with enough force to make her cry out in pain. Then Walter was bending down, his angry red face close to hers as he grated, 'You've a choice, the workhouse or Nathaniel Blackett.'

'Does . . . does he know?'

'He knows you're expectin' a bairn an' I've told him you were taken advantage of by a travellin' man, an' that's the story you keep to whatever road you choose. He's prepared to wed you quick an' say the child's his when it comes early so you keep your good name.'

Her good name! Eva stared into the blazing blue eyes, and she knew that if it were possible for her da to strike her dead at this moment and have done with her, he would have done so. All he was bothered about was what people would say if word got out she'd been taken down. He was leaving her with no choice, no choice at all, and they both knew it.

'What if he doesn't like me?'

It was said with a touch of her old defiance, and Walter's hand rose swiftly before he checked himself, breathing deeply as he glared at this young woman who, up until three days ago, he had always secretly considered was more like him than his son. 'You'd better make sure he does.' It was soft but deadly. 'Because I tell you one thing, girl: your life won't be worth a farthin' candle in the workhouse, an' you'll be in for a fourteen-year stretch until that' – he pointed at her belly – 'is old enough to keep itself.'

Eva married Nathaniel Blackett on an excessively hot day at the end of July. None of her family was present, and the only witnesses were Nathaniel's brother Eustace and his wife, Delia. The bride had met the groom twice before the wedding day, and on each occasion Eva's parents and the priest who was going to marry the couple – Nathaniel being of the Catholic faith – were present. This same priest had been given to understand Eva was expecting Nathaniel's child; a fact which did not concern him nearly as much as her converting to the one true faith, which Eva, heartsore and ill from the effects of the pregnancy and the savage beating she had endured, listlessly agreed to. She had no interest in religion one way or the other anyway.

Henry and Hilda, on their return from honeymoon, had been told only that Eva was getting married, and Henry, guilty and ashamed at the immense relief he felt that his sister would not be living in close proximity to his wife, asked no questions. He assumed Eva found their changed circumstances too painful to submit to, and Eva – mindful that the family home would ever be barred to her if she spoke the truth – did not disabuse him of the idea.

So it was that Eva found herself leaving St Mary's in Bridge Street, situated at the hub of the thriving town of Bishopswearmouth, on the arm of the stranger who was now her husband.

They had been married late on the Saturday afternoon – Nathaniel hadn't finished his shift at the Wearmouth Colliery until well after midday – and as they left the relative quiet of the church and stepped into the hot, busy street to begin walking towards Wearmouth Bridge, Eva blinked her distress at the noise and press of human bodies. She had rarely come into the town with her father – Henry or one of the farm hands had always accompanied him on market days – but the once or twice she had ventured away from the farm she hadn't been able to wait to get home, and now she felt as though she was being smothered alive.

Sunderland's huge population growth in the last seventy years and booming prosperity depended heavily upon the Wear, although as a harbour the river had disadvantages: it was uncomfortably narrow, shallow and exposed to north-easterly gales, with a difficult entry for sailing vessels. Nevertheless, thanks to the thriving coal trade, it was invariably crowded with shipping.

The river also lay at the heart of Sunderland's industry. Factories and workshops, roperies, glassworks, potteries, lime kilns, ironworks and, above all, shipyards clustered along its banks, competing with coal staiths, quays and warehouses. The noise and clatter and smoky pall was oppressive even to those who were used to it, and as the party of four reached the bridge and Eva gazed about her, the urge to start to run and keep running was so strong she had to bite her lip against it.

'You all right, lass?'

It was a moment before Eva replied to the small, wiry man in whose arm she had her hand, and then her voice was stiff when she said, 'I'm perfectly well, thank you.'

Her chalk-white face and bloodless lips belied her words, but after a swift glance at his brother and sister-in-law walking just in front of them, Nathaniel said no more. It was to be expected the lass was terrified out of her wits, and but for her condition he would have been only too pleased to give her more time to get used to him before they were wed. Mind, it was only that very thing that had put her across his path in the first place. In spite of her bulk, she seemed to him like a frightened young bairn that needed careful handling, and he wasn't averse to going slow. From the little her da had said, she'd obviously been took down against her will, and that was enough for any bit lass to come to terms with without her belly being full as a result of it. Aye, he'd go slow all right; he was no sackless lad still wet behind the ears.

Once they had crossed over the bridge into Monkwearmouth, passing the great cranes on the banks either side, they continued walking along North Bridge Street past the saw mills and then Monkwearmouth Station and the goods yard on their left, before turning left before the smithy and continuing into Southwick Road.

Coal dominated the western part of Monkwearmouth, and the Wearmouth Colliery in Southwick Road provided a livelihood for hundreds of Sunderland's working men. The company had raised a gridwork pattern of dwelling places for its miners, stretching north from Southwick Road, and now, as Eva entered the narrow, mean streets of terraced houses, the desire for flight rose hot and strong again.

She couldn't bear this, she couldn't. She breathed deeply, the soulless uniformity of the cobbled streets claustrophobic after the wide-open spaces she'd grown up with.

'Well, we'll be gettin' along, man.' Nathaniel's brother and his wife had turned on the narrow pavement to face them, their eyes studiously avoiding Eva's white face and stiff body.

'You'll not come in for a bite of somethin'?'

Although Nathaniel made the offer, it was with a marked lack of enthusiasm, and now it was Delia who said, 'We'd best get back, Nat,' before turning to Eva and placing a tentative hand on her arm as she added, 'I'll nip round the morrow, lass, an' see how you're doin'. Likely it'll all be a bit strange, you bein' a country lass an' all.'

There was no criticism implied, but it was a moment or two before Eva replied, and then her voice was cold when she said, 'I'm sure I'll be all right, thank you.' She had been half listening to a group of dirty-nosed barefoot urchins skipping in the road with a piece of old rope whilst the others had been talking, and the macabre rhyme the raggedy guttersnipes had been singing, drawn from the execution of the murderess Mary Ann Cotton in Durham Jail a few years back, had somehow seemed indicative of both her surroundings and her circumstances.

> 'Mary Ann Cotton
> She's dead and forgotten
> She lies in a grave
> With her bones all rotten
> Sing, sing, oh, what can I sing?
> Mary Ann Cotton is tied up wi' string.
> Where, where? Up in the air
> Sellin' black puddens a penny a pair.'

'Aye, aye, I'm sure an' all, lass.' It was hasty and embarrassed, and as Eva turned towards the children again the other three made their goodbyes quickly, before Nathaniel's brother and his wife crossed Southwick Road and turned into Pilgrim Street.

'She was only tryin' to be friendly; she didn't mean anythin' by it.'

'What?'

As Nathaniel spoke Eva turned to him, her gaze wide and vacant, and he stared at her for a few seconds before he said, 'Nothin'. Nothin', lass.' He rubbed at his coal-dinted nose, clearly out of his depth, before saying, 'You'd best come in an' take the weight off. Likely you could do with a sup o' tea, eh?'

She continued to stare at him as he opened the door of the house against which they were standing, the rear of which overlooked the sidings of the Wearmouth Colliery, but she said nothing as she stepped into the dwelling which was now her home.

It was later that night, and only after Nathaniel was snoring gently at the side of her in the big brass bed, that Eva let herself think. It could not possibly be just six hours since she had come into this house. It seemed like six days, six weeks, six months . . . Her body was stiff, every muscle straining in its effort to be still, and the unaccustomed softness of the flock mattress was too alien to be comforting.

Nathaniel had surprised her. Her eyes were wide and staring as she gazed into the darkness. She had expected him to take what was his right but he had made it plain, before the neighbour who had been looking after his boys had arrived on the doorstep, that he wouldn't touch her until after the bairn was born. Her large, full-lipped mouth twisted. He had made up his mind she was a bit lass, that was it, and as it suited her to let him think along those lines she'd go along with that for the time being. She had enough to put up with without him mauling her about.

Nathaniel's consideration brought no shred of tenderness into her thinking, only contempt for what Eva saw as his lack of gumption in asserting himself.

The hot summer night was stifling and the stench from the privies in the backyards drifted in through the partly open window, causing Eva to wrinkle her nose and swallow hard. The man at the side of her stirred slightly, grunting once or twice before he resumed his periodic snoring, and as she pictured the small, skinny body topped by wiry, dirty-coloured hair and indeterminate features, a wave of bitterness engulfed her.

This place and him, and his brats too. It wasn't to be borne, it wasn't, but what could she do? Nowt. Bad as this was, it was better than the workhouse. She breathed in and out very slowly as her heartbeat pounded in her ears. But that was all you could say for it. And her mam had said she was lucky. Lucky!

'What about if you'd bin promised to one of the Silksworth miners, eh, or Whitburn or Ryhope?' Alice had railed at her the day before. 'The hovels some of them poor devils live in aren't fit for pigs. There's no yards or washhouses or coalhouses or drains, an' the middens are shared by ten or more families with one tap atween 'em. Two rooms, an' the floors seepin' filth an' the smell enough to knock you backwards, an' here's you, goin' to have a two-up, two-down an' your own privy. You don't know you're born, girl, that's your trouble. You ought to be down on your knees thankin' God for your luck in landin' Nathaniel Blackett. Aye, you should that.'

Well, she knew who she had to thank for her present circumstances all right, and she'd see her day with her mam and da if it was the last thing she did. Eva's green eyes narrowed in the blackness and they were alive with hate. But she had to go careful if she still wanted to see Henry, and she had to see him. She *had* to. He was part of her, wound into her innermost being like parts of her own body. She would die if she couldn't at least see him.

She could have prevented him marrying that scrawny scarecrow if her mam and da had let them alone. She inclined her head to the thought, her face grim. If she'd been able to tell him about the bairn he'd have stood by her; why else would she have made sure she fell? She knew her Henry. She wouldn't have named anyone and likely her da would have gone mad, but he wouldn't have thrown her out, not if Henry had stood his ground and said she had to stay. And then they could have been together with no one knowing who had fathered the bairn but Henry, and the bairn would have been a means of keeping him tied to her forever. But now that cord had become a noose around her neck . . .

Acid hot tears burnt their way down her cheeks but she still remained perfectly still.

Oh aye, she'd see her day with her mam and da all right, her time would come. And now the bitterness became a tangible entity, lying heavy in the room. She'd never had no truck with religion – as far as she could see it was just a tool the preachers and such used on gullible folk who didn't bother to think for themselves – but if there was any truth in what her da had flung at her, seconds before he'd left her at the church door in the town, then she'd go along with that. 'The devil looks after his own.' Well, maybe she'd find out the truth of that statement in the years to come, because there certainly wasn't anyone else who would be looking out for her.

She slowly drew the sleeve of her heavy calico nightdress across her wet face as she sniffed and gulped a few times. Henry had treated her shamefully and she didn't deserve it, not from him, but it had been her da who had pushed for Henry and Hilda to be wed. It had. She clung on to the thought as though it was a lifeline and gradually, over a period of some minutes, her body relaxed and she slept.

Part 1 – The Children
1902

Chapter One

The new century, rung in amid claims by the financiers and politicians that the next hundred years would be even more glorious than the previous ones of unparalleled success and expansion, didn't appear so glowing to millions of Britain's working class and to the hard-pressed north in particular. And to Walter and Alice, the newspaper reports of the immediate capsizing of the new royal yacht, *Victoria and Albert*, as soon as it undocked in Southampton three days into the new year could have been an echo of the farm's fortunes.

There had been some significant changes at the farm in the last thirteen years and all of them bad, not least the ever-dwindling stock, empty farm labourers' cottages and reduction of produce to sell in the marketplace due to the severe flooding in the north of England through the winters of 1900 and 1901. But to twelve-year-old Polly Farrow, conceived on Henry and Hilda's wedding night, the farm was home and she loved it with a passion that matched her grandfather's.

Whether it was this which had endeared the child to the dour old man from when Polly was a toddler, or his granddaughter's sunny nature and bright, pretty face, no one knew, but it was clear to anyone with eyes to see that Polly was Walter's pride and joy.

Her sister, Ruth, born three years later after a difficult confinement which provided Hilda with the excuse she needed to take to her bed and become an invalid, was pretty enough, but had none of Polly's bounce and good humour, being an awkward, rather petulant child with a tendency to cry easily and complain incessantly.

And it was this last irritating attribute of her younger granddaughter that now induced Alice to swing round from skimming the milk and cry, her voice shrill, 'Give over yammerin' or so help me I'll skelp your lug, an' then you'll have somethin' to whine about.'

'But me *arms* are tired!'

As Alice raised her hand Polly quickly moved her sister behind her, her voice soothing as she said, 'I'll carry on churnin' by meself for a while, Gran. I'm not tired.'

'Well, there's more reason for *you* to be tired than that one. Over an hour collectin' the eggs this mornin' she was, an' that with your da needin' help with the milkin'. By . . .' Alice let her voice fall away as she eyed the two girls irritably. 'More artful

23

than a cartload of monkeys when it comes to avoidin' work, she is.'

This last brought to Polly's mind the organ-grinder who had accompanied the travelling fair when it had stopped at Silksworth a few days previously. Her grandmother had taken the two girls to view it setting up. This was exciting in itself and was the next best thing to going on the rides, for which both girls knew without asking their grandparents had no money. But as they had been watching the beautifully painted caravans and the flamboyantly dressed men and women arrive, the small, cheeky-faced little monkey, dressed in a tiny red blouse and trousers and belonging to the old organ-grinder, had jumped on her granny's shoulder. Bedlam had ensued. Gran had screamed and flapped her arms and had started running around with the monkey chattering and jumping as it held on to her straw bonnet, and then, when the organ-grinder had reached her, the monkey had whisked off her hat before the old man could grab him and taken off over the field to a nearby caravan, where it had sat on the roof laughing at them all with the bonnet in its little hands. Then it had danced backwards and forwards, pretending to put the bonnet on and making faces at them all, until Ruth had laughed so much she wet her flannel drawers and her granny had almost cried with vexation at the state of her bonnet.

Once the big fat woman who was billed as the bearded lady and had more whiskers than her grandda had coaxed the monkey down on to the ground with a bag of nuts, they had retrieved the bonnet – now distinctly the worse for wear – and made their way home, her granny muttering dire threats about the little animal and Polly and Ruth desperately trying to hide their laughter, which had continued to gurgle up every time they thought about the monkey's bright-eyed, wicked little face.

It had been a lovely, lovely day. Polly met Ruth's eyes and she knew from the sudden sparkle in them that her sister's thoughts had followed her own.

'We'll get the butter churned and the washing done, Gran.' Polly nudged Ruth meaningfully. 'Won't we, Ruth?'

Alice's thin, austere face softened in spite of herself. What would she do without this wee lass? she asked herself, and not for the first time. Polly's slender frame topped by a mass of glowing chestnut curls was deceptive in its apparent fragility. Her elder granddaughter did the work of a grown woman – two grown women – round the farm. It worried her that Polly and Ruth didn't get much schooling, but they were sore needed here. Aye, sore needed. Up at five o'clock in the morning they all were, and still there weren't enough hours in the day. And there was that one upstairs playing at being sickly and expecting to be waited on hand and foot!

24

The thought of her daughter-in-law brought the frown back to Alice's face, and her voice was abrupt as – having finished the skimming of the cream from the big earthenware bowls of milk set on the cold stone slabs in the dairy – she said to Ruth, 'Come on, you, an' we'll see about skinnin' them rabbits an' peelin' the taties afore the three of us get stuck in to the washin'.'

As her grandmother and sister left the small dairy for the scullery beyond, Polly heaved a sigh of relief and continued churning the butter. This might make your arms ache until you thought they were going to drop off, but she would rather do the churning any day than handle the rabbits or pheasants her da sometimes caught. She knew they were dead and couldn't feel anything any more, but their poor limp bodies and unseeing eyes always made her feel sad, and once the skins were off and needed scraping and salting and stretching she felt even worse. She hadn't told anyone she felt like this because she knew it didn't bother Ruth or her granny, same as they didn't turn a hair when her grandda killed the fattened pig each autumn to keep them going through the winter. And it had to be done, she knew that. She just didn't like to hear it squealing and know it wouldn't be rooting about for its food any more, or feeling the sun and the rain on its back or snorting for its mash.

Her granny was in a right tear the day. As her thin arms kept up the rhythmic churning, Polly allowed her thoughts to flow and ebb. But she knew why tempers were short on the farm: the barley hadn't done well – the torrential rain just before they'd harvested it had meant it was all but flattened – and it was Sunday tomorrow. Her granny was always in a mood when Sunday got near, and she knew – although she'd never asked her gran about it – that it was because her Aunt Eva and the lads might come. Her granny was always sharp on a Sunday until it had gone past three and she knew whether they'd made the journey from Monkwearmouth, although she was always nice to them when they got here. But it was polite nice, not real nice – to her aunt at least. Her gran loved Michael, though. A slight smile curved Polly's rosebud lips at the thought of her cousin, and she gave a little hop of anticipation at the thought of the forthcoming day. She hoped they'd come the morrow; they hadn't come last week and everything had seemed grey somehow.

Of course another reason why her granny couldn't take Ruth's whingeing might be because they hadn't had a lodger for ages. Gran always moaned about the work involved when they had someone staying in one of the old cottages situated a hundred yards behind the cow byres, but the extra money bought things like their boots and winter coats. But they only really had people staying in the summer and it was nearly October now, and her coat had been too short last year. Her granny had said they'd go to the old second-hand market in

Ryhope that all the colliery workers used. That had been last autumn, and then the bad weather and the floods had set in and they'd had some beasts drown, and her gran hadn't mentioned the market again.

'You nearly finished, lass?' Alice poked her grey head round the open door of the dairy, and without waiting for an answer continued, 'I've made a brew; take a sup up to your mam, hinny, while I finish off in here.'

'Aye, all right, Gran.' Polly's voice was without demur but expressed resignation. She knew full well neither her granny nor Ruth wanted the job of venturing into her mother's room and listening to the endless string of complaints that began the moment the door was opened, but although Ruth was her mother's favourite and therefore less likely to incur her displeasure, her granny was aware that if there was a choice between any work and enduring her mother's grumbling, Ruth would choose the latter and dally upstairs as long as she could.

Polly walked through the scullery, averting her gaze from the bloody skins of the rabbits lying in a tin dish on the stone slab under the small window. The poss tub was in the middle of the floor, half full of soaking washing, and out of habit she picked up the poss stick and gave the sheets a good pounding before continuing through to the kitchen, where Ruth was engaged in peeling potatoes at the scrubbed table.

The black kale-pot was already gently simmering with the rabbit pieces and other vegetables, and as Ruth looked up she said eagerly, with one of the mercurial changes of mood common to her when she had got her own way over something or other, 'Gran says we can have a shive of the sly cake she's made for tomorrow before we start on the washin', Poll, so hurry up an' take Mam's tea before she changes her mind. An' Gran said to fill the kettle for the washin' an' all.'

Polly stared into the round face framed by mousy-brown curls and her voice was flat when she said, 'You fill the kettle.' She didn't doubt her grandmother had asked Ruth to do it, and although she wasn't averse to doing more than her fair share for the sake of preserving harmony, she also knew that given an inch her sister would take a mile. 'I'm takin' Mam's tea.'

Her mother was lying propped up against the big feather-filled bolster when Polly entered her parents' small bedroom, and as Hilda raised herself slightly on her bony elbows and watched her elder daughter walk towards her, her expression was sour. 'About time.' She took the proffered mug with an abruptness that bordered on hostility. 'You could die of thirst up here and no one would care.'

The smell wafting from the china chamber pot under the bed informed Polly her mother had used it recently, despite the row that had erupted the last time her mother had refused to make the journey to the privy in the yard to do her business.

26

'No need for it,' her grandmother had yelled. 'It's bad enough gettin' the bairns to empty it normally without the other, an' you can't tell me you're unable to get down them stairs, my girl.' Her grandmother had been furious on that occasion, and although Polly and Ruth – sitting huddled at the bottom of the stairs with their ears straining – had been unable to hear what their mother was saying, the row had gone on for some considerable time, and had started again when the menfolk had come in for their dinner and her granny had dragged her da upstairs and told him to tell his wife what was what.

'I'll take the po down, Mam.' Hopefully she'd be able to empty it without her granny noticing, Polly thought as she reached under the bed. The room was smaller than her grandparents' bedroom, holding no more than her parents' three-quarter-size bed, which was pushed against the wall under the window, and a big rectangular metal strongbox in one corner at the foot of the bed. This contained a change of sheets, the spare patchwork quilt and items of clothing. The suit her father had been married in hung on a wooden peg above the chest, and her mother's Sunday frock, shawl and bonnet on the peg next to it. The room always seemed airless to Polly; her mother rarely had the window open even on the hottest summer day, insisting any breeze would be liable to give her a chill.

How could her mam, who was always going on about how grand life had been at Stone Farm before she was married and how nice everything was there, how could she bear to spend all her time up here in this smelly little box? And she didn't have to, Polly told herself silently as she carefully carried the pot out of the room without glancing again at the narrow-eyed figure in the bed. She agreed with her granny on this. Her mam was quick enough to come downstairs on a Sunday when she heard her stepbrother arrive, and she was always quite animated on those occasions.

Polly shut the bedroom door and hurried downstairs, walking through the kitchen and out into the yard, where she entered the privy. There were rarely any overpowering smells in here; her grandmother was meticulous in keeping the small stone-built hut fresh with ashes down the hole in the wooden seat extending right across the breadth of the structure, and her grandda cleared it out every other day by lifting the little wooden hatch at the back of the privy and evacuating the contents with his long shovel.

Once out in the fresh air again, Polly stood still for a moment, her grey woollen dress and white pinny flapping about her calves as she put the empty chamber pot down on the cobbles before straightening and lifting her face to the cool, keen breeze.

She could hear mooing from the cows in the field beyond the lane; they only had a dozen left now and she knew each one by name and all their little mannerisms. The geese and hens were occupied scratching about amongst the straw in one corner of the yard, and low grunts from the pigsty in its square of ground at the rear of the farmhouse told Polly the pigs had recently had their mash. The sights and sounds were like food and drink to her; they created a feeling that often made her want to whirl and dance and fling her arms into the air with the shivery, jumpy sensation that rose up and up in her at such times.

She was so glad she didn't live in the town like Michael. Poor Michael. The feeling diminished into one of aching pain. He hated it, she knew he hated it, and if he had to go down the pit like his da and Arnold and Luke . . . Her Aunt Eva wouldn't make him, would she? Michael thought she would.

Polly stood a second more staring into the distance, and then purposefully shook off the sad greyness that always accompanied thoughts of Michael descending into the bowels of the earth. That wouldn't happen for another eighteen months or so, until Michael's fourteenth birthday, and eighteen months was a lifetime away. Anything could happen before then. Michael had told her, the last time he had been at the farm, that Mr Sotherby – who Michael worked for part-time delivering milk in the East End – had said he would be willing to give him his own permanent round when he left school. Of course that wouldn't earn the same as working down the pit, but with Michael's da and Arnold, and now Luke this last twelve months, bringing in a good wage, her Aunt Eva didn't have to worry over-much.

Mind, her aunt was funny about Michael. Polly's fine brows drew together in a frown. She knew her aunt took all of the shilling and tenpence Michael earned a week and only gave him a penny or two back for sweets and things, because she'd heard her granny talking to her grandda about it and saying it wasn't fair. Michael had to carry twenty cans of milk at a time up two or three flights of tenement stairs, and last winter his hands had been cracked and bleeding with the frost and cold. He had cried one Sunday afternoon, and her granny had covered his hands with goose fat and made little muslin gloves to fit under his wool ones, but her aunt hadn't cared. She didn't like her Aunt Eva.

Polly bent down and retrieved the chamber pot from the cobbles, and now the shivery feeling was quite gone as she thought flatly, Aunt Eva's like my mam, she is, but in a different way. And although she couldn't have explained it out loud in words, she knew exactly what she meant.

Alice was busy dividing up portions of the sly cake as Polly entered the kitchen again after washing the chamber pot under the pump, and Ruth's mouth was already full of the sugared pastry liberally sprinkled with currants. Alice said nothing as Polly scurried past her for the stairs, but once her granddaughter reappeared in the kitchen, Alice's voice was soft as she said, 'Sit down an' have a sup, hinny.'

'Aye, ta, Gran.'

It was quick and relieved, and for a moment guilt was hot and heavy in Alice's heart. The load this bairn – this precious bairn – bore was enough as it was, without her having to act as peacemaker between her mother and grandmother. Alice knew she should have kept her mouth shut the last time she'd gone for Hilda, like Walter had said, at least until the bairns had been out of the road. But he didn't have to put up with Lady Muck, did he. Alice's mouth hardened. He and Henry might be out from dawn to dusk and doing the work of four men, but she'd take that any day compared to what she endured.

Alice brought her chin tightly into her neck. She had considered herself very fortunate when she had been sent to this farm from the workhouse, until she'd got here, that was. Walter's mother had been sickly and unable to see to the meals and household chores, but if she had been a kind mistress the hard work from five in the morning until late at night wouldn't have mattered. But she'd been a dreadful woman, eaten up with frustration at her enforced idleness, which had manifested itself in a cruel and biting tongue and an obsessional desire to see Alice crushed and brow-beaten. The missus, as Walter's mother had dictated she be addressed, had known that by hiring a chit from the workhouse she would be able to have free rein; before Alice a series of girls from the town had come and gone, staying a month at the longest.

And so, rather than be sent back to the workhouse in disgrace, which would have meant being incarcerated for a good few more years, Alice had cooked and cleaned, fed the poultry and calves and pigs, and suffered Walter's mother. And when some particular act of spite had been harder to stomach than normal, she'd repeated to herself that this wouldn't last forever. A few years and she would be experienced enough to work anywhere.

But then Walter's parents had died of cholera within a week of each other the third summer she had been at the farm, and on the night of the second funeral Walter had plied her with home-made cider and had his way with her. The next morning when she'd come to her senses she had known it was because he had sensed she was ready to leave the farm and didn't want to lose his workhorse, but as fate would have it she'd already fallen for Eva and she and Walter were married by September.

She'd been full of suppressed rage and bitterness all through the pregnancy, railing silently against the farm, Walter, herself, and when her daughter was born she'd barely been able to bring herself to look at the means of her entrapment. She had often wondered since if her rancour during those nine months had communicated itself to her unborn child, because she and Eva had always disliked each other.

'Gran? I'll carry the kettle through, shall I?'

Alice came back to her present surroundings to see Polly, having finished her mug of tea and sly cake, attempting to lift the kettle off the hob. 'Aye, hinny, an' you, Ruth, get up off your backside an' help her, an' careful mind, the water's boilin'. I'll flake up a wee bit more soap by an' by when I've finished me tea.'

As the two girls staggered through to the stone-floored scullery carrying the great black kettle between them, Alice sat on for a few moments more. By, she was tired the day; she hadn't the list to tackle the mounds of washing, but they wouldn't poss themselves. And there was that madam upstairs playing the old soldier again, and it was Sunday the morrow. Sunday seemed to come round quicker and quicker, and with Eva and the lads not visiting last week they were bound to make an appearance come the afternoon. She rose slowly, her thin shoulders hunched, and walked wearily through to the two girls to find Polly attacking the poss tub with enough gusto to make the water bubble, while Ruth scraped idly at the big hard chunk of blue-veined soap in a manner that guaranteed only the smallest of slivers fell into the tub.

'Oh, it looks grand, Poll, bonny, but do you think they'll come?'

''Course they'll come.' Polly smiled at her sister, standing pressed close to her side, before both girls turned again to survey the kitchen, which they had spent most of the day cleaning.

The fire was glowing a deep red in the shining blackleaded range to their left and it turned the newly polished brass fender rosy pink. It illuminated the hardwood saddle and hid most of its imperfections with the mellow flickering on the old wood, the flock-stuffed cushions appearing plump and soft for once. The kitchen table was sporting its white Sunday cloth over its weekday oilcloth, the six hardbacked chairs clustered round it all seeming to admire the bowl of wild flowers the girls had picked a few minutes earlier. And the colours of the flowers were reflected in the big clippy mat on the stone flags in front of the range. Polly and Ruth had lugged and pulled the mat into the yard that morning, beating the dust and grime from its cloth pieces for over five minutes before hauling it back into the kitchen.

'I hope they come, Poll.' Ruth ran across to stand in front of the mantelpiece, staring up at the little wooden clock in the middle of it. 'What's the time now?'

'Nearly three.' In spite of all Polly's help, Ruth still hadn't grasped how to tell the time, but now, as they heard their grandmother descend the stairs, their sense of expectation grew. Their granny always changed her working pinny for the fancy one with little daisies on before their aunt and the lads came, once she had made sure everything was ready for tea, which was prompt at four on a Sunday. The meal held part of the magic of this one special day in the week.

30

Every weekday – if they were at home and not at school, which was mostly the case – the routine never altered. Oatmeal porridge for breakfast, and then tea and bread and butter. This was at six o'clock, after the men had been out an hour milking the cows and feeding the horses – old Bess, and Patience, the last of Bess's foals, who was four years old now.

Then the men went off into the fields with the horses, taking a tin bottle of tea with them and two slices of bread and jam, and the girls worked with their grandmother in the house and dairy. The men came in for a cooked dinner at twelve, which they all ate together, and then at three, Polly and Ruth took their grandfather and father their tea in the fields – a can of strong black tea, two thick shives of bread and butter and a currant bun. Supper – bread, butter and cheese – was at seven o'clock, after the men had come in from the fields and milked the cows and attended to the horses. This routine never varied and the food never altered.

But on Sunday afternoons everything was different. After dinner the girls would help their grandmother fill up the tin bath in the scullery, and the menfolk would wash and change out of their rough working coats and soiled breeches into their Sunday clothes. Then they would disappear into the barn after donning thick hessian butcher's aprons and work on 'clean' jobs for an hour or two. On the arrival of any visitors they would leave the aprons in the barn and stroll in a few minutes later with their pipes alight, as though they had been taking the air after dinner.

It had taken Polly some years to understand that this act of apparent ease and relaxation was for her mother's stepbrother's benefit, and his alone. Frederick Weatherburn always arrived at or about the same time as her Aunt Eva and the lads and, like them, he rarely missed more than one week in a month. He was big and jolly and smelled of good tweed cloth and cigar smoke, and he was rich – or so her mam maintained anyway. Her grandda and da were always hearty and loud when Uncle Frederick was around, and Polly didn't know if she liked that – it made her feel uncomfortable and slightly embarrassed somehow, although she didn't know why. But she did know she liked Sunday tea.

Baked jam roll, cheese scones, fruit loaf, seed cake – they usually had the lot on a Sunday, along with slices of her granny's delicious white bread and butter, and a big plateful of their home-cured ham cut very thin.

Sometimes, when the farm had been going through a harder spell than usual and Polly had noticed her granny's stews and broths consisted mostly of taties, and that the flour was the cheaper kind – dark and with bits in it – which made the hard bread she didn't like so much, she thought they wouldn't have the white bread and plateful of ham on a Sunday afternoon. But they always did.

31

'All ready, me bairns?' Alice was smiling as she walked into the kitchen, but when Polly looked at her grandmother she saw it was her granny's Sunday smile.

This smile went hand in hand with her grandda and da being different, the elaborate tea, her mam coming downstairs and perching herself on the saddle near the fire, and her granny's face sometimes when she looked at Aunt Eva. But Sunday meant Michael too. Polly hugged the thought of her cousin to her and skipped across to her grandmother, burying her face in Alice's apron and holding her tight round the waist as she said, 'Look at the table, Gran. Isn't it bonny?'

'Aye, pet. Right bonny.'

'An' the rain's held off. I told you it would, didn't I?'

'That you did,' Alice said heartily, too heartily. Bad weather sometimes meant a respite in this weekly torture, although on more than one occasion she had known Eva drag the lads through a foot or so of snow on the two-and-a-half-mile walk from the tram stop. At least now the bairns were grown Frederick couldn't give them all a lift part of the way home in his horse and trap. She'd suffered the torments of the damned every time that had happened, although Walter had assured her Eva had more sense than to open her mouth to anyone. But Alice wasn't so sure. Seeing Eva sitting there week after week with her hungry eyes fixed on her brother's face . . . No, she wasn't so sure what Eva would do if the mood took her.

And then, as though the thoughts of her daughter had conjured her up, she heard a familiar voice call, 'Yoohoo, anyone at home?' seconds before the kitchen door opened and Eva stepped into the kitchen, closely followed by two youths and a young lad. And it was this young lad who ran over to where Polly was now standing by her grandmother and said eagerly, his thin, pale face alight, 'We came, see? And it's grand outside. Shall we go down to the stream and look for crayfish?'

'Can we?' Both Polly and Ruth were looking at their grandmother, who in turn glanced at the two tall lads either side of Eva. They added their own plea by saying, 'It's really warm out, Gran,' from the younger, and 'There won't be many days like this afore the weather sets in,' from the older boy.

'Aye, all right, be off with you.' Alice was laughing at them as she spoke, but once the door had closed behind the young folk and Eva had come fully into the kitchen, seating herself on one of the hardbacked chairs, which she pulled out from beneath the table and turned to face the room, Alice said flatly, 'Nathaniel not with you?'

It was her stock address and Eva answered as she did each week, her voice matching her mother's in tone. 'He's at his allotment.'

'Oh, aye.'

32

'Where's Henry . . . and Da?'

She knew Eva always mentioned Henry first to get under her skin. Alice turned quickly to the range, taking a cloth and pressing the ready-filled kettle further into the glowing embers before saying shortly, 'They'll be in presently. You ready for a sup?'

Eva opened her mouth to answer, but before she could do so the sound of a horse's hoofs on the cobbles outside brought her mother walking swiftly across the room, saying, 'That'll be Frederick.'

Oh, aye, that'd be Frederick all right, and give it another minute or two and in would come her da and Henry with their pipes smoking and their faces smiling as though they hadn't got a care in the world. Who did they think they were fooling? It was savage. This bit farm was shrinking each year, and there they were trying to play the gentlemen. It would be funny if it wasn't so pathetic. Her mam and da hadn't made such a good bargain as they'd thought when they'd got rid of her and kept Henry and his lady wife, had they! She had always done half of Henry's work along with hers; he was no farmer, Henry. But she hadn't minded working for both of them, and she still wouldn't. *Oh, Henry, Henry.*

Eva listened to the sound of her mother greeting Hilda's stepbrother and her expression was bitter, but by the time they entered the kitchen, her father and Henry following on their footsteps, Eva's face was wiped clean of all emotion. And Alice would have been more than a little surprised if she had known her daughter was echoing her own agonising when Eva said silently to herself, her eyes tight on her brother's beloved face, *Let the torture begin.*

Once outside in the late summer air that smelt heavily of the big pile of manure steaming gently in one corner of the yard, Polly had the desire to laugh out loud, but knowing the others would enquire why she was laughing, she restrained the impulse. She was just so glad to see Michael – and Luke and Arnold too, of course, she added quickly, as a dart of guilt pricked her – and it was such a canny day too.

'Come on then.' She beamed at the others, her heart-shaped face with its great violet-blue eyes alight with the joy of being alive, and as though her elation had infected the rest of them, the five went running madly out of the yard into the lane beyond. They climbed over the dry-stone wall without bothering to open the gate and then continued pell-mell across the field, leaping over piles of cow dung with shrieks and cries until they came to the stream bordering that field with the next.

As though at a given signal the boys were taking off their boots and socks and rolling up their trouser legs, wading in over the smooth rocks around which the crystal-clear stream tumbled and frothed. Polly and Ruth followed a little more cautiously. The stream was running high

33

– there had been several bouts of torrential rain throughout September which had created havoc with the crops – and their grandmother didn't like them plodging at the best of times; besides which, the icy water was stinging like pins and needles on their bare legs.

Within a few minutes Ruth had had enough and retreated to the bank, laughing and shouting to the others as they searched for crayfish and the little minnows that populated the stream, but although Polly's feet were numb and the bottom of her dress and her knickers were wet from the gurgling splashing of the water, she didn't want to miss a minute of playing with Michael.

Eventually, however, they were all sitting on the spiky dry grass on the bank, toasting their frozen feet to the weak rays of the dying sun. It was Luke, noticing how Polly's teeth were chattering, who said, 'Here, I've a bag of winter mixture, who wants one to keep the cold out?'

'Me, me, Luke!'

'An' me!'

'Have you got one of the red ones, Luke? I like to suck 'em until they're nowt but a little spike.'

As the others clamoured for one of the sweets in the small paper bag Luke had fished out of his pocket, it was Arnold, his dark eyes on Polly's bright laughing face, who said, 'Aye, I'll have one, man. I like a good sucker that puts fire in your belly now and again.'

'Shut your mouth, Arnold.' Luke's voice was low but weighty.

'What? I only said—'

'I said shut your filthy mouth, they're only bairns. Keep your double meanings for them as appreciate it.'

'Shut your own mouth.' Arnold had risen to his feet, his stance menacing, and as Luke handed the bag of sweets to Michael before standing himself, Polly felt a trickle of fear run down her spine.

She didn't understand the portent of what had been said or why the afternoon had gone wrong so suddenly; she only knew there was going to be a fight in a minute if she didn't do something to avert it. At fifteen and sixteen years old, Luke and Arnold had the tall, wide-shouldered physiques of lads a good few years older; they didn't take after their father at all. Michael was the small, slim one who appeared younger than his twelve years. If Luke and Arnold started to fight, it wouldn't be a bairns' scrap.

Polly grabbed the bag from Michael and stepped between the two brothers, her voice carrying a shrill note as she said to Arnold, 'Here, have one. Please, Arnold, have one.'

Arnold continued staring at Luke a moment longer before he lowered his gaze to the slender, chestnut-haired figure in front of him, and as Polly raised the bag a little higher he slanted another quick glance at Luke before he said, his eyes running all over her flushed face, 'You don't mind me funning, do you, lass? A bit carry-on never hurt anyone, did it?'

Polly blinked a little. There was something in his manner that she couldn't put her finger on but which made her want to take a few steps away from the big bulk of him, and she found she had to swallow before she could say, 'No, no, of course not.'

'See?' Arnold was again looking towards Luke, a smile curling his thick lips as he took in his brother's angry face.

'I'm warning you, Arnold—'

'It's time to get back.' This time it was Michael who put himself between the two antagonists and his voice was sharp. If Luke and Arnold had a fight they'd all suffer for it, and nothing must be allowed to interfere with their Sunday visits to the farm. 'Gran'll have the tea ready and she'll go barmy if we're late.'

It was Arnold, with a little hiccough of a laugh, who reached for his boots and socks first, thereby defusing the situation, but once they were all retracing their steps back to the farmhouse Michael kept close to Polly. He loved the farm. He glanced at the slim, straight figure next to him, and Polly, sensing his gaze, turned her head and smiled at him. And he loved Polly. He kept his eyes on her smooth, silky skin that was like thick cream, his gaze taking in the burnished copper in her glossy hair before he turned his eyes frontwards again. And now his thoughts were not those of a twelve-year-old boy but a grown man sensing his destiny as he told himself, Another eighteen months and I'll have left school, and two years after that we'll both be sixteen. Lots of people wed early . . . And when he took Polly's hand to pull her over a ridge of mud the cows had made with their hoofs and she didn't try to withdraw her fingers from his once they were walking on again, it was all the confirmation he needed.

Chapter Two

The tea things had all been cleared away and the bowl of flowers was back in the middle of the snowy-white cloth and had been for half an hour, but still no one showed any signs of wanting to leave. This was mainly due to the earnest debate which had been steadily gathering steam for the last twenty minutes between Frederick on the one side and Arnold and Luke on the other, Walter and Henry long since having left the fray.

'Aye, I know farming depends on the weather and such and can be a hazardous life, but it's not a patch on coal mining,' Luke was saying in answer to a comment of Frederick's. 'There's danger all around underground. The owners pay lip service to safety, and there's scarcely a week or so goes by without a fall or an explosion marking some poor devil's card. They talk about the Labour Party the trade unions created a couple of years back being the answer to the working man – well, I hope so, the unions need some backing.'

'It was one of your own, James Keir Hardie, who said the aim must be for a party in Parliament with flexibility for development,' Frederick reminded the younger man quickly. 'It was his proposal they took on board, and development happens slowly.'

'Aye, and he's a good man and a good Scottish miner, but when it comes to the unions taking on the owners it'll be like spitting against the wind without government help. Look at Silksworth, and that only eleven years ago. Them damn – sorry, Gran – them bailiffs had a key that'd open every colliery house door and they got the police to help them. Miners on the roof of every house, rioting in the streets, but the end result was the candymen entering homes and turning men, women and bairns out into the streets to starve. Hundreds evicted and for what? Daring to object to being buried alive while the owners and viewers are sitting pretty in their blood-bought fancy houses, that's what.'

'Aye, aye, well, I wouldn't argue with you there, lad,' Frederick said with a touch of the condescension that was habitual with him. 'Bad business at Silksworth, bad business.'

'One hundred and sixty-four men and boys killed ten years before that at Seaham, seventy at Ryhope; man, I could go on and on up to the present day. And there's always someone getting killed or injured or going down with silicosis and the like. And I've yet to

37

see a farm worker covered in carbuncles and open sores caused by years of working in hot salt water seeping down from the North Sea above the mine tunnels. Me da's covered in them. Isn't that right, Arnold?'

'Aye, aye, it is that.' Their altercation by the stream put to one side in the face of this common cause, Arnold nodded vigorously.

'I can see you're going to be a strong union man, Luke.'

The censure in Frederick's voice was not missed by the younger man, and Alice, having heard Hilda's stepbrother's views on trade unions before, squirmed slightly at his tone. This was going to turn nasty, she knew it.

Luke looked at the man sitting so comfortably on the saddle next to the fire who had his Aunt Hilda, Polly's mother, hanging on his every word. Frederick's plump hands were resting on his thick corduroy breeches, his leather boots were polished to a good shine and his coat was of the best woollen tweed. He looked like what he was – a prosperous employer who had never gone without a meal in his life – and now Luke's voice was flat and hard when he said, 'Aye, and I shan't forget me membership's bought with such as the Penrhyn quarrymen. Two years long, their dispute over union recognition, and them and their families destitute to the point where David Lloyd George asked the TUC for bread for their bairns last month. Lord Penrhyn wants shooting if you ask me.'

Frederick Weatherburn stared into the young, good-looking face of this callow upstart, as he thought of Luke Blackett. This was what came of education of the masses; they got ideas above their station and began to think for themselves. A working man was at his best when he could neither read nor write, everyone knew that. Hadn't his own father refused to employ any individual who knew their letters? And he'd been right. By, he had. But he must go carefully here. He'd other fish to fry than putting this ignorant numbskull in his place, and Luke was Eva's stepson when all was said and done. He had looked at the situation very carefully before he had given his consent for Hilda to marry Henry, but as it was, with the farm's steady downhill descent, things couldn't have turned out more satisfactorily. Aye, he'd hold his hand with this young understrapper, he could afford to.

Frederick rose somewhat ponderously to his feet before he spoke, noting with some satisfaction that Walter and his wife were looking anxious – as well they might; they relied heavily on his help at haymaking time and such like – and then he said coolly, 'Maybe, lad, maybe, but I doubt his family would thank you for the thought. Well, I must be off. That was a grand tea, Alice, as always.'

Sanctimonious, patronising so-an'-so, he didn't know he was born. Luke was red-faced and inwardly burning with righteous indignation as he watched the older man take his leave amid effusive goodbyes from Polly's mother and the family. According to his stepmother, there were a good few men and lads employed full time at Stone Farm, besides female staff in the house and the like. When had Weatherburn ever worked until he was fit to drop? Not often, he'd be bound, and he'd certainly not gone home at the end of a soul-destroyingly long shift to a wife who was as thin as a rake through taking in washing and any other work she could find, and bairns who were bow-legged with rickets and full of ringworm and impetigo. Of course Walter and Henry were a different kettle of fish; they had their own cross to bear in trying to keep this farm afloat, he knew that. He had no quarrel with Polly's family.

He glanced at Polly now – he had noticed she had been listening avidly while they had been talking, her huge blue eyes flashing from one to another – but she was looking at Michael. By, she was growing up fast, and she was going to be a stunner. What would she say if he told her that the main reason he continued to accompany his stepmother each Sunday was to see her? Laugh, most likely; she wouldn't understand, she was still just a bairn. And there was Michael. The two of them were as thick as thieves, always had been, and he wasn't sure if it was just bairns' friendship or a stronger bond that would develop into something more as they grew. The thought caused the familiar ache in his chest and he now rose abruptly from his seat at the side of the table, nudging Arnold sitting at the side of him to do the same.

Walter, Alice and Henry, along with Eva, had followed Frederick outside into the yard, where the horse and trap were tethered, and now Luke nodded at Hilda, who was still sitting on the saddle with her shawl drawn tightly across her thin shoulders, as he said, 'We'll have to be making tracks too. Goodbye, Mrs Farrow. Come on, Michael.'

Hilda inclined her head coldly but she said nothing, although inwardly she was seething. How *dare* this big, gangling half-nowt, this *pit-yakker* upset Frederick! Henry should have said something, put him in his place, instead of just sitting there with that silly look on his face, smoking his stupid pipe. She'd have something to say to him later, the weak, spineless fool.

Once Polly, Ruth and Michael had followed Luke and Arnold outside, Hilda rose to her feet, drawing her breath in through her teeth in a low hiss as her anger continued to burn. Where was the respect for Frederick's superior knowledge? He was well read; the study at Stone Farm was lined with books, and besides Frederick's taste in literature and the arts, he had an excellent knowledge of current affairs. Their father – Hilda was emphatic in claiming the paternity and never allowed herself to dwell on the reality – had always maintained it was education that made the difference between the working man and his betters, and he had been right. Oh, why had she allowed herself to become linked with these people? If only she had known then what she knew now. It would have been better for her to remain a spinster all her days than to be interned in this dreadful place.

She climbed the narrow, steep stairs slowly, the muscles in her legs being weak through lack of use. Once in the bedroom she sank down on to the bed as her thoughts continued to flow on. Henry had tricked her when he had married her and brought her here, oh yes, he had, he had. He had given her to believe that this farm, although smaller than the one she had grown up on, was a prosperous entity with plans for growth, but within a month of their arriving home from honeymoon Walter had dismissed his men and closed up the cottages. When she thought of those early days of marriage . . . She shut her eyes tight, swaying slightly as her arms crossed over her flat stomach and her hands gripped either side of her waist.

She had been expected to work harder than ever Betsy and the kitchen maid at Stone Farm had done, and the nights with Henry, the close proximity with this man who had changed from courteous, respectful suitor into someone with wants and needs that horrified and disgusted her, had been unbearable. She had never imagined that people did 'that' to procreate. Perhaps if her mother had lived longer she would have explained something of it to her, but the degradation, the utter *baseness* of the night hours had sickened her. And she didn't believe Henry when he said that some women found it acceptable, even pleasurable. It was too, too humiliating, too vile for that. And what was the end result? Months of wretched bloatedness, and then agonising pain as the thing planted in her had made its appearance into the world. But she had put a stop to all that.

The thought brought Hilda's head – which had been bent over her flat chest – slowly upright, and the rocking stopped as her cold pale blue eyes narrowed. Henry had always denied he married her to establish a solid link with Stone Farm, but if it hadn't been that, then what else? It certainly hadn't been because he loved her, she had realised that even before they had been wed; in fact from the first time they had walked out together. But she hadn't cared for him in a romantic sense so she hadn't been unduly concerned. Henry had been the only man of her acquaintance who had shown the slightest interest in her, that had been the plain fact of the matter, and she had known that if she'd refused him she would have been condemning herself to a life of spinsterhood – a life which appeared very sweet with hindsight. Frederick would have taken care of her; he wouldn't have expected her to soil her hands with low, menial work of the kind she had encountered here.

She undressed slowly, but her indolence was engendered more by the bitter nature of her thoughts than by fatigue, and when Henry opened the bedroom door a few minutes later and glanced across at

40

the thin, still figure of his wife lying primly under the worn, darned sheets, Hilda was ready for him, her invective flying forth before her husband had time to open his mouth. 'Well? I trust you're satisfied with your afternoon's work?'

'What?' He had been about to change back into his working clothes but now he paused, his brow wrinkling. She was in a tear about something, but then that wasn't surprising. That scrawny frame of hers held a capacity for venom that had used to amaze him in the early days of their marriage.

'Don't look at me like that, you big galoot. You know full well what I mean.'

Henry's mouth had thinned and now his voice was a snap when he said, 'I don't know an' I don't care, there's the cows to be seen to.'

'*The cows to be seen to.*' Hilda repeated the words with acid mockery, her lips curling back from her teeth in contempt. 'That's all you're fit for, to see to the cows, Henry Farrow. Well, for your information, I'm talking about the way you allowed that gormless yap to argue with Frederick.'

Henry said nothing for a moment, then, on a deep intake of breath, he growled, 'Luke Blackett has been workin' down the pit for nigh on fourteen months, he's no lad, an' furthermore, he's entitled to his own opinion same as everyone else.'

'His opinion!' It was said cuttingly, Hilda's plain, sallow face wrinkling in a sneer. 'How can someone like him have an opinion?'

By, he'd do for her one day, so help him. Lying in this damn bed twenty-four hours a day, making his life and everyone else's a misery, turning the screws whenever she had the chance . . . She was a devil of a woman, and yet she'd been so quiet, so contained when they were courting. Uppity maybe, but then she'd been entitled, being Frederick Weatherburn's stepsister. How often had the words he'd said to Eva come back to haunt him? 'Happy doesn't come into it.' By, if ever there'd been a self-fulfilling prophecy, that had been it. And Eva wasn't happy, he knew that, although they'd never spoken of it or the past. What he should have done, that day his mam found the pair of them, was to have taken Eva and gone far away somewhere. She'd have gone with him. Oh, aye, she would. Followed him to the ends of the world, Eva would have.

He brushed the thought aside as Hilda continued to rant and rave, divesting himself of his clothes and pulling on his grimy working breeches and shirt without looking at his wife again. He let her voice flow over him and around him but not into his head; he knew from such scenes in the past that his detachment was the one thing that reduced her to a heap of quivering frustration and then a stony silence that could go on for days, weeks maybe, if he was lucky.

But it was as Henry was leaving the room that his wife's voice,

41

now low, hissed at him, 'I'll make it my business to see Eva's brat and those other two hulks don't set foot in this house again, you see if I don't. They're a bad influence on the girls, especially Polly. She runs wild when they come, and Luke and Arnold aren't even family, and Michael looks as though he's riddled with the consumption—' Then she stopped with a surprised squeak as Henry swung round.

'Shut your evil mouth.' Henry's face was turkey red with temper and he no longer appeared to Hilda as the stoical, long-suffering, weak individual she thought she knew. He was staring straight into her startled eyes and his own were narrowed with hatred. 'Them little lasses don't have much of a life as you well know, but they look forward all week to seein' their cousins – an' they look on Luke an' Arnold as their cousins just the same as young Michael. You do anythin' to spoil the one thing that gives 'em a bit of pleasure, an' so help me, woman, I'll swing for you.'

'Don't you dare speak to me like that.' Hilda's voice was choked with outrage but threaded through it was a new emotion, one of fear, and it was this that Henry's sixth sense picked up and which he capitalised on.

'Oh, I dare, lass. Make no mistake about that,' he ground out slowly, walking across to the bed and bringing his head low until his face was no more than a few inches away from that of his wife. 'I've not much joy in me life, you've seen to that, but me bairns' laughter is somethin' I couldn't put a price on, an' I'll be damned if I let a spiteful bitch like you finish it. You say one word to stop them lads comin' or break up their friendship an' you'll have me to answer to.'

The hatred which was in his eyes was reflected in the narrowed, opaque orbs staring back at him, and after waiting a moment or two for Hilda to speak, Henry straightened, staring down at the rigid, furious figure in the bed as he said, his voice quiet now, even calm-sounding, 'I mean it, Hilda. I'd do it an' you know I'd do it, don't you.' It was a statement not a question, and Hilda remained silent as he turned and quietly left the room.

His bairns' laughter! Hilda ground her fleshless buttocks into the bed. His *bairns*. As far as Henry was concerned – and Walter too – she had only ever given birth to one bairn, their beloved Polly. Her mind conjured up the image of a bright, laughing face with great azure eyes set under fine curving brows, and again her buttocks churned the mattress. Always cheerful, always seeing the rainbow in the storm, the girl was enough to drive anyone mad. Ruth now, Ruth was different. Ruth understood her mother was a gentlewoman, that she had been born to better things than this miserable farm.

Henry had called her an unnatural mother once, and maybe she was. She considered the thought quite objectively. It had been when Polly was learning to walk and was always hanging on her skirts, and one day she had lost her temper and smacked the child's hands away. They had all gone for her on that occasion, Walter, Alice and Henry, and she had shouted back that she hated the farm and everyone and everything in it, including her daughter. And she had meant it, and Henry had known she meant it.

He had talked to her that night once they were in bed, his voice soft and flat, and she had known quite clearly that they had reached a crossroads in their marriage, and the way they would proceed from that point would depend on her. 'I know you're not happy, Hilda, an' bein' wed isn't all you thought it would be, but all I'm askin' is that you make some kind of an effort, if not with me an' Mam an' Da, then with the bairn. Can't you try an' love her? At least show her a bit of affection now an' again? Mam said you boxed her ears yesterday for nothin' an' shut her away upstairs, an' she was still bawlin' an hour later.'

'It's up to me how I deal with my own child, I've told your mother that.'

'Aye, maybe, but she's nowt but a babby still an' it's not fair to take out your disappointment with me on her.'

She had been surprised then, she hadn't credited him with such insight, but her voice hadn't mellowed when she said, 'She might be young, but she's wilful with a mind of her own and it needs breaking. Your parents are too soft with her, that's half the trouble.'

'It upsets 'em when you won't pick her up when she comes to you, or speak kindly to her, an' it does me an' all if you want to know.'

'I don't want to know.' The darkness had made it easier to say what had to be said. 'I don't care what you and your parents think either, Henry, and I shall continue to discipline Polly as I see fit. Spare the rod and spoil the child.'

'She's barely fourteen months old, woman!'

'And don't woman me!'

Things hadn't been the same after that. Hilda settled back against the bolster, and there was no regret in her thinking. But her frankness hadn't put an end to the disgusting business of the night hours as she had hoped; she had had to wait until after Ruth's birth for that. At least her children were both females. It wasn't the first time she had thought it, and now her bony chin came down into her neck as she inclined her head as though nodding to something spoken. She wouldn't have been able to bear the thought of producing something formed in her husband's image.

She hadn't meant to listen. Polly leaned against the door of her bedroom, and she was trembling from head to foot. She hadn't, she hadn't meant to listen, although her mother wouldn't have believed that if her da had found her outside their bedroom door, which had been open just a crack. Thank goodness she had nipped in here just in time. She glanced at the mug of tea in her hand she had been intending to give to her mother, some of which had sloshed over her pinafore in the hasty flight to her room. And as she continued to stare at the mug, she was aware of something strange happening deep inside where the muddled feelings concerning her mother lay.

She had brought her mam the tea because – when they had all been outside saying goodbye to Uncle Frederick, and then Aunt Eva and the lads, and she had heard a mistle thrush singing its heart out in the fresh, sweet air – she had felt sorry for her. She had always felt sorry for her mam if she thought about it. Oh, she knew, secretly, that her mam wasn't as poorly as she made out, but nevertheless, to stay in that little room all the time and never to run and jump in the fields and hills, or hear the chattering of the birds as they settled down for the night or the fox barking in the twilight . . . well, it must be awful. She wouldn't be able to bear it.

She raised her head, her gaze sweeping the small room she shared with Ruth, which was the same size as her parents' bedroom. The last of the sunlight was shining through the narrow window and making a pool of gold on the old faded quilt at the end of the bed; soon it would reach the stone wall beyond and then it would begin to get dark. While these thoughts were on the surface of her mind, her real self was tackling the issues raised by the conversation she had unwittingly overheard as she'd stood hesitating on the landing.

Her mam was nasty, spiteful – she had always known it, but because it was her mam it had been acceptable – but more than that, her mam didn't like her. She liked Ruth, but she didn't like her, and Mam knew that by stopping the lads coming on a Sunday she would hurt her. It might upset Ruth but it would hurt Polly, and that was why her mam had said what she had. Why did Mam always want to hurt her? Polly pressed her hand against her mouth. Ruth never took their mam her meals if she could help it, or picked her little bunches of wild flowers to look at while she lay in bed, or any of the other things she did to try and please her. And yet her mam liked Ruth and not her. She took a gulp of the hot tea by way of comfort.

Whatever she did to please her, Mam would never like her. The knowledge that had been at the back of her mind from a very young child couldn't be denied any more. Sometimes, when she was talking to her mam after she'd brought her something, and Mam shut her eyes as though she was tired, Polly knew it was because she couldn't bear to look at her. And then when she left the room after saying she'd let her mam go to sleep, but had the horrible sick feeling in her for the rest of the day, it was because she had known all along what Mam was thinking. She had, but she had thought that if she didn't admit it then it wouldn't be real. Which made her stupid. She blinked fiercely, refusing to allow the scalding feeling at the back of her eyes to turn into tears.

Well, she wouldn't try to make Mam like her any more. She drank the rest of the tea straight down. You couldn't anyway; people either did or they didn't, and if they didn't they'd find a hundred reasons not to, like Ann Boyce at school. Even though she didn't manage to get to school every day because of the farm and her granny needing her, she did better at her lessons than Ann Boyce, and that was why Ann hated her, although she tried to make on it was other things. But Ann Boyce, with her swanky airs and graces and her drippy nose, was one thing; her mam – *her own mam* – was another. For a moment Polly's slender shoulders slumped and she felt a desolation so deep as to be frightening sweep over her before she straightened, her arms going back and her chest expanding, as she said out loud, 'Michael likes me,' and then even more loudly, 'Michael likes me an' I like him,' and the declaration was of the same portent as the one Michael himself had made earlier.

Chapter Three

Nathaniel Blackett was proud of his two sons, although he would have allowed himself to be hung, drawn and quartered before he admitted to the fact. Now forty-three years of age, he had been working down the pit from the age of eight, and his face and body – scarred and stained with the blue marks stamped on it by the 'black diamonds' he mined – could have belonged to a man some twenty years his senior. His aged appearance wasn't helped by his small, wiry build, although in the job he did, his size worked to his advantage. Most of the roadways down the pit weren't made for the convenience of a full-grown man, and the smaller and nimbler a miner, the better he fared. Nobody at the pit ever got paid for travelling time, even if they had to crawl for over a mile from the bottom of the shaft, so the quicker they got to where they were working, the better for everyone concerned.

But at least his lads had had the benefit of an education and had been fourteen years of age before they'd gone underground. Nathaniel stretched, easing his aching back, which had been bent over his spade all afternoon, as he gazed up into the darkening sky in which the first stars were beginning to twinkle.

He still remembered his first day down the pit as though it was yesterday. His mam had shaken him awake at three in the morning and it had still been dark when he'd reached the pit and gone down in the cage. He'd walked along the horse-way for upwards of a mile before he'd reached the barrow-way, over which the young men and boys pushed the trams with the tubs on rails. They'd settled him in a little hole inside one of the trapdoors on the barrow-way, and it had been his job to pull a piece of string to open the door when a man or boy wanted to pass through. He'd been terrified; it couldn't have been darker than if he'd been born blind, but with candles at a penny a day out of his fourpence-a-day wage, his mam and da had told him he'd got to get used to it and he'd better start right off.

He hadn't been scared of mice and rats before that day, not when he could see them, but it had been a different kettle of fish when he could hear the rats squealing and fighting over some morsel or other and feel the mice running over his hands now and again. But bad as that had been, it was the great ugly flying beetles that had turned his bowels to water. Feelers as long as a cat's whiskers – you could stamp on them, jump on them, squash their guts out and still they'd crawl away. Aye, he'd never got used to them, still hadn't if the truth be known. One of them dropping down your neck was enough to spoil the best day.

By, he'd been right glad when the sound of 'Loose, loose!' had reached his ears and he'd known it was four o'clock and time to knock off. Nathaniel grinned up into the charcoal sky, taking a great lungful of fresh, clean air that carried the tang of woodsmoke from a neighbouring bonfire. Aye, he had that. As a trapper he'd waited until the last putter had passed with his tram and then he'd been off to the foot of the shaft. His mam had had a man's dinner waiting for him, he could smell it still. Baked potatoes and tripe and onions, followed by as many girdle scones as he could eat. He'd never forgotten the taste of them hot scones dripping with butter. His mam had been a canny body right enough. She'd known that his bait was eaten along with the muck, dust and sweat that went with working underground.

He frowned suddenly, the elation of working in the crisp northern air after six days of knowing nothing of the ascending or descending sun gone. She'd been a good mother and a good wife, his mam, and his da had known it. Her family had been her life and he'd never heard her complain, not over his da's gambling or drinking or the hardship that went hand in hand with being a pitman's wife. And Dora, Nathaniel's first wife, had been from the same mould, whereas Eva . . . Every night Eva created merry hell about banging their clothes against the wall in the backyard to get the worst of the muck off. There was no give and take with Eva. And to think he'd once thought she was a defenceless little lassie in need of love and protection! By, her da had seen him coming all right. Right fool old Walter had taken him for. Still, Eva had never refused him his rights as her husband once Michael had been born, even if she did lie there like a sack of flour, and he and the lads always came home to a hot meal. That was something. He repeated the thought as though he needed convincing. Aye, there were others worse off, he'd be bound.

He'd wondered how she'd be with the bairn once it was born, her supposedly having been taken down against her will, but she treated Michael no better and no worse than his two lads. Maybe, in hindsight, he should have asked her about the circumstances of her despoilment, but he'd thought it better to let sleeping dogs lie. He couldn't quite work her out if the truth be known. She'd got a tongue on her that could cut you to pieces and not an ounce of tenderness in the whole of her big frame, and when it came to bawling you out she was second to none, and yet sometimes he felt there was a softer side to her. Had she really been unwilling all those years ago?

Nathaniel stood for a moment more before pushing his lips outwards and shaking his grey head irritably. What did he know? Nowt. Double nowt. He'd never have taken her on if he'd had an inkling of what the last twelve years would be like, that was for sure, and one of the most ironic things in the whole set-up was that Michael looked more like his lad than his own bairns did. Funny, that.

He stretched again, glancing over the square of ground that had held the last of his crop of vegetables. Another week or two and he'd have to dig the land over, but he didn't mind that; kept him sane, this bit allotment.

There was still work to do up here in the winter, and the comradeship that went on in all the rough huts built from a mixture of old timber, corrugated iron, orange boxes and the like, made for some canny afternoons. Half the blokes were miners and well known to him, like old George next door.

Nathaniel glanced at the neat patch of land next to his, and an image of dour-faced, hoary old George flashed into his mind. He'd had to be carried home last Christmas Eve, old George, after they'd all brought a sup of something and a few mince pies to toast the occasion. That had been an afternoon to remember, right enough. They'd all been well oiled by the time they had left the allotment, but it had only been when George had tried to rise from his seat on an orange box and fallen flat on his face that they'd realised he was mortalious. And then he'd started singing. By, could he punch 'em out, and none of 'em for a lady's ears! They'd tried to gag him halfway home but he hadn't been having any of it, and when they'd finally plonked him down by his front door he'd staggered to a nearby lamppost and started doing an Irish jig under the dark night sky punctured with a million twinkling stars, holding on to the lamppost for support.

His wife Myra – built like a tank and with a face on her to frighten the devil himself – had given them all gyp for bringing her man home in such a state. Bit of a tartar, George's Myra, but the lass had got a heart of gold under that gruff exterior, although it hadn't been obvious that day. Not with the neighbours all peering out from behind their curtains and laughing. Sent them all packing with a flea in the ear, she had, after hauling George into the house by his ear and him yelping like a bairn.

Nathaniel chuckled at the memory, brushing his grimy hands against his old cloth coat before making his way out of the allotments, his cap pulled low over his forehead.

He was carrying a sack filled with the last of his crop of vegetables, but he still managed to light a Woodbine as he walked, drawing the smoke from the cigarette deep into his lungs as his rheumy eyes – caused by years of acrid coal dust and thick grime – narrowed with satisfaction. He'd had a good afternoon and he was more than ready for his tea; likely Eva and the lads would be back from the farm by now.

She was always in a funny mood come Sunday night, funnier than usual that was. His face straightened as he thought of his wife again. But he'd long since stopped worrying about the whys and wherefores concerning Eva's moods. As long as she put the dinner on before she went to Mass on Sunday morning – although Nathaniel kept his church visiting to high days and holidays, he made sure Eva kept the family's ticket to heaven up to date by her regular attendance – and hurried back without gossiping after, so she could dish up in time for him to have a clear run at the allotment, he didn't mind her visiting her mam and da. He never thought it did her any good, mind, but that was her business. He wasn't going to poke his neb in one way or the other; he'd got it bitten off too many times in the past for that.

It was almost dark when Nathaniel reached Bow Street, and the air had turned chilly. The nights were drawing in fast and winter was round the corner. Nathaniel had his head down as he passed a group of men hanging about at the corner of Southwick Road and he was thinking about his tea, but when one of them croaked his name, followed by, 'You're in a hurry the night, Nat. Who's on your tail, man?' he stopped and turned round, and the man left the others and walked over to him.

Nathaniel had known Bill Hutton all his life. They had played together as bairns and Bill had started down the pit just a month after him, but old as Nathaniel looked, the man in front of him appeared to give him twenty years. Bill had been in line for a few lungfuls of firedamp in an explosion at the pit some twelve months before which had brought the roof – continually weakened by dripping water from above – down on a bunch of miners making for their working point. It had been two days before they had reached Bill, the only survivor of the accident, and the company had refused to pay any compensation, as the miners had been travelling to their appointed place in the pit, not actually working, when the explosion had occurred. After they'd got him out and it had been apparent his insides were cindered and he'd never work again, some folk had said Bill ought to be glad he was still alive. Funny, but Bill had never seen it that way, and Nathaniel didn't blame him. When your bairns were starving and you'd lost every scrap of dignity you ever had, being alive wasn't all it was cracked up to be. How they'd stayed out of the workhouse this long Nathaniel didn't know, but Bill and his wife both came from large families scattered all around Monkwearmouth, so perhaps that was the answer. But handouts from families hard pressed themselves couldn't last forever.

'Just bin up the allotment, man, same as usual,' said Nathaniel.

Bill nodded. His days of working at an allotment or anything else were over; he was hard pressed to put one foot in front of the other most days. 'Aye, nice day for it.'

'Nice enough.' Nathaniel kept his voice casual as he looked at the broken, bent man in front of him whose scrawny wrists sticking out from the ragged cuffs of his jacket looked as though they'd snap with the slightest of pressure. 'Got a few veg I don't know what to do with; don't suppose you an' Peggy could use 'em?'

Bill looked at him, just looked at him for a good ten seconds, before he said, 'Ta, thanks, Nat. Aye, we could use 'em right enough, but won't Eva mind?'

Eva would go fair barmy like as not, but they had three wages coming in. 'No, man, like I said, I didn't know what to do with 'em.'

As the sack changed hands Bill muttered, in the wheezy, tight croak that was painful to hear, 'Things were as black as they've ever bin the night, man. You don't know what this means.'

Pray God, aye, pray God he never would neither. Nathaniel's hand reached in his pocket for the almost full packet of Woodbines and the couple of shillings beer and baccy money he had to last him till pay day, and now he stuffed these into the top pocket of Bill's worn jacket without saying another word, turning smartly on his heel and walking away before Bill could thank him further.

'Gave them away?' Eva's voice was rising. 'You gave them away to Bill Hutton? They were to last us the next month. You said there were enough to last us the next month.'

'Aye, there were.'

'And you gave them away on account of some sob story?'

'There was no sob story, I told you how it happened, an' besides, you've got money in your purse to buy vegetables, which is more than Peggy's got.'

'How do you know what Peggy's got? Soft as clarts, you are, believin' everythin' anyone says. Likely Bill's not as bad as he makes out and he's laughin' up his sleeve right now.'

'Saints alive.' It was said through gritted teeth. Was she really so stupid or was she trying to get under his skin? If ever there was a numbskull in this world it was Eva. 'His bairns' backsides are hangin' out an' him an' Peggy are walkin' scarecrows, so I doubt there's much laughter in that house.' Like this one, he added with silent bitterness.

'Peggy works,' Eva snapped.

'Aye, Peggy works all right, you never said a truer word there. Peggy was never one for sittin' on her backside.' This was sharp and pointed; Eva was far better off than most of the housewives thereabouts, who needed to supplement their family income by taking in washing or engaging in other menial work, and Nathaniel never missed an opportunity to remind her of the fact. 'Works her fingers to the bone by all accounts, an' she's lucky if she can pay the rent, as you well know.'

'I know nothin' of the sort.'

'Well, I've always said there's none so blind as them that don't want to see, an' I'm not discussin' this further. Where's me tea?'

They stared at each other and it was Eva's eyes that dropped away first as she sniffed before turning to the kettle sizzling on the hob. That was typical of Nathaniel, give away their last penny he would. Talk about a soft touch! She spooned three ladles of tea into the big brown teapot with tight, angry movements, and then poured water over the tea, leaving it to mash as she walked through to the pantry at the side of the kitchen and took the butter and cheese from its marbled slab. Once she had carved a whole loaf into thick slices and placed it with the cheese and butter and a small bowl of jam, she went to the foot of the stairs and called, 'Supper's on the table,' before returning to the kitchen, taking a plate of cooked pig's trotters and chitterlings from the pantry and adding it to the table.

She hadn't glanced once at Nathaniel sitting in his armchair in front of the hearth, and neither had they spoken, but at the sound of heavy footsteps on the stairs Eva said stiffly, 'You'd better come and get it before they go through the lot.'

It was an overture of a kind, and Nathaniel answered it by saying, 'Aye, I'll do that.'

It was another two hours before Eva had the kitchen to herself again once Nathaniel and the lads had gone up to bed. After putting the oats to soak for the morning's porridge and washing up the supper things, she made another pot of tea, but in the small teapot this time, which held two cups, and then seated herself in the armchair Nathaniel had vacated. She had started this habit just after Michael was born, claiming the baby's fretfulness late at night disturbed Nathaniel and it was better to let the child have his early-morning feed before she came up to bed, after which Michael always slept through until six o'clock. Whether Nathaniel had guessed she was merely postponing the moment she would have to lie down next to him in the big feather bed she didn't know and she didn't care, but when Michael had been off the breast and sleeping soundly alongside Luke and Arnold she had continued to stay down in the kitchen and Nathaniel had made no comment. When he wanted her he would normally wake her up with his fumbling early in the morning, and she never objected; she merely shut her eyes and pretended she was elsewhere and that the physical act wasn't really happening. It worked, mostly.

Eva now glanced round the kitchen, its shadowed cosiness creating no housewifely satisfaction. Nathaniel thought she was fortunate to be living here, she told herself bitterly, their altercation over the vegetables on her mind. And maybe she was at that. Five of them in a two-up, two-down with its own netty and washhouse was untold spaciousness and luxury compared to plenty, she had realised that soon after she'd been wed. A good many of Sunderland's working class lived in tenement poverty, with one terraced house providing accommodation for two or even three families, or in two-roomed, single-storey cottage rows sandwiched around their place of employment like insects round a dung heap. Women tirelessly cooked, cleaned, baked, washed and fought to keep their families afloat, rising at dawn to make bread and falling into bed late at night too exhausted to think. So, aye, maybe she was lucky compared to most. Nathaniel didn't drink or gamble his wage away like some, and now Arnold and Luke were earning she supposed they were in clover. But she'd give it all up for life in a stinking hovel with Henry, even if it meant ostracism from the rest of the world.

She leaned forward slightly, looking into the faintly glowing fire she had recently banked up for the night with slack and damp tea leaves. She had hoped, in her first hellish months here, when she had thought she was going mad, that Henry's child might prove a comfort to her, but that hadn't been the case. Not that Michael was any trouble – except when he started that ridiculous business about not wanting to go down the pit – but she had discovered her love for Henry filled every crevice and part of her heart, leaving no room for anything or anyone else. She lived only for Sunday afternoons. Aye, she could say that in all truth, she thought morosely. Without the promise of them she would have done away with herself years ago, and likely no one would have missed her.

By, Eva was a bitter pill, why did his da put up with it? Luke always referred to his stepmother by her christian name in his mind, even though out loud he addressed her as Mam because he knew it pleased his father. Or at least it had done in the early days, when his da had still been trying to make them into a family.

All that carry-on about the vegetables, you'd have thought they were dusted in gold the way she'd created. And she wasn't short of money, not with what he and Arnold stumped up, and his da's wage and all. But then nothing his da did was right, it never had been, so why had they married in the first place? Of course Arnold had his own ideas about that. He glanced across the room as though he could see Arnold's bed in the blackness. When you looked at the dates, Michael *had* arrived early, even being premature as his da and Eva had maintained. But he couldn't see his da taking a lass down out of wedlock himself; Da wasn't like that. Oh, what did it matter anyway.

Luke turned over in the narrow iron bed that was pressed close to the wall, conscious of Arnold's heavy breathing across the room, although there wasn't a sound from Michael's small pallet squeezed in between the two single beds. An hour or more she'd been down there by herself and it was the same every night; he knew exactly when she came up to bed because the floorboard just outside their room on the cramped landing creaked if you so much as breathed. By, he couldn't stand the thought of a marriage like his da's.

Across the room there came the sound of a grunt and a groan, followed by a long and loud passing of wind, causing Luke to wince as his insides tightened. He was a dirty pig, their Arnold. Always had been. But it wasn't that which made Luke dislike his brother, nor the loud-voiced bumptiousness and bragging; not even his foul language once he was in the company of his pals and other miners. He knew men that turned the air blue down the pit who were good blokes, decent. But Arnold . . . Arnold wasn't decent. What exactly Arnold was, Luke's mind couldn't find a name for, but he knew it was unclean, and there were times when his brother, his own brother, made his flesh creep. *And Arnold wanted Polly.*

He twisted in the bed again, but the reality of what he had seen in his brother's eyes had to be faced. He had tried to put it to the back of his mind all day, first by taking on that pompous fool Frederick, and then by focusing his thoughts on his father and Eva, but it wasn't any of them who were twisting his guts. The thought of Polly and Arnold – But it wouldn't come to that, of course it wouldn't, he reassured himself in the next moment. She was just a young bairn, as innocent as they came. He was letting his mind run away with him here. Look how she'd been that Sunday a few months back when Michael and Arnold had been doubled up with the skitters, and he'd made the journey to the farm with Eva alone, only to find Ruth laid low too with a bad cold.

Just he and Polly had gone to the stream, and it had seemed like an enchanted place that afternoon – at least to him. Without the others dashing about and splashing it had been quiet and still, and Polly had been content to sit with her feet dangling in the crystal-clear water without engaging in aimless chatter. It had been late May and the scent from the hedgerows had been heady. A flock of goldfinches had busied themselves, twittering sweetly, among the thistles and wild flowers on the far side of the stream, and at one point a green woodpecker had flown across their eyeline with a startled laughing call. He couldn't remember what they had spoken about that afternoon, or even if they had spoken at all; he'd just known it had been heaven on earth.

Aye, she was a child still and she didn't look on any of them in that way, but one thing was for sure. Luke stared up into the blackness that seemed light compared to the consuming darkness of the mine. He would kill Arnold before he let his brother touch such stainless purity with his filth.

Chapter Four

The hard, long winter of 1902 was nothing but a distant memory now as a hot July gave way to an even hotter August, but in the farm kitchen Polly was sick and tired of the heated discussion which had been raging for most of the afternoon, prompted by Labour's by-election victory some eight days before.

She didn't *care* that Labour had won the Barnard Castle seat in the Durham coal-mining constituency, thereby swelling the Labour representation committee to three MPs, she told herself fiercely, or that the new MP had switched sides from the Liberals, which branded him a traitor as far as her Uncle Frederick was concerned.

Her mother's stepbrother and Luke had been at it hammer and tongs for the last hour or so, with her grandda, Da, Arnold and even Michael joining in now and again. Even her mam and Auntie Eva had got involved; her mam on Uncle Frederick's side and her aunt supporting her da and Luke when they had said they thought more and more Liberal agents might change their allegiance in view of the big anti-Tory swing in the north. Everyone was cross with each other and tempers were running high, and it was such a *beautiful* Sunday afternoon and soon it would be Monday again and a whole seven days before she'd see Michael once more.

Polly caught her granny's eye across the room, and as the old woman wagged her head Polly got the impression Gran had read her mind and moreover agreed with her. Then, as Alice beckoned to her, she left her seat on the cracket next to Michael and made her way to her granny's side.

'Help me put the food on the table, hinny. That'll stop their blatherin', an' why don't you an' Ruth an' Michael take your plates outside, eh? It's too bonny a day to waste indoors.'

'Can we, Gran?'

'Aye, me bairn. This lot'll be at it all afternoon now they've started. Out to change the world, they are.'

They walked backwards and forwards between the scullery and pantry and the kitchen amid such snippets of conversation as, 'Oh, aye, aye, great gentlemen the mine owners, an' no doubt their lady wives look bonny enough when they attend their fancy balls an' such

55

like, but it's thém same folk that shed crocodile tears over the dead an' don't you forget it. Why, only last week . . .'

'. . . and refuse the chance of education when it is offered to them. What can you do if a lad would prefer to play the wag and earn a bob or two rather than be at his lessons, now you tell me that? It can't be so bad a life if they're breaking their necks to start it . . .'

'Aye, I said beyond belief an' I mean beyond belief! Of all the half-baked notions I've heard this afternoon, that takes the biscuit, Frederick. Sure sign you've never bin down a pit . . .'

'. . . get the wrong end of the stick because they don't understand the finer points, that's the thing. Most of them can't even read or write . . .'

'. . . tell you I've heard pitmen arguing the toss on everythin' from politics and pigeons to women and whippets, now then, so don't tell me they're all ignorant halfwits . . .'

'. . . nothing but trouble since the first trade union in 1851. Aye, I mean it, Luke, whatever you say. Mob rule, that's what it boils down to, and it'll ruin the country if the unions get the upper hand. The mines, the steelworks, the shipbuilding yards and factories; they're all hotbeds of discontent, whereas the workers used to know their place and everyone was happy. Well, I'd like to see someone try to tell me what to do on my own farm.'

Frederick's face was as red as a beetroot and the mood in the kitchen had turned dark. Polly knew a little of the ins and outs of what the others had been talking about, and she sensed there was none of the normal Sunday jollication flowing, and that her Uncle Frederick looked more than a little upset. And if he was upset that would mean another bout of her mam and da's quiet fighting and her mam being impossible for days, besides which – she looked across at the big burly figure sitting next to her mam on the saddle – her uncle had been very kind to her of late. The severe winter had meant she and Ruth had got to school even less than normal, but it hadn't mattered so much because her Uncle Frederick had taken to bringing her books and newspapers from Stone Farm when he visited. This had become more frequent, often encompassing an evening or two in the week. And he usually sat and talked with her, discussing what she had read and explaining all manner of things. She liked those times and she was glad they had continued even when the winter had finished.

So now, aiming to diffuse the electricity in the air as much for Frederick's ease of mind as to avert her mother's wrath from her father, she reached for a plate of sliced buttered fruit loaf and walked across to the saddle, offering her uncle the plate as she said smilingly, 'I don't know if you dare try a shive, Uncle Frederick, 'cos I made it meself. Gran's rheumatism has been playin' her up so me an' Ruth did the cookin' yesterday.'

56

For a moment she didn't think it was going to work, and then, as her uncle brought his eyes from Luke's grim, tight face to her own, Polly watched him take a long, hard pull of air before he relaxed, saying, 'Did you now? Well, I'll have to be trying a piece in that case, won't I?'

'Gran thought I was a sight over-generous with the fruit, but I like it nice an' claggy.'

'Nice and claggy, eh?' A smile was spreading over his face, widening his mouth and giving his eyes the crinkled look she liked best. 'We're two of a kind then, you and me, because there's nothing I like more than a sticky fruit loaf. Betsy, bless her heart, is a mite sparing with the currants.'

'I can make you one any time, Gran won't mind.'

'No?' His voice was soft now, and low. 'Well, that's right nice of you, lass. And what do you think of your reading for this week? Is *Nicholas Nickleby* to your taste?'

'Oh, yes.' Her voice was bright now, and eager. 'It's more cheerful than *Great Expectations*, isn't it, and I can understand it better.'

'Good, good.' He nodded, his eyes wandering over the sweet face in front of him. 'We'll discuss it in the week, eh? Maybe Tuesday? Would you like that?'

Polly glanced at her mother. Hilda had subjected her daughter to a ten-minute lecture the previous week on the merits of being seen and not heard when visitors were present, but she had known it was only one visitor in particular her mother had had in mind. Ever since her Uncle Frederick had started to bring books to the farm and tell her about literature and the classics and such, her mother had played up. She had even made Ruth sit with them every time her uncle called, and her mam knew how much Ruth disliked reading and writing. Ruth hated all that stuff as much as her sister loved it. 'Can I, Mam?' Polly said now.

Hilda's voice was as low as her stepbrother's had been when she said, 'Can you? You don't have to ask me, girl, you know that. If your uncle is kind enough to spare his time, the least we can do is to be grateful.'

Oh, her mam. Always twisting things round.

Polly could feel the colour flooding into her face as she turned away from the saddle. Mam had made it seem as though she had asked permission because she didn't want to sit with her uncle and learn about everything, and that wasn't the case at all. Uncle Frederick had told her numerous times that he looked forward to their discussions, and that she was a bright, intelligent lass, and much as she loved her grandparents and Da, it was nice to have a grown-up *listen* to her like her uncle did.

They'd read *Great Expectations* throughout the winter months, along with a book of poems for what her uncle termed 'light relief'. He'd told her he had been pleasantly surprised at how quickly she'd taken to Dickens, and when he encouraged her to discuss and comment on different newspaper articles and such, he never laughed at what she said or made fun of her, but said her slant on things was refreshing. She liked her Uncle Frederick. And her mam would like to spoil those precious times if she could.

Polly's small chin rose at the thought, her blue eyes darkening as she watched the others filling their plates. This had been a horrible afternoon up to now. Well, she was going to take her plate outside and she wasn't going to ask *anyone* to come with her. If they wanted to, then that was fine, but if no one followed her . . . She'd know. Quite *what* she would know, Polly wasn't absolutely sure, but it was all to do with Michael's fascination with the others' conversation and his obliviousness to her presence beside him on the cracket.

Once outside in the cobbled yard in front of the house, Polly stood still for a moment, the hot sun beating down on her uncovered head and the smell from the pigsty at the back of the building wafting on the summer breeze as it was wont to do when the wind was in the wrong direction. She glanced down at her plate of food and then back towards the farmhouse door, which was slightly ajar. She could hear Ruth laughing inside, which meant one of the lads was teasing her, probably Michael. Ruth always made up to Michael.

This last thought, along with the smell of the pigs, brought Polly skirting the edge of the yard and passing through the small opening into the area beyond. She passed the stable, rubbing Bess's velvet nose and then Patience's, as the two horses peered enquiringly out, then continued past the empty cow byres and on to the barn beyond. The air was fresher here, clean, carrying the scents of the hedgerows and the apple trees and fruit bushes which bordered her granny's vegetable plot. Her da had once told her that when he was a boy, and the farm had employed some four or five men, Gran's little orchard and plot of land had been a picture, but it was mostly overgrown now, and a couple of the trees were diseased and needed cutting down.

Nevertheless, she never came this way now without thinking about one of the poems in Uncle Frederick's book. Like so much of what she read, it made her feel sad and happy at the same time.

> I remember, I remember
> The house where I was born,
> The little window where the sun
> Came peeping in at morn;
> He never came a wink too soon,
> Nor brought too long a day,

But now I often wish the night
Had borne my breath away.

There were more verses, all about flowers and trees and birds, but the melancholy running through the poem always made her think of her granny.

The barn door was wide open, and Polly sat down on a bale of hay a couple of feet inside and gazed at the view. Past the tangle of the orchard and unkempt ground there was the lane, and beyond that a field of grazing cows and then more fields. It was peaceful and quiet, nice, but she didn't feel nice inside. She closed her eyes and shook her head. She was barmy. Ruth had called her that the other night. She had been leaning out of their bedroom window and looking up into the night sky, and she'd said she'd like to make a necklace of the stars and give it to her granny, and Ruth had laughed and called her barmy.

'Got you!' As Arnold's voice sounded loud in her ear, the start Polly gave almost sent her backwards off the bale of hay, and as her legs flew up and the plate fell from her lap it was only Arnold's hands shooting out and grabbing her shoulders that saved her. 'You can't hide from me, you know.'

'I wasn't hiding!' Her voice was indignant.

'No?' He was laughing, but his brown eyes were hard on her face and he hadn't let go of her, and when she wriggled in his grasp he said, but softly now, 'You sure about that, Polly?'

'Of course I am.' Her tone was still strident, but inwardly something deep inside registered that there was an element of truth in his accusation. If she had thought Arnold was following her she would have made sure he didn't find her. Since that day last summer at the stream she had become aware of this older cousin in a way that made her slightly afraid. She had shot up in the last six months – her granny had done nothing but bemoan her sudden growth and the fact that her hems had been let down as far as they would go and still her two dresses were only just below her knees – but Arnold was a good head taller than her, and broad with it.

He seemed to tower over her now as he said, 'Funny, but I got the idea you think you're too good for us now you've got a bit of book learnin'. Am I wrong?'

'Yes, you are.' Her voice was quieter; she sensed something here that wasn't right and instinctively knew she needed to keep her wits about her.

'Prove it.'

'What?'

'Prove it.' His voice had a slight tremble to it now and his fingers tightened on her shoulders, his thumbs stroking the soft, warm skin of her neck above the collar of her dress.

59

'Let . . . let go of me.' It wasn't as forceful as she would have liked, but her stomach seemed to have curdled in the last few moments.

'You're a pretty lass, but then you know that, don't you? Oh, aye, you know it all right.' He gave a low laugh deep in his throat. 'Blossomed out just as I expected. You ever kissed a lad, Polly? You kissed Michael?' His tongue came out and wetted his fleshy lower lip.

'No.'

'I don't think I believe you.'

'I don't care what you believe, Arnold Blackett.'

'Don't see anything of life stuck on this bit farm, do you?' His upper body was bending forward, and although she had her hands either side of her thighs in the hay, her balance was precarious with his fingers pressing her slightly backwards, and she knew without thinking about it that she mustn't fall on the floor. 'If you're kind to me I'll take you to the Olympia in Borough Road, you'd like that, wouldn't you? It's got roundabouts and gondolas and a big menagerie, it's right bonny.'

'Gran . . . Gran wouldn't let me.'

'Oh, aye, she would, if we played it right. We could all go, you and me and Luke and Ruth and Michael, see? Or there's the Victoria Hall, they're doing moving picture shows. You ever bin to a moving picture show, Polly?'

'You know I haven't.'

'No, that's right, stuck on this bit farm you don't go nowhere, but you're not as ignorant as you make out either, not with all the animals around, eh? Bin brought up with it, haven't you? No, you know what's what all right.'

Polly didn't have the faintest idea what he was talking about, but from his tone she knew he wouldn't talk this way if her da or any of the others were present. He was acting like he had that day when Luke had gone for him – nasty. Her neck was aching from the strained position he'd pressed her into, and then suddenly he moved with a swiftness which caught her unawares. He jerked her forwards so she was forced to slide off the bale and on to her feet in front of him, whereupon she found herself enveloped by his brawny arms.

Polly lowered her head instinctively as his mouth sought hers, and then all her fighting instincts rose in an angry rush and she thrust outwards with both hands, taking Arnold completely by surprise. He reeled backwards, almost losing his footing, and then when he would have come at her again they both heard a voice calling her name. Arnold glanced about him and then sat on one of the sacks of taties at the side of Bess's harness, which her father had been cleaning when everyone had arrived, swinging one leg idly as he surveyed her from under glowering brows.

Polly continued to stand exactly where he had left her for the

60

simple reason that her legs felt weak and she needed the support of her buttocks resting against the bale of hay, but she glared back at him, determined to hide every trace of the trembling in her stomach.

'What's been going on here?' It was Luke who walked round the side of the barn door a second later, his dark eyes flashing from Polly's white face to Arnold sitting on the sack.

'Nothing.' Arnold's voice was casual – too casual – and when Ruth and Michael appeared at the barn's entrance Luke was already hauling his brother to his feet, his face close to Arnold's as he growled, 'I warned you, didn't I, and I meant it.'

'Pack it in, man.' There was only a year between the two brothers, and although Luke was the younger, he matched Arnold in height and breadth. 'I didn't do anything, I tell you. Ask Polly.'

Luke's hand was gripping the front of Arnold's shirt as he turned to glance at Polly, and now her brain was racing. If Luke and Arnold fought, her grandda would want to know why, and then this whole thing would mushroom like a snowball rolling downhill.

'We were talking,' she said flatly. 'That's all.'

'See?' Arnold jerked himself free.

'Oh, aye, I see all right,' Luke said grimly. 'I see a frightened little lass, that's what I see.'

'You all right, Poll?' Michael had sidled to Polly's side, and now, as he took her hand, she felt sufficiently recovered to smile at him and say in a normal voice, 'I'm fine, I am. There's nothin' wrong, really.'

'You dropped your plate.'

This was from Luke and an accusation in itself, and now Polly said quickly, 'It was a rat. It ran right in front of me an' made me jump.'

'We've bin havin' trouble with rats.' It was Ruth who unwittingly gave credence to the lie. 'Da was tellin' us the other night he was workin' in here when one squeezed itself under the barn door, then another an' another until they were passin' through in a line. They crossed right in front of him and then out that hole' – she pointed to a broken timber at the bottom of the barn – 'to go down to the pigsty. Gran said when she empties the pigs' food into their trough there's three or four rats in it afore she's finished sometimes. Da's bin meanin' to get another cat since Kitty died an' Uncle Frederick's lettin' us have a couple of kittens from one of his cats in a week or two.'

It was a long speech for Ruth and had the added advantage of being the truth, and now, as Polly saw Luke was hesitating, she added, 'They come down from the cow byres and calf pens mostly, but the odd one lives in here an' all. I *hate* rats.'

'Aye.' Luke still wasn't totally convinced. 'Especially the two-legged kind.'

61

'What's the matter with you?' Arnold's righteous indignation was more forceful now he knew Polly wasn't going to give him away. 'Always having a go about something or other, you are.'

'And there's usually just cause.'

'Aye, well, there's not today.'

'Maybe.'

'Oh, for cryin' out loud!' Arnold shook his head, and no one looking at him would have guessed his irritation was feigned. 'What are we wasting time for? It's a right bonny day and I'm for the river. You told 'em what we've brought the day?' And as Luke shook his head, Arnold turned to the others, a smile on his face, and said, 'Bandy nets. Thought we'd try for some tiddlers.'

'Bandy nets?' Ruth was jumping up and down in her excitement. 'Where are they?'

'Down by the wall in the lane.' It was Michael speaking now and his eyes were on Polly. 'We thought it'd be a surprise, and you can keep them here so we can use them again.'

'Come on then.' Arnold turned and walked out of the barn, and as the others followed him, Michael caught hold of Polly's hand once more and said in a low undertone, '*Are* you all right, Poll? Really?'

His concern and the feel of his fingers holding hers made Polly's voice light as she said, 'Aye, I'm fine,' and she was – now. But she'd make sure she was never alone with Arnold again. He would have kept trying to kiss her if Luke hadn't called, and she knew she'd have bruises on her shoulders tomorrow from where his hands had gripped her flesh.

The sun was beating down out of a cloudless blue sky as the five of them picked up the nets and climbed over the wall, and in spite of the way her stomach was still churning, Polly's spirits lifted. Everything was so much better when the sun shone.

She and Ruth could get up early tomorrow and have the weekly wash soaking in the poss tub before breakfast, and out drying over the thorn hedge skirting the field sides once the sun was really up. The worst job was wringing out the sheets and towels – they always made her hands ache for ages afterwards – but even that didn't seem so bad when the sun was shining. They had a mangle in the scullery at Stone Farm. That must be wonderful, a mangle. Still, with a bit of luck she'd have everything dried and damped down and ready for ironing by tea-time tomorrow – that'd please her granny. She gave a little skip, the incident in the barn fading to the back of her mind as the afternoon regained its normality.

Once at the stream, Luke and Arnold followed the flowing water some way until they came to the point where it joined another inlet and the whole widened into quite a substantial river. Michael had been holding back a little, his hand still clasping Polly's, but now, as Luke and Arnold took off their black hobnailed boots and then their socks before rolling up their trouser legs, they called to him to join them on the large rocks, the tops of which formed stepping stones across the river just in front of the really deep water.

As Michael turned to Polly she answered the unspoken request on his face with a smile. 'Go on, you go. Me an' Ruth'll plodge.'

Once the lads were in the middle of the river, casting their nets, the two girls sat down on the thick grass and unbuttoned their boots before rolling down their black stockings and slipping their garters into their pinafore pockets. Ruth said nothing whilst they did this, and after a moment or two Polly glanced at her sister's sulky face. 'What's the matter?' Her voice was resigned. Ruth was in a tear about something. She knew the signs.

'Nothin'.'

'Yes there is. You look as if you've lost a penny an' found a farthin'.'

Ruth shrugged. She was fed up with everyone making up to their Polly, and they did. They did. Sun shone out of her backside, as Nellie Cook at school would say. All that fuss in the barn and all she'd done was to drop her plate; if Ruth had dropped hers she'd have got wrong for it, not all that attention. And Michael, Michael liked Polly better than her, she knew he did. He was always talking nice to her and sitting near her, and look at today – him holding Polly's hand and everything.

'Come on.' Polly had scrambled to her feet and was holding out her hand, but Ruth ignored her. 'Come *on*, Ruth. It'll be fun fishin' with our nets. Oh, don't be mardy, not today.'

Ruth looked up then. There had been a catch in her sister's voice as though she was upset about something, but when Polly smiled at her and held out the bandy net, Ruth decided she must be mistaken. Anyway, what could Polly be upset about? Ruth asked herself bitterly. Everyone was always falling over backwards to be nice to Polly. Nevertheless, she too rose to her feet and took the net Polly proffered, saying mutinously, 'I'm going on the whale's teeth' – their nickname for the stepping stones – 'with the lads.'

'You mustn't, you know you mustn't; they can swim and we can't, and it's deep one side. We've promised Gran—'

'I'm going an' you can't stop me, you're not Gran.' And as Polly reached out to take her arm, Ruth darted away defiantly.

Polly followed her sister to the edge of the bank. She knew it was quite deep even on the shallower side of the whale's teeth – when Michael had fallen off into the water the year before, it had come up to his shoulders – but the other side fell away in a sharp downward slope and looked murky and dark. So now, as Ruth went to put a tentative foot on the first rock, over which the water frothed now and again, Polly yanked her back with enough force to make her cry out. 'Don't you dare, Ruth. I'll tell Gran and Da'll skin you, you know he will.'

'Oh, you! Tellypie tit, your tongue will split an' all the little dicky birds'll have a little bit.' Ruth sang the rhyme tauntingly, her body bent forwards towards her sister and her neck stretched out. 'I'm not scared.'

'Well, you should be,' Polly shot back. 'Remember Clara Ramshaw? She drowned at Farrington burn an' her da an' her brothers were there but she dropped like a stone, her da said, an' by the time they got her out she was dead.'

Ruth was silent for a moment. Clara had been in her class at school and her death had shocked everyone. 'Oh, you, you spoil everythin'.' But it was weaker and Polly, satisfied that her sister wasn't about to launch herself on the slippery rocks to impress the lads, continued to walk along the bank a little way more to where the water wasn't swirling quite so much. If they were going to catch anything in their nets it was more likely to be here, in this deep water away from the rocks and the noise the lads were making. She glanced behind her once and saw Ruth was following her, her face still querulous.

Polly sighed, and then called over her shoulder as she bent to skim her net through the water, her voice both laughing and conciliatory, 'Come on, kiddar. It's too nice a day to be moany. Come an' see what you can catch.'

Kiddar. They all thought of her as just a bairn, and Polly always made out she was miles and miles older than her instead of just three years. And she was fed up with Polly telling her what she could and couldn't do.

Ruth was never really sure afterwards if she meant to push Polly into the fast-flowing river or just frighten her sister, but the end result was Polly seeming to hover in the air for a second as she gave one shrill, terrified scream, and then disappearing under the surging flow in a flurry of arms and legs and spray. And then Ruth was screaming herself and the lads were shouting, and Luke gave her an almighty shove backwards as he leapt into the river exactly where Polly had gone down. Ruth landed with such a bump it knocked all the wind out of her and she lay gasping but silent, listening to the voices above her head but unable to respond.

When Polly felt the waters close over her head her mouth was still open in a scream and she immediately took a great mouthful of the river before she knew what she was doing. It filled her airways and her eyes and ears as she sank – like Clara, like Clara had done at Farrington burn, her mind screamed. But then she felt her feet land on the river bed, and weeds and other things wrapped round her legs and she kicked out furiously, putting all her strength in

64

aiming for the light she could see far above as she thrashed wildly with her arms.

She was aware the current was carrying her along and that its pull was aiming to keep her under, but she fought against it with all her might, her lungs beginning to ache as she held her breath. And then her head broke the surface of the fast-moving water and she managed to gulp a breath before she felt herself submerged again, and terror like she had never felt before gripped her.

It could only have been a second or two later that she felt her hair being torn out by its roots, the pain forcing her to open her mouth in a cry that made her swallow more water. But then she could breathe air again and her face was staring into Luke's contorted features, whereupon she flung her arms round his neck in a stranglehold that threatened to drown them both.

'Let go, Polly! You have to let go. I've got you, I won't let you slip. Trust me.'

It was the hardest thing she had ever done, to follow his instructions and relax her hold sufficiently for Luke to turn her round against his chest, and her eyes were wide with fear as he struck out for the bank with one arm, towing her body behind him. And then she felt other hands reach down and grasp her, and she realised Luke had reached the edge of the embankment and Arnold and Michael were kneeling there waiting to help.

As she was hoisted to safety, Polly felt herself enfolded into Michael's arms as Arnold heaved his brother on to dry land, but she was too spent to say anything, as was Luke.

'Polly, oh, Poll. Poll . . .' Michael was murmuring her name over and over as he cradled her in his thin arms, his legs either side of her limp, water-soaked form and his arms tight round her as he endeavoured to stop her shaking with the warmth of his slight body.

She was covered in mud from being dragged up the bank; her granny would go mad when she saw the state of her Sunday dress and pinny. Polly was aware of the thought at the same time as her senses sucked in the heat of the sun, the smell of the warm grass and wild flowers dotting the riverbank and the twittering of the birds in the trees surrounding the water, who were blissfully unaware of the drama which had been enacted beneath them.

She raised her head to see Luke kneeling on the grass a yard or two away. He looked strange; he, too, was covered in mud and gunge, and there were bits of twig and more mud causing his wet hair to stick out at all angles. And then everything began to recede and she felt sick, and she rolled out of Michael's hold as the nausea overcame her and her stomach rebelled against the river water she'd swallowed.

'Polly?' When she eventually pulled herself into a sitting position,

Ruth was crouched at the side of her, and her sister's face was ashen. 'I slipped, Polly.'

'It's all right.'

'No,' said Michael, who had stripped off his shirt and now wrapped it round Polly's shivering body. 'No, it isn't all right. You don't act the cuddy near water, you know that as well as anyone, Ruth. You could've drowned her.'

He looked into Polly's dirt-smeared face, in which her teeth were chattering so hard they could all hear it, and she managed a small, reassuring smile when she saw the expression in his eyes. He'd looked at her like that a few times since that time at the stream nearly a year ago, but never so long or so openly. 'You look like a stranded little mudlark nymph,' he said very softly, his narrow, thin chest rising and falling with the force of his emotion.

And then, as their shared glance became absorbing, shutting out everyone and everything else and making them oblivious to the three pair of eyes watching them, it was Arnold's voice that broke the bubble as he said sharply to Ruth, 'You oughta be whipped to within an inch of your life, you.' His eyes had left Polly and Michael and were now glaring at the younger girl, and they resembled cold black chips of the coal he worked. 'You'll be in for a leathering tonight if I have anything to do with it.'

'No, no, she couldn't help it. You heard her, she slipped.' Polly struggled to her feet as she spoke, walking across to Luke, who had also just risen to his feet as she said, 'Thank you, Luke. Oh, thank you.' She took his cold hands in her equally cold ones. 'I wouldn't have got out of there without you, I know I wouldn't. You saved me.'

Luke stared at her for a moment. He was as aware as his brother had been of all that had passed between Polly and Michael, and for a moment the pain in his heart said, Oh, aye, I saved you all right, and it looks like it was for Michael. But then the bitterness was gone as the rational side of him added, Well? Wouldn't you do the same again without thinking about it? Aye, aye, he would, by, he would. 'I've never understood why lasses are discouraged from learning to swim.' He smiled at her, allowing himself a brief touch of her face before he added, the smile turning into a grin, 'Just give me a bit of notice the next time you decide to take a dip, eh?'

'Oh, Luke.' For a moment Polly leant against this big brother of hers – as she'd always thought of him. It seemed natural somehow that Luke had been the first to see the danger and dive into the water; he was like that. He might go on a bit about the unions and politics and education for the working classes and all, but there was something about this tall, big-shouldered miner that made you feel safe. You could walk into the worst of situations with Luke beside you and not be afraid.

And then she felt herself gently put from him as he said quietly,

'Let's see about getting you home and in the warm, eh? Can you walk?'

'Of course I can walk.' It was a touch indignant and told the others more clearly than anything else could have that no real harm had been done.

They looked a sorry bunch on the way back to the farm; Arnold stalking ahead with a face as black as thunder, Luke and Michael either side of Polly, who still had Michael's shirt wrapped round her, and Ruth bringing up the rear with the four bandy nets – Polly's having been lost in the river.

Several times on the walk home Polly turned and called for Ruth to join them, but each time Ruth shook her head and kept her eyes on the ground, so eventually Polly gave up trying, finding it was all she could do to put one foot in front of the other without worrying about how her sister was feeling.

And how Ruth was feeling was changing minute by minute. At first she had been overcome with horror at what she had done and terrified that one of the lads might have seen exactly what had happened. That fear allayed and Polly safely out of the water, relief had been paramount, along with the desire to make her part in the proceedings as innocent as possible. Then Michael had gone for her, and Arnold, and Michael had been all over Polly. Well, they all had, fussing and carrying on.

She hadn't meant for Polly to actually *fall* in the river. Her conscience twinged for a second and she answered it vehemently: *she hadn't*. It had been Polly's fault, she'd been too near the edge, showing off in front of the lads. She was always showing off, although the others couldn't see it. She scowled at the grass beneath her boots.

And now everyone was cross with her and she'd get wrong from her da and her grandparents when they got back, especially if Arnold had anything to do with it. She hated Arnold. She glanced straight ahead and saw Michael had his arm round Polly's waist. And she hated Michael, and Luke, but most of all Polly. She always had to be *the* one, their Polly did.

Their entrance into the kitchen at the farm caused pandemonium, and in spite of Polly saying she was perfectly all right, Alice, and to a lesser extent Henry and Walter – lesser in the sense that the two men didn't show their disquiet quite so verbally as Alice – were beside themselves with what might have happened. It caused an immediate exit of all the visitors, Luke sluicing himself down under the pump in the yard and insisting his clothes would dry on his back before he was home, and then the tin bath was brought out for the second time that day and filled to capacity with hot water and mustard.

How long Polly soaked in the steamy solution she didn't know, but by the time Alice was satisfied her granddaughter could get out, Polly was glowing from head to foot and the cold stone slabs on the scullery floor felt wonderful beneath her bare feet.

Ruth had been sent straight upstairs by her furious granny and for once she hadn't argued or complained, being wise enough to know she had got off lightly. However, once Polly was also in bed and their da and grandda and granny had all squeezed into the small room and told them that today marked the end of any more jaunts to the stream when the lads called, she had been less subdued.

'That's not *fair*.' Ruth wrinkled her nose at the three grown-ups, but Polly, lying at the side of her, said nothing. She had been feeling constantly nauseous since vomiting the river water, and the hot mustard bath had made her feel worse. There was the washing to be done tomorrow morning, and all the ironing if the linen and clothes dried in time, and her granny couldn't do much lately, not with her rheumatism so bad. She *had* to be well. But she felt like she was going to have the skitters.

Once the grown-ups had gone downstairs, Polly turned on her side away from Ruth's quiet ranting and raving, and closed her eyes, but long after Ruth's rhythmic breathing told Polly her sister was asleep, she continued to lie awake, the cramps in her stomach worsening. And then she felt something sticky between her legs and, after feeling cautiously, was horrified to discover what looked like blood on her fingers. She climbed out of bed carefully, her heart thudding fit to burst, and after wiping herself carefully with her handkerchief, padded downstairs to find her granny.

It was only sometime later, after listening to Gran's brief and embarrassed explanation after she had fetched out some wads of calico to the ends of which were attached lengths of tape, that Polly realised this bleeding signified her entrance into womanhood, and that worse, it was going to happen to her every month from now on.

However, once she was snuggled up to her granny on the old saddle with a thin blanket over her legs and a mug of hot sweet milk in her hands, everything didn't seem so bad. The room was quiet with the shadows of evening slanting across it, and the red glow from the fire was comforting. In spite of the heat of the day, the stone-floored farmhouse was never over-warm, and Polly had been feeling a mite chilly in her linen nightdress.

Her da and her grandda were seeing to the beasts out in the fields; they'd be in soon for their supper. Polly felt a wave of well-being and contentment relax the tightness in her stomach and her eyelids became heavy. In her semi-sleep state her mind drifted to Michael. She was going to be his lass; his face had told her so today. She hugged the thought to her, a small smile curving her delicately shaped lips. And once Michael told Arnold, he wouldn't try and kiss her any more – not that he'd get much chance anyway now she and Ruth had to stay around the farmhouse when the lads came. He was horrible, Arnold, as horrible as Luke was nice.

Her granny had said she'd begin to get more of a woman's shape now this thing had happened to her. She thought she would rather like that; you couldn't stay a bairn forever and you had to be a woman to get wed. And she wanted to get wed, oh, she did. She would walk down the aisle on her da's arm and Michael would be waiting for her . . .

She snuggled more comfortably into the flock cushions. All in all, it had been something of an eventful day.

Chapter Five

'Aye, well, you might think as I'm over-reactin', woman, but I know what I know. He's playin' it tighter than a duck's arse an' twice as canny, but I'm tellin' you he wants her.'

Alice had to suppress a smile. Walter's way of putting things could be funny, but as her husband had no sense of humour whatsoever she knew better than to show amusement. And especially today, in view of what they were discussing. 'Frederick?' she queried doubtfully.

'Aye, Frederick, an' don't tell me you haven't suspected somethin', with all the books an' such he's bin bringin' the bairn?'

Alice raised her eyes to her husband, and in the flickering light from the oil lamp she saw his level gaze was fixed on her face as he waited for her answer. *Had* she harboured any suspicions regarding Frederick Weatherburn's apparent charitableness and kind-heartedness towards Polly these last months? she asked herself silently. Well, she might have, now and again, but she wasn't going to admit it to Walter, with him in this mood. 'She's nowt but a bairn, Walter.'

'You've told me yourself this night she's a bairn no more, so think on, lass. An' don't tell me he's old enough to be her da either, I know that right enough,' he ground out irritably. 'But there's plenty of 'em get the urge for something young to warm their bones.'

'Oh, Walter!'

'An' while we're on the subject, I'm none too happy about some of the things the pair of 'em talk about neither. I'm as broad-minded as the next 'un, an' if he wants to bring the local papers an' have a debate till he's blue in the face I've nothin' agen it, but I don't want our little lassie's mind filled with anythin' mucky.'

'Mucky?' Alice didn't have the faintest idea what Walter was talking about, but she knew the incident that afternoon, with its potential for tragedy, had upset him, and so her voice was indulgent.

'Aye, mucky. I caught Frederick discussin' what he called the "merits" of that dancer, her with the fancy name who's none too particular about keepin' herself to herself. Isadora Duncan, that's it. Flauntin' herself an' prancin' about in the altogether with her you-know-whats jigglin' about.'

'I don't think she was in the altogether, Walter,' Alice replied stolidly, aiming to keep the gurgle of laughter out of her voice.

'Well, the woman's nowt but a brazen hussy nevertheless!'

Alice nodded. It was always better to nod and keep quiet when Walter was on his high horse.

'Takin' Paris by storm!' Walter gave a very good imitation of a pig snorting. 'A young lass like her'd be better occupied settin' her sights on marriage an' bairns. By, I don't know what the world's comin' to, I don't straight.'

'Aye, well, our Polly's got her head screwed on all right,' said Alice, aiming to placate him.

Walter looked long and hard at his wife for a full ten seconds before he turned from her and took up the poker. Crouching on his hunkers, he stirred the embers of the fire. He wasn't sure about Alice, what she was thinking, he never had been. His uncertainty had been the reason he'd resorted to the measures he had to make sure she didn't leave the farm after his mam and da died all those years back. Most women of his acquaintance would jaw their heads off all day given half a chance and always be ready for a good crack, but not Alice. Silent as the grave most of the time, Alice was. But she was a good worker, aye, and a canny lass in her own way.

Still on his hunkers, he glanced up at her, sitting on the saddle, and as his gaze fell on the blanket at the side of his wife it brought him back to the main point of their conversation. 'He's too old for her, you know it an' I know it, an' he could come here covered in gold an' I'd still say the same. Do you hear what I'm sayin'?'

'Aye, I hear you.'

'An' that's all you've got to say on the matter?'

'We don't know for sure if Frederick is feelin' the way you say.'

'An' if he is? If he's pavin' the way, so to speak, what say you then?' Walter asked with quiet persistence. 'Do you want to see our lass wed to Frederick Weatherburn?'

If he had asked her that question this time yesterday she could have said in all truth that the answer was no. Alice's hands were lying on her lap, her fingers entwined, and now she worked her thumbs one over the other whilst keeping her eyes downcast. But she had seen the way Polly and Michael were looking at each other when the lot of them had come back this afternoon. She had been coming out of the privy and had stood and watched them crossing the field, and what she had seen had turned her bowels to water. Polly and Michael. *Polly and Michael.* She'd known the bairns thought a bit of each other, but bairns formed attachments, it didn't mean anything. But *this*, this meant something. She felt her stomach turn right over and stood up quickly, her voice urgent as she said, 'I need the privy.'

She hurried out, across the yard, where the night air was muggy and heavy and smelt of an imminent thunderstorm, and into the lavatory. Walter had cleaned it out that morning ready for their Sunday visitors and she had put a fresh load of ashes down the hole after lunch, so there were no bad smells as she shut the door and sat on the scrubbed wooden seat.

Why hadn't she seen something like this happening? She swayed backwards and forwards a few times before bringing herself stiff and straight. She mustn't lose control or imagine the worst, not yet. They *were* still bairns, of course they were, she told herself silently, the thought one of desperation. In another few months Michael would be leaving school and joining the lads he thought of as his half-brothers down the pit, and that alone would bring about changes. He'd have to toughen up, get harder, and the appealingly winsome side of the lad that was so like Henry would be knocked out of him.

Alice felt a momentary pang of guilt. She had been pressing Eva for months to let Michael stay above ground in some job or other, and now she couldn't see him down the mine quick enough. She shook her head at her own fickleness. But she knew what it was that attracted Polly to the lad, and of necessity, if Michael was going to survive as a miner, that side of him would have to die. Maybe a stronger individual would be able to remain true to his real identity underground, but she sensed in Michael the same inherent weakness that always caused his father to take the line of least resistance. Neither of them was a fighter. Even if her two grandchildren hadn't shared the same father, she still wouldn't have wanted Michael for Polly. He was a sweet lad, gentle and kind, but she would have had to carry him the whole of her married life.

Alice hunched her shoulders. It was a full moon outside, but inside the lavatory the darkness was complete, and in her hurry she had forgotten to bring a candle. But it didn't matter; nothing mattered except Polly and Michael. It was ironic, when you thought about it, that of the two people she loved best, one had to be sacrificed for the sake of the other. Michael was Henry as a lad, but purer, sweeter than his father had ever been, but then Henry's Achilles heel in the shape of his sister had meant her boy had never stood a chance.

Somewhere nearby a fox barked its raucous cry, and Alice leant back wearily against the stone wall of the lavatory. Perhaps if she'd been kinder to Eva, shown her daughter some affection, none of this would have happened. And if Walter hadn't tricked her into marriage in the first place but asked her proper—

Here her thoughts were interrupted by a bang on the door that made Alice nearly jump out of her skin, followed by Walter's voice, gruff and somewhat embarrassed, as though his show of concern was in some way unfitting, saying, 'You all right, lass?'

'Aye, aye, I'm fine. I'll be in in a minute.'

'It's likely that milk you insisted on finishin' up. I told you you should have thrown it out an' had the same as the rest of us, but you won't be told.'

'No, well, I'll know next time.'

'I'll sort out that bottle of stuff I fetched for Ruth when she had the skitters bad a while back, a drop of that'll sort you out. You'll be right as rain come mornin'.'

Feelings were funny things. As Walter returned to the farmhouse Alice's thoughts were with her husband. Thirty-four years she'd been wed, and the first twenty-two of them she had been hard pressed to tolerate Walter. And then their Polly had been born, and she'd expected him to be uninterested in the bairn, her being a little lassie and not the grandson she knew he'd been hoping for. But he'd loved her from the first, dangling the babby on his knee and showering her with affection in a way he'd never done with his own bairns. And with Hilda rejecting the child and then taking to her bed once Ruth was born, she and Walter had virtually brought both little lassies up – Henry being a loving but distant father.

And somewhere along the line a strange thing had happened, because she'd found herself warming to Walter, and in turn that had seemed to release something in him he'd hitherto kept hidden. And she was right fond of him now – she balked at the word love, her contained, repressed upbringing inherent in her thinking – and he of her. Polly had brought a lot of joy into both their lives, and yet life was harder now than ever it had been. Strange that. But the bairn was special right enough. Alice's eyes narrowed reflectively.

And if Hilda's stepbrother *had* got his eye on their lass then Alice wouldn't be backwards in tipping Frederick the wink that she was for him. He might be considerably older than Polly but he was well set up and Polly would want for nothing. Her lass, mistress of Stone Farm! Aye, she'd certainly do all she could to steer Polly in that direction and pray God, aye, pray God He would cause this other thing to die while it was still in its embryo state. Walter would go mad, stark staring mad, if he got an inkling of it. She'd had to do battle to get him to agree to Eva and the lads visiting the farm once Eva was wed, and it was only the fact that they couldn't have trusted Eva to keep her mouth shut if they'd cut her off altogether that had persuaded Walter. She knew Michael was a constant thorn in his grandfather's side, and Walter had never taken to the lad like she had.

Alice reached for a couple of the squares of newspaper hanging on a nail driven into the stone wall of the lavatory. She'd have to get back; she was feeling better now and she'd been daft to panic when there were still years before Polly would be ready to marry anyone. What was it the parson had said the last time they had got along to church? She'd found it comforting, sensible, at the time and had repeated it to herself until she'd got it off by heart. Oh, aye, she had it now. 'Take therefore no thought for the morrow: for the morrow shall take thought for the things of itself. Sufficient unto the day is the evil thereof.'

74

Part 2 – The Family
1906

Chapter Six

'Grandda says there'll be a fresh fall of snow before nightfall, and he's never wrong, so I wouldn't go on one of your treks today, Miss Collins.'

'Really?' Gwendoline Collins wrinkled her long, aristocratic nose before nodding resignedly at Polly. 'In that case I will have to concentrate on painting those sketches of catkins and common gorse I took a few days ago on Hasting Hill. It's probably just as well I have a day by the fire; I walked as far as Seaham Harbour yesterday and I have to confess it was somewhat taxing in places in the snow. I wanted to see how they had fared with enlarging and rebuilding the South Dock from when I was in these parts seven years ago, and it is quite different now, Polly. The harbour I remember has all but disappeared save for the North Dock.'

Polly smiled at the tall, thin woman in front of her but said nothing. She knew Seaham Harbour was one of the mushroom towns created by the nineteenth-century coal boom, because Frederick had been educating her in much of the local history, but she had never been there herself although it was only some four miles south-east of the farm.

Indeed, it was only in the last two years that she had begun accompanying her father into the town of Bishopswearmouth on market days; a procedure that had come about of necessity due to her grandfather's increasing ill health. This had begun one day after Walter had lifted a cart stacked with produce in order for his son to replace a broken wheel. The resulting seizure – which Walter insisted to referring to as 'nowt but a funny turn' – had put the old man in bed for a week, although he had refused – and still refused in spite of other attacks – to see a doctor.

Polly was now approaching her sixteenth birthday, and she appeared a fully grown woman and a beautiful one at that. She was tall compared to most of her female contemporaries at five foot seven inches, and her slender figure and fine-boned frame belied her strong constitution.

She had put her hair up the year before, although the thick chestnut curls were forever struggling to escape the bun on top of her head, and her eyes – which were of a deep violet blue and heavily lashed – seemed to carry an inward light which drew and held the onlooker. Her lips were red and full although her mouth was not large, and her teeth were very white and evenly spaced.

To Gwendoline Collins, whose plain face and sharp, angular body hid an acute appreciation of beauty in all forms, Polly was the perfect encapsulation of youth as it should be and the main reason she had taken one of the farm labourers' cottages in the autumn of the previous year, some six months ago.

Born late in life to wealthy upper-class parents who had doted on their only offspring, Gwendoline had inherited a considerable fortune at the relatively tender age of twenty. This had enabled her to follow her first love – that of painting – and combine it with her second – that of ardent naturalist – for the last eighteen years. She had travelled the country and made numerous trips abroad in spite of the raised eyebrows and horrified whispers her independence had called forth from her peers, and she had had a wonderful time, never staying in one place for more than a few months for fear of putting down roots.

In her first few weeks at the farm she had followed Polly around and sketched her about her everyday chores, and in the process an unlikely friendship had formed between the formidable, blue-blooded lady and the young, ingenuous farm girl. Gwendoline was an eccentric but a fascinating one, although her fiercely feminist views had not endeared her to the menfolk at the farm, or Alice for that matter. Gwendoline, in her turn, considered that the only person worthy of an intelligent conversation was Polly, which meant she rarely visited the farmhouse.

Polly attended to the cleaning of the two-roomed cottage Gwendoline was renting, and which – once Gwendoline had decided to stay for the winter – the older woman had had furnished by H. C. Askwith, cabinet maker, of 59 High Street West, Bishopswearmouth. Polly also brought the farm's lodger a cooked meal each evening, and fresh bread, milk and other produce daily, along with a supply of logs and coal and clean water. The very generous sum of money Gwendoline paid on the first day of every month was sorely needed, but the extra work involved in having a permanent lodger in one of the cottages – not to mention a lady who required everything doing for her – tried Polly to the uttermost.

Since Walter had been ailing it had become more apparent that Henry was no farmer and couldn't manage, and so Polly had taken it upon herself to work outside; dealing with the milking, seeing to the pigs, hens and geese, working in the fields alongside her father when necessary and even tending to the horses some nights. Her granny and Ruth worked in the house and dairy, but the old woman and the sulky young girl frequently clashed, and it was not unusual for Polly to come in from outside when it began to get dark to find Ruth had stomped off somewhere or other in a paddy, leaving her granny coping alone.

At those times Polly would force Ruth – often to be found in her mother's room – back to the kitchen to finish her tasks, whereupon the fur would fly and Ruth and Hilda would label Polly a heartless tyrant amid much bitterness. Polly's day started at four thirty in the morning and rarely ended before ten at night, and sometimes she was too tired to even undress when she fell into bed beside Ruth.

But there were good times too, little nuggets of pure gold amongst the harsh daily grind which made life a joyous thing if only for a short time; not least Polly's new closeness to her father.

On the frequent occasions when her grandfather was too middling to do any work at all outside, Polly had found her father to be quite a different individual to the withdrawn, remote man she had always known. She had come to realise that her grandfather's strong, taciturn nature caused her father to retreat into a shell of his own making. She had first discovered this through a less than happy incident which had occurred in the weeks after Walter's first attack. A calf had been born to a cow that was a particular favourite of hers, the animal in question being a gentle, doe-eyed creature who never lunged out with her hoofs during milking as some were liable to do. The birth had been long and difficult and the cow had moaned and cried almost like a human as they had tried to help her along, and Henry had talked to her as though she was a person too. And then the calf was there on the straw in front of them, the wind moaning as it whipped round the open door of the byre and the night's bitter chill seeping into their bones as they stared down at the perfectly formed, beautiful little creature. It was quite dead.

And the cow had known, the sound coming from her throat grief-stricken as her long, coarse tongue had licked and licked at her tiny baby in an effort to make it draw breath. And her da had cried, as much for the cow as the calf. They had both sat on the straw watching the poor creature's efforts and howled their eyes out. And then her da had sat and talked to the cow with the calf in his arms, for hours it seemed, explaining that she would have another chance, reassuring her as though she could understand what he was saying, petting her, and Polly had realised she was seeing a side to her father that he normally kept hidden when her grandfather was about. And she had loved him for it – for the compassion and understanding he had showed to the poor dumb creature. That had been the start of a new relationship between father and daughter.

They enjoyed some right good cracks from day to day too, when they were partaking of their bread and tins of tea at their breaks. Old Bess and Patience would be standing by, swishing their long, thick tails to keep the flies off and relishing the brief respite from their equine labours as they waited for the morsels of bread which inevitably found their way into the horses' gentle mouths.

Polly found she liked her father as a person very much as well as loving him as her da, although she often wondered – especially after the incident with the cow and calf – how on earth a dreamy, impractical, quietly compassionate individual like her father had come to marry a woman like her mother.

Frederick continued to call regularly, bringing an ever-changing supply of books and newspapers, some of which contained knowledge about places Polly had never even dreamed existed. Through her uncle she shared the excitement of the Wright brothers flying a curious-looking heavier-than-air machine over the beach at Kitty Hawk, far away in North Carolina in the United States of America. She learnt a little about the mystery of radio-activity when Madame Curie became the first woman to win a Nobel Prize for her work in that area of physics; and much, much more. And since Gwendoline had been living in the cottage and they had discussed such things as Mrs Pankhurst's new militant movement to gain the vote for their sex, the Pope's – Gwendoline was a lapsed Catholic – banning of low-cut evening gowns and any form of what he called provocative clothing for women, and the general views by a male-dominated society that women were put on earth solely to please and serve their 'betters' – namely men – Polly's eyes were being opened wider and wider.

She sometimes felt, after an evening when Frederick had called or a Sunday afternoon at the farm, or yet again after a conversation with Gwendoline – often when Polly was on her hands and knees cleaning out the ashes of the previous day's fire and relighting a new one – that she was living in two worlds.

One was a place she had always known, familiar, safe and monotonous, a place of hard daily grind and backbreaking work that, however, was not without its shafts of delight. Flowering grass, soft and shimmering in the evening light as the breeze ruffled it. Crops of wild strawberries amid dark leaves in the fields. The silver film caused by the morning dew when the fields were an enchanted sea of mist and a lark was calling high in a silent sky. Sunsets and sunrises, when the sky turned to fire and the birds sang a song of salutation to their Maker.

And the other world, the place of adult awakening that her uncle's – and lately Miss Collins's – help with education was enhancing, that too was a delight, but more often disturbing to boot. Polly was finding within herself a deep well of questioning, even criticism of all the concepts and values she had imbibed as a child, and although Miss Collins assured her this was normal, that it was her time to become her own person, there were occasions when Polly wondered what that person would be like. She felt different from the rest of her family, and it wasn't simply to do with age, as the older woman had suggested, because Ruth didn't seem to challenge the class system and social injustice and the rest.

She liked listening to the men talk on a Sunday afternoon now, and more and more she found her views corresponded with those expressed by Luke. Why should Sunderland have the highest infant mortality rates in the country? Why should it be acceptable to those in governmental power that whole communities be forced to exist in unimaginable depths of squalor in the north-east, when huge investments in the south were readdressing such problems? When Luke got on his high horse the farm kitchen fairly buzzed, and more often than not Polly felt her Uncle Frederick was out of his depth with the younger man.

'A hundred and twenty-four dead in the Glamorgan pit disaster last July, thirty-two in a pit in South Wales four months before that, accidents are happening all the time to a greater or lesser extent.' Luke had been burning with anger a few Sundays ago. 'The owners and viewers look on miners as expendable; there's always plenty more when a few die, so why bother to spend money on making the mines safe? And the men know it, they know it all right, but they've no choice but to work death traps if they want to feed their families. It's all very well for Lord Londonderry to spout that it's the parental duty to feed bairns, and school meals and such are unnecessary; what does he know about hunger and starvation, eh? When was he ever out of work? You answer me that, man.'

Luke's gaze had swept round the kitchen and his eyes hadn't been their normal warm chocolate brown but fiery and hot. 'The trade unions have been calling for old-age pensions, eight-hour days and universal suffrage for years, and *that's* why the working-class man is supporting them, Frederick. Not because they want to bring down the establishment. James Keir Hardie wants reform *within* the establishment, and so do plenty more. Why do you think Labour upped their seats from two to twenty-nine in the General Election in February, if not because the working man is waking up to the fact that he's got to fight back?'

There had been more talk of the same, and Frederick hadn't called for the last three Sundays, but tomorrow was Polly's sixteenth birthday and she knew her uncle wouldn't miss her special tea.

'You'll come to my birthday tea tomorrow, Miss Collins?' Polly now rose to her feet and dusted her skirt as the fire she had set began to crackle and shoot flames. The older woman had been living in the cottage for the whole of the winter but she had only entered the farmhouse twice in all that time, and had never stopped more than a minute or two. Polly knew that once the inclement weather improved their lodger was planning to move on, and she did so want her friend to meet Michael before she left.

81

'That's very kind, my dear, but a birthday is a family occasion,' Gwendoline said with a smile to soften her refusal. And then she added – with a twinkle in her eye that told Polly she was aware of more than Polly thought she had divulged in their conversations – 'But why don't you bring Michael across to see me at some point? You mentioned he is very fond of ornithology and I have one or two fine books on the subject he might like to borrow.'

'May I?' Polly was blushing; she hadn't realised she'd been so transparent.

'Of course.' And then Gwendoline's voice became brisk as she reached towards a package wrapped in brown paper on the sofa beside her and said, 'I was going to give you this tomorrow, but then I thought that was silly, as you would perhaps care to wear it on your birthday.'

'A present? Oh, Miss Collins, thank you. I don't know what to say.'

'It's not new.' Gwendoline brushed aside the thanks with a flap of her hand. 'But I thought you could do something with it as you are nearly as tall as I am, and slim, although you have more shape. I have never had any shape. But you might not like it; I won't be offended if you don't like it. It's one of several I brought with me.'

'Don't like it?' Polly had carefully unwrapped the paper and was gazing at the thick rich fabric in russet brocade the parcel had held. The dress had a small, neat collar and wide cuffs in fine cream lace to complement the warm autumn shade, and as Polly reverently shook it out, the folds of material seemed to shimmer in the light from the cottage window. She had never seen anything quite so beautiful in all her life. 'Oh, Miss Collins.'

Polly's voice was small, for the words had to negotiate the lump in her throat, but the expression on the young face seemed to satisfy the other woman, because Gwendoline said gaily, 'You'll need to let it out a little over the bust and possibly nip in the waist a mite, but otherwise it should do. Yes, it should do very well.'

Polly practically floated back to the farmhouse kitchen. She paused in the yard before entering the house, looking up into the low-laden sky heavy with snow as she whispered, 'Please don't let it snow too much before tomorrow. Let him come. Please, please, *please* let him come.' She would be sixteen years old tomorrow, and that was grown up, really grown up. Her granny had been married at seventeen, after all. She had been waiting for this birthday and she knew Michael had been waiting for it too. And when he saw her in this beautiful dress . . . She shut her eyes tightly, her joy constricting her breathing as it filled her chest. He'd say something, he'd ask her. She knew he'd ask her.

Her granny oohed and aahed over the dress, but Polly sensed the enthusiasm was forced, whereas Ruth's response – one of barely concealed resentment and indignation – was, if hurtful, at least genuine. And she could understand Ruth being envious, oh, aye, she could, because the dress was right bonny.

And it was later that evening, when her granny was making griddle cakes for supper and Polly was sitting at the old scrubbed table altering the dress while the menfolk smoked their pipes in front of the fire, that Alice said, in a tone that aimed to be casual, 'Miss Collins given you any idea when she'll be movin' on, lass?'

Polly liked the rare occasions when her granny cooked griddle cakes for supper. There was nothing nicer than hot griddle cakes with butter melting into the pastry and a warm sup of tea, especially in the winter, when the oil lamps were casting a comforting softness to the battered surroundings and the fire was glowing in the blackleaded range. She felt happy at such times, contented and at peace, but she didn't feel that way tonight, in spite of the beautiful dress beneath her fingers. And the reason for her unsettledness was summed up in her grandmother's words.

Polly raised her head slowly, and looked straight into the old woman's eyes as she said quietly, 'Her rent makes all the difference, Gran. I don't know how we would have survived this winter without it.'

'Same as we always do, lass.' This was from Walter, and it was sharp.

'Things are getting worse, Grandda.' She glanced at her father to add support to her words, and when none was forthcoming, she sighed deeply. She didn't want to have to say it, but they had to face facts. And she knew why her granny was itching for Miss Collins to leave: Gran had decided long ago, along with her da and grandda, that Miss Collins was a bad influence on her. Polly had walked in on a discussion about it more than once, and in spite of the quick change of subject that always followed, she had known what it was all about.

And when she thought about it, she felt her grandda and da didn't like her Uncle Frederick bringing her books and such, although she had nothing concrete to base the feeling on. But her granny – and this was surprising in view of Gran's views about Miss Collins – her granny was for her Uncle Frederick. Overtly so. In fact, there had been times lately when she had thought her granny made more of a fuss of her uncle than her mother did.

And then the unfamiliar caress of the soft, rich material in her hands brought her eyes downwards and delight flooded her once again. What did it matter anyway? Her grandda was fond of saying, 'There's nowt so queer as folk,' and the older she got the more she agreed with him, but none of it mattered beside the fact that Michael was coming tomorrow. It was snowing again but not heavily, not yet leastways, and it mustn't – it just *mustn't* – get too bad.

'Sixteen years old tomorrow, lass, an' I can remember the night afore you were born clear as yesterday.' Her granny was aiming to lighten the atmosphere, and as Polly raised her head again and glanced across at the small, thin figure by the range, at the work-lined face and the hands knobbled with the complaint that kept her grandmother in constant pain, she smiled into the waiting eyes.

'You want me to call Ruth, Gran?' she asked softly.

'Aye, aye, you do that, lass.'

Ruth was upstairs with their mother. Her sister spent most evenings thus occupied these days, and whatever the two talked about it didn't seem to do Ruth any good, because the younger girl's disposition was becoming more and more querulous. This was reflected when, in answer to Polly's call, Ruth walked into the kitchen and, her voice loud and holding a note of peevishness, said, 'Griddle scones? No one told me we were having griddle scones.'

'I wasn't aware I had to check with you what I'm a-cookin',' Alice returned tartly. 'Butter a couple an' take 'em up to your mam along with a sup of tea.'

'I'll have mine up there an' all.' Ruth's tone of voice and the venomous glance she threw at the dress in Polly's hands left no doubt as to her present source of discontent.

'For cryin' out loud!' Alice had caught the look. 'Can't you be glad for your sister for once? But no, not you! That'd be like askin' the devil to sing in the church choir. Born whinger, you are, girl. An' don't forget Polly only took on the job of lookin' after Miss Collins because you created merry hell about the extra work when I asked you to do it.'

'Huh.'

'An' don't huh me unless you're askin' for a skelp o' the lug.'

'It's not *fair*.'

'By, you've got a lot to learn about life, lass!'

'Ruth, I've told you you can share it once you've grown a bit and it'll fit you,' said Polly appeasingly. 'Now let it alone.'

Ruth's reaction to Polly's offer was a toss of her light brown curls as she gathered up the tin plate of griddle scones she had been buttering, and two mugs of weak tea, and flounced out of the kitchen.

'She'll drive me to drink that one, you see if she don't.' This from Alice, a staunch teetotaller, caused the menfolk to glance wryly at each other and Polly to hide a smile. Her granny!

The next day dawned bitterly cold, with flurries of snow showers that stung and smarted in the raw wind. Everyone at the farm went about their work as normal after breakfast, when Polly had thanked her family for her birthday presents: a studded comb for her hair from

84

her grandparents and a box of toffee and a long cream velvet ribbon from her parents and Ruth.

'The ribbon was my idea.' Ruth had mellowed a little now the shock of Polly's good fortune had faded. 'Nellie Cook brought her mam's periodical into school – *The Lady*, that the woman who her mam does for gives her when she's finished with it – and it showed a picture of a lady with a ribbon threaded through her hair that looked right bonny. I could do it for you after dinner when we've changed, if you want.'

'Would you?' Polly hugged her sister and for once Ruth didn't stiffen or draw away but returned the embrace. Oh, this was going to be a *wonderful* birthday!

Outside the farmhouse the icy air was enough to take your breath away, and the inch or so of fresh snow which had fallen through the night on to ground already lethal with black ice made walking treacherous. Nevertheless, the cows still had to be milked and all the animals fed and watered and cleaned out, and the eggs collected and such, besides the hundred and one other jobs the farm engendered.

Even with her old coat buttoned to her chin, her hat pulled well down over her ears and an old worn blanket tied shawl-fashion about her shoulders, Polly's teeth were chattering as she went about her work, visiting the labourer's cottage first and lighting the fire for Miss Collins, who was still snuggled under layers of covers in the bedroom.

'I'm just going to help me da milk the cows and then I'll come back with some more coal and logs.' Polly had just finished smashing the ice on the water butt outside the cottage, and now she placed the filled kettle on the small shelf which jutted out from the chimney above the burgeoning fire. 'The pump's frozen up again but grandda's seeing to it, and once you've had your wash I'll bring a pan of drinking water, Miss Collins.'

'Thank you, Polly.' Only the tip of their lodger's nose was visible, the thick bedspread pulled right over Miss Collins's head cocoon-fashion.

Mid-morning, Polly and her father had a mug of hot ginger and a shive of lardy cake in the warmth of the farmhouse kitchen before returning outside, Henry to the task of rebuilding part of the dry-stone wall that had crumbled over the last week, and Polly to mucking out the stable.

She was worried about her grandda. Even the relatively minor job of melting the build-up of ice on the pump had seemed to tire him, and she had insisted the old man stay in front of the brightly glowing fire in the kitchen the rest of the morning, much to Walter's disgust. But he hadn't argued *too* vehemently, and that in itself was indicative of how he was feeling. It was strange: there was her granny, all shrivelled and frail-looking compared to her grandda, who was big and solid and

85

hearty, and yet of the two, Gran was in the better health. She wished her grandda would let them call the doctor, just once. She would feel better if the doctor had seen him. She knew it would cost a few shillings; even if Da took her grandda into Bishopswearmouth in the horse and cart it wouldn't be cheap and it was money they could ill afford, but with what Miss Collins paid, they would find the money somehow.

However, three hours later, bedecked in the new dress and with the cream ribbon which exactly matched the lace on the collar and cuffs wound amongst her chestnut curls, Polly wasn't thinking about anyone but Michael.

This was a special day, a momentous day, she knew it. Even the weather had conspired to make it so, the heavy snow which had been forecast holding off and a tentative, weak winter sun breaking through the grey clouds now and again.

'You look right bonny.' Ruth's voice was a little awestruck – the finely dressed, beautifully coiffured young woman in front of her was almost a stranger.

Polly smiled at her sister but said nothing, her gaze returning to her hands, which were sticking out of the fine lace cuffs like two swollen pieces of red meat. It was a shame about her hands – this was the sort of dress that should have lily-white soft hands complementing it – but she couldn't remember the last time her hands hadn't been chafed raw. Still, the dress was bonny, and perhaps no one would notice.

When Polly walked into the kitchen, Ruth following her down the stairs a moment later, she found her grandda and da hadn't followed their normal procedure on a Sunday and retired to the barn after they had washed and changed, but were sitting in front of the range smoking their pipes. Knowing they had waited to see her in the new dress, Polly felt suddenly shy, and this was reflected in her voice when she said, 'It . . . it fits all right now.'

'By, lass.' Henry rose slowly to his feet, his stunned expression widening into a beaming smile. 'You look a picture, aye, you do. A real picture. Doesn't she, Da?' And then, calling to his mother, who was slicing the ham on the stone slab in the scullery, he said, 'Come an' see your bonny granddaughter, Mam.'

Her grandfather had added his praise to that of her father, but when her granny came through she stopped on the threshold for a moment or two before walking slowly over to where Polly was standing. 'Oh, hinny.' Alice's hand came out and touched one sleeve of the dress but the faded eyes were on Polly's bright face. 'Hinny.'

'Do you like it?'

Like it? Alice continued looking into the face she had always considered beautiful but which now – under its array of carefully positioned rich burnished curls – had taken on a new dimension. The large, thickly lashed eyes were intent on hers and Alice knew she had to say something, but the fear that had gripped her made her voice weak when she said, 'You look bonny, lass, real bonny.' Pray God she was wrong about the other thing, *pray God*, because this was no bairn or slip of a lass standing in front of her, but a full-grown woman who was arrestingly lovely. She had watched Polly and Michael over the last three years – for the first twelve months after the incident at the river she had felt she'd thought about nothing else – but although there had been times when a certain glance between the two young people or an inflexion in their voices had disturbed her, there had been nothing specific to pin her worry on. And so she had comforted herself with the assurance that she was imagining things, fretting unnecessarily because of what she knew about their parentage.

And Frederick wanted Polly. Oh, aye, now she was sure about that – not that she'd ever have admitted it to Walter. And although the lass still thought of her mother's stepbrother as an uncle, he was no relation to her at all. Looking like Polly did, it was only a matter of time before she was spoken for; it was against all nature that she wouldn't wed early. How they would cope without Polly, Alice didn't dare to contemplate, but Frederick would see his own wife's kith and kin all right – Polly would make sure of that.

Polly felt disappointed. She didn't know why exactly, but there had been something in her grandmother's manner, a flatness almost, that was puzzling and hurtful. Her granny didn't like Miss Collins's dress, but couldn't she at least be glad her granddaughter had something new and bonny to wear on her birthday? Polly was standing straight now, her face unsmiling, and then she flinched inwardly – although no trace of it showed on her face – as, in another break from tradition, Hilda's slow footsteps informed those in the kitchen that Henry's wife had taken the unprecedented step of venturing downstairs before her stepbrother arrived.

Polly quite literally braced herself for the moment when her mother entered the kitchen, and as she half turned her head and saw Hilda standing looking at her, she forced herself to smile naturally and say, 'Hallo, Mam. Thought you'd come down early for the birthday celebrations then? The others aren't here yet.'

'I'm well aware of that.' The narrowed blue eyes looked her up and down, their pale opaqueness like thin ice, and then Hilda walked across to the hardwood saddle, adjusting the flock cushions before she seated herself and said, 'It's too old for you, that dress. I can't think what Miss Collins was about, thinking that colour would suit you.'

Polly heard the others, even her sister, protest, but funnily enough, her mother's spite had the effect of putting iron in her backbone. 'I disagree.' It was cool and cutting. 'But then I've heard it said that beauty is in the eye of the beholder, and we both know exactly how you view me, don't we, Mother?'

87

It was the first time in Polly's life that she had ever addressed her mother by the more formal title, and everyone in the room was aware of it, along with the fact that the young woman standing so proudly in the middle of the room had an authority about her that had been made all the more noticeable by the fine clothes. She neither looked nor sounded like young Polly.

To say that Hilda appeared taken aback was putting it mildly, and Henry had the unique – and very pleasant – experience of seeing his sharp-tongued wife lost for words in the moments before the sound of a horse and trap outside in the yard indicated that Frederick had arrived.

Michael was feeling sick with a mixture of nervous excitement and apprehension, and this feeling had been mounting steadily over the last weeks. He had known for years he was going to ask Polly to marry him, and for almost as long that she would accept when he did, but now the day was here – now it was actually *time* – the reality was overwhelming; not least how he could contrive to get her alone for a moment or two to pop the question.

It was like a menagerie every week in that farmhouse kitchen. He frowned to himself as he looked ahead into the snowy landscape where his mother and half-brothers were striding ahead, their footsteps making deep indentations in the virgin snow. Since Ruth had pushed Polly into the river that time, his grandparents had been adamant they all stay in the kitchen or about the farm buildings, and such close proximity with the others had made any courting impossible. Courting! He gave a mental snort at the word. He hadn't even held her hand in years. Every Sunday, come rain, hail or snow, they'd have politics and religion and every other subject under the sun raked over until its bones were showing. He hadn't minded at one time, but since the urge to be alone with Polly had grown, he'd got sick of the sound of the others' voices.

'You all right, Mike?'

As Luke turned round and called, Michael raised his hand in response, saying, 'Aye, I'm fine, man.' Luke was the only one who called him Mike; to nearly everyone else he was Mick or Michael. And Luke was the only person – apart from Polly and his father – he had any time for. He was a good bloke, Luke, and intelligent too. How he and Arnold came from the same mother and father he'd never know. His eyes now fastened on the back of Arnold's head and narrowed with dislike. He was a big ignorant nowt, Arnold, but nasty with it, and cunning. Michael was afraid of this brother, and he knew Arnold sensed it and used it to his advantage. Same as Arnold had sensed he and Polly liked each other, and never missed an opportunity to make snide comments about her. Never when Luke was around – Arnold had a healthy respect for Luke's fists and caustic tongue and he knew Luke looked on Polly and Ruth the same as sisters – but when they were alone that was a different matter.

Michael brought his eyes from the big bulky shape of Arnold but his thoughts continued to flow on. He was a vindictive so-an'-so, his eldest brother, and nothing would convince him other than that Arnold's carping about Polly – which had grown with the years – was a result of Polly making it clear she had no time for him. And she could do that, Poll; with just a glance of those deep blue eyes she could put you in your place all right. He grinned to himself. But if things went right today he'd soon be away from Arnold and the town and the pit. Aye, the pit . . . His stomach knotted at the thought of it. What was the betting the talk in the kitchen would touch on the mine explosion in France again? Three weeks running they'd had that, and aye, it was criminal that over a thousand miners had died and that it could happen here as easy as winking, but Sunday was his day away from that hell-hole. He felt for the families in Courrieres as much as the next man, but he didn't want the pit rammed down his throat every minute of every damn day.

And he knew exactly how many days he'd been underground. They were engraved on his mind, his soul, and his innards still broke loose from the casting of his stomach every time he descended in the cage the same as they had that very first morning he'd gone into hell.

The blackness, rats the size of small cats, the foul language, men reduced to animals as they squatted a bit away from where they were working to do their business, which created a smell – especially in-bye, where it was particularly warm – that was unimaginable; that was bad enough. As was crawling along on his knees under a roof held up by props that looked like matchsticks when you thought about the tons of stone and coal and muck above you, and always – *always* – with an ear half cocked as you listened to what the roof was doing. The 'bowking' noise that different layers made when they cracked, the 'fissling' noise which meant the floor was beginning to creep and the warning rattle that meant you'd got seconds to get to safety. Michael brushed his hand across his face, which his thoughts had caused to become damp with sweat, and then pulled his cap down more firmly over his forehead.

And still there were the explosions that gave no warning at all, especially in bad weather, when the atmospheric pressure was low. He had learned not to vomit when he saw a man injured by a fall of stone or coal, or trapped by a pocket of gas that had exploded when a hewer's pick had released it. Death and injury and roof-falls and foul air had been part of his life for two years now, and he knew he would go mad if he didn't get out of there soon. The terrible feeling that he'd kept under control all that time, when his heart started to pound against his ribs and reverberate in his eardrums until his head felt it was going to explode and the sweat ran in his oxters, that feeling was going to take him over one day soon.

He breathed deeply several times and then lifted his head to see the farm in the distance. But it wouldn't take him over would it, because there was Polly and the farm, and they both meant life and sanity. He knew his da didn't feel the way he did about the pit, nor Luke and Arnold, and he didn't understand why he was so different. He'd fought against it at first until he realised he wasn't going to win, and it had only been the thought of marrying Polly and them moving into one of the farm labourers' cottages and working on his grandda's farm that had kept him going. And the good Lord had kept him safe. Aye, he praised God for that. He'd spilled out his guts many a time to Father McAttee in confession and it had helped him get through the next week. *And now it was time.*

The thought spurred him on to catch up the others, and as he neared them Luke turned and waited for his approach, whereupon they stood together for a moment, their faces turned to the clean, crisp wind that carried the scent of snow in its biting embrace. 'Canny, eh?' Luke's eyes were sweeping the white fields and snow-dusted trees and hedgerows before his gaze lifted to the wide expanse of light-washed sky. 'Makes you want to breathe it all in and let it wash all the styfe of the pit out of your lungs.'

Michael nodded, and then turned to look Luke full in the face. He was good-looking, his half-brother, and he certainly had enough lasses giving him the eye, but Luke also possessed something Michael knew he didn't have which had a drawing power all of its own. There was a well of life in him, a virility that was strong and potent, and even without his attractive features and big solid frame, Luke would have been compelling. Luke would never be beaten. Michael acknowledged a pang of admiration that was tinged with envy. Luke would fight and keep fighting until his dying breath and always get what he wanted.

'Look at your mam.' Luke brought Michael's attention to the large, formidable figure of Eva that even Arnold was having difficulty keeping up with. 'She can fair move when she wants to.'

'And she always wants to when we're going to the farm.' The two exchanged a grin before Michael added, 'I can understand it, mind. There's nothing I like better than being out here.'

'Aye.' Luke nodded but said nothing more as the two started to walk again. He knew Michael loved the farm as much as he hated the pit, and he had seen what working underground was doing to his young brother. He also knew how Michael felt about Polly. He felt his guts twist in spite of himself. If it had been anyone else but Michael, anyone else, he would have used every trick in the book – fair means or foul – to supplant him in Polly's affections. But he couldn't set himself up against Michael, not Michael.

Apart from the fact that Michael was his baby brother and the link between them had always been strong, he recognised that in the slight, almost willowy figure of the young lad at the side of him there dwelt an intrinsic goodness, a gentleness, that was rare. And Michael needed to get out of the pit; it was killing him slowly, inch by inch.

Why Luke himself came to the farm every week, however, was a different kettle of fish. How often had he told himself he was barmy, doo-lally, to put himself through it? But he couldn't stay away, that was the heart of the matter. Perhaps when the thing was settled, when Michael had asked her – and Michael *would* ask Polly to be his lass, and soon – it would allow him to cut the thread that pulled him back here week after week. It didn't do him any good, that was for sure. His body burned for nights afterwards and many a time he'd been tempted to ease himself with Olive Robson or Nancy McClean, or lately Katy Chapman. But he didn't want Nancy or Katy, or any of the others who made it clear they were willing.

He might move away altogether. As they came within fifty yards of the farm, Luke's eyes narrowed thoughtfully. That was the answer. There was always one of the Newcastle pits, or maybe Harton Colliery in South Shields. Harton was a particularly wet pit and subsequently the wages were higher. One of his da's brothers lived in Boldon Lane; he could board with them until he got sorted, and from what his da had said in the past, South Shields wasn't so different to Sunderland. There were the same huge steamships coming up the river, many with foreign names, blowing their horns and whistles ready for their bales, crates and barrels to be offloaded on to the docks in big rope nets, with hundreds of men shouting to the fellers operating the slings, telling them where to set them down and grabbing them with hooks as they descended. The same Sunday-morning markets at the quaysides where you could buy anything for a few pence, and the quacks and tricksters would be gathered selling their wares and doing their acts; and rowing races on the river itself – be it the Tyne or the Wear – when everyone would be shouting and cheering, and once the winner passed the finishing line, the foghorns blasting and the ships' whistles blowing was enough to deafen a body, and everyone went mad jumping up and down.

Aye, he wouldn't want to move to a little village pit, not after living in Monkwearmouth close to the Wear. He'd got used to the parks with their shuggy boats and swings and lakes chock full of tadpoles and tiddlers, not to mention the beach, where all the local lads and lasses did their courting.

The thought of the evenings when he had watched young couples sedately marching the sands brought his mind back to Polly, and now,

91

as Luke followed Michael across the farmyard to where the open kitchen door was emitting the sound of chattering voices, he gave a mental nod to the prospect of Harton Colliery.

Nothing was going to change here; he could forecast exactly how the next months and years were going to develop. He had no wish to exist on the perimeter of Polly and Michael's life as a benevolent uncle figure to their bairns, and that was what would happen sure enough. It was time to leave Sunderland. He'd miss his da, though. He paused at the kitchen door and raised his eyes to the grey-white sky above, in much the same way Polly had done the day before. But his da had seemed happier of late. He looked younger, lighter, somehow, and Luke had even caught him singing 'Wait Till the Sun Shines, Nellie' the other night, when his da'd been having his wash-down in the tin bath in front of the fire. He couldn't remember ever hearing his da sing before and he'd wondered if he'd got a load on, but his breath hadn't smelt of beer or whisky. So maybe things were looking up at last between him and Eva.

Luke brought his head down into his neck and narrowed his eyes as he heard his name called from inside the room. They were waiting for him. His hand fingered the small package in his jacket pocket. And as it looked as though this was the last birthday party he'd attend here for quite some time, he'd better put a brave face on it. So thinking, he pushed the door wide and walked into the house.

Chapter Seven

The bedroom was not overly small, being the whole of the upstairs of the three-roomed cottage, but crammed full as it was with old, somewhat battered furniture, it gave the appearance of such. But as Nathaniel stretched and wrinkled his toes, flexing his arms before his hands made a pillow for his head, he reflected that a king's palace wouldn't suit him better. And it was all to do with the woman who was now nudging the bedroom door further ajar with her foot, her hands being full with two cups of steaming-hot tea.

'Thanks, lass.' Nathaniel sat up straight as he took his cup, and as she slid under the covers beside him and he felt the nearness of her, her soft, warm voluptuousness under the old flock dressing gown she'd pulled on before leaving the bed some minutes before, his body hardened in spite of the fact they'd only just made love. But she did that to him, his Tess. He had never met anyone who was so big, and he didn't mean in the physical sense, although she had plenty of meat on her bones – she made two of him at any rate. No, he meant the fount of loving, of tenderness, of generosity that made up the core of her. Even his Dora, God rest her soul, hadn't loved him like Tess did.

'There'll be a bite of panhacklety later on when your dinner's got down, if you want it.'

'That's like askin' a dyin' man if he wants the lifeline thrown to him.'

'Oh, you.' Tess smiled as she wriggled against him, her head coming to rest on his shoulder. She took a sip of her tea before saying, her voice quieter now, 'Doesn't she wonder why you don't want any tea come Sunday night these days?'

He'd wondered about that himself until he had realised Eva probably didn't notice what he ate and drank. 'I always have a bite of somethin' on me plate to show willin', and the lads wolf down the lot fast as blinkin' anyway. Besides' – the tone of his voice changed, a bitter note creeping in – 'Eva wouldn't care if I slowly starved in front of her, lass, an' that's the truth.'

'Oh, Nat.' Tess bit on her lip for a moment before she said, 'I've said it afore and I'll say it agen, she doesn't know when she's well off.'

'Aye, maybe.' What had he ever done to have this woman love him like she did? The thought swept away all the bitterness the mention of Eva had caused. He could hardly believe there was a time when he hadn't been coming to this house and losing himself in the great warm expanse that was Tess, but it had only been the last twelve months, since the accident at the pit had taken her man. Nathaniel had been working with Perce when it had happened – a piece of roof had fallen on his skull and split it in two – and although he'd never liked the man, he'd felt obliged to go and see his widow and offer a little comfort in telling her Perce had died instantly and without suffering. And that had been the start of it.

Tess had made him welcome with a cup of tea and a piece of lardy cake when he'd called to see her at the house in Carley Road at the side of the Carley Hill wagonway, and by the time he'd left – some two hours later – he had known her marriage had not been a happy one. He hadn't known Perce had regularly used her as a punch bag, that had come later, along with the fact that Tess – in spite of her big hips and buxom appearance – had had one miscarriage after another all through her ten years of marriage. Mind, Perce's fists had helped them along.

Nathaniel drew in a long, hard breath and, reaching down, put his tea on the bare floorboards before doing the same with Tess's cup. 'I love you, lass.' He folded her into his arms as he spoke, his voice thick. 'You know that, don't you? An' all this skulkin' about don't sit well, you deserve better than that.'

'I don't mind, lad.' Tess twisted in his arms, her hand coming up to his face, which she stroked softly. 'I don't mind anything as long as you keep coming here. The last twelve months have been the happiest of me life, and though I know I shouldn't say it, Perce being dead an' all, I thank God everything happened as it did. But I don't want to cause trouble for you, that's the last thing I want. If Sunday afternoons and the odd evening in the week is all we have I'll be content with that, aye, an' count meself lucky. But I'm worried it'll get back to her some day soon.'

'There's not much chance of that.' He wished there was if the truth be told; it would take the decision of what to do out of his hands. 'She's never had anythin' to do with anyone, you know that. Kept herself to herself an' even got on the wrong side of our Eustace's wife, an' that's no easy thing to do.'

Tess nodded. Carley Road was separated from the gridwork of streets that fanned out from Southwick Road by the Cornhill glass-works, but one of her neighbours – married to a miner – had a sister who lived next door to Nathaniel, and she had some stories to tell. In a community where a woman's lot involved a constant fight against poverty, dirt, disease and the dreaded words 'laid off', good neighbours and family sometimes meant the difference between the workhouse or struggling through. 'But that Eva, she'd see you in

94

hell afore she'd lift a finger,' Joan had said more than once as they had gossiped over the backyard wall. 'There was our Mildred, just had the bairn an' right poorly with it, an' did Eva offer to take the other uns, even for an hour or two? Did she blazes. Not even a pot of tea an' a comfortin' word when all she's got to do all day is sit on her backside with the menfolk down the pit an' her youngest at school, an' they're not hard up, not compared to most. An' it was Nora on Mildred's other side – God bless her – who took the bairns an' fed 'em an' brought in an evenin' meal once Don was home from the pit. An' Nora's not got two pennies to rub together, not with her brood to feed an' clothe. By, she's a crabby, tight so-an'-so, that Eva. I pity her menfolk, I do straight.'

That conversation had occurred some years before Tess had met Nathaniel, and Joan had related other incidents over the years about 'Lady Blackett', as she referred to her sister's neighbour. Bearing in mind her own unhappy marriage and the misery that went on behind closed doors, Tess had always kept an open mind about such matters, however. Who knew that this Eva was putting up with in private? Most folks thought Perce was a good bloke – salt of the earth, she'd heard him referred to as more than once. And suffering and despair affected different people different ways. By all accounts this Eva was one of them who kept everything just so – Joan said that according to Mildred, Eva didn't just stone the front step with a scouring stone to give it a smart cream-edged finish, but scrubbed the footpath outside the front door to boot – so maybe she had her own problems and keeping herself to herself and her house like a new pin was her way of coping.

And then Tess had met Nathaniel, and within the space of a few weeks life had become a beautiful thing. When he kissed her she felt like a goddess, aye, she did. And the things he said and did . . . He was the most caring man alive, he was, and whatever had gone on in his wife's life before Eva had met him, she ought to be on her knees thanking God every night for such as him.

Tess had worried at first, knowing how house-proud his wife was and how he must be used to everything looking nice, because she was not like that and she knew it. Dirty mare, Perce had used to call her before he'd swiped her one. But she wasn't dirty, just untidy, and it didn't worry her if a bit of dust mounted up now and again. For years – with the constant misses month after month, sometimes three a year – she'd felt too tired and washed out to do much, but she wouldn't think of them times now. They'd gone, they were dead and buried along with Perce.

'Joan, next door, I reckon she's got a good idea about us.' Tess's big brown eyes with their flecks of green were anxious as they looked up into Nathaniel's face. 'She doesn't miss a thing, that one.'

Nathaniel said nothing for a moment. Tess was thirty-one years old but she looked nearer forty; she'd had a hell of a life with Perce. And he wanted to make her happy, he *ached* to make her happy. He wanted to fill her life with joy, with laughter, with all the things she had missed in being married to a drunken thug of a man. He wanted to wake up beside her in the morning and lie down beside her at night, to sit with her in front of the fire in their own place with the front door keeping the rest of the world out. But there was Eva, and he was a Catholic. If he asked Tess to come away with him it would be to live a life of sin, and she was a respectable woman, a good woman. He couldn't ask her to do that; even if they moved far away where no one knew them it wouldn't be fair on her. But this, this carry-on wasn't fair on her either. 'I'm sorry, lass.' His voice was heavy.

'Oh, I don't mind, not for meself, I'm thinking of you,' Tess said quickly and with an earnestness that was genuine. 'I don't know if she's said owt to her Bert, but with him knowing you and the lads . . .'

Nathaniel shook his head. 'He's not one for jawin', Bert, but whatever happens we'll face it together, lass. All right? An' the lads aren't bairns any more, they'll understand. They've lived with Eva for years an' all, don't forget.' But would they? Would they understand him taking up with another woman, because that was the way they – anyone – would look at it. But Tess wasn't just another woman, she was – well, she was his other half. That was the way he felt about it. He was incomplete without her and since meeting her he knew he had felt like that all his life. Oh, he'd have been happy enough with Dora if she'd lived, and he'd have never looked the side another woman was on, but what was between him and Tess transcended words. Maybe if he'd been an educated man he could have found words to describe it, but he just knew he wouldn't want to live a day without her. Not an hour, a minute.

'Here, finish your tea, lass.' He bent down and lifted up Tess's cup, but before she took it from him she looked at him lovingly and touched his face again, her voice as soft and enveloping as her body as she said, 'If it ever gets too difficult for you, if it meant losing the lads or something, I'd understand if we had to call it a day, Nat, and I'd be thankful for what we've had. More than thankful.'

And now the tea was put down again swiftly and she was being held so tightly in his arms she couldn't breathe, as Nathaniel said hoarsely, 'Never, lass, never. You're me sun, moon an' stars, always will be, an' whatever happens – *whatever happens* – this is it for life. I'll sort out somethin', I will. An' I don't want you workin' in that laundry for ever neither.'

'I don't mind the work, lad. I'd go barmy sitting looking at these four walls seven days a week, and it helps with the rent. The bit I got for Perce paid for the funeral and tided me over for a while, but it won't last for ever.'

'Aye, I know.' He buried his face in her thick springy brown hair that was liberally sprinkled with grey. If anyone waited for the colliery to look after a dead miner's wife and family as they deserved they'd be waiting a damn long time. Sometimes he thought they were seen as less than men to the owners and the viewers; certainly the owners' dogs and horses were treated a darn sight better than the minions who worked their mines for them. Still, it was the way of the world and had been for as long as he could remember. It might get better with all this talk of trade unions and the Labour Party and all – certainly according to their Luke it was the only answer, though he wasn't too sure himself. It was the same everywhere, the rich got richer and the poor got poorer. Them with money made sure of it.

Tess was saying, 'As long as we can see a bit of each other then I'm happy, Nat. I mean it. And who knows what the future holds? One day at a time, lad. One day at a time.'

He brought his face from her hair, squeezing her one more time before reaching down for their fast-cooling tea without speaking. One day at a time. That was the philosophy Tess had lived her life by and it hadn't got her much. A husband who had knocked her into next weekend and robbed her of the chance to be a mother – something Nathaniel knew had created a deep and abiding sadness in her. She was born to be a mam, his Tess. Everything in her spoke of warmth and tenderness and kindness. Why, she'd even endeavoured to find excuses for Perce, going on about how he'd had a wretched childhood even before he was sent down the pit at six years of age. Huh! The mental exclamation of disgust was loud in Nathaniel's head. His own da had knocked him and his mam and his four brothers about when he wasn't gambling or drinking or working down the pit, but he'd sooner cut his right arm off than raise it to a woman, so you couldn't tell him Perce had acted like he had because he'd seen it in his childhood.

He became aware she was looking at him over her tea cup, and as he raised his head and met the soft greeny-brown gaze that was openly adoring, he smiled at her. Her loving was something a man dreamed of, and he knew he was the luckiest man alive. And maybe the future was something you had to take by the throat and make work for you. But there was Eva, and no matter how she was – how she had always been – she was his wife, and she'd had a rotten introduction into the ways of men, if her father's account of what had happened was true. But she'd stuck to it all these years, so what could he do but accept it?

By . . . He settled himself more comfortably on the lumpy flock mattress beneath him, the empty tea cup loose in his grasp and Tess's big body fitted into the side of him. He could go mad thinking about this lot. Aye, he could, because there was never a clear answer however much he racked his brains. But one had to present itself one day. His eyelids were heavy and he closed them, a contentedness settling on him despite his thoughts. And when the answer did come he'd know, and he'd grasp it with both hands.

Chapter Eight

'Oh, Luke, it's lovely. Thank you.' As Polly opened the small oak box Luke's package had contained and saw the exquisite hairbrush set with mother-of-pearl, she raised a glowing face to the man in front of her. She couldn't believe how wonderful this day had been. All her presents – a set of the complete works of Charles Dickens from her Uncle Frederick, two fine lawn handkerchiefs embroidered with flowers from her aunt, chocolates from Arnold, and now this beautiful hairbrush from Luke – had been lovely, but Michael taking her aside and showing her the small velvet box in his hand had been the most thrilling thing.

'I want to give you your present when we're alone,' he'd whispered. 'Make some excuse, suggest we go and see Bess and Patience or something, won't you?'

She'd nodded, her face alight but her manner decorous as she endeavoured to conduct herself in the seemly manner her sixteen years warranted. But it had been hard, very hard. She knew what he was going to say, what he was going to ask, and that box! She felt a well of emotion rise up in her that turned her cheeks pink and her eyes to sparkling sapphires.

If the others noticed Michael hadn't given her a present no one commented on it, but once everyone was sitting down drinking the first of the many cups of tea they usually consumed over the space of a Sunday afternoon, Polly found she couldn't wait another second. 'Miss Collins has asked me to take Michael to see her.' She was talking to the room in general but her eyes were on Michael across the paper-strewn table. 'She has some books on ornithology she thought he might like to look at, and as she'll be leaving once the weather is better, if he is going to borrow them it had better be soon.'

'Miss Collins?' Alice's voice was sharp. 'How does she know Michael likes birds?'

'Because I told her,' Polly said simply. The words themselves meant very little, but as a statement of things unsaid they meant a great deal.

Polly watched her grandmother's face stretch slightly, her eyes widening, and then Alice said, 'You, Ruth, it's been a while since you've seen Miss Collins. You go an' pay your respects along with Michael an' Polly.'

'Aw, Gran.' Ruth was sitting at her mother's feet in front of the roaring fire, and now she turned to look up at Hilda as she said, 'I don't have to, do I, Mam? Miss Collins don't like me, I can tell, an' I haven't drunk any of me tea yet.'

'Of course you don't have to.' Hilda's voice dared anyone to disagree with her, and now her tone was both bitter and pointed when she added, 'I didn't see any dresses handed out last month when it was *your* birthday.'

'We won't be long.' Polly rose quickly, Michael following suit, and she was conscious that although the others seemed oblivious to the interchange between her grandmother and herself, Luke's eyes were tight on the pair of them as they walked out of the kitchen.

'Whew.' There was laughter in Michael's voice. 'That was close. I thought we were going to have Ruth tagging along.'

Polly smiled back into his bright face but said nothing. It was cold, very cold; the air had a bite to it that nipped at your nose and fingers and would turn them blue within minutes, but she was warm inside.

'Did Miss Collins really ask to see me?' Michael moved away from the door, which he had shut firmly behind him, as he spoke, and as Polly joined him she said, 'Yes, of course.'

'And you've spoken about me to her?'

Polly's blush deepened but she said, 'Aye, I told you.'

'Why did you mention me?' They had reached the end of the farmhouse and were moving through the small break in the wall, beyond which lay the stables and the barn and the cottages.

'You know why,' Polly said, a trifle stiffly now.

And then the stiffness vanished as Michael caught hold of her hands, the laughter sliding from his voice as he said, 'You look right bonny today, Poll, beautiful in fact. You're the most beautiful lass in the world.'

'Oh, Michael.'

'I love you, Poll. Do you love me?'

'You know I do.'

'I've loved you forever.' His arms went round her, but gently. 'For ever and ever. I can't remember a time when I haven't known I love you.'

She gazed back into his face, which was on a level with hers, her eyes starry as they took in every contour of his sweet, serious features: the finely shaped nose and chin, the midnight-blue eyes with their long thick lashes, the silky brown hair just visible beneath his cap, which he had pulled on as they had left the kitchen. 'I know, I feel just the same.'

'Aw, Poll, Poll.' It was a hushed whisper, almost a sigh, and then he drew her against him and kissed her, a soft, lingering kiss, before putting her carefully from him and fetching the little brown velvet

100

box out of his pocket. 'This is your present,' he murmured. 'Will you marry me, Poll, and be my wife?'

The small ring the box held was clearly not expensive, the stones semi-precious, but to Polly it was the most wonderful ring in the world. 'Oh, Michael! Yes, yes, I'll marry you.' She flung her arms round his neck, her voice ecstatic.

'I'll have to ask your da.'

'Oh, me da loves you, you know he does. They all love you.'

Their voices were excited, their breath mingling in the icy air as they stood closely facing each other, and then Michael took the ring out of its snug box and slipped it on to the third finger of her left hand. 'We'll have a good life, Poll. I promise.' His tone was rushed now, feverish, as he kept his eyes on her vivacious face. 'I can work on the farm and try and get things round a bit, it needs another man here.'

Neither of them was aware of the incongruity of his words, considering that Michael had the build and frame of a lad much younger than his sixteen years.

Polly nodded. They needed another man, they needed several, but everything would be all right now Michael had asked for her. The world could be taken on and conquered now Michael had asked her to marry him.

'Do you mind if we visit Miss Collins a bit later?' Michael was whispering despite the fact that they were alone, but it seemed right somehow. 'I'd rather go back and ask your da before we see her.' He was feeling slightly nervous about asking her father if the truth be told. And yet no, that wasn't quite right – it wasn't so much his Uncle Henry's reaction he was uneasy about as his grandfather's. He didn't know why, but he had always felt, deep in the heart of him, that his grandfather didn't like him, probably because he was his mother's son. It was as clear as the nose on your face that there was no love lost between his mother and her father. And along with this feeling had come another, of resentment towards the dour old man, who – Michael felt – was harsh and cold. With everyone but Polly, that was. But no one could be harsh or cold with Polly, Polly was just perfect.

His heart lifted again on this last thought, and now he tugged at Polly's hand, saying, 'Come on then, let's go and tell them.'

They burst into the kitchen like two excited children on Christmas morning and immediately Alice guessed. As they came to a halt in the middle of the kitchen, Michael's arm self-consciously round Polly's waist, Alice's heart turned right over and her mouth went dry with panic. But she said not a word, merely sitting like a stone statue as Michael, with touching boldness, made his little speech to an amazed Henry.

'Well, this is a turn-up for the book.' Henry sounded as nonplussed as he looked. 'But you're still nowt but bairns—'

'No we're not, Da.' Polly's voice was quiet but very firm. 'Michael has had two years down the pit and I've had even more working on this farm. We left our childhoods behind years ago. And don't forget' – she slanted a glance at her grandmother now, only to become transfixed for a moment by the look on the old woman's face. It was another second or two before she managed to continue – 'Gran was married at seventeen, and that's just a year older than I am now.'

'That was different.' Hilda's voice was sharp.

'No it wasn't, Mam.' Polly's was just as sharp. 'I do the work of two women, three, out in them fields, and you know it, so don't tell me I'm not old enough to know my own mind.'

'By . . .' Henry shook his head. 'By . . .'

'Aren't you going to say something other than by?' Hilda snapped tightly. 'It's ridiculous, absolutely ridiculous, an engagement at sixteen. Eighteen maybe, or nineteen, with marriage in twelve months or so, but sixteen!'

'I'm not waiting three or four years, Mam.' Polly felt Michael's arm tighten round her waist. 'Michael doesn't want to and neither do I.' She turned to her grandfather, intending to appeal to him, but his thunderous face warned her it would be a fruitless exercise. She looked at her uncle and his red, angry face seemed ready to explode, and Arnold's was no better. Her Aunt Eva appeared stunned, her hand pressed over her mouth so tightly it was distorting her face, and Ruth was sitting goggle-eyed on the cracket, her mouth gaping open. It was only Luke, his eyes warm, who said, 'Young or not you'll do just fine, I'd bet me life on it.'

'*You can't get married.*' Alice's voice bordered on the hysterical.

That her grandmother was in shock Polly had no doubt, but it still was like a knife twisting in her ribs. Gran loved Michael, she knew she did, so why was she taking this tack in front of them all?

'Why not?' Michael's arm had become like a vice. 'Why not, Gran? We love each other, surely that's all that matters in the long run? What difference will waiting a few years make? We know how we feel, we always have.'

'Dear God, dear God.' It was a soft moan as Alice's face crumpled. 'Oh, for this to happen.'

'*Gran.*' Adrenalin born of anger was sweeping away all the hurt now, and Polly's voice was loud. 'Why can't we marry? What have you got against it?'

'Oh, lass, lass.' Alice's streaming eyes turned from Polly to Michael. The poor lad, the poor, poor lad. She wanted to say something but it was beyond her to do it with the wee lad standing there so innocently. The sins of the fathers – and the mothers. Oh, aye, oh, aye, dear Lord, the sins of the mothers right enough. What were they going to do?

102

What was going on here? Henry's eyes flashed from his mother – who was now wringing her hands as her tears ran unchecked – to his father, whose countenance was black with rage. Walter was glaring at Eva, his lips drawn back until they all but disappeared, and Henry found himself wondering what his sister had to do with his parents' obvious distress.

As Henry's gaze was turned on her, Eva raised her eyes, her hand still pressed over her mouth, and stared back at him. And suddenly he knew. He knew. 'No.' He had risen during Michael's little speech requesting Polly's hand in marriage, and now he took a step backwards as his thin face drained of colour. 'No, I don't believe it.'

'Henry.' Eva's voice was a whimper as her hands came together tightly across her ample bosom. 'Henry, they made me—'

'That was the reason for her wedding?' Henry swung round to confront his father. 'All this time you've let me think . . . That was the reason?' He was shaking, his voice hoarse. 'And I swallowed the tale of a quick marriage because she needed to get away! He's mine, isn't he? He's my bairn.'

'Who's your bairn?' Hilda asked, confused. 'I don't understand, Henry. What are you saying?'

'Henry, it wasn't my fault, it wasn't.' Eva was desperate to make him understand. 'They said they'd put me in the workhouse if I told you, and they would have, you know they would have. And afterwards they said that if you knew you'd go away, far away, and I'd never see you again. Oh, Henry, *please*. It wasn't my fault. I tried to tell you—'

Henry's whole face had screwed up as he had listened to his sister, who was talking as though there was no one else in the room; indeed, it was doubtful if Eva was aware of anyone else but her beloved brother. 'He's my bairn.' His eyes were wild as they swept over Polly and Michael's confused young faces. 'And now— Oh, what have I done, what have I done?'

'What *have* you done?' Hilda stared at her husband and it was clear from the look on her face that the awful truth was dawning. 'Henry, you aren't saying Michael is your son? You're not saying that, are you? You can't, you *can't* be saying that. *Eva is your sister!*'

There was absolute silence after Hilda had finished speaking, but Henry didn't break it for some seconds, and then he said, after dragging his eyes from Polly's white, horrified face, 'I should've been told. I should've been *told.*'

'Oh, oh, I need my smelling salts!' As Hilda went limp in Frederick's grasp, no one moved. They were all standing or sitting as though frozen in time. The expressions on Frederick, Arnold and Luke's faces were ones of stunned shock and disgust; Walter's face was fiery, the whites of his eyes red; and Alice was still a huddled, weeping heap. Henry's gaze had locked with Eva's, who was standing with her fists pushed against her chest, and Ruth was staring at her father open-mouthed.

This couldn't be happening, it wasn't real. Polly felt as though she was going to sink into the ground, and she wasn't even conscious that Michael's hand had left her waist. It was like a play, a Greek tragedy, something that exercised your brain as you struggled to keep pace with the plot. But this wasn't a play, it was real. Her da and her auntie. Oh, dear God, dear Lord Jesus, let it not be true. Please, please let it not be true.

'You, you've done this.' Henry was addressing his father before his gaze swept over his mother and he added, 'Both of you. How could you keep it from me?'

'We didn't know, lad, not until after you were wed an' then, then it was too late.'

'It was never too late to tell me!' Henry's voice was a bark. 'But it didn't suit you, that's the thing.' His gaze narrowed, and, his tone changing into thin bitterness, he said, 'You forced her to wed a stranger to save your own faces, knowing that the bairn was mine. She could've gone away where no one knew her, we could have said she was wed and then widowed, anything, but no, that wouldn't have done, and now look. Look! You've ruined both bairns' lives—'

'*Don't you take that tack with me, lad.*' Walter rose up out of his chair like an avenging angel, his voice thunderous. 'If anyone's ruined their lives it's you an' that Jezebel there! No decent man or woman could countenance what you've done; I tell you, it don't bear thinkin' about. That me own flesh an' blood could behave worse than the animals!'

As Henry's fist shot out, it was only Polly – springing forward and holding on to her father's arm – that stopped the blow from reaching its target. 'No, Da, no!' She was pleading with him as he continued to eye the furious old man in front of him. 'Please, Da, don't. Don't, Da.'

It was a full twenty seconds before Henry's arm dropped limply to his side, and during that time no one had moved a muscle. Hilda was whimpering and moaning, Frederick's arm round her shoulders, but other than that, the only sound in the deathly quiet room was the odd crackle and hiss from the fire.

'I'm sorry, lass.' It was a low, broken whisper and then, as Henry's eyes moved to Michael, standing stiff and still at the side of Polly, his face worked soundlessly before he said, 'Michael, if I'd known, things would've been different. I promise you things would have been different.'

As his hand stretched out towards his son, Michael took an involuntary step backwards, his lips curling back from his teeth as though he was surveying something foul and unclean, and this was reflected in his voice when he said, '*Don't touch me.*'

104

They continued to stare at each other for another moment or two, and as Luke watched them he thought, Why haven't I seen it before? Michael was the spitting image of Henry. The same nose, the same slight build and silky wavy hair, even the way they held their heads at a slight angle when they were listening to others conversing. Why hadn't he seen it? And then he answered himself. Because who on earth would be thinking anything like what had emerged today could be real? And plenty of nephews take after their uncles. Besides, Michael's build was the same as their own da, his and Arnold's. Saints alive, his da! Did he know Michael wasn't his? He couldn't have married Eva knowing she'd been taken down by her own brother, could he? Luke felt the bile rise up in his throat.

'Michael. Please, lad, listen to me—'

'I said don't touch me!' Henry's hand had moved towards his son again, and now Michael's voice was ugly as he smacked it away.

Polly was in a state of shock. She knew she was in shock because she felt as though she was back in the cow byre again and her da was looking at the newborn calf and stricken cow. She could almost feel the searing wind and bitter chill of that night reflected in the expression of raw defeat and helpless compassion on her father's face as he looked at Michael, and it made her want to reach out to him. In spite of everything. But what they had said, what he and her auntie had done, it was horrible, *horrible*. Her da couldn't have done that, he couldn't, there had to be some mistake. But there wasn't. Oh, Michael, Michael. And . . . and this meant Michael wasn't her cousin. He was – *Oh, Michael.*

'Let me explain, please.' Henry was openly pleading.

'There's nowt to explain.' Michael's voice was low but of a quality that made those listening want to cover their ears against it. 'You're vile, filthy, the pair of you! You make me want to vomit. I'd rather be dead than have you as a father.'

Polly saw Michael's words hit her father between the eyes, but even as she opened her mouth to say something – she knew not what, just something – another voice called from just outside the kitchen door. 'Hello there!' The tone was gay. 'Anyone at home?'

Miss Collins! Her granny's audible groan and her grandfather's muttered curse brought Polly spinning round, but Henry reached the door before her, jerking it open and passing through into the yard. He neither glanced at Miss Collins nor acknowledged her presence; indeed, it was doubtful if he heard her startled greeting.

'Polly?' Gwendoline Collins didn't need to be told all was not well as she stared at the ashen-faced girl in front of her. 'Polly, what is it?'

'Can . . . can I talk to you later, Miss Collins? There's . . . We have a difficulty that's arisen. I'm sorry.'

105

'Of course, my dear, of course.' And then, as the sound of raised voices from within became louder, Gwendoline said quickly, 'You go in, Polly, and we'll talk another time, but if there is anything I can do please don't hesitate to call. Goodbye, and . . . happy birthday, my dear.'

Happy birthday! As Polly stepped back into the kitchen it was to see Michael bodily restraining his mother from leaving as he shouted, 'You'll stay here and explain to me rather than run after him!' only to be shaken off like a leaf from a tree in autumn by one of Eva's powerful forearms.

'What do you want me to say?' Eva's voice had changed. The frantic entreating with which she had addressed her brother had been replaced by a low growl that came from deep in her throat. 'That it isn't true? That that numbskull of a pit yakker is your da? Well, Nathaniel has no claim on you, none, do you hear? Henry is your da.'

'Don't you know what that means?' Michael stared at the woman who had given birth to him, but who he felt at this moment was the devil incarnate. 'It makes Polly my sister, my *sister*! And me a bastard born of incest.' And as Alice gave a long, low moan, he swung round to look at his grandparents, his eyes moving from one to the other as he said, 'And you knew. All the time you knew.'

'Aye, they knew all right.' Eva brought Michael's attention back to herself. 'Sacrifical lamb, I was.'

'Michael, please.' Polly had moved to his side and now she put her hand on his arm, only to find it shaken off as violently as Eva had dealt with her son. She stepped back a pace, her face expressing her hurt surprise, before she said, and quietly, 'We need to find my da, Michael, and let him explain. He wouldn't . . . There's got to be an explanation.'

'*Our* da, you mean.' The words were coated with a terrible bitterness. 'And he can talk until he's blue in the face but it won't alter the facts. We're brother and sister, Polly. *Brother and sister!*' And as though the words had to be repeated to be believed he said again, 'Brother and sister.'

Polly had her hand to her mouth now and she was dimly aware of Frederick comforting her mother on the saddle, her grandfather rigid in his seat and Luke saying to the room in general, 'Look, we all need to calm down, all right?' before her aunt brought all eyes back to herself as she said, her voice once again coming deep and guttural, 'I'm not ashamed of it and I'm not going to pretend I am. I love him. I always have and I always will, so there.' As she glanced round the room her eyes were fierce. 'We should have been together, we would have been if it hadn't been for our mam and da interfering. And as for you!' Her gaze fastened on Hilda and it became demented, and Ruth, who was huddled on the floor against Frederick's

106

legs, whimpered with fright as Eva growled, 'You were never a wife to him.'

'Oh yes she was, Mam, a legal wife all right and proper.' There was no vestige of the shy, gentle, sweet lad they all knew in Michael's voice or manner now. His head was forward, his upper lip curled right back, exposing his teeth, and his chin uplifted. 'Whereas you . . . You're nothing, nothing! You don't care you've robbed me of everything I thought was mine, do you? Me da, me brothers, who I thought I was, but I could have taken all that if you'd left me Polly. But now—' For a second Polly thought Michael was going to hit his mother, and it was clear everyone else did too because she saw Luke make a sudden movement towards them, but Michael's fist merely hit into the palm of his other hand. 'Now everything is gone. You've never been much of a mother, not to any of us, but I didn't think you capable of this.'

'Well, now you know.' Eva stepped back from her son, making a wide sweep of her arm to embrace the room as she cried, 'Now you all know, and I'm glad it's out in the open. I am! No one has thought of me for years.' She wagged her head as though someone had denied it. 'No, no one. I was packed off and got out of the way and I've had to put a face on things for the last sixteen years. Well, I'm tired of it, do you hear me? Tired of it!' She fairly spat the words into her mother's face, and as Walter rose and – so it seemed – in the same movement brought his open hand in a ringing slap across Eva's face, pandemonium reigned.

In the mêlée, no one noticed Michael turn and leave the kitchen except Polly, and she was hot on his heels as she followed him out into the bitterly cold afternoon, grabbing her coat from the back of the kitchen door as she left.

'Michael! Wait, Michael!'

She caught him up as he left the yard for the lane beyond, but his stride didn't alter, his voice terse as he said, 'Go back, Polly.'

'No, I have to talk to you. Please, wait a minute, Michael.'

'All the talking in the world won't make any difference. I hate them, I hate them both, an' Gran and Grandda. I can see now why he's never liked me, and he hasn't, you know.'

He was walking with his head and shoulders hunched forward and his cap pulled low over his forehead, and so quickly Polly found herself running and stumbling to keep up with him. 'You can't go, not like this.' She almost went headlong, and when he still didn't slow down she said again, her voice desperate, 'Please wait a minute, *please.*'

The appeal brought his face round to look at her, and she saw his teeth clamp down on his lower lip before he said thickly, 'It's no use, don't you see, Polly?' Nevertheless he slowed his stride, enabling her to come alongside him on the path without slipping and sliding.

'What are you going to do?'

107

'What can I do?' The sob in his voice wrenched at her heart, but when he stopped and turned to face her on the snow-covered path she saw his eyes were dry and burning. 'I can't go back home, not now I know. I'd kill her, I would, I tell you.'

'Oh, Michael. Michael.'

'I . . . I don't know what I'm going to do, where I'm going to go. It'll have to be far away, far far away, that's for sure, because Arnold won't keep his mouth shut about this little lot. He hates me, he always has since he knew you an' me cared for each other, and he won't miss the chance to put the knife in.'

'He won't,' Polly said feverishly. 'Luke won't let him say anything.' A separate part of her brain that seemed to be working quite independently at the moment noticed he hadn't said the word love – that they loved each other – but cared instead, and she realised in that moment he had already gone from her. And he had to go – she knew he had to go – but how was she going to be able to bear it? She would never love anyone other than Michael, *never*.

'I have to go anyway.' His eyes were moving over her face now, his own face very white and strained. They seemed to drink in each feature, each little chestnut curl dancing free of its confines in the icy wind. 'You know I do. I can't stay here and not see you, and . . . and I can't see you.'

He bowed his head and began to cry. It was silent crying at first, evident only in the shaking of his body, and then as Polly gave a little moan and put her arms round his waist with her head resting against his chest, he gave vent to his despair, holding her close for the last time as they both sobbed against the cruelty of fate. It was Polly who pulled herself together first, raising her head and sniffing desperately as she wiped her eyes with the back of her hand. Her deep blue eyes looking almost black in her white face, she said brokenly, 'You can't just go, Michael, without knowing where.'

'It doesn't matter where.'

The agony in his voice was too much and it brought Polly's hands to her eyes to press her tears back. She mustn't cry any more, that could come later when she was in bed and Ruth was asleep. For the moment she had to make Michael see that he wouldn't be able to cope if he just went off, he wasn't made that way. Her lips moved hard, one over the other, before she said, 'It does matter, to me. If you did anything silly . . .'

'I don't intend to top meself if that's what you mean.'

She didn't know what she meant.

'Goodbye, Polly.' He was backing away from her as he spoke and the look on his face checked the involuntary movement she made towards him. She had to let him go, she couldn't make this any harder for him than it was, but oh, she loved him so much. And terrible though this was for her, it was a hundred times worse for Michael, with his da not being his da and Luke and Arnold not even half-brothers, and his mam having done *that* with her da. *Her da.* How could he? *How could he?*

She knew Michael was crying again as he walked away and she felt her heart was being wrenched out by its roots. Her words were just a whisper on the wind when she said softly, 'I love you, I love you so much.' And contrary to her earlier resolve, she found she was watching the small, bewildered figure through a mist of tears, her thoughts whirling and bouncing in her head as her stomach churned and various emotions battled for pre-eminence. She felt utterly grief-stricken and angry and confused and wretched, but overall the anger was growing and taking control. And she welcomed the bitter rage, it was a temporary opiate against the hurt and pain.

And then she blinked to clear her eyes. She thought she had seen another figure on the path walking towards Michael. It was Miss Collins. She must have decided to take a walk after the brief visit to the farmhouse. Polly tensed as the two met, mentally preparing herself to run and join them. The last thing Michael wanted in his present state was to have to talk to a relative stranger.

Miss Collins was bending down slightly, her head close to Michael's, and to Polly's surprise there was no sudden and offended jerking away indicating that Michael had told her to leave him alone. In fact it seemed as though the two were conversing.

'Polly!' On hearing her name called she turned to look towards the farm and to where Luke was making his way towards her, but she didn't raise her hand in recognition or make any movement other than turning back to the two figures some way down the path, who were now walking away from the farm together. She strained her eyes to where they were being swallowed up by the snowswept landscape. Of all the people in the world, Miss Collins would know what to do and say in a situation like this. Her travels and independent spirit had given the older woman an edge that Polly called self-possession but others, less kind, would label worldliness, though Polly wasn't conscious of that right at this moment. She only knew that Miss Collins would talk to Michael and that she would help him without expressing undue shock or disgust. And that was what her beloved needed right at this moment.

'Come on, Polly.'

How long Luke had been standing at her side Polly wasn't sure, she was only aware that when he eventually took her arm to lead her back towards the farmhouse she was very cold and the two figures in the distance had long since disappeared. 'Miss Collins was with him.'

'Aye, I saw.'

'I hate my aunt and my da.'

'No you don't, you only think you do.' Luke's voice was quiet as he looked down at the beautiful young girl beside him. It had been an afternoon of revelation in more than one direction. He had discovered he wasn't quite the big fellow he'd always liked to think he was when, amid the surprise and revulsion at what had been revealed, and the sympathy he had felt for Polly and Michael's circumstances, there had been an element of gratification too. This meant the unthinkable had happened and Polly was free. Free to fall in love with someone else. Someone else? Who was he kidding? Free to fall in love with him was what he had meant. And he'd been sickened that amid all the hurt and pain and horror of those he loved – and he did love Michael as a brother – he had been thinking of himself, and worse, of taking Polly when Michael had been dealt such a killing blow.

'I'll never love anyone but Michael, Luke.' It was said in a low voice but with passionate intensity.

'Never is a long time.'

'Be that as it may, I mean it.' She didn't sound like young Polly, in either her choice of words or the way she spoke them, and Luke felt his blood chill in his veins. Women were different to men in their attitude to love, or at least most of them were. Of course there were the types down at the docks or in the bars in Monkwearmouth who could give any man alive a run for his money, but most women seemed to love with a sacrificial devotion at the heart of their emotions, whereas with a man the feeling was much more physical and – he admitted somewhat ruefully – therefore more necessary on a day-to-day level. Look at the old Queen, devoted to the memory of her beloved Prince Albert and wearing the black clothes of mourning for more than forty years before her death five years ago. Somehow he couldn't see a man in such a position of wealth and power doing that.

Was Polly another Victoria? As they came to the farmyard his eyes ran over her lovely tragic face and the stiff, determined set of her slender shoulders under the faded coat. Only time would tell, she was such a young lass still and it was natural to tell herself now she would never love again when the object of her devotion had been so painfully wrested from her. Nevertheless, the chill deepened inside him and was only put to one side when, on opening the kitchen door, he was hit by the barrage of raised voices from within.

It was impossible to determine who was shouting at who. Eva had the appearance of a wild woman as – one hand pressed to the side of her face, which was flaming red from Walter's blow, and her long thick hair falling down from the bun at the back of her head – she faced Hilda and Frederick, the three of them yelling for all they were worth, with Arnold and Alice apparently joining in. Walter was sitting in his chair and he looked ill, and Ruth was crouched at the side of the range wailing and crying. The noise was indescribable.

110

And then Luke nearly jumped out of his skin as the young, slight girl at the side of him screamed for silence with enough force to bring every voice to an abrupt halt.

'Where's Da?' Polly was talking to Ruth, and when her sister shook her head she turned to the others and said again, her voice urgent with the strange presentiment which had swept over her on entering the farmhouse, 'Has he been back?'

'Back? No, he hasn't been back and I shouldn't think so either. How he thinks he can ever hold his head up again after what's come out this afternoon I don't know, and I tell you—'

What Hilda was about to tell her Polly never found out, because she left her mother in full flow and spun round, clutching at Luke's arm as she said, 'We must find him, Luke. He was in such a state.'

How much of a state Henry had been in became obvious two minutes later. The body was hanging by the neck from a rope thrown over one of the old beams in the barn, and the blue face and grotesquely extended tongue told Luke at once that Polly's father was dead. 'Go on out, Polly. *Now.*' He tried to shield her from the sight of the gently swinging figure but Polly shook him off, gazing up at her father as she murmured, 'Oh no, no, Da. No. Don't go like this, not like this.'

But it was too late. It had been too late on a sunny summer evening sixteen years ago in this very place, or maybe even six years before that, when a giggling fifteen-year-old girl had led her fourteen-year-old brother into a sweet-smelling hayloft and taught him what passion and desire were all about. Or perhaps the death bell had slowly begun to ring when a bitter young mother had looked into the face of her newborn child and seen only entrapment and a life of toil and relentless drudgery, and had hardened her heart against her firstborn.

Or perhaps such tragedy never has a finite beginning.

Chapter Nine

It was long past midnight, but Polly was still sitting in front of the fire in the kitchen in a state of exhausted numbness. The house was quiet now, and in the dim light from the one oil lamp she had burning, the blackleaded range with its big iron kettle on the hob, the clippy mat on the scrubbed flagstones and the hardwood saddle with its flock-stuffed cushions all looked the same as usual. The battered table covered with an oilcloth and the stout wooden chairs, the big black frying pan and other pots and pans sitting on their steel shelf above the hob were items she had known since babyhood, and yet somehow, tonight, she felt as though she was looking at them all through someone else's eyes. Because she had changed. All these familiar objects were the same, but she had changed out of recognition to the girl she had been this morning. At least that was how she felt.

As the kettle began to sing, Polly roused herself. She went to the tall, narrow cupboard on the right-hand side of the range and extracted the big brown teapot from one newspaper-covered shelf, along with the tea caddy and a small glass bowl of sugar. After warming the pot, she spooned in three teaspoonfuls of tea and then added the hot water, sitting down once more whilst the tea mashed.

Once the tea was ready she stood up again and walked through to the pantry, taking a jug of milk from its stone slab and returning to the kitchen table. Her movements were slow and steady, almost ponderous, and they continued to be the same when she poured two cups of tea and climbed the stairs to her grandparents' room.

'How is he?' As Polly silently entered the room she looked at the inert figure of her grandfather in the bed, and Alice raised her head from where she had been dozing on one of the kitchen chairs Polly had brought up earlier. 'Same.' Alice shook her head wearily. 'What are we going to do, lass?'

'First off, you're going to drink your tea.' Polly's voice was gentle. The heart attack her grandfather had suffered on hearing of the death of his son had aged her grandmother ten years, or so it seemed. Her granny seemed to have shrunk inwards since that moment when Grandda had collapsed on the kitchen floor. 'I'll leave Grandda's here. He might wake up later and want a sup.'

'If the doctor's right an' your grandda's going to be bed-ridden, what'll happen to us?' Alice asked pitifully, her lips trembling.

'Gran, Grandda hasn't worked much outside for years now,' Polly said quietly. 'You know that.'

'Aye, but there was your da then.'

Yes, there had been her da then. And now his body had been taken to Bishopswearmouth by the same doctor who had attended her grandfather. 'We'll manage, Gran. Ruth can leave school, it's nearly time anyway, and she'll have to help me outside a bit as well as helping you in the house. You'll have your work cut out with Grandda until he gets better.'

'Do you think he'll get better?' It was pathetic in its hopefulness, and now Polly lied stoutly as she said, 'Of course he will, Gran. You know Grandda, built like an ox, as he's so fond of saying.'

'Oh, lass, lass. An' where will we find money for the doctor's bills an' the funeral an' all?'

'We can't deal with everything tonight, Gran.'

'I'm sorry, lass.' Her grandmother wasn't speaking about her agitation over money and they both knew it, and now Polly shook her head slightly as she said thickly, 'I can't believe me da did that, Gran. Not with Aunt Eva. It's . . . it's unbelievable.'

'Aye, it is that, me bairn. But don't blame your da, Polly. Your aunt was the one. Aye, she was. Even if she is me own daughter, she's a fiend from hell, that one.'

Polly stared at her grandmother for a moment or two. She didn't say what she wanted to ask, which was *why*? Why was her aunt like that? There must have been something that made her that way, surely? Instead she just inclined her head before setting her grandfather's cup on the floor by her grandmother's chair and quietly leaving the room. No one had mentioned Michael. Not once, since her Uncle Frederick had gone for the doctor in his horse and trap before taking her aunt home, had anyone referred to him. Not Luke or Arnold, who had stayed until the doctor had come; not even Miss Collins, who had paid a brief visit as the doctor was leaving. It was as though Michael had ceased to exist. *But he hadn't*. And Polly wanted him, she so wanted to see his face and comfort him, love him. She was frightened for him, terribly frightened, because she had understood something this afternoon that had hitherto been hidden from her. Michael took after his da, *their* da. They were dreamers, impractical and gentle, in a world of their own half the time.

Polly opened the door of the bedroom she shared with Ruth and looked in on her sister, who was fast asleep and snoring gently under the covers, then she closed it again quietly, after taking her calico nightdress off her side of the bed. She didn't open her mother's door, neither did she call to her to ask if she was awake and wanted a cup of

114

tea. There had been a scene between her mother and her grandmother after the doctor had left, and both women had said too much, the result of which being that Hilda had taken a heavy dose of laudanum and gone to bed, leaving them all to it.

On returning to the quiet shadowed kitchen, Polly poked the fire into a blaze and added some more wood, before pouring herself a strong cup of tea, which she drank straight down. She poured another, this time adding more milk as the previous one had burned her mouth, and drank this cup sitting on the saddle watching the leaping flames lick at a piece of partially burnt wood, which sizzled now and again. Then she took off all her clothes but her shift. There was something she had to do tonight before she tried to get some rest. It wasn't sensible and it certainly wasn't practical, but she had to do it nevertheless.

She pulled on her rough calico nightdress, which felt doubly stiff and shapeless after the soft, yielding material of the dress, and then her coat, as the night's bitter chill was making itself felt. Then she returned to the saddle with the russet brocade dress in her hands, and slowly and systematically began to rip it to pieces. She burned the fragments on the fire one by one, watching steadily as they flared brightly for a few moments before dwindling away to ashes.

When nothing remained of the dress, she sat quietly for a full minute before reaching up to her hair and pulling the ribbon out of her tangled curls, but just as she was about to send it the same way as the dress, her hand stilled. Her da had gone all the way into Bishopswearmouth with instructions from Ruth about the ribbon, and he had bought her this. His face had been so bright, so proud this morning when he had seen her in all her finery. She ought to hate him for what he had done; she actually *wanted* to hate him because then this raw, gut-wrenching pain might lessen a little, but she couldn't. She couldn't. Her hand hovered for a moment more and then she rolled the ribbon up, thrusting it into the pocket of her coat.

One thing that would remain from this day, one thing she would wear proudly until her dying day was Michael's ring. She sat staring down at her hands – the ring on the third finger of her right hand now – and the three small garnets in their band of gold twinkled back at her, their brightness mocking her misery. Michael was gone and her da – their da – was dead. The future that had been so radiant just hours before was now like the dress: destroyed, dark, nothing but a pile of ashes.

She lifted her head and glanced round the silent kitchen, and as she did so the weight of her family bowed her shoulders. Her da was gone and her grandda would never leave his bed again, although the doctor had indicated he might linger on for months if not years. There was her granny and Ruth, and her mother, and they had all – in their different ways – made it plain to her over the last few hours that they were looking to her. She didn't mind that so much with her sister and her granny, one still so young and the other old and frail, but her mother . . . Polly's mouth hardened. She wasn't at all sure just how ill her mother really was.

What was she to do? What was to become of them? It had been an uphill struggle even with her da alive and her grandda doing the odd job outside. They had sold off a couple of cows each winter just to get through, and even then, without Miss Collins's rent money, they had barely managed. And now their once bonny herd was down to just six beasts and their winter feed all gone.

She would have to sell them at market. She shut her eyes tightly at the thought. All except Buttercup. She couldn't bear to part with Buttercup, her favourite cow; besides which, they would need fresh milk each day. Buttercup would have to stay. But if they were to keep the two pigs and the hens and geese, the rest of the herd would have to go. There was her da's funeral to pay for and the doctor's bills, and her da had said only last week that the farmhouse roof needed attending to. With flour at two shillings and ninepence a stone and tea at sixpence a quarter-pound, they were going to be hard put to even buy the essentials. They would have to cut right down where they could.

She glanced at the flickering lamp on the table. No more lamp oil at over thruppence a quart, they could manage with candles from now on. And her mam could do without sugar in her tea, although no doubt she'd create a bit. For someone who was supposed to be constantly at death's door, Mam held on fast to all the little luxuries the rest of them rarely tasted.

The urge to cry suddenly swept over her and she had the desire to put her head in her hands and give in to it, but something Luke had said more than once in the discussions on a Sunday afternoon came back to her. 'No good bubblin' about the injustices and the unfairness, that serves nothing. We've got to fight and do it without letting 'em crush us.'

Well, she felt crushed at the moment. She raised her head as though in protest to the thought. And all things considered, she had good reason for feeling so. Her chin moved a fraction higher. But all the self-pity in the world wouldn't bring back her da or allow her to marry Michael or make her grandda like he had used to be. And if she thought of all those things now she wouldn't be able to carry on, so . . . she wouldn't think of them. Not now. She would wait a while, that was what she would do.

She breathed out slowly through her nose and, pulling her coat tighter about her, walked out of the kitchen into the blackness of the yard. Through memory rather than sight she made her way to the privy, shivering now in the bitterly cold wind whipping across from the open fields beyond, but once she had finished and was outside in the yard again, her eyes having adjusted to the darkness, she stood still for a moment despite the raw night.

116

Luke was right, she had to fight, and bad as this was, there were others worse off the night. Look at the poor souls in the workhouses or those families living rough on the fells round Gateshead way. They might be mostly tinkers and hawkers and the like, but they died in their dozens during the winter in their makeshift dwellings of earth cottages with sod or turf roofs. Mind, she'd take her chance on the fells any day rather than set foot in the workhouse. She shivered, but it was more to do with her thoughts than the icy wind.

What was Michael doing right now? Was he awake too? Did he know about her da? The thoughts had sneaked into her mind unbidden but almost immediately she clamped down on them, saying out loud, 'None of that, none of that.' That wasn't the way to be strong. She took a deep breath, her shoulders coming back under the old coat. She was glad Miss Collins had talked to Michael. Her eyes turned in the direction of their lodger's cottage. And she would see her tomorrow . . .

For the first time since she had decided to rent the cottage for the winter, Gwendoline Collins was experiencing a sensation of being confined on all sides. It had happened in the past several times before, but then it had been due to a physical restriction such as when she had been incarcerated in her cabin in a boat on one of her journeys, or yet still when she had made the mistake of venturing underground into a cave in Greece in order to see some fine specimens of stalactites and stalagmites. But there was no physical limitation now to make her feel so dreadful.

She twisted under the heaped covers on the bed, but on flinging one arm free quickly pulled it back under the blankets again as the cold hit. This place! She hadn't known what real cold was until she had made the mistake of renting this cottage. It had seemed like an adventure in the autumn when the air had still been redolent with the remains of summer and the crisp, bracing nights had merely been enough to make the roaring fire seem cosy. But in the depths of winter . . . How did Polly stand it? The hard, continuous grind, the harsh conditions, and it would all be a hundred times worse now her father had killed himself. *Killed himself.* Gwendoline's thin mouth became thinner as her lips moved one on top of the other. The man was a weakling, a coward on top of his other sins. Or had been.

The last amendment brought her twisting again, and now she faced the reason for the agitation that had her wishing herself a million miles from the farm. She had broken her cardinal rule and got involved with the people about her. And it troubled her, it troubled her greatly, the more so since she was not at all sure how Polly would view matters when they spoke tomorrow. And Polly would expect her to expound at length on the conversation she had had with Michael after he had left the farm, that was only natural. Had she been right to advise the boy as

117

she had? Her brows drew together, her face screwing up for a moment as though she was suffering pain. Here she was, a lapsed Catholic, and yet she had advised him as she had. But they had talked together at some length and the boy had been desperate; it had seemed right at the time. And he had a faith, there was no doubt about that. He was what her father would have called a good Catholic. Whatever that was.

Oh, what was the matter with her tonight? She made a little moue with her mouth in the pitch blackness. She had taken up residence here for a while because she had wanted to; no one had persuaded her into it, and it was she who had made the overtures of friendship towards Polly which had resulted in her becoming better acquainted with the workings within the family. She liked Polly. No, more than that, she admired her. The girl had a strong spirit that moreover was hungry for knowledge and enlightenment. Born to a better class with the benefits of education to set her free from narrow thinking, the girl could have gone far.

Gwendoline's blue-grey eyes, which had a piercing quality all of their own and were her best feature, suddenly opened very wide. And why not? she thought excitedly. Why shouldn't Polly have the chance to rise above the trappings of her working-class beginnings? Gwendoline herself could provide that chance. She had taken to the girl – her feelings hovering somewhere between those of a mentor and a friend – and certainly Polly was the only person she had met in a long, long time that she could envisage having as a permanent companion. The business with this boy who now turned out to be her half-brother had effectively finished all thoughts of romance for the time being, and if she took the girl in hand – gave her all the advantages of travel and experience and such – who knew what fine match she might make in the future when her heart had healed. If she was inclined towards matrimony, that was.

Of course, the matter of her family would have to be dealt with, but then it was clear they couldn't carry on here without menfolk. The farm would have to be sold, and if there were any debts, as well there might be, they could be cleared and then a small dwelling of some kind purchased in the town of Bishopswearmouth. Failing that, there were places which catered for the old and infirm, as the grandparents undoubtedly were, and possibly the mother too, while the sister appeared old enough to be put into service or work of some other kind. So Gwendoline disposed of Polly's family without a qualm, and after she had done so she fell immediately into a deep sleep.

'I'm . . . I'm sorry, Miss Collins. I don't want to appear ungrateful.'

'I'm aware of that.' It was stiff and cold, nearly as cold as the black frost which had fallen the night before and turned the snow-covered ground into glass.

Polly sat back on her heels in front of the fire she had recently lit and which was beginning to blaze, and surveyed the figure sitting up in the bed with a thick eiderdown draped about it. Miss Collins was angry with her for refusing the offer to be her companion and travel the world. They had been discussing the matter for some five minutes since Miss Collins had first made the incredible suggestion, and although at first Miss Collins had been smiling and soft-voiced as she had countered Polly's objections, she had gradually got stiffer and stiffer and was now very much the aristocrat.

She couldn't deal with this today, not on top of everything else. For the first time since she had known the other woman, Polly felt a dart of dislike pierce the high regard she had for Miss Collins. It was like a mausoleum back there in the house and she had a hard day's work in front of her; didn't Miss Collins realise how things were? And she couldn't just walk away from her family, the idea was unimaginable, but because she hadn't immediately fallen in with the suggestion it was as if a wall had been erected between herself and this woman she had thought of as her friend.

Polly now took a long, deep breath, curbing her bewilderment, and said quietly, 'Thank you for talking to Michael yesterday, Miss Collins. Was . . . was he all right when you left him?'

It was a silly way to put it in view of the circumstances, and Gwendoline's voice reflected this when she said, 'Hardly.' And then, as if realising she was being grossly unfair, Gwendoline added quickly, 'But I'm sure he will be. Time is a great healer.' Oh, hark at her! She despised platitudes.

'Did you talk for very long?'

Gwendoline hesitated. She was aware of her character deficiencies, and unlike most people made no excuses to herself regarding them. She knew she was rather a passionless person – except where her love of naturalism and art was concerned – but this did not trouble her. Neither did her recognition that from a very young child she had fought constantly to have her own way and heartily disliked being thwarted. In fact if pressed she would have confessed to thinking it an advantage in the solitary life she had chosen. She had been excited this morning before Polly had arrived to carry out her normal duties; somewhat carried away with the idea of Polly as her companion, she confessed silently to herself. And now the girl had made it quite plain she could not be induced to leave her family or this miserable farm. And it had annoyed her. It had annoyed her greatly. But if Polly was closing her eyes to the wonderful opportunity being offered to her, she must accept her decision with grace. Nevertheless, Gwendoline's voice still had a slight edge to it when she said, 'I suppose so, some twenty minutes at least. He was in some distress.'

'Did he say what he is going to do?'

119

'Not exactly.'

Polly stared at the other woman before rising to her feet and standing perfectly still for a moment. She was glad she had burnt the dress. It was a ridiculous thought to come to mind in the present situation, but it lifted Polly's chin and narrowed her eyes. And this woman wasn't a friend, not in the true sense of the word. Real friendship was unconditional. This reticence regarding Michael was a punishment because she had refused to go away with Miss Collins.

And then Gwendoline disabused her of this idea when she said quietly, 'I am not being mealy-mouthed through choice, Polly. Michael and I discussed the present state of affairs, the hopelessness of your attachment. You do know it is hopeless?' And at Polly's nod, she continued, 'And then we spoke of other things – his family, life, God.'

'God?' said Polly blankly.

'His father – his mother's husband – is a Catholic and Michael has been brought up in the faith. He has not questioned it as I did at about his age. His religion will be a comfort to him.'

'He means to go away, doesn't he?'

There was a pause before Gwendoline said, 'That was his intention, yes. I understand he was going to collect his belongings and leave before his mother returned home last night. He felt he couldn't see her without . . . wishing her harm.'

He had gone. The women's eyes held across the expanse of the small two-roomed cottage, and it was Gwendoline who looked away first. He had gone. *Gone.* The word was reverberating in Polly's head, before a stern inner voice checked it, saying, Well? You knew he was going, didn't you? He told you so. 'Did he say where he is going to live?'

This time the pause was longer, and Polly had her answer even before the other woman said, 'I think he thought a clean break was best for everyone concerned.'

But Miss Collins knew. Michael barely knew her and yet he had confided in her. *What had she said to him?*

After another exchange of glances, Polly turned and made for the door, saying over her shoulder, 'I'll bring the drinking water and fresh milk shortly.'

'Thank you, Polly, and . . . and I think it would be best if I left shortly, perhaps at the end of the week? You are going to have enough to do without tending to my needs too.'

Polly had stopped at the threshold but she hadn't turned round, and now her slender shoulders stiffened just the slightest bit but her voice was quiet as she said – still without moving – 'As you wish, Miss Collins,' before she stepped out of the door, closing it firmly behind her.

Chapter Ten

'An' you're seriously tellin' me you can't get out of that bed for your own husband's funeral? Is that what you're sayin'?'

As her daughter-in-law stared back at her, Alice acknowledged that if the power of thought had any say in the matter she would be six foot under at this very moment, the same as her lad was going to be shortly. Hilda's eyes told her as much.

'I'm ill.' Hilda's voice was thin and cold. 'And it's hardly surprising with everything that has happened. Even you must see that.'

'What I see is a lazy, vindictive—'

'Don't you call me names! Not you! When I think of what I have endured since I was tricked into marrying Henry to cover the goings-on here, it makes me sick to my stomach.'

'Aye, well, there's plenty that makes me sick to me stomach an' I'm lookin' at one thing right now.' Alice was standing in the doorway to Hilda's bedroom, her small, slight body appearing even smaller in her black funeral clothes. It had taken all of the big pot of black dye Polly had purchased in Bishopswearmouth to turn their Sunday clothes into those of mourning, but new ones – even purchased from the second-hand market in the East End at a fraction of the original cost – had been out of the question.

'Gran, come away.' Polly's voice was firm as she took her grandmother's arm and led her away from the doorway. 'Uncle Frederick is waiting outside.' She pushed the old woman towards the stairs before returning to her mother's room and saying quietly, 'Ruth is here to take care of you and Grandda until we get back, and there's bread and cheese and brawn for midday. We'll have a hot meal tonight.'

There was no reply from the figure in the bed, but then, just as Polly was about to close the door, her mother's voice stopped her.

'It's disgraceful, you not having folk back here after for a bite. What will people think?'

'I don't care what people think.'

'Well, that's true enough. Cheapest funeral you could get; just one horse, and not even a closed carriage.'

Polly stared at her mother and wondered how her father had managed to live with such a stupid woman for seventeen years without doing her physical harm. Her mother had ranted and raved for the last week since her da's death, calling him every name under the sun, so it certainly wasn't any tender feeling for the departed that had prompted her complaint. Keeping up appearances, that was all her mother was concerned with. No matter that her da's death and her grandda's collapse had revealed to the unsuspecting womenfolk that the farm's finances were in an even worse state than they had imagined. It appeared the two men had been borrowing off Frederick for the last few years and the amount they owed was now considerable; added to which, with the remainder of the cows gone – excepting Buttercup – the farm was reduced to little more than a smallholding, which left no chance of recovery. The farmhouse and barn were in desperate need of repair, their livestock was almost nonexistent, their debts were overwhelming and her mother wanted to spend money they didn't have on a lavish funeral and wake! It would be funny if it wasn't so tragic.

'Goodbye, Mother.' Polly shut the door on her mother's voice as it began another lament, and stood on the landing for a moment, biting hard on her lip. Then she nipped along to her grandparents' room and opened the door very quietly, only to find her grandfather wasn't asleep as she had thought he might be. For the last week it seemed he had barely been awake.

'Hello, me bairn.' He was lying quite still on the big feather bolster doubled behind his back which brought him almost sitting upright in the bed. The doctor had advised his patient to lie in such a position, and Polly and her grandmother had found it helped his breathing.

'We're just going, Grandda.' Polly walked across to the bed and took one of the big, bony-knuckled, blue-veined hands lying limply on the bedcover. 'We'll be back before you know it.'

Walter said nothing, but as a drop of moisture slid out of the corner of one eye and down his weather-beaten face, Polly said thickly, 'Oh don't, don't, Grandda. It'll be all right.' She had never thought to see her grandfather cry, not her big, burly, tough grandda, and it hurt her as much as anything that had happened.

'I'm sorry, lass.' Walter wiped his hand across his face before sniffing loudly. 'I'm a bit down the day.'

'Aye, I know, we all are, but we'll get through, Grandda. Once the spring is here and the weather's warmer everything will look different. You'll see.'

'He wasn't a bad man, lass, an' he'd have sooner slit his own throat than bring such pain on you. I know that. I should've stopped your aunt comin' to the farm, I know that now an' all, an' weathered whatever came from that direction. As it is . . .' He shook his head slowly, his voice trailing off.

'It'll be all right,' said Polly again, squeezing his hand between her own. Her grandda loved her, he always had, and it had been

122

his hands that had lifted her high on to his shoulders and carried her round the farm as a small child, his hands that had mopped her tears and fashioned little wooden toys for Ruth and herself. Her granny and her grandda might have made mistakes with their own children, but with her mam as she was and her da always having been a remote father until the last couple of years, it had been her grandparents she had always relied on for security and love. She couldn't let them down now when they needed her the most, and whatever it took she intended to keep what was left of this family together. She bent over the bed and kissed the old man's furrowed forehead before hurrying out of the room and down the stairs to the kitchen, where she found Frederick and her grandmother waiting for her, Ruth purring like a kitten over the box of toffee their mother's stepbrother had brought her.

'You've got plenty to keep you occupied until we get back. There's the leek pudding to do; mind you wash and trim the leeks well and split them to get rid of any grit, Ruth. Start boiling the pudding as soon as it's ready and we'll have it for our dinner tonight with mashed potatoes and gravy, all right? And make some bread while you're about it, and keep enough back for a stottie cake after the dough's had its first rising and you've knocked it down, so we can have that with the pudding and gravy tonight.' Polly's voice was brisk; she had found that was the best way to handle her sister, who had cried on and off for the whole of the last week. 'Then see if there's any eggs, and feed the pigs their mash. It's cooling down in the scullery.'

Ruth nodded sulkily. She hated their Polly; her sister was always keeping her at it.

'And don't forget to keep checking on Grandda, mind.'

'All *right*.' She was only showing off in front of Uncle Frederick. Ruth looked at her sister through narrowed eyes. Her mam said Polly was trying to take over as mistress of the house and make everyone jump through hoops, and she was right. Look how Polly had shouted yesterday when she'd come in from milking Buttercup. Just because she had gone for a lie-down on the bed and fallen asleep and the bread-and-butter pudding had burnt away to nothing. Her gran had nodded off in the chair sitting next to her grandda, but Polly hadn't said a word to her. No, everything was always Ruth's fault.

'Well now, are we ready?' Frederick spoke almost as though the occasion was some kind of pleasant social outing, and he must have realised this because his voice carried a more sober note when he added, 'It's a quagmire out there, lass, so be careful.'

Aye, it was a quagmire all right since the thaw had set in four days ago and the thick snow and ice had turned to slush and mud. Polly had to wade through that same quagmire umpteen times a day, her feet constantly wet and cold and her flesh chilled through to the bone. Didn't he realise that? Who else was going to milk Buttercup and see to the horses and the hundred and one other jobs outside? And then she checked the momentary irritation as she thought, He's only trying to be kind.

She was forced to remind herself of this several times during the course of the next two hours. Her uncle persisted in holding her arm and that of her grandmother as he positioned himself between them at all times, acting as though he was in charge of the proceedings to the small collection of family and friends who had gathered at the tiny cemetery just outside Silksworth. Because of the circumstances, and the doctor removing her father's body from the house rather than it being laid out at home as was customary, there was no cortège following behind the funeral conveyance as the black-plumed horse clip-clopped its way inside the cemetery gates.

Parson Dodds was standing to one side of the open grave, a single gravedigger behind him. Polly, her grandmother and her uncle stood at his side, with the rest of the mourners scattered behind them. Polly was touched to see her Uncle Nathaniel there with Luke and Arnold, but there was no sign of her Aunt Eva.

The sickness in Polly's chest deepened as the service began. It was short, very short. It had been decided, in the few minutes before her uncle had gone for the doctor a week ago Sunday, that the story the family would stick to was one of an unfortunate accident on the farm. Whilst taking a close look at the hole in the barn roof, which was in urgent need of repair, her father had slipped, inadvertently entangling himself in his safety rope and causing his own death by hanging. He had been the victim of a tragic mishap. There was no point in putting out their dirty washing for everyone to see, Frederick had insisted when the others had expressed initial misgivings. Henry was dead, nothing could bring him back, and at least this way he could be buried with dignity.

However, Polly felt the good parson's short service was indicative of the scepticism with which he had made it clear he viewed the 'accident'.

'Ashes to ashes, dust to dust . . .'

It was over.

'Eee, I'm sorry, miss, right sorry. I got to know Mr Henry a bit when he was courtin' Miss Hilda, an' the master said I could come along today an' offer me respects.'

Polly raised tear-blurred eyes to the figure who had spoken, but she had to blink several times before she could see the plump, pleasant-faced woman in front of her. 'I'm Betsy, miss. Your uncle's housekeeper.'

'Oh, oh, I see. Thank you. Thank you, Betsy.' She knew of Betsy McKenzie – the stout Sunderland-born lass had worked at the farm all her life, first as a kitchen maid, when Hilda's mother had been alive, and then as housekeeper when the second Mrs Weatherburn and Frederick's father had died – but this was the first time she had met her. Once Hilda had taken to her bed, of necessity it had been Frederick who had visited his stepsister's home, and although Polly had apparently been taken to Stone Farm in the years before the birth of her sister, she had been too young to have any memory of it.

'He was a grand man, your da. A grand man.' Betsy nodded her head so vigorously her hand had to shoot up to catch her hat. 'Me an' Cook – Mrs Duffy it was in them days, although she's gone now, poor soul, food poisonin' of all things – we used to always make sure there was a batch of singin' hinnies cookin' on the girdle when we knew your da was callin'. Liked 'em hot with butter on, he did.'

Polly hadn't thought it was possible she could raise a smile today of all days, but there was something so comical about the little plump body with her rosy red cheeks and button nose that her mouth twitched in spite of itself. A cook that had died of food poisoning indeed!

'An' him as thin as a rake too. Me an' Cook used to say he could eat like a horse, Mr Henry.'

Mr Henry. Her da had been Mr Henry to this little woman and the staff at Stone Farm. It was a strange thought, disturbing somehow. 'Mr Henry' lifted her father into the league of gentlemen, but he had just been an ordinary working man, a farmer. There were farmers and farmers, though, and suddenly her Uncle Frederick's wealth wasn't a remote thing but was staring her in the face through the eyes of the plump little personage in front of her.

'My granny always said my da had hollow boots,' Polly said now, glancing across at her grandmother, who was in conversation with Parson Dodds.

'Come along, Polly.' Her uncle's voice was a little abrupt, and his face was straight when he said to his housekeeper, 'Croft is waiting to take you back in the horse and cart. I shall be bringing Miss Polly and Mrs Farrow home for refreshments before we return to Low Farm; see to it, would you?'

This was the first time Polly had heard of it! She stared at Frederick, and although she didn't wish to be rude, her voice was slightly curt when she said, 'That's very kind of you, Uncle, but I need to get home as soon as possible. My grandfather is still quite unwell.'

Her uncle had drawn her to one side as she had spoken, and now he said, his voice very low and having lost its previous peremptory note, 'It was your grandmother I was thinking of, Polly. A visit to Stone Farm, just a short one, will do her the power of good, and when I took the liberty of mentioning it to her earlier she was all in favour of the idea. It will take her mind off things.'

His eyes moved to the gravedigger, who was busy shovelling earth, and as Polly's gaze followed that of her uncle before moving to the

125

small, bent figure of her grandmother, she nodded her acquiescence. She had lost her father but Gran had lost her only son, and that must be worse. If a brief respite from the farm was what her grandmother needed then she wouldn't deny her such a small pleasure, even though Polly herself had no desire to pay a call to Stone Farm or anywhere else for that matter with her grandfather still so poorly.

'Frederick. Polly.' Polly came out of her thoughts to see Luke standing in front of them, and as her uncle's grip on her arm tightened she drew purposefully away, disengaging herself. 'I'm deeply sorry, but then you know that,' said Luke quietly.

'Thank you.' Polly was aware of a disturbing feeling of shyness as she looked into the dark brown eyes staring down at her. Luke had been at the farm that day, he had heard it all, and although it wasn't her fault what her father and aunt had done, she felt ashamed and embarrassed. She gulped once and then forced herself to speak naturally as she said, 'My aunt decided not to come, I take it?' For which she thanked God, oh, aye, she did. Rightly or wrongly she hated, she *loathed* her Aunt Eva.

'She isn't well, Polly.'

She ought to have said she was sorry to hear it and enquire further, but she couldn't be that hypocritical.

Frederick fidgeted at the side of her, clearing his throat loudly, and for a moment Polly thought Luke was about to say something more about her aunt, but instead he swallowed hard, jerked his chin out of his stiff collar, then said quietly as he looked hard into her eyes, 'Anything I can do to help, I'll do it, Polly. You only have to say.'

'Thank you.' She didn't know how else to respond.

'Would you mind if I—' He stopped abruptly. 'I mean we, Arnold and I, called occasionally to see you all?'

'No, of course not.'

Luke looked away from her and to Frederick, his voice stiff now as he said, 'Goodbye, Frederick.'

Frederick inclined his head but did not respond in kind, and Luke stared at the other man for a moment more before he turned away and walked over to join his father and Arnold.

Polly noticed Alice was looking white and exhausted, and after asking her uncle to take her grandmother to the trap – something he seemed to acquiesce to almost unwillingly, she felt, which surprised her – she spent a few minutes thanking each person who had attended the funeral. She was making her way quickly out of the cemetery, and had almost reached its gates, when a hand on her shoulder and a voice in her ear brought her turning around. 'Polly? Wait a minute, lass.'

'What is it?' She had just finished talking to Nathaniel, which had not been easy in the circumstances, and now all she wanted was to get far away from the cemetery and its newly filled grave so that the lump in her throat would not dissolve into tears in front of them all.

'I only wanted a quick word, that's all, lass.' Arnold's voice was low and soft, almost conspiratorial, and his eyes were moving all over her face as he spoke. Their expression made Polly want to scrub at her skin wherever they touched, but although her heart was racing her gaze was steady and unblinking as she faced him. 'You know Michael's run off? Left home?'

When she did not answer but continued to stare at him, he said, 'Same evening the . . . accident happened.'

The pause was deliberate and in a way almost menacing, and when she still did not speak but continued to stare him out, he said, his voice louder now, 'You hear what I'm saying?'

'Yes, I hear you, Arnold. I'm just wondering what you are really trying to say, that's all.'

He gazed at her, his mouth slightly agape and his eyes narrowed, because this young woman with the icy voice and cool eyes was not the young lass he had watched grow from a bairn, but someone quite different. Someone he couldn't quite fathom. He had expected to see her crushed and broken this morning, overwhelmed by the tragedies which had followed from the announcement of her engagement to Michael. He had savoured the idea, turning it over in his mind as he had imagined the ease with which this latest development would allow him to have her. And he intended to have her, oh, aye, he did. The longing to touch her had become almost irresistible. He had had women since the age of fourteen, when he had earned his first wage packet, and he had learned they would put up with almost anything if the price was high enough, but each one – since the day Polly had refused to kiss him – had had Polly's features superimposed on theirs in the worst acts of degradation. If she'd allowed him a bit of slap and tickle likely this desire for her would have faded, or maybe not. Whatever, he *would* have her.

And with this in mind he said now, 'What I'm saying is that to my mind you've had a lucky escape. The lad's a milksop, always has been, and you know it at heart.'

'Don't tell me what I know and what I don't know, Arnold, because you might not like to hear my mind on certain matters. Michael is ten times, a hundred times the man you are.'

He continued to stare at her, his face darkening, and now his voice came rapidly as he stretched his neck out and almost spat, 'And who are you to tell me that, with the sort of scum you had for a da, eh? His own sister! I know all about you now, don't forget, it's all out in the open, so don't play the high and mighty lady with me, Polly Farrow.'

The nastiness of the confrontation and the fact that she hadn't been prepared for anything like it on this day of all days was making her muscles fluid and her stomach feel loose, but she didn't betray her inward agitation by so much as the flicker of an eyelash. 'What my father did or didn't do before he was married to my mother is no business of yours,' she said coldly, turning away from his furious face and passing through the cemetery gates on to the mud-filled lane beyond before he could say anything more. She knew he was watching her as she carefully picked her way to Frederick's horse and trap – she could feel his narrowed eyes burning into her back – but she carried herself stiff and straight, and she didn't glance towards the cemetery once Frederick had helped her into the seat beside her grandmother and they were on their way.

The cocky little upstart! Arnold's teeth were grinding even as he inwardly berated himself for getting on the wrong side of her. It should have been easy today to set the course, and with a family like hers she should have been falling on his neck for showing a bit of interest. At the very least he had thought to hold his knowledge over her, but it seemed she was having none of it. But it was early days yet. His chin went down in his neck as he continued to watch the horse and trap until it disappeared out of sight in a bend in the lane. Give it a couple of months without her da, and the old man worse than useless, and she'd be crying a different tune. Begging him to take her away out of it, she'd be.

'What did you say to her?'

A drizzle had started to fall and the wind was keen, and Arnold pulled his cap further on to his forehead and adjusted the muffler tucked in his cloth jacket before he turned to Luke. 'Offered me respects, that's all. I saw you get in afore she came over to talk to Da.'

The tone was belligerent, but Luke's voice was just as aggressive as he said, 'Leave her alone, Arnold. I'm warning you.'

'Warning me?' Arnold's head went back and he slanted angry eyes at his brother, whose gaze was on a level with his. 'I'm trembling in me boots!'

'She's not one of your dockside trollops.'

'No, I'll give you that, man, but since that day at the farm a lot of things have become clearer in my mind at least.'

'Meaning?'

'Meaning, dear brother, that she's pulled the wool over all our eyes, including yours. She's kept us all hanging on, now hasn't she, from when she was nowt but a bairn – you, me and Michael. She takes after her da, if you ask me.'

'You shut your filthy mouth—'

'Or?' Arnold said softly. 'By, you're a fool, our Luke, you always have been. You want her every bit as much as I do, admit it, but

Michael got in there first – for all the good it did him. And she must have given him plenty of encouragement to work up the nerve to ask her; the lad's always needed help to blow his own nose. I dare bet they've been at it on the quiet for a good couple of years.'

'Don't talk such rubbish.' Luke's fists were clenched at his sides in an effort to stop himself from attacking his brother.

'Rubbish, is it?' Arnold smiled slowly. He knew full well Luke wanted to hit him, and if they had been anywhere else but in a cemetery with the parson and his da and everyone around, he might well have done so. 'What about all those times Michael took off on a Saturday afternoon once his shift was finished, eh? Or them summer evenings when he wasn't back afore we were in bed?'

'He used to walk into the country and watch his birds, he's got books galore on the subject.'

'Birds!' Arnold's laugh was acidic. 'Birds be damned. She's a little scut, she's been ripe for it for years—'

As Luke's fist shot out and connected with Arnold's jaw, the older man stumbled back against one of the iron gates of the cemetery, making it rattle on its hinges, but then he was at his brother's throat and the two were grappling ferociously.

Nathaniel was there within moments, his little wiry body straining to separate his two sons, who were a good six inches taller than their father. 'Cut it out, the pair of you! What the hell are you thinkin' of?'

'Ask him.' Arnold's voice was a snarl.

'I'm askin' both of you. This is a funeral, for cryin' out loud; show a little respect. I can't believe me own flesh an' blood could show me up like this.'

'Show you up?' Again Arnold's head went back, but this time his mouth opened in a loud, bitter laugh that caused Nathaniel to wrinkle his eyes and say urgently, 'Shut up, man! What's the matter with you?'

Luke's body had deflated, all the fight leaving him as soon as his father had driven himself between them, but now, as Arnold said, 'You talk about us showing you up with a wife like you've got?' his brother said savagely, 'Keep your big mouth shut, Arnold.'

Nathaniel looked from his elder son to his younger, and what he read in their faces caused him to manhandle their now unresisting bodies away from the cemetery entrance and down into the lane running at the side of the grounds, whereupon he said, 'All right, let's have it. You've got somethin' to say, so spit it out.'

'I've got nothing to say.' This was from Arnold, and it was sullen.

'Oh, aye, you have, lad, an' if we have to stand here till nightfall I've a mind to do it. You think you know somethin' about Eva, is that it?'

129

'I don't "think" anything.'

'You never said a truer word,' Luke cut in bitterly from where he stood staring at his brother, the hate in his eyes matching that of Arnold's as his sibling's gaze turned to him. 'You just open your gob and to hell with the consequences.'

'Aye, well, maybe he ought to know, you considered that, eh? If he don't already, that is.'

'I'll bang your bloo—' Nathaniel stopped, glancing back towards the cemetery and crossing himself, before he continued, 'I'll bang your heads together if I have any more of it. You've somethin' to say, so say it, Arnold.'

'Michael's not your bairn, is he? He's no relation to any of us.'

That Nathaniel was prepared in part was evident when he sighed, drawing in a long breath as though begging for patience, before he said, 'So that's why he took off, eh? I thought there was more to do with his goin' than just bein' upset at findin' his uncle. There was a row at the farm that Sunday, is that it?'

'Michael didn't find Henry.'

'No?' Nathaniel's eyes narrowed. 'That's not what you all said.'

'Aye, well, the fact is, Michael might not know about Henry's death; he'd gone before we found him. And it wasn't an accident, you might as well know that an' all. Henry killed himself. He threw a rope over one of the beams in the barn and hanged himself,' said Arnold grimly.

'Henry did himself in?' Nathaniel's face had stretched and his mouth hung in a wide gape for a moment before his lips came together with a little snap. Again his gaze moved from that of his elder son, and he held Luke's eyes for what seemed like a long while before saying softly, 'You want to tell me why he did it?'

It was the last thing in the world Luke wanted to do. He had gathered that the mystery about Michael's paternity was not a surprise to his father, but it was also clear that Nathaniel had no idea of who had really sired Michael. 'He was depressed; the farm's been failing for a long time—'

'He'd just found out Michael was his bairn.'

There was total silence after Arnold's voice had cut in on Luke's, and then, as his father's eyes turned to him, their expression made Arnold gabble as he said, 'He didn't know, Henry didn't know. Apparently the old uns had told Eva to keep it quiet or else they'd turn her out; with Henry just being wed they didn't want to rock the apple cart. It all came up 'cos Polly and Michael had said they wanted to get wed . . .'

Arnold's voice trailed away. Nathaniel was shaking his head in the manner of a boxer who was having a job to stay on his feet.

'Satisfied?' Luke's voice was a low hiss.

130

'He had a right to know; he's married to her, isn't he?'

'All these years.' Nathaniel's voice was so low they could barely hear it. 'I've made allowances, put up with her rages an' her sulks, an' all the time . . . Her brother, her own brother. Was she willin'?'

He was talking to Luke, and now Luke nodded silently and again Nathaniel shook his head, lowering his chin into his neck.

The parson came out of the cemetery gates in his horse and trap, the gravedigger sitting alongside him, and when Luke took his father's arm and gently pulled him to the edge of the lane Nathaniel didn't demur but went as obediently as a child. They stood in silence as the parson passed with an inclination of his head, and remained there while the other mourners dwindled away. There were only a few of them; most men couldn't afford to lose a day's work to go to a funeral unless it was someone in the immediate family, and it wasn't fitting that women should attend without their menfolk.

The rain was heavier now, wetting the ground, which was already claggy with mud, and they had a four-mile walk in front of them, through High Newport and Low Newport until they came to Humbleton Hill and the outskirts of the town of Bishopswearmouth, but neither Luke nor Arnold urged Nathaniel to get moving.

'By, I've bin a fool. Do y'know that?' Nathaniel raised his head as he spoke but didn't look at either one of his sons, his eyes moving aimlessly over the fields surrounding the tiny cemetery. 'Saw me comin', old Walter did, an' I swallowed the story of a travellin' man takin' his innocent daughter down. Aye, I swallowed it all right, although I've often wondered since if she was willin'. But her own brother!' His lips came away from his teeth in an expression of disgust.

'What are you going to do, Da?' There was something in his father's reaction – now the initial shock had faded – that was puzzling Luke.

'Do?' And now Nathaniel looked at his younger son before he began to walk, Arnold and Luke falling in either side of the smaller figure. 'I'm goin' to do somethin' I should've done a while back if I'd had me head screwed on straight, lad, but I think it's only right I tell your stepmother the glad news first.'

'You're not going to do anything silly?'

'Silly?' There was a harsh grunt of a laugh that carried no humour. 'No, I'm not about to do anythin' silly, lad.'

He could kill Arnold. Luke's thoughts were hot and fierce as they trudged – silently now – along the narrow lane, passing the Silksworth Colliery after some twenty minutes or so before reaching Tunstall Hills Farm on their right. He needn't have said anything – they had agreed that after all this time it was pointless to rake up the dirt and perhaps cause their father pain. But because of spite – and it was spite sure enough, for whatever had passed between Arnold and Polly hadn't

131

pleased his brother – he had wanted to do some damage. Arnold had always been like that, venting his own disappointments and failures on others, and it wasn't only Luke who recognised his brother's weaknesses. Arnold wasn't popular down the pit.

Take last week, for instance, when they had been moving the conveyor belt towards the new face, withdrawing the props from the old face so the roof dropped. Arnold had taken one risk too many and nearly brought the roof down on a few of them, and then he'd wondered why old Gilbert and Neville had given him an ear-bashing for the rest of the shift. And when Neville had come in a couple of days later and said a cat had wrought havoc amongst his prize pigeons, Luke had happened to glance Arnold's way, and had got the impression the news was of no surprise to his brother. Mind, he could've been wrong. Aye, he could have, but he doubted it. Neville had blamed his little lad for leaving the door to the birds' cage open and had given the bairn a leathering, even though the boy had apparently insisted he'd been nowhere near the enclosure in Neville's backyard, and his missus had got involved and now Neville and his wife weren't talking.

The silence between the three men continued right until they passed the smithy at the corner of Southwick Road, and it was Nathaniel who broke it a moment later when he said, 'Well, lads, likely the eruption that's goin' to break in a minute or two'll be on the lines them poor so-an'-so's in Italy suffered last week when Mount Vesuvius blew its top, but there's no need for you two to bear the brunt of it. This is atween me an' Eva, all right?'

'Da, you know she's not well.'

Luke's voice had been low and Nathaniel looked at him for a second before he said, 'Makes no difference, lad. What needs to be said needs to be said, an' likely it'd have happened a while back if I'd had the sense I was born with. I've got a good few years in front of me yet an' I want to enjoy 'em afore they put me six foot under like what we've seen today.' Nathaniel paused in front of his house, his eyes moving out over the lines of regimented terraced dwellings stretching north from Southwick Road. 'All me life I've lived here,' he mused softly, 'here in Monkwearmouth, an' for most of me life I've bin down the pit. It took me da an' two of me brothers in 1870, just a year after the big strike. Mind' – he turned to Luke now – 'the upshot of the strike was the establishment of the Durham Miners' Mutual Association, like I've told you afore. You have me da an' men like him to thank for startin' the fight, Luke.'

'Aye, aye, I know, Da.' Luke's eyes dropped to the doorstep and he was conscious of thinking, It's looking dingy. First time he could remember it looking that way, but since the incident at the farm Eva had been strange and in a world of her own half the time. His da had been patient to date, sympathetic, because – as he'd said only first

132

thing that morning on the way to the funeral – it was her brother, for crying out loud, and no one deserved to die like that. But Luke had a feeling his da's patience with his wife was all used up now.

'Our da when he was alive, an' Eustace an' Lonnie an' Douglas an' Martin, we all used to be out of here like a dose of salts of a Saturday afternoon an' over to the football ground in Newcastle Road. By, we had some good afternoons there, lad, but it lost somethin' when they moved it to Roker Park. Aye, it lost somethin' all right.' Nathaniel stood for a moment more, chewing on his lip as he looked back down the years and saw, in his mind's eye, the figure of his father with five lads of varying ages fleeing pit and cottage to Sunderland AFC's ground.

And then he straightened and his voice had lost its wistful note when he said, 'I'm forty-seven years old, lads, an' you know what I've learned today? I'm not goin' the way of me da an' our Lonnie an' Martin without savourin' somethin' of life first. An' I've just bin markin' time the last sixteen years, or the first fifteen of 'em at any rate.'

He'd got a woman. Why the penny dropped at that precise moment Luke didn't know, but suddenly his father's happiness over the last year – which Luke had put down to a mellowing of Nathaniel's relationship with his wife – took on a whole new meaning. There was amazement on his face, and a slow, dull, red seeping across his cheekbones as he stared at the small, wiry figure at the side of him. When? And who? He continued to stare at his father with new eyes as Nathaniel opened the front door and stepped inside the house, but Luke found he was quite unable to move.

'What's the matter with you? Get going.'

Luke couldn't reply to Arnold's grunt for a moment. The new knowledge which had burst forth into his consciousness was creating a strange sensation made up of a hundred and one emotions, none of which had precedence except the one of envy. And then, as Arnold made to thrust him roughly aside, Luke turned with a lightning movement of his body and said, 'Don't shove me around, Arnold, I'm warning you. You've done enough the day already.'

'Huh!' It was a small sound in Arnold's throat; he had read the signs accurately and wasn't about to press the angry man in front of him any further.

Once inside the house, Luke and Arnold came to a halt in the kitchen. The usually spick and span surroundings were cluttered and untidy, and the kitchen table still held the remains of the men's breakfasts, which they had got themselves. Eva had still been in bed when they had left the house early that morning for Silksworth; since Henry's death she had taken to rising long after they had all left for the colliery.

There was a roaring fire burning in the range and Eva had obviously been sitting in front of it before they had arrived home, but she was now standing facing her husband. Nathaniel's manner was not quiet but neither was it as aggressive as one would expect in the circumstances, and he was saying, 'So you admit it, then? You don't deny you'd bin carryin' on with your own brother?'

'Why should I?' For the first time in over a week there was an element of life in Eva's voice. 'And let's call a spade a spade. We were lovers, right from when we was bairns we were lovers. There, you have it. And I loved him, I never stopped loving him.'

'An' the travellin' man?'

'There was never any travelling man, there was only Henry.'

The exultation in Eva's voice caused Luke to lower his head and screw up his eyes. The woman was deranged, she had to be.

'An' Michael leavin'? He found out?'

'Aye, he found out.' Eva's head was back and her chin was up. 'And to my mind he ought to be glad Henry was his father and that a weak-kneed little nowt like you had nothing to do with his birth.'

'You were quick enough to accept all this weak-kneed little nowt gave you.' Nathaniel had been determined not to lose his temper, but Eva's reaction had not been what he had expected. If she had shown an element of remorse or any of the brokenness of the last few days he would have tempered his words accordingly, but now his voice was low in his throat as he growled, 'But rest assured on one thing, woman, I wouldn't touch you now with a barge pole. You've made me life a misery over the years an' I was dim enough to stand for it, but no more. An' when I walk out of them doors it'll be wipin' the dust off me feet for good.'

'Walk out, he says.' Eva turned to the two silent figures watching them, her eyes narrowed and her mouth ugly, before she again looked at her husband. 'And where do you think you're going?' she scoffed tauntingly.

'I'm goin' to a good, clean woman who's worth her weight in gold, that's where I'm goin'.' Nathaniel saw the meaning of his words hit Eva full in the face, causing her eyes to widen and her mouth to become slack. 'Aye, that's right, I've got someone. Now you chew on that.'

'I don't believe you.' Eva's face was looking fiendish now. 'What about your precious church, what would Father McAttee say? And who would have you anyway?'

'You've got a woman on the side?'

It was the first time Arnold had spoken since they had entered the house, and his voice was high, and now Nathaniel turned to his elder son and nodded, his face set. 'Aye, I have, lad, an' proud of her I am. She's a good woman, a fine woman, an' I don't intend to carry on with her bein' me bit on the side. She's worth a darn sight more than that.'

'I don't believe you.' Eva's voice was hard. 'I don't! You're saying this to get back at me.'

'What do you care anyway?' Nathaniel looked his wife full in the face. 'From the first moment I took you on you've made it plain you see me as less than the muck under your boots. There are a hundred an' one ways to make a man squirm, an' you've used 'em all through the years. Aye, an' relished doin' it. An' as far as Father McAttee goes, he don't know the half of it, does he – Michael bein' your brother's bairn, you bein' less than the worst whore down at the docks an' never bein' a wife to me in any sense of the word. Mental adultery you've been indulgin' in all these years an' you know it. Well, as far as I'm concerned I'm free of you for good an' all, an' whether the Church sees it that way don't matter no more. Me an' Tess'll take ourselves far away from here, somewhere we can make a good life for ourselves with no tittle-tattle, an' she'll be me wife as I see it afore God.'

The mention of a name seemed to tip Eva over the edge. Whether it was the pent-up rage of years or her desolation and agony over Henry wasn't clear – perhaps it was a combination of both – but one moment she was standing glaring at the man she had loathed and despised for years, and the next she was beating him furiously about the head, shouting unintelligibly as she did so.

Nathaniel's face was partly protected by his forearm, which he had raised instinctively at Eva's first blow; nevertheless, one cheek bore evidence of a deep scratch by the time Luke and Arnold manage to drag Eva away. She continued to fight the brothers for all she was worth for some moments more, but eventually the superior strength of the two men prevailed and they were able to restrain their stepmother in such a way that Eva could barely move. And then she became limp in their grasp.

Nathaniel had a tea towel to his cheek as he watched his sons subdue his wife. The damage to his face had been caused by the ring Eva was wearing next to her wedding band, which had been his first wife's engagement ring. Eva had come across it one day shortly after they had been married, when she had been clearing out the dresser, and when he had walked in from the pit she had been wearing it.

He had felt that evening – and oft times since – that he should have insisted Eva return the ring to its little blue velvet box. It had felt like a desecration to Dora's memory to see it on another woman's hand, but he had been weak. Eva's eyes had dared him to object – as had her aggressive stance – and in an effort to appease his new wife, and for the sake of the fragile harmony sitting so uneasily in his small home, he had taken the easy way out.

He dabbed at his cheek now, his eyes still on his wife before they lowered to the cloth in his hand, and he saw it was stained red. Aye, well, maybe in this – if nothing else that had happened since the first day he had set eyes on the woman across the room – he had got exactly what he deserved. But it was over with at last. Finished. Done with.

Luke had pushed Eva down into the chair she had vacated when Nathaniel had walked in, and now he kept one hand on his step-mother's shoulder as he said, 'Da? What are you going to do? You aren't really going now?'

'It seems a good time, lad.'

Aye, it seemed a good time as far as his father was concerned right enough. Luke stared at the older man, rubbing his hand tightly across his mouth as his thoughts raced on. If his father went now, who would take care of his stepmother in the years ahead? She certainly couldn't return to her family – that boat was well and truly burned – and Arnold's first priority would always be Arnold. It would be Luke who would bear the responsibility for a woman who – if he were being truthful – he would have to say he had always disliked.

'You can't just walk out.' Arnold had obviously been thinking along the same lines as his brother, and his tone was aggressive. 'Whoever this woman is, you've got a duty to your wife.'

'Wrong.' Nathaniel's brusqueness was decisive rather than hostile. 'I brought Eva into this house sixteen years ago for your sake, yours an' Luke's, an' she knows that as well as me, and I was prepared to make it a marriage in every sense of the word, but she was havin' none of it. She's made a monkey out of me but enough is enough, an' neither you two, nor her, nor Father McAttee, not even the good Lord Himself, will stop me doin' what I intend to do this day. An' that's final, Arnold.'

'I'll never divorce you.' This was from Eva, who was sitting stony-eyed but quiet now.

'That's neither here nor there. I was more married to my Tess on the day I met her than I've ever bin to you.' Nathaniel was walking towards the door leading to the stairs as he spoke, and when Eva said, 'Where do you think you're going?' he didn't pause in his stride as he answered, 'To get me things together. I haven't much an' you're welcome to such as the house holds, but there's certain things I'm takin' with me an' no blighter'll stop me.'

'Stay with her.' Luke nodded at Eva as he spoke swiftly to Arnold, and then he followed his father out of the room, mounting the stairs two at a time and walking into the bedroom his father and Eva shared to see Nathaniel sitting on the bed looking as though the stuffing had been knocked out of him.

'You all right, Da?' He walked over to his father and knelt in front of him, moving the tea towel away from his cheek and shaking his head at the sight of the nasty scratch, which was still oozing blood. 'You'll need some salt on that.'

'I'll sort it when I've seen Tess.'

'You think a bit of her then?'

'Oh, lad.' Nathaniel had never been a one with words, but now he looked into his son's deep brown eyes – his favourite son, although he had never voiced it – and said softly, 'She's everythin' I ever wanted an' more. What she sees in me I'll never know, but I thank God every day for her, I tell you straight.'

His father thanked God for her, this other woman he was putting in the place of his lawful wedded wife. All Luke's life, until he had earned his first wage packet and was considered a man by his da and therefore old enough to choose his own road, he had been forced to go to church with Eva and his brothers. His da might miss a few weeks or months if he felt like it, but his wife and his children must attend Sunday Mass no matter what. His father wouldn't have been able to hold up his head otherwise. He had endured the Catholic school with its demented old-maid schoolmistress, Miss Potts. Potty by name and potty by nature, all the bairns had said, but it still didn't prevent the screaming nightmares which featured her dire warnings about that dreaded place, purgatory, where the fires never went out and naughty bairns were forced to sit on sizzling red-hot gridirons on their bare backsides.

And what fear the good Miss Potts hadn't been able to instil mentally had been accomplished physically, with the lethal cane she'd wielded with all the considerable power of her big fat body. Luke could feel it still. A nasty, mean-minded tartar Miss Potts had been – he had often wondered if the priests, Father Gray and Father McAttee, had known what their schoolteacher was like with the bairns, because they'd been decent enough men on the whole.

But he'd put up with it – and no doubt imbibed a certain amount of indoctrination he'd carry with him until his dying day – because he'd known how his father felt about the 'one true faith', as he referred to it, all apparently overseen by a fiercely jealous – and definitely Catholic – God.

And now . . . Now this same God was apparently approving of his father taking another woman in adultery, because dress this up as you like, that was what it boiled down to. Not only approving of it – if his father was to be believed – but receiving thanks each day for having orchestrated the event in the first place.

'You don't think this is right.'

His father's voice was still soft, but there was a note in it Luke had never heard before, a plea for understanding. It created a feeling of uncomfortableness. His father had married Eva to keep his family together and he had put up with hell on earth – Luke himself knew that

137

– to continue to keep it together. If his father had been a different kind of man he might well have stuck his bairns in the workhouse; there were many who did just that in similar situations. And what Luke was feeling now wasn't so much righteous indignation or anything like it; he was worried about how his father leaving would affect him. And – and here Luke's disquiet deepened into self-disgust – he was resentful that his father was going to walk off into the sunset with his Tess when there was no chance Polly would ever look the side he was on.

'You go, Da.' Luke thrust out his hand and Nathaniel gripped it hard. 'You couldn't stay now anyway, so go and be happy with your Tess. But let me know where you are. Promise me that, Da.'

'Aye, aye, I'll do that, lad.' There were tears in Nathaniel's eyes for the first time Luke could remember. 'It'll have to be on the quiet, but I'll find a way. Likely one of Tess's neighbours'll tip you the wink.' He let go of Luke's hand as he got to his feet, and as Luke rose too, Nathaniel looked about him helplessly.

The big battered trunk containing the spare blankets and sheets for the household stood at the end of the bed, and now Luke opened the lid and took out a pile, saying, 'You'll need this.'

'Aye, that's an idea. There's not much bar me clothes an' a few things of your mam's an' mine, but I'll need somethin' to carry 'em in.'

The packing was accomplished in minutes, and again the two men were standing looking at one another. 'Not much for forty-seven years, is it?' Nathaniel gestured at the trunk. 'But then there's only ever bin two things in me life I'm proud of, you an' our Arnold.'

Never had Luke seen a look such as was now on his father's face. Their relationship had always been a good one but devoid of what Nathaniel would term 'soft blathering', but the fierce love his father had always kept hidden beneath the rough northern exterior was now blazing forth.

It made Luke humble and brought the pain of regret for a hundred things left unsaid, and his heart was crying out with the simplicity of a child as it silently begged, Don't go, please don't go, Da, stay. We can get to know each other, really know each other before it's too late. But the awareness of his father's selflessness through the long, bitter years of internment with the woman downstairs kept him silent, and instead he said, 'I'll miss you, Da. I wish things could be different.'

'Aye, me an' all, lad. Me an' all. But this isn't goodbye, not really. You'll meet Tess one day an' likely then you'll understand.'

'I do understand.'

'No you don't, lad, not yet. You're young, you've yet to taste the bitter dregs, an' that's how it should be, that's right an' proper. But Tess is a good woman, believe me on that. She's Perce's widow, you remember Perce?' Luke nodded. 'I met her when I

138

went round to offer me respects after the accident, an' it all came from there.'

'You'll be all right?' Luke was aware he was talking for the sake of it now, saying anything to delay the inevitable. Why couldn't he tell his father he loved him? Why couldn't he take him in his arms and hug him? What was this crippling code of honour that said such actions were womanly, daft? Were working men like this the world over, or was it only the north that produced such weakness? Because it was weakness. Anything that paralysed normal responses like this had to be such.

'Aye, me an' Tess'll be all right. She's young, darn sight younger than me, an' we can both work an' build up a home together. But not round here. I'm not havin' her treated as a brazen hussy by them not worthy to lick her boots, an' you know some of the wives round these parts when they get goin'. Tarred an' feathered a bit lass only a couple of months ago in Thomas Street North near the tram depot 'cos they'd got wind she was carryin' on with a married man.'

Luke nodded again. Oh, aye, he knew how it would be all right, and ten to one it would be this Tess who would bear the full brunt of righteous disapproval from all and sundry. He could hear them now. 'Have you heard about Nat going off the rails, then? He's walked out on his wife and taken up with her that was married to Perce! Lost her own man a while back, she did, so bold as brass she sets her sights on Eva's, poor soul. Now granted, Eva might be something of a tartar, but give her her due, she kept that house spotless and brought them two lads from his first wife up as if they were her own. She don't deserve this. Ought to be horse-whipped, that Tess. Someone should do something.'

And no doubt a few of the women would do something, and ironically it was often the foul-mouthed and coarse element among them who were the most voracious in their self-righteousness. It was rare a mob got together and went as far as they had with the lass in Thomas Street North – most of the women were too worried about what their menfolk would say if they got to hear about such goings-on – but someone in Tess's position would regularly have a handful of filth thrown at her or muck smeared on her doorstep. And the decent housewives – the ones who minded their own business and got on with looking after their menfolk and families – would simply ostracise the lass in question with a relentlessness that was perhaps more cruel than all the verbal and physical abuse. Women could be the very devil.

'No, I see you have to move away, Da.' He stared at his father and Nathaniel stared back before he bent and lifted the trunk, refusing Luke's offer of help as he lugged it out of the room and down into the kitchen, where Eva was still sitting in the chair, Arnold standing alongside her.

139

Whether they had been conversing Luke didn't know, but when Nathaniel held out his hand to Arnold and his elder son refused to take it, his father's body remained absolutely still for a moment before his head turned to glance at his wife. Eva stared back at him, her eyes full of deep loathing, but again no one spoke.

Luke followed his father out of the house and into the street, where they stood for a moment in the icy drizzle that carried the odd snowflake in its midst. 'You got far to go, Da?'

'Carley Road, lad.' And now Luke felt his father's arms about him for the first time that he could remember since he had been a very young child, and Nathaniel's voice was thick as he said, 'Look after yourself an' our Arnold. He's not like you, Luke. He'll get into trouble, he's too easily led.'

The embrace only lasted a matter of seconds, but although every pore of Luke's body was straining to return it, he remained like stone, his hands at his sides and his limbs stiff. And then he was watching his father walk down the street, his small body bent with the weight of the trunk, and he was glad of the sleet wetting his face because it hid his hot tears. *I love you, Da.* As Nathaniel neared the corner his pace quickened, and Luke could feel the sense of release that was filling the other man's soul. Through blurred eyes he saw him turn and raise his hand, and he lifted his own in response, and there was a long moment when they just looked at each other through the mist of sleet and rain. Then Nathaniel turned again and walked on, and he was gone.

Chapter Eleven

Stone Farm was as different from the one Polly had been born on as chalk to cheese, and the full realisation of this had been sweeping over her in waves of increasing amazement ever since the horse and trap had turned off the lane and into the long stony track bordered by her uncle's fields on both sides.

Although the boundary of her grandfather's farm joined that of Frederick Weatherburn's, the divide was in the nature of a high dry-stone wall beyond which rose a steep and sudden incline – whether natural or man-made Polly had never ventured to ask. As bairns she and Ruth had climbed the hillock to see beyond, but the acres of grazing cattle and sheep had deterred the two girls from exploring further.

Now, as the horse and trap bowled along, Polly reflected that her uncle's farm could swallow her grandfather's paltry forty acres whole, and morever, there was an air of prosperity abounding that was in stark contrast to the desperation at home.

'There we are.' She came out of her musing to see her uncle pointing to a large thatched house in the distance, which looked to be mainly three-storey except for what appeared to be an addition to the original house which was a third of its size and two storeys high. The size of the dwelling place brought Polly's mouth open for a moment. 'You can't remember anything of Stone Farm, can you?' Her uncle was speaking directly to Polly, leaning slightly forward in order to look round her grandmother, who was sitting next to him on the hard wooden seat, and when Polly shook her head he continued, 'Your mother was always very happy here, from the day my father brought her and her own mother to stay. I was eight years old at the time, so I remember it well.'

'You've always bin kindness itself to Hilda, Frederick.' Her granny's voice was loud and she nodded as she spoke. 'Especially considerin' she's no relation of yours, not in the blood sense.'

'I've always prided myself on being a man who takes his responsibilities seriously, Alice.'

'Aye, there's not a soul as could say different.'

There was something in the exchange, normal though it was, that caused Polly to glance sharply at her grandmother, but the old woman

141

was looking directly ahead, and although she must have been aware of her granddaughter's eyes, she made no effort to meet them.

As they neared the farmhouse, Polly saw that the winding stone track they were following opened up into a large cobbled yard, but unlike the one at home, this did not lead directly to the house. Instead the yard was bordered by a small stone wall with a wooden gate set in it on the far side, beyond which – and directly in front of the farmhouse – stretched an area of regimented flowerbeds some twenty yards long. As though he had been waiting for them, a figure materialised from the barn to the left of the muck-free farmyard and, as the horse and cart drew to a halt, took the reins from Frederick and stood at the horse's head.

'Thank you, Croft.'

Frederick did not look at the man as he spoke and his voice was very much that of master to man, and again Polly found herself glancing at her grandmother after they had alighted – with Frederick's help – from the trap.

'Come along, you must be in need of a warm drink.' As her uncle made to usher her in front of her grandmother, something in Polly rebelled. He was making her feel uneasy – odd somehow – and the need to assert herself was strong. She half turned, taking her granny's arm as she said somewhat pointedly, 'Be careful you don't slip, Gran. These cobbles are like glass with the rain.'

'I'm all right, lass. You go ahead.'

'No, we'll go together.'

Frederick made no comment to this, but hastily opened the little gate in the wall, standing aside as the two women passed through into the garden beyond.

As they reached the front door it was opened from the inside and Betsy stood in the doorway, her round eyes commiserating as she glanced at Polly's white face. 'Everything's ready, master, an' I've lit the fire in the sittin' room,' she said hastily. 'Shall I bring a tray of tea through while Mrs Farrow an' the miss warm up a bit?'

'Splendid.' Frederick's voice was hearty, and once they were all standing in the wide hall after wiping their feet on the thick rope mat on the threshold, he said, 'I'm glad you're seeing Stone Farm, Polly, although of course I wish it were in happier circumstances,' before opening a door to his left.

The sitting room was large, very large, and for a moment Polly just glanced about her. The furniture was dark and old, but nice old, not like at her grandfather's farm, and the two sofas and three chairs were covered in a chintz fabric, the red of which was reflected in the drapes at the two windows. A big rug lay in the middle of the wooden floor, with another smaller one set in front of the fire, which was piled high with burning logs and coal, and it was this which drew her gaze.

The range at home was kept burning day and night, even in the summer, providing as it did their means of cooking and heating water, but this fire was serving no useful purpose except to provide warmth. And coal burned away so much faster when mixed with logs, everyone knew that. It was the fire in the sitting room – more than anything else she saw and experienced over the next two hours at the farm – that emphasised to Polly the difference between the Uncle Frederick she had always known and this new individual who was the lord and master of his own little world.

After a cup of tea in the sitting room, Betsy called them through to the stone-flagged dining room. This room was half the size of the sitting room and again warmed by a substantial fire, but although the light repast the housekeeper had prepared was tasty, Polly found she could eat very little. She had been bracing herself for the ordeal of the funeral service for days, but nevertheless, the sight of the coffin being lowered into the ground had upset her profoundly, and the confrontation with Arnold afterwards had left a nasty taste in her mouth. But that wasn't all of it. Her uncle's attitude was unsettling her, but quite why she felt such a strong sense of unease, she wasn't sure.

The sense of disquiet continued all through the brief tour of the farmhouse after lunch, and although her grandmother oohed and ahhed over everything, Polly was mostly silent, although she acknowledged the house was a fine one.

The old part of it dated back to 1725 and consisted of the sitting room, the kitchen and the dairy on the ground floor, above which were three good-size bedrooms, with a large attic room on the top storey which was Betsy's living space plus storage. The new part of the farmhouse had been built by Frederick's grandfather over a hundred years later; the lower floor consisting of the dining room and Frederick's study and office, above which the space had been divided into one large master bedroom and a small dressing room leading to a tiny night water closet, all accessed by the original staircase.

'Well, what do you think?' They had just entered the sitting room once more, and again Frederick's voice was hearty as he addressed Polly. 'Was it what you were expecting?'

'Expecting?'

'Stone Farm, the house.' He made an expansive gesture with his hands, flinging his arms wide.

Did he really think she cared about his fine house on this day of all days? 'It's a beautiful house, Uncle Frederick.'

'Oh, I think it's high time we dropped the "uncle".' Frederick turned to include Alice in his glance. 'What do you say, Alice? Our little lass is a full-grown woman now, and as you so rightly pointed out earlier,

143

I'm no relation to her at all. "Uncle" seems out of place these days, wouldn't you say?'

There was a sick feeling growing in Polly's stomach, but it was accompanied by a voice that was saying, You're imagining it, you must be. He doesn't mean what you think he means, not Uncle Frederick. He was there when Michael asked for you in marriage. He knows you love *him*. 'I . . . I wouldn't feel right calling you anything else but Uncle,' Polly said quietly, forcing her voice into a calmness she was far from feeling.

'Nonsense.' This time the tone wasn't so much hearty as cavalier, and when Frederick's glance again swept over her grandmother, Polly's eyes followed it, but Alice was staring down at her hands, the thumbs of which were working one over the other. 'I've always considered us to be the greatest of friends, Polly, and it would please me if you called me Frederick, all right?' He smiled at her from his stance in front of the fire, his hands now holding the back of his long, beautifully cut black jacket away from his backside as he swayed slightly from side to side. 'Now I'm sure that isn't too much to ask, is it?'

Polly's back stiffened. He couldn't be suggesting what she was thinking, but that look on his face . . . She lifted her chin slightly, taking a long pull of air through her nostrils before she said, very coolly and without smiling, 'Of course not.'

'There we are then, it's all settled. Frederick it is from now on.'

A knock at the sitting room door signalled Betsy's entrance with their outdoor clothes, and Polly had never been so glad to see someone in all her life. She needed to get away from this place – or more particularly from the man standing looking at her so intently – and she was dreading the journey home in the horse and trap.

As it happened, the ride was uneventful, and Frederick confined his conversation to Alice, who was again sitting next to him. He refused Alice's offer of a cup of tea when they reached the farm, his manner so normal as he said goodbye that Polly told herself she had completely misunderstood a perfectly innocent conversation, which had just been friendly and nothing else. Anything else was too absurd, too *preposterous* for words. Of course it was. She stood for a moment after her grandmother had entered the house, staring after the horse and trap, and in her mind's eye she pictured her uncle's – *Frederick's* – round, red-cheeked face and bright black beady eyes, his big rotund body and large hands, the backs of which were liberally covered in thick brown hair. He was as old as her father, slightly older in fact, so she understood. Of *course* she had been mistaken . . .

That had gone well in the circumstances. Frederick Weatherburn settled his fleshy backside more comfortably on the wooden seat and clicked his tongue to the horse as he jerked on the reins, the animal immediately responding by falling into a steady trot. Yes, it had gone very well, all things considered. If nothing else, she had been forced to recognise that he was a man of substance, someone not to be sneezed at. Of course, it was early days yet. He narrowed his eyes on the back of the horse, a handsome chestnut he had bought in the summer at Durham horse fair. As far as Polly was concerned, at least; for himself, he had been thinking about marriage to Hilda's elder daughter for some two or three years and educating her for that purpose.

Polly was intelligent and amusing, and she had all but run that household since old Walter had had his first bad turn – and not just the household. Henry had never had any farming skills.

Yes, Polly would make an excellent wife. She was young and robust and would produce strong, healthy heirs, which was important. He was forty-one years old; it was high time he got on with the business of procreating. Not that he had much heart for it, if the truth be told. He had never been able to understand this primeval urge regarding the act of copulation that most men seemed to feel. He preferred an enjoyable evening wining and dining at the Gentlemen's Club on the corner of Fawcett Street any day, or a brisk gallop over his land on his favourite filly.

But it was time to take a wife, and Polly fitted the bill for one reason above any other: she was his means of securing Walter's farm without laying out another penny. He had encouraged Walter and Henry to fall more and more heavily into debt to him over the last years, and he didn't apologise for the fact. No, by gum he didn't. And things couldn't have worked out better. The farm was crippled, they all knew it, but if he played his cards right he could acquire that forty acres – along with a wife – as well as being seen to fulfil his Christian duty by taking in his new wife's family and giving them a roof over their heads.

And the Farrows' forty acres meant he had access to old man Nicholson's land beyond, and it was common knowledge that Nicholson had lost interest in everything since his only son had been taken with the fever five years ago.

Frederick breathed in deeply, drawing the raw air full into his lungs as a feeling of well-being quickened his blood. Land. Land meant power, and it was the only thing that really excited him. He had thought to wait another couple of years before he showed his hand with Polly, but the events of the last week or two were urging him to get things settled. By, he'd got the gliff of his life when that young whippersnapper had marched in and stated that he and Polly wanted to get wed, but as it was, it had furthered his course more effectively than anything else could have done. But there were still those other

145

two sniffing about; he couldn't afford to rest on his laurels. His upper lip curled at the thought of Eva's stepsons, whom he considered vastly beneath him in every way. Aye, he needed to press on sure enough, and now that interfering, hoity-toity baggage who had been lodging at the farm had hightailed it, it left the road even clearer.

The Women's Political and Social Union indeed! Unnatural they were, the lot of them. What did women want the vote for anyway? They didn't have the faintest idea of what it took to run a country; their minds weren't made that way. And just last week the Independent Labour Party had called for female emancipation! Keir Hardie wanted shooting, he did straight. Fuelling the silly notions put forward by these Pankhurst women, who would be better applied trimming their bonnets or whatever it was ladies did.

But no matter, no matter. He consciously wiped the frown from his brow and forced himself to relax. The Collins woman was gone, and as far as he could ascertain Polly had expressed no sorrow at her leaving. He would soon make sure any stupid notions she had put in Polly's head were dealt with; his wife would know her rightful place sure enough.

There was a ground mist hovering over the land and everything was soaked with the icy drizzle that was falling, the road beneath the horse's feet glutinous mud, but as the horse and trap approached the turn-off for Stone Farm, the going became easier.

His grandfather had had the foresight to have a thick layer of pebbles and small stones laid on the drive up to the farm, and Frederick never drove down the stony path without a feeling of well-being enveloping him. The drive signified wealth and prestige – it had taken two men three months to complete it to his grandfather's satisfaction – and prepared any visitors for the prosperous and thriving farm and imposing farmhouse they would see at the end of it.

And now Polly had seen it. He gave a grunt of satisfaction as the farmhouse came into view. Next time he would show her the labourers' cottages, which he prided himself were better than most, and certainly cleaner than she'd find on any other farm hereabouts. No stinking cesspools or foul-smelling middens outside the back door for his workers; the middens were at the end of their strips of garden, which were a good hundred yards long, and the contents of the small wooden boxes were collected every five days by Croft or one of his workers in the farm cart and dumped in the old quarry a mile away. His workers were well looked after, and they knew it, and gave him the absolute obedience and respect he deserved.

Yes, Polly would appreciate that an alliance with Frederick was a feather in her cap, but just in case she proved to be difficult, her Achilles heel, in the form of her family, would provide him with all the persuasion he needed. He smiled to himself, his lips exposing teeth of a surprising whiteness. 1906 was going to be his year, he felt it in his bones.

Luke's thoughts were the very antithesis of Frederick's as he sat at the kitchen table the next morning feeling as sick as a dog. For the first time in his life he had gone out and got mortalious after his father had left, staggering home just after ten, whereupon he had vomited his heart up in the deep glazed sink in the scullery and all but passed out on the cold stone flags.

He had been vaguely aware of his stepmother and Arnold looking in on him at some point, but he had come to a couple of hours later to the realisation that they had left him where he had dropped and gone to bed. He'd been chilled to the bone and feeling like death as he'd pulled himself to his feet, grimacing in self-disgust at the mess in the sink.

Once he'd cleared up in the scullery, he'd stumbled upstairs, there to fall on his bed fully dressed as the grinding pain in his head and the nausea in his stomach took the last of the strength from his legs. And to think some of the men he worked with got into this state every pay day. He didn't know whether to feel sorry for them or give them a medal!

'You had a load on last night.'

Arnold had always been one for stating the obvious, and Luke didn't bother to reply, but he winced slightly as his brother sat down at the table with a steaming bowl of porridge with a big dollop of jam in the centre of it.

'You thought what Da clearing off means to us, then?' Arnold took a great spoonful of porridge, half of which dribbled on to his chin.

'Aye.' Luke had leaned back in the chair and shut his eyes after one look at the porridge, and he didn't open them as he said, 'Strikes me it's a pity you didn't afore you opened your big mouth. What did you think he was going to say? Thanks for telling me, lads, and he'd leave it at that?'

'Now don't you pin this on me, our Luke.' Arnold's voice was without heat; he had been thinking along the same lines himself. 'How did I know the old man had a woman on the side? I mean, Da of all people.'

'What do you mean, Da of all people?' Luke's eyes had snapped open at the derogatory note in his brother's voice.

'He's wind and water, always has been.' Arnold was too busy spooning in the porridge between words to notice the expression on Luke's face. 'I'd have knocked me wife into next weekend many a time rather than put up with a quarter of what he's put up with. She wouldn't have been so cocky with her face bashed in.' After a moment Luke's utter silence brought Arnold's attention from his bowl, and when he saw his brother's tight, deep gaze fixed on his face, his eyes flickered.

Luke saw Arnold's Adam's apple jerk up under his chin and then fall again, but his voice was aggressive when he said, 'What? What have I said now? It's true, isn't it? She called him a weak-kneed nowt, and to my mind she wasn't too far from the truth.'

'You say that again, ever, and I'll do for you.'

Arnold stared at his brother. Luke's voice had been low, eerily low, but it had felt like he had been yelling.

'You're a nasty, filthy-minded, selfish swine at the best of times, but you're stupid too.' Luke carried on talking and Arnold sat as though mesmerised. 'You can't recognise goodness, can you, because there's not an ounce of that quality in the whole of your body. Da got her in because of us and he stayed because of us, and everything he put up with he put up with because of us and Michael too. Even knowing Michael wasn't his he never showed it, not once, not ever. And you look at all that and you take him for a mug. I tell you, man, you're not worthy to lick his boots.'

'No?' Arnold had jerked to his feet, two spots of colour high on his cheekbones. 'Well, I wonder if you'll still be saying that when you're left with her. He thumbed towards the ceiling. 'Because I tell you straight, I'm out of it as soon as I get meself a room somewhere. I'm not getting landed.' He snatched up his bait can on the last words and stalked out of the house without waiting for his brother.

Aye, well, he wasn't surprised. Luke sighed wearily and then got to his feet, wincing again as a hundred little men with hammers pounded at his temples. He was under no illusions about Arnold's capacity for tolerance and understanding; it was nonexistent.

By, he felt rough. He reached for his own bait can, and as he did so the smell of smoke on his clothes was heavy. Mind, it wasn't surprising – the air had been so thick with it in the pub last night that he hadn't been able to see from one end of the room to the other. The smell of Shag tobacco smoke, McEwan's bitter or Burton's bass had been coming off every man's breath, and they'd all breathed it in, coughed and spluttered it out and repeated the business over and over for hours. The cards, the dominoes, even the old fox terriers lying under the tables had all stunk with it, and in the corner there had been a whiff of vinegar with old man's pee added to it. And he knew plenty of pitmen who lived in the place more than their own homes. They would sit there, kneading their dark brown baccy twist with the juice still in it to fill their pipe, a pint of Bass in front of them and a smile on their face as they peered through the thick haze.

Luke shook his head and then wished he hadn't as his brain objected. He wanted more than that from life. And he wanted more than the pit had to offer too. The air in that pub had been fresh compared to where he worked all week, and with one in every fifty Durham miners killed in the pit and ten times that number expected to have a serious accident

148

at some time, life could be short. Every miner expected to lose fingers or bits of them, but they were considered minor injuries, and the owners and viewers would have laughed at any miner who tried to say that such accidents deserved compensation. But Luke had yet to see one of the managers or owners with half a hand gone or eyes full of disease because of the coal dust. And he didn't want to end up like that, or under tons of coal and stone either.

Oh, stop your blathering. The voice in his head was caustic. All this because his father had gone, and yet no, it wasn't that, not really. If he thought he had the faintest chance with Polly, if he was coming home to her each night, and their bairns, he would work down the pit till he dropped.

There was a movement from upstairs, and not wishing to face his stepmother until his head belonged to him again, Luke made hurriedly for the front door, pulling his cap low over his forehead as he stepped into the raw northern air.

He was on foreshift this week – six o'clock in the morning until two in the afternoon – and normally he didn't mind the early start, but with his head drumming a tattoo and his stomach loose from its linings he could have done with another few hours in bed.

Once at the pit he joined the group of men – of which Arnold was one – waiting to go down in the cage, automatically tilting his head to the side as he entered because of the low roof. As soon as everybody was in, the gate was slammed shut and the cage took off with its normal clash, tearing down faster and faster until it clanged to a stop.

There was the odd bit of good-natured bantering as the forty or so men – twenty from the top half of the cage and twenty from the bottom – began to walk down the road. Within minutes it had got narrower and narrower, the roof lowering sharply until the big men – like himself and Arnold – were doubled up. It was pitch black, a blackness so consuming that it seemed to swallow the light from the lamps whole. It had unnerved Luke when he had first come down the pit, this blackness. He had felt it sucked the thought process out of him, that the essential part of himself which made him what he was had been submerged in a drowning flood of fear that reduced him to animal level. But he had got used to it. You could get used to anything if you had to.

A group of men sectioned off into a side road leading to their district amid more banter, the main recipient of the witticisms – a young lad of eighteen who had got married the day before – taking the jibing in good part.

'You just make sure you've enough strength left at the end of the shift, Lenny, all right?'

'Aye, he'll need it sure enough. She won't be happy till you've given her a bairn, lad. They're all the same.'

149

'Fair wore me out, my missus, until she'd got three or four hangin' round her skirts, an' even now she keeps me at it.'

'In your dreams, Rob. In your dreams.'

Luke smiled to himself as he and a good number of men continued along the road. Robert Finnigan was what the man himself described as a good Catholic, meaning he gave his missus a bairn every year regular as clockwork, and it was common knowledge that she'd said every baby for the last five years was the last one. But still they kept coming. Fourteen of them now packed into three rooms, and to look at Rob you'd think a breath of wind would blow him away. But he was a tough little customer.

The mental image of the five-foot-nothing little Irishman brought his father into Luke's mind; Rob and Nathaniel had been good friends from bairns. His father had been on the backshift this week; Luke would have to let the deputy know he wouldn't be coming in. Would his da go to his brother's place in Boldon Lane and try to get set on at the Harton pit? Or would he take his Tess further afield than South Shields? One thing was for sure, gossip travelled faster and with more deadly accuracy than any knife in these parts. In lives made up of hard, grinding labour from morning to night it was the one thing that cost nothing and provided the most pleasure – unless you were the victim, that was.

Luke smiled again, but it was a cynical twist of his lips this time, and the man at the side of him – an old miner who had been down the pit some forty years – glanced his way. 'Somethin' amused ye, lad?'

'Down here? That'd be the day, Pete.'

'Aye, aye.' Pete gave a hoarse laugh. 'Nowt doon here to tickle yor fancy sure enough. Old Bob had two of his fingers off yesterday, hangin' on by a thread they were, an' yer know what Harley told him? Go home an' put a clooty bag on 'em. Damn fool doctor! How does he think a flour bag filled with hot bran'll help? Bob's missus snipped 'em off an' did the necessary an' that with the so-an'-so's keepin' a penny of our pay for the doctor. Doctor! He couldn't doctor the pit ponies, that one.' Pete swore, loudly and with great fluency, and the last word was still on his lips when the blast hit.

For a moment all Luke was aware of was that his eardrums felt like they had exploded and clouds of gritty dust were hitting his face and filling his eyes and ears. Everything was shaking and moving but the ringing in his own head was taking precedence, and it was some seconds before he realised he'd been flung to the floor, where he was sitting in total blackness, a blackness so absolute that it felt like a live entity in itself. How long he sat there he didn't know – it could have been seconds or minutes such was his stunned state – but then outside sounds began to filter through what had become a giant waterfall roaring in his ears.

150

He felt himself all over, breathing out a long sigh of relief when he knew he still had two arms and two legs. Shouldn't there have been some warning? The old miners said there was always a warning – a rush of air, the scurrying of rats, *something* – before an explosion.

'Pete?' Luke and the old miner had been the last two of the shift through the mother-gate – Arnold had been one of the first out of the cage and had stalked off after giving Luke a glare that told him their earlier conversation was still rankling. Luke remembered now the feeling of someone thudding down against him when he'd been knocked to the floor, and he felt about him cautiously.

When a voice at the side of him said, 'Keep yor hands t' yerself, lad,' he knew Pete was all right.

'What are we going to do?' Luke gasped thickly.

'Get out them as can move.' The shuffling indicated that Pete had risen to his feet, and now Luke joined him, swaying slightly, as the older man said, 'It's in-bye where it's happened, an' them nearer the tailgate'll have fared worse. We'd better see what's what with our lot. Where's t' deputy?'

Luke felt his head cautiously. By, but he felt dizzy, and he could hardly hear a thing – had his eardrums shattered? As he groped his way in the pitch blackness, he had only gone a few steps when he tripped over what turned out to be Ernest Burns. He recognised him from the loud swearing that followed. 'Ruddy good down here. If the firedamp don't get you, a boot in the head'll do the trick.'

More shuffling and groaning and muttered curses indicated that men were moving now, and Pete was encouraging those who could to get back to the roadway. The air was choking and fetid, and when Luke again stumbled over a prostrate body – which this time made no response – Pete told him to haul it back towards the roadway. 'Aa'll join thee in a minute, lad. All reet?'

The dust-filled air was thick and heavy as Luke, now crawling as he lugged the dead weight behind him, made for the air door. As he reached it, he thought for a moment the relief was going to make him lose consciousness. And then he was through, and the first thing that struck him was that there was light – blessed, wonderful light – from the lamp of the shift foreman, who must have run from the other section when he heard the blast. And the second reaction was to look round the men standing or sitting or, in some cases, lying in the roadway.

'They're all out bar Pete, Jack, Bart an' your Arnold.' Sam Williamson, the shift foreman, read Luke's mind, before kneeling beside the unconscious figure of Eric Armstrong, the miner Luke had brought out with him. Then he rose, saying, 'Get moving to the shaft, the lot of you, and those that can't walk must be carried. I've notified up top and they're sending in a rescue crew. It seems bad, but I've seen worse.'

151

The air was cleaner out in the roadway, with the air door shut against the suffocating coal dust, and Luke continued to breathe it in for a moment before he said, as the rest of the shift began to shamble off, 'I'm going back in. Pete's all right but he'll need help to find the others in there.'

Sam looked at Luke. 'Aye, well, I won't argue with you, lad, and I'd be glad of the help. It'll take time for the rescue crew to get here, and maybe there's more in store. The sooner we get 'em out and up top the happier I'll feel, and there's still the section at the tailgate to see to. The roof's down there, so I understand, and I reckon it's bad.'

Luke nodded. He didn't quite understand the desperate urgency he felt regarding Arnold – he had never liked his brother, and he knew full well Arnold didn't like him – but nevertheless it was there. Perhaps it was as simple as blood being thicker than water. But it wasn't just Arnold. To leave any man lying in that pitch-black hellhole was unthinkable.

They reached Pete after a short way and he was hauling Bart Hopkins, who looked to have two crushed legs, along with him. The man's groans were blood-curdling.

'He says Arnold an' Jack were afront of him.' Pete didn't stop moving as he spoke, and Luke and Sam Williamson had to press against the walls of the tunnel as he passed. 'Seemed to me the roof's doon, but one of 'em was groanin' like.'

'The others are moving to the shaft; can you manage to take Bart?' the foreman asked.

'Aye.' It was pithy, but the grit-laden air was not conducive to conversation.

They had gone some way when they found them. Arnold's head was bleeding and he was unconscious, but the prop that had wedged itself above his head and which was taking the weight of a huge slab of stone had certainly saved his life. Jack Davison, the deputy, was quite dead, the life having been crushed out of him by the unforgiving, hard black rock he had worked for most of his forty-three years.

It was when they came to move Arnold that the two men realised one of his legs was broken, the bone sticking through his torn trouser leg and gleaming with macabre whiteness in the dark. Nevertheless, whatever other injuries he might have also sustained, they knew time was of the essence. It wasn't unusual for one explosion to be followed by another – firedamp was the very devil – and they could do nothing for Jack; it would take machinery to lever the body free.

By the time they reached the roadway, Luke and Sam were sweating and gasping, but then they were breathing the clean flowing air again in great hungry gulps.

'He was lucky.' Sam Williamson nodded down at the comatose figure at their feet. 'Give it a while and likely he'll be as right as rain. Jack was the only breadwinner in his house, it'll hit his missus hard.'

'Aye.' Luke said nothing more. They needed all their strength to make it to the shaft and the cage that would take them out of this mausoleum, but Sam's words had kicked him in the stomach. Eva, and now Arnold. The ties holding him to this town, to the pit, were tightening like the tentacles of a giant squid which was determined to suck the life out of him. He was the only breadwinner now that his father had gone, at least until Arnold was better, and who knew how long that would take?

At a movement from Sam he turned, taking his brother's upper body as Sam lifted Arnold's legs, and the two coal-encrusted figures, their eyes gleaming strangely in their black faces, began to stumble along the rough roadway towards the box that would carry them upwards into the daylight.

Chapter Twelve

It was a blazing-hot day in early September, and the country had been in the grip of a heatwave for weeks, the temperature now reaching ninety-three degrees Fahrenheit in the shade.

At the beginning of August the weather had made the bank holiday one of the busiest ever, thousands of Durham's working class escaping to the parks and beaches in horse-drawn trams and farm carts and by shanks's pony, there to buy song sheets and listen to the bands and eat bread and fish for a penny. The farthing fairs, bathing machines, cockle wives, Punch and Judy shows and donkey rides did a roaring trade, along with the portable stage shows by pierrots and comedians, and the inevitable open-air services by the temperance sand missions – the preachers giving it hot and strong to their restless audience. Down in the capital, London's parks had reported record business; the beautiful Australian Patsy Montague delighting more cosmopolitan crowds at the London Pavilion with her tasteful impersonation of a living marble statue.

None of this pleasure-seeking had touched the farm at all. Since the day of the funeral in April the relentless daily drudgery which made up Polly's life had become almost mind-numbing, with little to distinguish one day from another as she laboured from sunrise to sunset. She had heard nothing from Miss Collins beyond a brief note two weeks after her departure, when the older woman had thanked Polly for her ministrations when she had been residing in the cottage. A horse-drawn flat cart had arrived at the farm the next morning, the contents of the cottage had been cleared and that had been that.

Luke had made one short visit to acquaint them with the facts of his father's departure and the accident at the mine, emphasising that with Arnold laid up and Eva's mental and physical health causing concern, he felt obliged to curtail his visits to the farm for the time being. Polly rightly assumed – more from what Luke didn't say than from what he did – that conditions at home were dire, and she expressed her understanding of the position Luke now found himself in whilst adding that he would be welcome any time he could call. That had been in April, and since then Luke had written twice to say he hoped all was well at the farm and that he would try to visit eventually, but as yet he had not made an appearance. Of Michael there had been no word at all.

Frederick hadn't called for a full month after the funeral, and when he had arrived one mild, sunny afternoon in late May he had offered no explanation for his absence. He had brought a pile of newspapers with him for Polly 'to catch up with current affairs', as he had laughingly put it, along with his copy of *Poems* by Currer, Ellis and Acton Bell, the book the Brontë sisters had published under their pseudonyms. Polly had thanked him for his kindness but she had felt constrained in his presence and it had showed, which had thrown all Frederick's carefully thought-out strategy to the wind. He had delayed his visit under the old adage of 'absence makes the heart grow fonder', and had been extremely put out to find Polly wasn't falling in line with his plans.

He had brooded over the conundrum all the way back to Stone Farm, and had eventually decided on the policy of letting Polly stew in her own juice. The farm was failing fast and she couldn't carry them all for ever – his time would come. He had lent all the money he intended to lend, and the slightest disaster on top of all their current debts would send the farm and its occupants into a rapid downward spiral from which there would be no escape. He would restrict his visits to the minimum and wait, that was what he would do, and when calamity hit . . .

Calamity hit in the form of the torrential rain which ended the heatwave. It was the last straw for the old farmhouse's dilapidated, weather-beaten roof, which had been crying out for attention for years.

It was a Tuesday afternoon, but it could have been any day of the week as far as Polly was concerned. She had been labouring in the fields for the last two weeks; the corn had ripened early and needed to be harvested before the arrival of the rains – forecast by Walter every night when he looked out into the baking farmyard. The corn harvest was always a worrying affair, as the grain couldn't be cut or otherwise handled when it was wet, and when the rains came the grain could go rotten or even start to germinate in the ear before it could be harvested. It was also a time of intense and continuous hard work, but in other years Frederick had sent his labourers to the farm to help once his own corn was safely stacked and in his barns. A couple of his men were experts at making a good corn rick with walls that leaned outwards to avoid the rain and a roof which was perfectly pitched and thatched. This year, however, the men hadn't materialised in spite of Polly's repeated requests for help, and although Ruth and their grandmother had spent some hours each day helping, the half-acre of corn a good man with a sickle could harvest in a day had taken three times as long, and there had been several acres to mow.

When the first drops of rain fell out of a steadily darkening sky, Polly straightened her aching back and looked about her. She had shown her sister and grandmother how to stook the sheaves in the hours they could afford in the fields, and most of the short double-rows of barley they had done so far were now in the barn. Thank goodness they hadn't planted oats; oats would have had to be churched three times in the stook – stood for three Sundays – before they could have been brought in. But there was still more to do.

She adjusted her big straw hat wearily. The last two weeks had seen her hands and arms scratched to ribbons, her face raw with sunburn in spite of the hat and every muscle of her body screaming for relief. She had risen at half past four every morning and worked until twilight, but it had been worth it. Most of the barley was safe. In a few weeks she could harness old Bess and plough the stubble, once she had had Ruth gleaning the last of the grain. They couldn't afford to waste a single stalk that would mean food for the chickens.

She raised her hot face to the fat raindrops, the scent of the thunderstorm beginning to permeate the cracked ground, and then, with a suddenness that quite literally took Polly's breath away, the heavens opened and a solid sheet of water enveloped everything. She gasped, blinded and stunned for a moment by the cloudburst, and then bent to retrieve the sickle before heading in the direction of the farmhouse.

The straw hat had fallen limply about her face and she took it off, carrying it against her soaked body as she trod over baked earth which was steaming as though the fires of the underworld were trying to break through. Her long linen skirt and calico apron impeded her progress as she stumbled along, the torrent of water not letting up for a moment, but then she reached the gate and passed through into the area beyond where the pigsty was, the back of the farmhouse looming up in front of her. She skirted the side of the house, the ground awash with a stream of water, and turned into the farmyard, and just as she did so the door opened and Ruth emerged pell-mell.

'Oh, Poll! Poll!' As Polly placed the sickle at the side of the wall, Ruth grabbed her. 'Quick, the water's pouring in.'

'What?'

'Upstairs. Grandda's bed's soaked and Gran's trying to move him, and it's all in Mam's room too.'

By the time Polly had raced up the stairs, the devastation was worse. They had placed various pots and pans under the slate-tiled roof the previous winter, once they had realised just how bad the deterioration was, emptying them every so often, but the lath and plaster ceilings had shown evidence that the rain had been dripping in for some considerable time before that. Slates were broken and in some cases missing altogether – the whole roof needed retiling – but there was no money for what would prove an expensive job, and Henry had made the decision that they would manage

157

for the time being until he could do some repairs in the summer months.

Now, as Polly stood on the threshold of her grandparents' bedroom, she saw there was a very real danger that the whole ceiling could come down on top of the old man, who was sitting gasping for air on the side of the bed, his wife standing by the side of him, wringing her hands ineffectually.

She could hear her mother yelling for attention in her own room and now she spun round, saying to Ruth, 'Strip the clothes off the bed and quick,' before she sprang across the landing and wrenched open the door of Hilda's room.

'About time! I've been calling—'

'Get out of that bed, Mam, and come and help me with Grandda.' Polly totally ignored her mother's outraged face, and as Hilda began to say, 'How dare you! I can't—' she flung back the covers from her mother's thin body and yanked her out of the bed. 'Get in there and help Grandda,' she said again, 'or I'll make you, Mam.'

'You'll pay for this, Polly Farrow.' Hilda was beside herself but she did as she was told, and after Polly had sent her grandmother down the stairs in front of them, she and her mother and sister lifted Walter into a standing position and then carried him, staggering under his considerable weight, on to the landing. They were halfway down the stairs, the whole lot of them having nearly gone from top to bottom twice, when the crash from upstairs alerted them to the fact that the ceiling had finally reached the end of its life.

'It's all right, Grandda.' Polly was less concerned with the state of the bedrooms than the old man fighting for breath. 'We'll sort it.'

We'll sort it. Once she had got her grandfather lying on the saddle and her granny had given him a spoonful of his medicine – the medicine that was bought with the proceeds from the items Polly had been forced to spirit away from the house and take to the pawn shop in Ryhope, which catered mostly for the colliery workers – Polly went upstairs to survey the damage. It was beyond sorting. She stared at the soaking, dirty, tangled mass that had once been her grandparents' bedroom, her mind numb. And then she walked slowly to the room she shared with Ruth.

It had stopped raining now, the deluge finishing as suddenly as it had begun, and as she opened the bedroom door a shaft of sunlight was falling on the debris within. Several chunks of the ceiling was down, although the damage was not so severe as in her grandparents' room. Nevertheless, the room was uninhabitable and distinctly unsafe, her mother's bedroom proving to be the same.

After leaving the third bedroom, Polly stood quietly on the landing, her mind struggling to take in the enormity of the ruination. What was she going to do? *What was she going to do?* Over the last few months anything of the slightest value had been pawned: the spare bedding, her father's wedding suit and other clothes, the few bits of extra cutlery and crockery – there was nothing left to take. And even if there had been, the money she could have obtained would have been a drop in the ocean to what was needed now.

She leant against the rough stone wall, her head spinning with exhaustion. All the shame and humiliation involved in slipping into Raymond Vickers's shop and seeing her parcels unwrapped and the meagre contents inspected had been for nothing. They were worse off now than they had ever been. She had died a little each time she had walked into the fusty-smelling shop, the contents of which held stories of personal tragedies and poverty, but she had always emerged with her head held high and her chin jutting out, daring any passer-by to look at her with scorn or pity. But her fight to keep the farm alive, the hours of back-breaking work, the constant chivvying to get Ruth to do her fair share, had been thwarted by the most relentless of a farmer's enemies – the weather.

She pushed back the mass of chestnut-brown curls that had worked free from the bun at the back of her head and were curling damply round her face, and looked down at the floorboards beneath her feet, her mind's eye seeing the room below wherein her grandfather was lying. Grandda was so frail now, and Gran looked as though a breath of wind would blow her away. The heart attack her grandda had suffered when her da had hanged himself seemed to have aged his wife as much as himself; they were both painfully old and vulnerable.

The workhouse. The words loomed up from nowhere and caused a constriction in Polly's throat, but in that moment she recognised that they had been lurking in her subconscious for months. *Never.* She bit down on the sick feeling as bile rose in her throat. Never, no matter what it cost, would she see her grandda and granny in that place. There was a way out of this, there had to be. She had no idea how much the farm was worth in comparison to the debts her da and grandda had run up, but her Uncle Frederick would know. Her mother had been brought up at Stone Farm – the ties which connected them were family ones.

'Polly?'

She became aware of Ruth just behind her, and as she turned, Polly saw her sister had been crying. 'What's the matter? Is it Grandda?'

'No, no.' Ruth stopped her when Polly would have pushed past her. 'It's just . . . what are we going to do?'

Ruth looked much younger than her thirteen years as she asked the question she had verbalised many times over the last months when any problem had hit. Polly stared at the face which would have been pretty but for the petulance which had become a permanent feature, and as she did so, she shivered. But the chill she felt was less to do with her

159

damp clothes than with the weight of the responsibility bearing down on her. All of them, her grandda and granny, Ruth, even her mam, were looking to her to provide a way out of what had become the shambles of their existence. They told her – and had been telling her for the last months – in a hundred little ways, spoken and unspoken, that they were depending on her, and it wasn't *fair*. She was sixteen, she was young, she had her whole life before her, and she missed Michael so *much*. Missed him and worried about him and—

'Poll?' Ruth moved a step closer, burying her head in her sister's chest, and Polly's arms went round her. For all Ruth's fierce hostility, she was capable of warm moments like this now and again, and as her sister's arms went round her waist Polly sighed inwardly and nuzzled the top of the mousy-brown head. Self-pity was an indulgence she couldn't afford, it was too weakening. As Luke always said, you had to play the cards you were dealt. She wished he wasn't so bowed down by troubles of his own; she would have liked to talk to him. It wasn't just Michael that she missed. The thought was a surprise; she hadn't recognised that part of the ache in her heart was a yearning for the tall, dark miner she had always regarded as a brother, but it was there and it was very real.

'We haven't got any money to mend the roof, have we?' Ruth's voice was small and muffled.

'No, we haven't,' Polly agreed briskly, hugging Ruth tightly before she pushed her away and looked down into the tear-stained face. 'But it's got to be done, so I'd best go and see Uncle Frederick and see if he can help. You dry out the bedding you took from Grandda's room and make sure he's comfortable on the saddle, and see if you can get the blankets off our bed and Mam's while I'm gone, but be careful. And bring down any clothes you can salvage, anything you can. Mam can help.'

'Huh.' Ruth grimaced. 'She says the shock's given her the skitters and she's been out in the privy since we got Grandda on the saddle.'

'She'll be sleeping out there too if she doesn't muck in,' said Polly grimly, but with a twinkle in her eye.

'Oh, Poll.' Ruth grinned weakly. 'Anything else you want me to do?'

'Pray it doesn't rain again.'

The bright and breezy manner Polly had adopted for the benefit of the others back at the house vanished the moment she was on her way to Stone Farm. She had taken the time to wash her face and hands and tidy her hair, and she was now wearing her spare clean blouse and her winter felt hat – the straw bonnet had all but disintegrated. Her skirt was grubby from her labour in the fields, but her spare one had been hanging on the back of the door in her bedroom and was in a worse state from the effects of plaster dust and rain.

Ruth had helped her to harness Bess to the cart, and now, as the old horse clip-clopped her way along, Polly didn't hurry her. The sunshine which had followed the torrential downpour was intermittent and more storm clouds looked to be gathering – the heatwave had definitely broken – but in spite of this, Polly was in no rush to reach Stone Farm. She knew she had to face certain facts she had been putting off since her father's funeral, the main one being the knowledge that the man she was on her way to see wanted her. And her granny knew. Oh, aye, her granny knew all right, although they had never talked about the visit they had made to Stone Farm that day in April.

Polly narrowed her eyes as she stared over Bess's broad back to the lane beyond, the puddles it contained being swiftly absorbed into the thirsty ground. A kestrel cried, sharp and shrill, in the sky above, and for a moment the sound reflected something deep in her heart. It was a cry of freedom, of independence, and as her eyes followed the small falcon she could sense the glorious liberty displayed in the powerful wings as the bird swooped and glided in the thermals.

She would ask her uncle what the farm was worth, that was the first thing to ascertain. He had been good to them in the past, very good, but if his generosity had exceeded his normal astute business acumen, that would mean the farm was his in essence anyway. She shifted on the hard wood of the cart, her stomach churning. Of course if her father had been alive and her grandfather well they could have continued to live at the farm as tenants working for Frederick, but as it was . . . She squared her shoulders, knowing she had to come to terms with what Frederick might ask of her before she came face to face with him.

The man she had always regarded as her uncle had metamorphosised into someone else over the last months, someone with an unsmiling, determined mouth and hungry eyes, but he was still the same man who had brought her books and spent time talking to her. She had only ever known kindness at his hands, she must remember that. And she liked him, she had always liked him. There were four people relying on her to provide a roof over their heads back at the farmhouse, four mouths to feed and four bodies to clothe. The last thoughts were intrinsically linked. They brought to mind the expression on her granny's face when Polly had looked at them all in the kitchen and told them she was going to see Frederick. It had pained her, that look, because along with the hope and relief etched on Gran's countenance, there had been shamefacedness. Her granny suspected what the outcome of this visit would be but she hadn't said a word to stop her going, because they both knew, at bottom, that it was the only avenue left open, with the house falling down about their ears and their livelihood swallowed up.

Surprisingly, she found the last thought quelled the nervous fluttering in her stomach. Her mind was no longer desperately racing back and forth, nor was there present in her that weakening feeling of self-pity, but instead strength to see through what had to be seen through. But she would be honest, completely honest, whatever happened.

A vivid flash of lightning followed by a low, deep roll of thunder told her more rain was imminent, but she didn't hurry Bess to move faster. Instead she lifted her eyes to the gathering clouds that were darkening the sky and obscuring the last of the blue, and breathed in the smell of the approaching storm, allowing the old horse to saunter on at her own pace.

Frederick sat gazing down at the accounts spread out in front of him on the leather-topped desk, but the normal satisfaction the rows of neat figures gave him was absent.

Four months. Four months and she still continued to persist in her stubborn refusal to acknowledge what he was offering. She must know. Women sensed these things, didn't they? But of course she knew. He ground his teeth together and flung down his quill pen, whereupon it splattered ink in a small arc of black droplets. There was talk that Nicholson's wife was pressing the old man to move down south near Grimsby where her people came from; he wouldn't be surprised to see the Nicholson farm up for sale in the near future. Now was the perfect time to get in first and pre-empt other offers, but it would still cost him a pretty penny.

He rose abruptly, walking to stand in front of the small tiled fireplace, where he stood staring down at the cold ashes left from the fire Betsy had lit the previous evening. He had been working until late at his desk, and in spite of the heat outside the building, the thick stone walls and flagged floors guaranteed the interior of the farmhouse never really got warm.

Had he played this affair with Polly right? A waiting game was all very well, but she had seemed to get more stiff and unyielding in her manner each time he had seen her of late, which hadn't been often. The last two times he had called she had been out working in the fields like a common labourer. The thought irked him, but his irritation was not tempered by any tenderness; he couldn't countenance the thought of his future wife behaving in such a way. Running the household was acceptable – useful experience for the time when she would be instructing Betsy and Emily, the kitchen maid – but any outdoor work beyond collecting the eggs and such was totally unacceptable. He had never dreamed, when he had withheld his labourers from the hay-making, that Polly's stubbornness and headstrong attitude would lead her to the measures she had adopted. Any other girl of

162

his acquaintance – and she was little more than a girl still – would have accepted defeat gracefully.

Frederick's eyes narrowed. In the past he had congratulated himself on the fact that it was Polly who was the elder daughter – her intelligence and beauty would reflect on him among his social peers once she was his wife – but recent events had persuaded him otherwise. Ruth, had she been older, would have been much more realistic and appreciative of the advantages of such a match; she had more than a little of her mother in her, did Ruth.

A knock at the study door interrupted his musing, and he turned as Betsy opened it and, popping her head round, said quickly, 'It's Miss Polly, master, an' she's soaked through an' as cold as clay. I've put her in the sittin' room an' lit the fire.'

'*Miss Polly?*' And then, as he stared into his housekeeper's round bright eyes, Frederick took hold of himself, saying quietly, 'Thank you, Betsy. Tell Miss Polly I'll be along shortly, and see about some refreshments, would you.'

It was a full minute more before Frederick left the study, and when he opened the door to the sitting room it was to see Polly ensconced in front of a now roaring fire with a thick fleecy blanket draped about her shoulders. Her rich brown hair was curling about her face in tiny tendrils and her magnificent eyes were wide as she rose to her feet. She looked young and delicate, her slender body enveloped in the cream coverlet, but he knew her apparent vulnerability was an illusion – the last months had taught him that her fragile exterior covered a will of steel.

Polly's stomach muscles had tightened when she had seen Frederick standing there, but her manner was quiet and contained as she faced him. 'I'm sorry to come so unexpectedly,' she said quickly. 'I hope I haven't interrupted anything important.'

'Of course not.' Frederick smiled as he strode forward and took her hands, which were still icy cold. 'I would like to think this is a call in answer to the repeated invitations I've made over the last months, but I suspect something is amiss.'

Polly felt herself flushing. He knew full well she couldn't afford time on social calls, and the intonation of his voice had aimed to make her feel guilty. She heard her voice, sounding to her own ears tight and defensive, saying, 'Yes, something is amiss. The rain has brought the ceilings down at home.'

He was staring down at her and he did not say, as one would have expected in the circumstances, 'Is anyone hurt? Is everyone all right?' but, 'I am not surprised. The farmhouse is in a severe state of disrepair. You must realise that?'

'Yes, of course I realise that.'

It was clear from his deep breath and the stiffening of his face that he did not like her tone, but he continued to hold her hands in his own as he said, 'The whole roof needs replacing and all the window frames are rotten, and that is just the start of it. Too much has been left for too long.'

'My father and my grandfather did what they could.'

'I'm sure they did.'

Their glances held for some seconds before Polly said, 'Grandda . . . Grandda needs to be looked after properly.' He waited, his gaze concentrated on her face. 'I wondered, if we put the farm up for sale, how much money would be left after we had paid our debts?'

Frederick felt a quickening in his body but he strove to hide his excitement as he said, 'Very little, if anything at all. The farmhouse itself is a liability as it is, and forty acres is not a great deal of land, as you know.'

'So you virtually own the farm now?'

Frederick was taken aback, albeit slightly, by the forthright question. He let go of Polly's hands and turned away, aware he had to choose his words carefully, but before he could do so Polly said quietly, 'The farmhouse is almost uninhabitable as it is, certainly in the winter, and Grandda's medicine is expensive.'

'Aye, I know.' He was facing her again, and now he took her hands in his once more, shaking them slightly as he said, 'But your grandda doesn't have to live there, none of you do. You must know how I feel about you, Polly. I want nothing more than to make you happy, and if you would consent to be my wife it would make me the happiest man on earth.'

It was not in Polly's nature to play the coquette, and Frederick was again flummoxed by her straightforwardness when she answered quickly, 'But I don't love you, not in that way. You know about Michael and my feelings for him remain the same even though we'll probably never see each other again. I don't want to hurt you, you've been so good to us all, but I would never be able to love you as you deserve.'

All this talk about love, thought Frederick, and what was the emotion when it all boiled down to basics? A biological urge to procreate. That was it at bottom. But of course women couldn't bring themselves to accept that; they had to fabricate their own niceties about the act. He adopted his most understanding face as he pushed Polly gently down into the seat she had vacated a moment or two earlier before pulling another chair in front of her and sitting down himself. 'You mustn't worry about that, my dear,' he said kindly. 'I understand what you are saying, of course, but I want you for my wife, and I know if I don't marry you I shall marry no one.' That was a good line; he had been told that one by a friend of his who had assured him women couldn't resist such a declaration. 'And putting aside my love for you, there are so many other reasons why a union between us is right. Your family will become my family and come under my protection here, you have my word on that, and the two farms can join together as one. It will wipe out any debts and I might even be able to make something of the land.'

She had to try, just one last time. She had read something recently, and although she wasn't sure of her facts, she understood banks sometimes lent money to businesses in situations like this. 'I could try to borrow the money to pay you back, from a bank, perhaps? If Grandda put the farm up as surety on a loan—'

'A bank?' Frederick's laugh was harsh. 'A bank wouldn't touch you, my dear, not in your present circumstances, besides which, you can't trust banks. It's only land and bricks and mortar that mean anything, and money you can see in your hand. Never set foot in a bank if you know what's good for you, that's my advice. Besides . . .' He looked at her almost sorrowfully now. 'When they knew of the extent of your debts . . . Oh, Polly' – he now took her hands again, his face earnest – 'say yes to me, my dear, and make me the happiest man alive.'

She had known, hadn't she? From the moment she had seen the devastation at home, she had known. She had been sitting with her head bowed as she stared at their joined hands, but now Polly lifted her blue gaze to his waiting eyes. 'I . . . I can't promise you that I will come to love you, but I can promise that I will try, and also that I'll be a good wife,' she said in a small but clear voice. 'If you are satisfied with that, then yes, I will marry you, Frederick.'

And so it was done.

Chapter Thirteen

The banns were read out for the first time two Sundays later, on the sixteenth of September, the day after the newspapers reported that twenty-five men had died in a Durham pit disaster. Although the accident was big news, it couldn't compare to the extensive spread the TUC conference at the beginning of the month had merited, with nearly five hundred delegates representing a million and a half union members attending and causing waves of concern to flow in high places up and down the land. What was the country coming to, with workers demanding their 'rights'? Rights? The only rights they should be allowed were the ones given them by their betters. Such was the mood among many of Britain's mine owners and land owners, and many northern pits were feeling the bite of increasing hostility between management and union members. It was unfortunate that it was in this charged climate that Luke and Arnold first heard of Polly's impending marriage.

Polly had written to Luke to inform him that the family were now residing at Stone Farm due to extensive damage to the farmhouse, and that she had accepted a proposal of marriage from Frederick – the ceremony to take place at the end of October. The letter caused a row between the two brothers that made all their previous altercations appear mild.

'The dirty little baggage.' Arnold was all but foaming at the mouth when he finished reading the short note Luke had passed silently to him. 'She's fooled us all, you see that, don't you? She never intended to marry Michael, she was just using the milksop to get Frederick interested. She fancies herself the lady wife of that upstart, does she? By, I see it all now. The filthy, conniving whore—'

'That's enough.' Luke had leapt up from his seat so suddenly the chair had gone flying back against the wall, and he was glaring down at his brother, who was sitting with his injured leg propped up on the cracket.

The two men were just about to eat their evening meal which one of their neighbours, Elsie Appleby, had prepared and dished up for them before disappearing to see to her own family's dinner. Luke was now paying this same neighbour to tend to Eva during the day – his stepmother had suffered a complete breakdown, according to

167

the doctor – and take care of the washing and ironing, and all their meals. Elsie did what she was paid to do, but with her own large family of ten children to look after, it meant the shine and sparkle of Eva's houseproud days were a thing of the past.

'You're determined not to see it, aren't you? It's staring you in the face in black and white, and still you're too damn stubborn or stupid to see what she is. She's had her sights set on Stone Farm all along, that's what this letter says.'

'The letter says they have been forced out of their home through no fault of their own, and Frederick's done the Christian thing and taken them in.' Which was more than he himself would have been able to do, Luke reflected bitterly. He was working extra shifts now when he was able to get them – Arnold's compensation money wouldn't stretch far, and with his father's wage gone it meant they were hard pushed, even without Elsie Appleby to pay.

He'd thought of Polly often in the last weeks – dreamed of her both when he was awake in the bowels of the earth and when he was asleep – but he had told himself he had to give her a chance to get over Michael and for his situation to clear before he could even begin to attempt to persuade her to see him as something other than a big brother type figure.

'Christian thing?' Arnold swore loudly before he continued, 'By, man, you're as thick as two short planks if you think that. All them books and things he's brought her over the years has been a means to an end. She knew what he was about all right, and now she's got what she wanted. I wouldn't be surprised if she caused the damage at the farm on purpose to give him a jog to get a move on, and once she was sitting pretty at his place she brought him up to scratch. And how? You asked yourself that then? I bet his bed's been warm the last few nights.'

'If you could stand on two legs I'd ram that last remark down your throat.'

'Maybe, but it don't alter nothing. She's scum, like the dockside dollies an' such, but at least they're honest enough to admit what they are. I'd sooner trust them any day than Polly Farrow.'

'The trouble with you is that your mind is a sewer, it always has been, and it taints everything it touches.' Luke's face was white but his eyes were dark with fury, and the two brothers stared at each other with absolute loathing before Luke snatched up his cap and stormed out of the house. If he stayed there a minute – a second – longer he would forget Arnold's leg had been broken in three places and land him one to take him into next weekend.

Arnold's teeth continued to grind together for some moments after Luke had left, his eyes staring blindly across the room as he inwardly cursed Polly. The trouble that trollop had caused; leading them all on, acting the innocent! But he'd known, he'd known what was at the back of those great blue eyes of hers, and he'd been proved right, hadn't he? By, he had. He could see now why she had acted the virtuous maiden with him when he had showed his hand – bigger fish to fry than a common miner for Polly Farrow. Didn't think he was good enough, did she? But he'd show her. If it was the last thing he did, he'd make her regret the day she turned him down. No one treated him like muck and got away with it.

The plate of thick rabbit stew in front of him was slowly congealing, its sweet smell suddenly rising up in his nostrils as he glanced down at the table, and he reached out, his face savage as he threw the plate across the room. It smashed against the range, shattering into pieces and causing the fire to sizzle as the stew cascaded into the flames. He'd see her like that one day, broken and crushed. The thought took the tenseness out of his body and he slowly relaxed back against the chair, taking a piece of bread from the plate in the middle of the table and beginning to chew on it. Aye, he'd see his day with Polly Farrow all right, and he'd teach her a lesson she'd never forget. And in the mean time, if there was any way he could make her life just a little bit less hunky-dory, he'd do it. There were more ways to kill a cat than skinning it, and this particular little alley cat would be crawling to him on her knees before he was finished.

Once outside, Luke crossed Southwick Road and plunged into the warren of streets the coal industry had spawned. The smoke from Wearmouth colliery and countless industrial chimneys hung over the rooftops like a black pall, but Luke had lived in Monkwearmouth all his life and he didn't notice the smoke and stench which poisoned vegetation and human beings alike. The town depended on its collieries, riverside industry and shipping, and the busy clangour meant growth, and growth meant wages, and wages meant food in hungry bellies.

The evening was oppressive; the whole month had been a stormy one, and Luke could feel the weather pressing against his eyeballs as his head pounded. There were numerous bairns playing their games on the pavements and in the gutters, some of them barefoot and most none too clean as they threw their pebbles or bits of coloured glass for hopscotch or careered madly round in the air hanging on to a piece of rope one of them had tied from the iron arm of a lamppost.

The occasional open door omitted strong smells of cabbage and other unsavoury odours as Luke walked by, and on one doorstep a girl was busy fixing her younger sister's hair into tight rag corkscrews to the accompaniment of vigorous protest from the infant in question.

It was just after he saw one little mite – who couldn't have been older than six or seven – staggering along under the weight of one of the stoneware jars known as a grey hen that Luke decided to make

169

his way to Carley Road. The jars carried up to a gallon of liquid when full, and it looked like the local beer shop had filled this particular one to the brim from the crablike walk the child had been forced to adopt under its weight. The little girl had just reached a doorway in front of Luke when a blowsy, dirty woman appeared on the threshold. She grabbed the child by the ear, making her squeal, and lugged her into the house, crying, ''Bout time an' all! Your da's bin callin' for this for half an hour an' more. You'll feel the side of his hand the night, Tess me girl.'

Poor little devil. Luke had stopped, he couldn't help himself, and as the woman went to close the door she noticed him looking at her, and read the condemnation written all over his face. Their glance held for a moment, and then she looked swiftly up and down the street before tossing her head and stepping backwards into the filthy interior, banging the door shut behind her.

By, in spite of everything he had a lot to be thankful for. His family life might never have been much to write home about, but at least it had been devoid of the shame and humiliation some of these bairns suffered. What was it David Lloyd George had said recently during some address or other? Oh, aye, he had it now. 'Britain is the richest country under the sun, yet it has ten million workmen living in conditions of chronic destitution.' Well, there weren't many of Sunderland's poor that would argue with that, Luke thought bitterly. It was the next bit of the speech, 'The imprudent habits of gambling and drink cause sixty per cent of the poverty', that had caught him and others on the raw. 'Drink is the most urgent problem of the hour for our rulers to grapple with,' Lloyd George had continued. Luke had actually laughed out loud when he had read that. Drink was the most urgent problem? What about the hopelessness and desperation caused by families of fifteen and more being packed into two rooms along with an army of rats and bugs and cockroaches? Why did the powers that be think men and women drank themselves silly anyway, if not to escape their miserable lot? But it was the bairns, like that little Tess back there, who were the real victims. She'd be lucky to survive to adulthood.

The name stayed with him and brought his father into his mind, and he turned left at the corner of Bond Street into Wallace Street, before cutting through at the back of the vicarage of St Columba's Church, off Swan Street. He skirted round the side of the Cornhill glassworks into the street where his father's woman had lived before the pair of them had left town, and then stood aimlessly for a moment or two as he looked up and down Carley Road. Tess's next-door neighbour's husband, Bert, had taken him aside at the pit a couple of weeks after his father had left and muttered that Tess had got word to Joan that they were all right and could his wife let Nat's lads know, but it had been evident that Bert had been uncomfortable in the role of go-between and Luke hadn't mentioned his father to Bert since. But now, suddenly, the need to hear if they knew any more was strong.

He thrust his hands into his pockets as he considered whether he should go the next step and make enquiries as to which house was Bert's, but before he could come to a decision he heard his name called by a familiar voice. Stifling a groan, he turned, his eyes alighting on Katy Chapman and another young lass who were coming towards him, their arms entwined and their faces bright. 'Look who it isn't.' Katy dimpled at him as she got closer, and Luke reflected, and not for the first time, that she was a bonny lass, with her fair fluffy hair and dark eyes. But forward. Definitely forward.

'Hello, Katy.'

'Hello yourself.'

Luke sighed inwardly. Katy's manner was coy, it was always that way around him. The Chapmans lived next door but one in Southwick Road, and Katy was a few months older than Polly, but it could have been a few years older, such was the knowledge shining out of her big brown eyes. And then he checked the thought sharply. It wasn't Katy who had just got engaged to a man old enough to be her father, and a wealthy man to boot. The censure was savage and sharp, and he acknowledged that he hadn't realised until that very moment how bitterly disappointed he was in Polly, or how Arnold's words had struck home. If she had really loved Michael she wouldn't be marrying Frederick a few months later; she didn't have to do that. If they were finding it difficult to cope with Henry gone and Walter laid up, they had only to sell up and move into town – they'd get a fair bit for the farm as it stood. But Polly liked farm life. Luke's eyes narrowed. And she obviously liked Frederick – enough to agree to share the marriage bed with him. His guts twisted and tightened and it was a second or two before he realised that Katy had been talking and he hadn't heard a word.

'I'm sorry?' His eyes focused on the pretty pert face in front of him, which was looking distinctly put out.

'I asked how your mam was.' Eva was always referred to as such by their neighbours and friends.

'Not too good.'

Katy stared at him for a moment, then bit on her lip, her face straight as she said, 'Me an' Gert are going to the Picture Hall.'

It was both an invitation and a question, and Luke replied to both as he said, 'I'm on my way to see a friend of me da's. He lives round here.'

Katy paused for a moment. She was glad he wasn't going to meet a lass, but she'd spoken to Luke Blackett umpteen times in the last twelve months or so and he had never followed up. Why was it you

171

only had to look at some lads for them to take liberties, and others – or more especially Luke – didn't seem to cotton on? She wetted her full red lips and fluttered her eyelashes a little as she adjusted her brown felt hat more securely on her curls, before saying, 'You ever been to the Picture Hall, Luke?'

She was a brazen little piece. Luke hid a smile as he looked more closely into the big brown eyes set in skin that resembled thick, warm cream. But she certainly had something. Nevertheless, the thought of accompanying Katy and her friend to Sunderland's first permanent cinema – opened four months previously at the north end of the bridge in Bonnersfield, and billed as 'the Premier Picture Hall in the North of England' by its owner, George Black – was like a betrayal to Polly. 'No.' It was succinct, but he softened his abruptness with a smile – he found Katy's boldness amusing in spite of himself.

'No?' Katy's eyes widened as she pouted prettily. 'Oh, me an' Gert are always going, aren't we, Gert?' Gert – a plain, tall and painfully thin girl who had been chosen to be Katy's best friend for those attributes alone – nodded quickly. 'We've seen *An Irish Eviction* an' *A Moonlight Dream* an' *Oliver Twist* an'— Oh, loads. You ought to go, it's packed every night. 'Course, the seats are a bit hard with them bein' old chapel pews, but we don't mind that. It's *The Game at Athens* on tonight, an' it's only tuppence in the pit. You'd love it, Luke. Wouldn't he, Gert?'

Gert nodded again. She hoped Luke wouldn't come. She was fed up with waiting about on street corners after evenings such as these when Katy disappeared down an alley or one of the back streets with a lad for a while. Katy's mam would kill her if she got the wind of half of what she was up to.

'And you really think I'd enjoy *The Game at Athens*?' Luke was laughing openly now; Katy's blatant flirtatiousness was a balm to his sore heart. Here was one lass who wasn't averse to being seen with him, he told himself, as he ruthlessly pushed the mental image of a sweet, blue-eyed face topped by a mass of burnished curls out of his mind. Polly had chosen her path, her letter had made that abundantly clear, and it was about time he did something other than working down the pit and returning home to those four walls and his stepmother and Arnold. He'd had a bellyful the night, he had straight. A little diversion would keep him sane.

'Aye, 'course you would.' Katy had picked up the different note in his voice and she sensed victory. 'You can give it a try anyways. There's no knowin' what you'll like until you give it a try, is there?' The innuendo was blatant, and Luke would have found it shocking in any other girl, but spoken as it was in a laughing gurgle he found himself chuckling again. And when Katy linked her arm through his – indicating for Gert to do the same – he made no protest.

As they made their way to the Picture Hall, Katy was animated. She might not get a chance like this again; she had to get him sufficiently interested so he would want to see her again, she told herself silently. She was on the verge of getting something of a name for herself – she knew that well enough without Gert going on about it all the time – and she needed the respectability of a steady beau, although there hadn't been anyone up to this point she had really wanted. But she wanted Luke Blackett, she had always wanted him, although up to now he hadn't looked the side she was on.

But she had to be careful. Luke wasn't like Edward Thornhill or Archy Stamp, interested in one thing and one thing only. He was different. She glanced at him under her eyelashes and her heart gave a little jump. She would have to play it cautiously with Luke, but it'd be worth it. Oh, aye, it would be worth it all right if she could bring him up to scratch.

Luke paid for both the girls at the pay-box, and as they took their seats on the wooden pews facing the large white sheet hanging at the front of the hall, he was already regretting the position he had put himself in. What was he doing here? he asked himself as the hand-cranked kinematograph started the programme rolling and Katy giggled at something Gert said. Katy was old Stan's daughter, and Luke had worked on Stan's shift until recently, when the veteran miner had had one accident too many and injured his back. Now Stan was on top in the line of young lads, old men and miners such as himself who were crippled who worked the huge, slow-moving conveyor belts carrying the coal and stones from the tubs that came up the pit shaft. Sorting the coal wasn't hard work but it certainly didn't require any brains, and old hands like Stan found it hard to be relegated to the 'screens'. Luke had liked Stan – he liked him still – and he couldn't mess about with his daughter. Besides which – and here Luke grimaced to himself in the darkness – Katy had five brawny older brothers who also worked down the pit and were handy with their fists and feet.

'What do you think? You like it then?' Katy leaned towards him slightly as she spoke. She had taken her hat off once they were seated, and now wispy tendrils of her hair, which was very fair and curly and had escaped the shining coil at the nape of her neck, brushed his cheek.

'Give him a chance.' Gert, seated on Katy's other side, spoke before Luke could answer, and it was as though she had said something very witty as the two girls giggled together.

By, the sooner he was out of this lot the better. Luke shifted uneasily on the wooden bench and then stopped abruptly as his thigh touched Katy's, and he was glad of the cover of darkness as he felt his face begin to burn. Still, there were two of them, that

173

was one good thing. It didn't look so bad with there being the two of them.

Katy made sure there weren't two of them later that night. Considering the Chapmans only lived a door or two away, Luke found he couldn't argue with Katy's suggestion that they see Gert home to Lower Dundas Street on their way to Southwick Road, and when they left the other girl and Katy put her arm through this – ostensibly because of the greasy pavements, which were wet and slippy after another downfall – it seemed crass and churlish to object.

He could feel the rounded curves of her body against his as they walked, and he began to sweat a little, his eyelids blinking rapidly as his body hardened in answer to the subtle stimulus in spite of himself. The smell of her was in his nostrils, and it was faintly cloying but not unpleasant. He realised, with another little shock, that she must be wearing perfume. He had never been close to a woman who was wearing perfume – most lasses didn't have the money for such indulgences – but then he remembered Stan had been full of the fact that Katy had been taken on at Binns on the west side of Fawcett Street some months earlier, in their ladies' department, so likely that was where it had come from. Whatever, it was nice. More lasses should wear it. He was sweating more now, and he would have liked to adjust the bulge in his trousers, but that was out of the question.

'You haven't got a lass, have you, Luke?'

They had just reached Thomas Street North, and Katy was smiling up at him, her pretty face innocently enquiring as her thick eyelashes fluttered. Luke swallowed, stretching his chin out of his collar as he said, 'No, no, I haven't.'

'I haven't got a lad.' She still had her face upturned, and he swallowed again before he said gallantly, 'I can hardly believe that.'

'It's true. I've had offers, lots of 'em, but I wanted to wait until I met someone I really liked. You know what I mean?'

'Aye, I know what you mean.'

They'd reached the inn at the end of the street, and now Katy came to a halt, forcing Luke to do the same. She paused a moment and then glanced up at him again, her face serious now and her eyes deep black pools as she said, 'Have . . . have you ever thought of me in that way, Luke? As a lass?' And then she put her head down immediately, giving a little twist to her body with her arm still through his, 'Oh, I shouldn't have said that, should I? I'm . . . I'm sorry. It's just . . .'

'No, no, it's all right.' His body was burning, and when she raised her head again and he saw her lips were trembling, it seemed natural to lower his head and kiss her. Quite how they came to be in the shadows at the back of the inn a few moments later Luke wasn't sure, but by then Katy was kissing him back and her arms were tightly round his waist, and the unspoken declaration was done.

Chapter Fourteen

The banns had been called for the third time some weeks before, wedding invitations had been issued and replies received and now the day was here. There was to be a barn dance with refreshments at the farm following the afternoon wedding, and all the arrangements had been left in the very capable hands of Betsy and the farm staff. At one point Frederick had liked the idea of a big tent on the lawn at the back of the farmhouse – he had heard Squire Bentley had done the same when his daughter had married the year before – but in view of the October weather being inclement at best, he had regretfully shelved the notion. Nevertheless, it was to be a grand occasion, with guests invited from near and far, most of whom were unknown to the bride.

Polly had met Luke once since the announcement of the forthcoming marriage, and that had been when he had paid a visit to Stone Farm to personally deliver his thanks for the invitation to the wedding and to say that although he and Arnold would be pleased to accept, he was afraid his stepmother would still be too unwell to attend.

Polly had received him in the sitting room with Frederick at her side and the visit had been a short and tense one. It had been when she had shown Luke to the door and they had been alone for just a minute or two that he had taken her hand, and, as she had looked into his face, said, 'You want this, Polly? This marriage? You're absolutely sure you want it?' and she had replied, her face stiff with the control she was exerting in order not to crumple into tears in front of him, 'Of course I'm sure, Luke.'

He'd nodded, his face unsmiling. 'Then I wish you every happiness together,' he had said politely, letting go of her hand and stepping back a pace before he had turned and opened the heavy oak door and passed through the opening, walking away without once turning to look back.

Why had she felt so devastated after he had left? Polly stared into the pale face looking back at her from the dressing table mirror in the room she had been sharing with her sister since they had all come to live at Stone Farm, and then answered herself immediately with, Because you don't want him to think ill of you, that's why. And it doesn't matter – it really *doesn't* matter what other people think. You know why you are marrying Frederick and other people can think what they like. Other people except Luke – for some reason his good opinion *did* matter, however much she tried to persuade herself otherwise. But she had to go through with this and she couldn't explain herself to a soul, not even her granny. But then her granny knew anyway. Polly turned on the upholstered stool and glanced across the wide, pleasantly furnished room to where her wedding dress was hanging on the back of the wardrobe door, surrounded by clouds of chiffon from the veil at the back of it. There was eight yards of satin and silk in the dress and it was a beautiful thing. It had been Frederick's mother's, and he had been delighted when she had consented to wear it. It had mattered little to her one way or the other, although she hadn't said that, of course.

The door to the bedroom opened and Ruth walked in, already resplendent in her pale lemon bridesmaid's dress with her brown curls arranged high on her head and threaded through with lemon ribbons. No one would guess, looking at her this day, that her sister had had tantrum after tantrum since the wedding had been announced, Polly thought as she looked into the young face smiling at her. Although their mother was behind Ruth's paddies, of course. Polly couldn't understand why Hilda had been quite so furious at the prospect of her elder daughter's marriage – especially when it was the means of installing her back in her old home with all the added little luxuries that entailed – but since the moment her mother had been told, the venom had flowed. Secretly, of course – there had never been a word breathed against the match in public – but Ruth didn't have the intelligence to hide what went on behind closed doors, and Polly had soon had a good idea of the bitterness and resentment her mother was feeling and, worse, feeding into her younger daughter.

'How's Grandda?' Polly asked softly. She had just sent Ruth to her grandparents' room to say she would be along shortly, once she was ready. Her grandfather had had one of his turns during the night and even talking was beyond him that morning.

'All right.' Ruth admired herself in the mirror, pirouetting round a few times to get the full effect of the billowing skirt. Wait till Cecil Longhurst saw her today! Cecil was the brother of Betsy's assistant in the kitchen – Emily, the kitchen maid – and as such, Ruth had decided, was far beneath her notice, but the tall, good-looking boy of sixteen was clearly smitten with her, and Ruth was enjoying every moment of her new-found power.

'You told him I'd pop in before we leave for the church?'

'Aye, I told him.' Ruth stopped her spinning and flicked the wedding dress from the back of the wardrobe door, fingering the beads sown on the V of the bodice as she said grudgingly, 'This is such a beautiful dress, Poll.'

Ruth had envied her a dress once before, and look how that had

176

ended. The thought was like a poisoned dart straight into Polly's heart, and it took her a full ten seconds to be able to say, 'Aye, it's lovely, but I'd have preferred to choose my own,' as she fought the chill of foreboding that had flickered down her spine.

Once Ruth had helped her to get ready, Polly stood for a moment staring at the fairy-tale figure reflected in the mirror. If things had gone according to plan it would be Michael she was going to meet at the altar today. Her heart jumped with pain at the thought and she put a hand to her breast, her face white. Of course, she wouldn't be dressed in all this finery; a simple white dress would have been all they would have been able to afford. She shut her eyes for a moment, hating the exquisite stranger in the mirror. *Michael, oh, Michael.* Where are you? Do you think of me? Do you feel it when I cry out to you? Please don't forget me, because I won't forget you. She tried to picture his face in her mind, but already the image was blurring, and that caused more pain.

'You feeling all right, Poll?'

She opened her eyes quickly, forcing a smile to bleached lips. 'Bit nervous, that's all,' she lied quietly. 'Let's go and see Grandda.'

Walter's eyes were waiting for his granddaughter, his precious bairn as he thought of her, and when the door opened and he saw her he thought his heart would break. Alice was sitting at the side of the bed, her hand grasping his resting on the coverlet, and as he felt his wife's fingers jerk and tighten he knew she was experiencing the same sense of bitter shame and guilt he felt. He was sick at heart that his bairn had sacrificed herself to save them, and whatever Alice said, however she tried to explain away this marriage to a man old enough to be Polly's father, that was what it amounted to. He had been a fool, a stubborn fool. He should have sold the farm years ago, when he would still have got a fair amount for it. Never mind it had been in his family for generations, or that town life would have slowly strangled him; what did that matter beside Polly having to do this to keep them out of the workhouse? First Michael and now this – how the lass was still standing, he didn't know.

'Hallo, Grandda.' Polly had pulled at her cheeks and bitten her lips before she had entered the room, trying to put a little colour into her chalk-white face, and now she forced a bright smile to her lips and a lilt into her voice as she walked across to the bed, the fine dress swishing and rustling as she moved. She had read what was in the old man's eyes – it had been the same thing that had been there for weeks but had never been spoken of – and all she wanted to do was to alleviate his despair. 'I wish you were coming to the church.' She included her grandmother in the words before turning again to the still figure in the bed, and now she took her grandfather's other hand and stroked the big gnarled knuckles gently, pausing on

177

the finger that had been broken years before and was now slightly twisted under.

'Remember when you saved me from the bull we'd hired to service the cows, Grandda?' Her voice was soft and she kept her eyes on the large hand between her own. 'You'd warned me and Ruth to stay with Gran in the house until the men came to collect him, but I wanted to see what he was like for myself and so I went into the paddock. When I started to scream you ran from the barn and got in front of me just as he charged, and he knocked you to the floor and trod on your hand. Everyone said it was a wonder he didn't kill you, but you couldn't use your hand properly for months and this finger never did heal right. You remember?'

She raised her eyes now and looked into her grandfather's, and the look which passed between them made the tears spurt from Alice's eyes.

'I cried and cried until I made myself sick because I was so sorry you had been hurt because of me, and you came up to my room later that night. You said . . . you said it didn't matter, that you loved me so much you'd tackle a hundred bulls and win if they dared to attack me because the important thing – all that mattered – was that we were still together at the end of the day. You wouldn't be able to bear it without me, you said.' Polly's spirit was shining out from her eyes now, everything in her wanting to absolve her grandfather from this agony of mind that was making him more ill. 'That's how I feel, Grandda,' she said quietly, 'about you and Gran. All that matters is that we are together, because I wouldn't be able to bear it if we weren't.' And now she called on all her strength to lie convincingly as she said, 'I want to marry Frederick, Grandda. I love farm life, you know I do, and with Michael gone I want to make a fresh start, but I couldn't bear it if you and Gran weren't with me. Please be happy for me.'

The tears were running down Walter's cheeks and into his whiskers now, and she rested her head against his for a moment, careless of her veil, before raising his hand to her lips and kissing the twisted finger. Then she stepped back from the bed. 'I'll come straight up to you and Gran once we're back, all right?'

'All right, me lass.' It was a slow, tortured whisper from labouring lungs, but the old man's face was more at peace than when Polly had come into the room, and as far as she was concerned it made what was to follow bearable.

They came out of the small parish church to a hail of rice, the sound of the bell-ringers working themselves into a frenzy, and shouted congratulations from what appeared to Polly's dazed mind to be hundreds of people.

The October day was a sunny one and unseasonably mild, but when Frederick took Polly's hand to help her up into the flower-bedecked horse and carriage, he found it to be icy.

She was married.

Polly glanced at the big, jolly figure seated next to her as they waved at everyone before the uniformed driver clicked to the horse. This was her husband. She was now Mrs Frederick Weatherburn, and Polly Farrow had gone forever. She continued to tell herself the same thing all the way back to Stone Farm as she endeavoured to take it in.

Once back at the farm Betsy – after offering her congratulations – took another look at her new mistress and said firmly, 'It's frozen you are. Come away in the house while the rest of 'em arrive an' have a sup, won't you. Everythin's ready in the barn, an' once everyone's seated you an' the master can go in an' we'll start servin'.'

'Aye, that's a good idea. You go and warm up, lass, and I'll just have a word with Croft about the beer barrel,' said Frederick heartily.

Polly looked at him. He had kissed her – once – in the church after the pronouncement that they were man and wife, and it had been neither pleasant nor unpleasant, merely a pressing of his lips against her closed ones. During the drive home he had rubbed her cold hands between his a few times and talked about who had been present at the ceremony and other such niceties, but he had made no attempt to kiss her again, for which she had been grateful. But later tonight . . .

She shivered convulsively, and Betsy said again, 'Come on, Miss Polly—' before stopping abruptly and giving a little giggle. 'Oh, I can't call you that no more, can I, miss!'

'Mrs Weatherburn is your mistress, Betsy, and must be addressed as such.' Frederick's voice was faintly reproving, although he was smiling.

Betsy's face lost its smile and she bobbed her head quickly. Always on his high horse about something, he was. 'I'll bring you a hot drink in the sitting room, ma'am,' she said flatly now.

Ma'am? Oh no, there was no way she could stand that, but over the last weeks Frederick had made it very plain he expected her to be aware of her position in his household. Nevertheless, 'ma'am' would drive her mad! Polly smiled into the plump face of the housekeeper as she said, 'I think I would like to be called missus, Betsy, as that's what I am now. Mistress or ma'am doesn't sit right.'

She knew Frederick disapproved; 'missus' was a title the farmers' wives on the smaller farms adopted, and he considered himself a cut above them, but she was determined on this. 'Missus' was warm, nice, besides which, Betsy and Emily and all Frederick's employees had shown her nothing but respect and kindness.

Betsy darted a quick glance at her employer. She had never known any other life but the one at Stone Farm, from when her mam had first found her a place as kitchen maid to the second Mrs Weatherburn. She'd been a little lass of eleven then, and within the year her mam and da had been taken with the fever and her two younger brothers had gone to live with relatives in North Shields and she had never heard from them again. She had watched the master grow up, and by the time the second Mrs Weatherburn and the master's father had died, she had been experienced enough to take on the role of housekeeper at the farm. She had done it willingly, but she had always known – deep inside – that she didn't like the master. He wasn't like his father had been, he was difficult to get on with and uppity. Aye, that was the word, uppity. But it didn't look as if the little mistress was going to follow suit.

Frederick swallowed heavily, and then said, in a hearty, jovial voice that covered his irritation, 'As you like, m'dear, as you like,' before turning away and striding off in the direction of the massive barn set next to two smaller ones.

The big barn had been transformed by the farm hands in the last few weeks. All the farm equipment and stores had been moved into the smaller ones until they were packed from floor to ceiling, and then the barn had been swept clean and the inside painted and rush matting placed on the floor. Four long trestle tables, set out in the form of cricket stumps, and numerous wooden benches had been brought in for the wedding feast, and the tables were now covered in clean, crisp white sheets and groaning with food and jugs of home-made wine. At the far end of the barn stood the huge beer barrel and a table of tankards waiting to be filled by Croft. Frederick had hired a party of fiddlers for the dancing later that evening – no expense spared, as he had said more than once in the last weeks until Polly, and everyone else if the truth be known, had become sick of the phrase.

A grand affair, that was what he wanted people to remember when they thought of this day – a grand affair, Frederick told himself as he let his eyes wander over the interior of the barn. Polly was a fine-looking little wench, and young, young enough for him to be envied by more than a few of his peers, but more importantly he now had old Walter's land. Once he finalised a deal with Nicholson, he'd be sitting pretty. Oh, aye, sitting pretty, right enough. But he deserved it, he'd been patient for years. He sucked the air through his teeth in satisfaction, his chest puffing out and his eyes narrowing.

Voices and laughter told him the first of the guests who had followed from the church had arrived, and he glanced round his surroundings once more – his mind calculating the cost of what he saw – before he swayed once or twice on the heels of his fine leather boots and then turned to greet them.

*   *   *

180

Everyone had been dancing for three hours or more since the tables had been carried out; just one, holding the remnants of the food, remaining at the side of the barn. The fiddlers were in fine form and so were most of the guests, courtesy of the home-made wine and beer, not to mention the bottles of whisky Frederick had had brought out once the meal was over.

Polly had had the first dance with her new husband, as tradition demanded, but since then she had barely seen Frederick as he had chatted to first one, then another, then another of his more influential and prosperous guests. She had lost count of how many times she had been whirled about the dance floor and by whom, but now, as she sat on one of the forms next to the table with the last of the food, two things stood out from the dizzy confusion of the day. The first was that her mother and Arnold had seemed to have a lot to say to each other as they'd sat in a corner of the barn, Arnold with his injured leg resting on an upturned bucket; and the second was the expression etched on Luke's face when he had danced with her earlier. She couldn't get his face out of her mind. It had made her want to tell him everything, to gabble it all out and – ridiculously – ask him for absolution – and to combat the feeling she had been very stiff and proper, which wasn't at all as she'd felt inside.

'It's a grand do, Miss Pol— I mean, missus.' Betsy had sidled to her side in a break from the dancing as the fiddlers downed yet another tankard of ale. Frederick had conceded that his workers and their families, along with Betsy and Emily, could join the jollifications once the food had been cleared away, mainly because Polly had insisted on it. She had been amazed a few days before when she had discovered, through something Betsy had inadvertently let slip, that an invitation hadn't been proffered to the farm hands and indoor staff.

'Aye, yes, it is.' Polly smiled at the plump little woman.

'The master'll be pleased.'

'Yes, he will.'

Betsy was bending slightly towards her, her face level with Polly's and her eyes bright, and as they exchanged a look in perfect understanding, Polly was suddenly aware she could have a friend in this bustling little housekeeper if she wanted it. And she did. She did want a friend.

'Thank you for all you've done to make the day so successful,' Polly said quietly. 'You haven't had a minute to yourself lately.'

'Oh, it's all in a day's work.' Betsy smiled warmly at her as she rose from the bench. 'I'll just be away to look in on your grandda an' granny. It's bin an hour or two since you went last, hasn't it?'

Polly nodded. 'But I'll go, Betsy, I'd like to.' She had asked Ruth to pop over to the farmhouse twice in the last hour, but her sister was too busy flirting with Cecil Longhurst – or perhaps teasing him would be a better description, Polly thought wryly. The poor lad didn't know if he was on foot or horseback with the little minx. But she did want to escape the noise and merriment for a few minutes; her head was pounding fit to burst and the comments flying around were becoming increasingly ribald – and all concerning the wedding night.

'I'll come with you,' said Betsy as the fiddlers began another spirited polka. 'There's one or two here who've imbibed a bit too freely an' they're not too particular where they put their hands. Mr Shelton, him that runs the public house in East Herrington, he'll get it when his lady wife gets him home. She's sittin' there with a face like a smacked backside.'

Polly glanced across at the woman in question and saw Betsy's description was more than a little accurate. It was as she was turning away that her gaze became arrested by a pair of eyes across the room. In the split second before Arnold's lids came down and hid the malevolent blackness, Polly felt the full force of his hatred, the shock of it causing her stomach to turn over. She stared at him, unable to believe she had seen what she had, but his gaze was on the dancers now and he didn't meet her eyes as she rose slowly to her feet before following Betsy out of the barn.

Arnold knew the second Polly left. He had been aware of every movement, every glance, every slight turn of the head the white-bedecked figure had made all day.

The conniving little strumpet; wearing white and looking as though butter wouldn't melt in her mouth when she'd been at it for years with everyone but him. The festering nature of Arnold's thoughts, made all the more virulent by the long hours of sitting idle since the accident at the pit and his inability to visit a certain house in Monkwearmouth for physical relief, made him want to writhe. And her mam had said nothing to allay his suspicions when he'd talked to her; it was clear Hilda suspected her daughter was no better than she should be.

The black gaze swept the room again before alighting on Frederick. Look at him, self-satisfied, posturing little nowt. Arnold ground his teeth together as his nostrils flared. Frederick hadn't said a word to him all day, or Luke for that matter, but he'd been buzzing round all his fancy friends like a bluebottle round dung. Well, perhaps it was time to take that smile off his fat face. Aye, aye, he'd give Frederick Weatherburn something to chew on all right.

Arnold rose to his feet, and as he began to hobble in Frederick's direction, Frederick noticed him out of the corner of his eye and silently groaned. He'd been putting this off all day, talking to Eva's stepsons; he still didn't see why Polly had been so adamant they had to have an invitation. When all was said and done they were no relation at all to the Farrows, being the sons of Nathaniel's first wife. And

182

miners! Ignorant, quarrelsome agitators, that was what most miners were, but then they did know the truth about Polly's aunt and father, so maybe it was prudent to keep them sweet.

'Arnold, lad.' As the other man reached his side, Frederick's voice was genial. 'How's the leg now?'

Lad? The patronising swine. 'So-so, Frederick. So-so.'

'It'll be a long job, I understand? Still, you can't rush these things, not if you don't want trouble.' Even as he was speaking, Frederick's eyes were roaming the crowd to make sure any leading lights in the assembly had their glasses filled.

And then Arnold brought the older man's eyes very definitely on to him when he said, his voice low but clear, 'You've done a decent thing in taking her on, man. There's not many that would have, not when they're well set up like you are.'

'What?'

'Polly.' Arnold's voice expressed a combination of commendation and sympathy. 'Still, I'm sure you can turn her round, and most lasses settle down when they're wed, so I'm told.'

'Turn her round?' Frederick glanced over his shoulder and then took Arnold's arm, manhandling him over to a quiet corner away from the dancers as he said again, 'What are you on about, turn her round?'

Arnold's eyes opened wide for a second and then he forced an uneasy laugh as he said, 'I thought you knew. Are you telling me you didn't know?'

'Know *what*?' Frederick hissed.

'About Polly.'

'*Arnold.*'

'Look, I'm sure half of it isn't true, and most girls can be free with their favours when they're young and pretty like she is. It doesn't mean anything, and when all's said and done you're the one she's marrying, aren't you?'

'Are you trying to tell me she's been—' Frederick stopped abruptly. 'That she has had liaisons?' he finished tightly, his face turkey-red now.

'Look, man, I shouldn't have said anything.' Arnold's tone had changed subtly and now held commiseration at its root. 'Forget it.'

'I don't believe a word you're saying.'

He believed it all right, it was there in the bulging veins in his forehead and the hunted look in his eyes. 'Aye, I've got it all wrong,' Arnold said soothingly, reflecting that nothing had given him so much pleasure for years. 'Forget I said anything, man, and enjoy your wedding day.'

Frederick stared hard into Arnold's face before turning and once more looking about him, and then he said, his voice rapid and his tone low, 'Who? Who's she supposed to have gone with?'

183

You for a start. Arnold kept his eyes steady and his face expressing nothing but faint embarrassment. And clearly she fooled you that you were the first. But they could do that, some women. How many times had the whores in Monkwearmouth acted a part for him when he'd asked for it, making themselves tight and pretending they were as pure as the driven snow? But at least they were doing it knowing what they were, whereas that one . . . His eyes flickered. Thought she was Lady Bountiful now, did Polly. Michael had been the first, he'd swear that on oath. All those evenings when the little half-nowt was supposed to be studying his blasted birds! Aye, she'd had a bit of fun with Michael all right, but all the time she'd got her sights set on Frederick and an easy life. He dared bet that farce of an engagement announcement had been to bring Frederick up to scratch, and as things had worked out it'd all fallen neatly into her lap. Had she known about Eva and her da? He wouldn't put anything past her.

Arnold worked his lips in and out for a moment or two, his head hung in apparent disconcertedness. 'Like I said, I shouldn't have mentioned it,' he mumbled at last. 'It's none of my business. Get yourself another drink and have a good time. This is your day, man.'

In the next couple of hours before the guests began to depart in their various conveyances, from carriages and traps to horse and carts – some, like Arnold and Luke, having arranged for horse-drawn cabs from the town to call at a predetermined time – Frederick had more than one drink. In fact the general consensus of opinion among the male guests as most of them staggered to their appropriate mode of transport seemed to be that the new bride was going to have a pretty disappointing wedding night.

Luke and Arnold were among the first to leave – Luke was paying Elsie Appleby by the hour to sit with Eva. It was left to Polly to bid them farewell, Frederick having all but passed out as he sat in a morose drunken stupor with half a bottle of whisky in front of him. Polly couldn't understand what had happened since she had returned from seeing her grandparents. Frederick had been merry when she had left and definitely well-oiled, but on returning to the barn she had found him pouring tot after tot of whisky down his throat, and had been able to get no more than a grunt out of him. She had never seen him intoxicated before, and the change from the affable, somewhat pretentious figure he liked to cut was frightening.

'I'd get Croft to get him up to bed.' Arnold nodded at the slumped figure as he spoke, and his voice was full of scornful laughter. 'Enjoyed his wedding a sight too much by the look of it.'

He hadn't met Polly's eyes since the incident in the barn earlier, and he still didn't look fully at he until the tone of her voice saying, 'I think he is entitled to,' brought the black orbs up to meet violet-blue.

'Oh, aye?' He kept the smile on his face with some effort as he surveyed her coolly uplifted chin and haughty gaze. By, she had it coming, this one. 'Let's hope a touch of brewer's droop don't make you regret saying that.'

'That's enough of that talk.' Luke's voice was thin and cold.

'It's a wedding, man!'

'I know what it is.'

'For crying out loud.' Arnold almost lost sight of the part he was playing, and then he forced his voice back into jocular mode as he made a helpless gesture with his shoulders and said to Polly, 'If you can't have a bit of funnin' at a wedding then when can you?' continuing before she could make any retort, 'Good night, then, lass, and pass on me best wishes to your husband when he's able to receive them. He looks like he'll need 'em before the night's finished.'

'Possibly, but then when Frederick is sober he'll revert to being the nice, kind man he always is, whereas you will still be you,' Polly said so quietly and sweetly that for a moment Arnold didn't take in what she meant.

'Think you're clever, don't you?' His face had darkened and he would have said more but for Luke's hand giving him a push that nearly sent him on to his back.

'Get out of it, man.' Luke's voice was a growl now. 'Like you said a minute ago, this is a wedding and she's the bride; show a little respect.'

'Respect? Huh.' Arnold stared at them both for a moment, and the black light she had seen emanating from his eyes earlier was stronger than ever, but this time Polly didn't allow herself to show the shock and fear she was feeling, but glared back, her eyes narrowed and her mouth tight.

'I'm sorry, Polly.' As Arnold swung round and hobbled out of the barn Luke's voice was low. 'Sometimes I think he's not all there the way he behaves, and he gets worse as he gets older.'

'I can't believe he's the same lad we used to play with when we were little,' Polly said with a slight tremble in her voice. 'He's changed so much.'

Changed? Luke looked down into the delicate face swathed with clouds of white chiffon, the beauty of which had been a torment all day. Arnold hadn't changed. He was still the same cruel so-an'-so who had enjoyed pulling the wings off dragonflies when they were small lads, and had set mouse traps in the cellar that he'd engineered to make sure the rodents weren't killed cleanly but died in agony. There was something missing in their Arnold – call it conscience, a soul, whatever – and the only difference between when they were lads and now was that his brother was more dangerous. He should have left him in that mine. That was what he should have done. It

185

wasn't the first time the thought had occurred to him, and it made his voice abrupt as he said, 'We're none of us little any more, Polly. Those days have gone and we can't get them back.'

'No . . .' There was a note in his voice that brought an ache to her heart, and she wanted to press her hand against her chest to combat the pain. Their eyes caught and held, and as the moment lengthened Polly found it difficult to breathe. More to break the quivering silence than anything else she found herself saying, 'Have you heard anything from Michael? Has he been in touch?'

Michael. Always Michael. How could she have married Frederick feeling as she did? By, he didn't understand women, he didn't straight. They were a breed apart. There was Katy wanting to devour him alive every night, and Polly as cool as a cucumber asking after another man on her wedding night. Luke shook his head, not trusting himself to speak as pain and resentment and anger and a hundred and one other emotions flooded his chest. It didn't help to recognise that part of the feeling that was twisting his guts – a big part – was jealousy, jealousy that she was marrying Frederick instead of him, which took him down to Arnold's level when you thought about it.

'Good night, Polly.' He leaned forward, brushing her cheek with his lips, and left in the same manner as on his previous visit to the farm – when he had asked her if she was doing the right thing in marrying Frederick – without looking back.

It was much later in the night, and Polly was lying stiff and still in her marital bed, Frederick's snores shaking the thick flock mattress and causing the floorboards to creak in gentle protest. She was hurting; all over it seemed, but especially in the juncture between her legs where an hour previously Frederick had forced his way into her body.

Her eyes strained wide in the darkness but they were sand-paper dry, the shock of Frederick's brutal consummation numbing her normal responses for the moment. This thing that she knew happened between married couples, that her granny had told her about vaguely just once, the night she had started her monthly cycles, hadn't been at all like she had expected. Or perhaps it had been Frederick who hadn't been as she had expected him to be.

When they had come upstairs after the very last guest had departed – which had seemed like an age after Luke had gone – Frederick had been stumbling and falling over, and she had thought his muttered curses and incoherent ramblings had been a result of too much drink. Perhaps they had been, she didn't know, but if every night of their marriage saw a repeat of what had happened tonight she wouldn't be able to bear it. She wouldn't.

He had fallen on the bed and seemed to go to sleep, and she, unsure and nervous of what to do, had left him there while she had struggled with the intricate fastenings of the wedding dress before completing her toilet and slipping into her new satin nightdress with lace cuffs and collar. She had plaited her hair into one coil down her back, and when she had crept under the covers Frederick had still been snoring loudly, much as he was doing now. But then he had begun to stir, and she'd been aware of him rubbing himself over and over.

She shut her eyes now, her legs instinctively coming tightly together and her body shuddering. There had been no talking, no kissing or cuddling or anything to lead up to what had followed. He had simply fumbled with his clothes and rolled on top of her, cursing again when her nightie hadn't allowed him immediate access. She had felt all the breath squashed out of her body with the weight of him, and when his knee had prised her thighs apart she hadn't been able to resist, the fumes from his whisky breath causing her to shut her eyes tightly. And then he had torn into her, that was what it had felt like, as the huge rod between his legs had driven seemingly into the core of her, pinning her to the bed and causing her to scream and struggle. But he'd just kept pounding into her until something warm and sticky had spilled out and Frederick had given a long, hoarse groan of satisfaction.

And then she'd felt the merciful release of that thing from her bruised flesh, and he had rolled away from her, muttering disjointed words, among which her name featured. Then he had immediately gone to sleep. Fully clothed, and still undone and gross in the flickering light from the oil lamp, he had lain there on top of the rumpled covers and slept like a baby.

When the spasms in her legs and belly had died down a little, she'd slipped off the bed and gone through to the dressing room, cleaning herself up as best she could in the near darkness with the bowl of water, soap and towel that was kept in there. Then she had come back into the bedroom and blown out the lamp before sliding under the covers as far away from Frederick as she could.

Why couldn't she cry? Polly blinked her eyes in the darkness. She didn't understand why she couldn't cry, but it was as if a giant hand was squeezing the place where the tears were and preventing them from bursting through.

This, then, was marriage. Frederick gave a particularly loud snore, then coughed and spluttered before the steady monologue continued again, and it was only then Polly realised she had tensed so much her fingernails were biting into the palms of her hands.

What had she done? *Oh, what had she done?*

Part 3 – The Marriage
1911

Chapter Fifteen

'You spoil them cats an' the crafty things know it an' all.'

'Aye, maybe.' Polly had just taken a bright red cinder out of the fire in the kitchen range, and now she dropped it into the thick earthenware bowl full of milk at her feet, where it sizzled briefly. 'But they like their milk warm.' As though on cue, the three purring felines grouped round the bowl bent their heads as though they were connected by a wire, and three small pink tongues licked daintily at the creamy liquid in front of them.

'Well, they're good mousers, I'll say that for 'em.' Betsy's voice was indulgent and her face smiling as she met the eyes of the tall, beautiful woman in front of her. She was just as guilty as her mistress of treating the farm cats as pets rather than the working animals Frederick insisted they were, and both women knew it. The two large tabbies and the white-footed black cat weren't supposed to set foot – or paw – in the farmhouse, but it was one of the many areas in her relationship with her husband where Polly followed her own star.

Their marriage – if the state of semi-hostility they existed in much of the time could be termed such – had never really recovered from the disastrous wedding night, or Frederick's self-justification the following morning when he had blamed his brutality on the whisky whilst mentioning some rumours he had heard as to her morality.

Polly had been deeply hurt and then furiously angry, the more so when Frederick had repeated what had been said. 'But that's just innuendo,' she'd said sharply. 'Surely you had the sense to see that? You should have asked me about it. And Arnold of all people isn't to be trusted. How *could* you believe him, Frederick?'

It hadn't helped the situation in the weeks ahead when Polly had discovered her husband had to prime himself with alcohol each time he pursued his quest for a son and heir. This action had created deep humiliation in Polly at first. Although she did not desire any physical contact with Frederick, the fact that he had to fortify himself before the act of copulation could take place made her ask herself if she was at fault in some way. He was a good, kind man, wasn't he? A man who had always helped her family, who was gentle and considerate. True, he might have rigid views on some subjects, but then everyone had their own way of looking at things. She must have failed in some way.

191

It was towards the end of their first thirteen months of marriage that Frederick's way of looking at one particular thing opened Polly's eyes to the fact that she had never really known the true nature of the man she had married so innocently, and a rift opened between them that was never to be healed.

Since their arrival at Stone Farm the summer before, her grandmother had taken to spending most of her time in the spacious room in which her husband was bedridden, and Polly's mother had continued to keep to her bed most days. However, in the evening, all of the family, apart from Walter, tended to gather in the sitting room, where Frederick would often read aloud to them from his newspaper or one of the books from the library, or they would listen to the gramophone he had bought two years before the wedding.

Polly hated the evenings. Apart from the strain of having to pretend all was well between herself and Frederick – as much for her grandmother's sake as anything else, as she didn't want either her or her grandda upset – she was forced to listen to Frederick pontificating about this, that and the other at length, with Ruth and her mother hanging on his every word. Furthermore, she knew the arrival of five more people into the farmhouse had created a great deal more work for Betsy and Emily, and she had made it clear very early on that she would do more than merely supervising menus and such, and that she expected Ruth to do the same. This had not gone down well with Ruth, who had had visions of seeing herself play the gracious lady, and when she had gone crying to Hilda, and Hilda had intervened on her younger daughter's behalf with Frederick, Polly had been furious. Frederick had been diplomatic – less to save either side's feelings than because he realised he would have to pay for more house staff if his wife and her sister weren't prepared to lend a hand – and the end result had been an agreement that whilst Polly and Ruth would work during the day, their evenings would be free for social intercourse and 'bettering themselves'. This meant Betsy and Emily were often on their feet until gone ten o'clock when four pairs of hands could have finished the chores before eight.

It was during one of these evenings in the November of 1907 that Polly, who had been listening – along with the others – to Frederick's views on the strikes that were sparking off all over the country, found herself arguing with her husband. 'I don't see why all the strikes are wrong,' she'd said quietly in response to a sweeping statement from Frederick. 'And just the amount of them, from the cotton mill workers to tram drivers, must mean there's a certain amount of justification in their claims.'

'Nonsense.' Frederick had adopted the patronising tone he used at such times as he stared into the lovely face of his wife. Her beauty held no pleasure for him these days; he had realised within weeks of his marriage that Polly wasn't going to be as malleable as he had hoped, and to add insult to injury – in Frederick's eyes – she frequently used her knowledge of current affairs and literature to argue against him. Considering it had been he, Frederick told himself, who had awakened her intelligence and taken it upon himself to educate her out of her beginnings, she should be more grateful and keep quiet. Polly was so different from Hilda; his stepsister held him in great esteem and moreover understood him. 'The working class is rife with agitators and you know it.'

'I beg your pardon, but I know nothing of the kind.'

'Then you are purposely ignoring the facts,' Frederick had snapped tightly. 'Just like those disgraceful women who shouted Asquith down last week.'

'They weren't disgraceful,' Polly shot back just as quickly, 'and again, in my opinion, they are perfectly justified. The bitter clashes between the suffragettes and mounted police in February could have been averted if the government had just *listened* to what the Pankhursts were saying. It was only the next month that women in Finland won seats in the Finnish parliament the year after they got the vote, and it wasn't just the female sex that voted them in either. What sort of message do you think it sent to women all over the country when Keir Hardie's Women's Enfranchisement Bill was defeated in the Commons in March?'

'I don't care what message it sent.'

'Exactly! And that's why we have the sort of scenes that erupted in Nuneaton last week, but shouting insults and chanting slogans didn't justify the harsh physical treatment the women received at the hands of the stewards. Even most of the men present objected to that.'

'I am not discussing the militant attitude of a certain type of woman as though it bears credible examination.'

'You were the one who brought the suffragettes into the equation,' Polly had reminded the cold-eyed man in front of her sharply.

'That's enough, Polly.' How dare she, how *dare* she display such an attitude in front of the others like this? Frederick asked himself bitterly, the ever-present inadequacy in his sexual prowess which his marriage had forced him to recognise colouring his thinking and making it imperative he was seen to be given due authority by his wife. She was a young, ignorant girl, not only of politics but of life in general beyond the narrow confines of Sunderland. 'Emmeline Pankhurst and all her kind should have been drowned at birth. She is a lure to silly, gullible women to get involved in things of which they have no concept, and all this talk of hunger strikes and marches and such should be an affront to the delicacy of any respectable woman. Women's minds are not capable of understanding important state issues and so on, they simply weren't made that way.'

193

'I don't believe that. People are capable of anything they aspire to, be they men or women, it's just that most women are not given the chance to prove themselves.'

'That is idealistic clap-trap,' said Frederick coldly, 'and evidence of your youth and immaturity.'

'I am young, yes.' Polly had been very aware of her mother and Ruth staring at them, and her grandmother's bent head as the old woman plucked at the shawl covering her knees, but both Frederick's tone and his scornful face had caught her on the raw. For months now she had striven to make this marriage work – putting up with his boorish behaviour in bed and out of it, turning a blind eye to his ridiculous indulgences where her mother and sister were concerned, and the fact that the three of them seemed set against her at every turn was just the tip of the iceberg. This wasn't the first time he had ridden rough-shod over her and attempted to make her look foolish in front of her family, and even his friends on occasion, but young as she was – and aye, aye, maybe immature too – she had a mind of her own and she intended to use it. 'But times are changing, Frederick, and you know it at heart. The vote *will* come for women and I, for one, will welcome the opportunity to make up my own mind about who I want to see in Parliament. As present things stand, it'll likely be a Labour man, like the candidate who won the Jarrow by-election from the Liberals.'

Polly had stopped then. Frederick's face had flushed to a deep red – the subject was still a very sore one with him – and his voice had been a loud bark as he'd shouted, 'Never! I'd rather see you dead first. No wife of mine would disgrace me in such a way.'

'Please, please.' Alice was attempting to pour oil on troubled waters. 'It'll probably never happen anyway.'

'It will happen, Gran.' Polly's voice had been stiff and unyielding. 'The ball is rolling faster and faster, like the one asking for pensions for the elderly, and a stop to women working eighty- and ninety-hour weeks in the factories and mills, and families being so destitute that the bairns are barefoot in winter and even the bread knife is in the pawn. Things like that aren't *right*.'

She had glared at them all before she had risen abruptly and walked from the room, ignoring Frederick's 'Come back here, woman, I'm not having this!' He had followed her, his face thunderous, and once in the hall had caught at her arm so angrily she had winced with pain.

'Take your hands off me.'

'Don't you take that tack!'

'I said, take your hands off me.' Her voice had been soft and low but of a quality that had seemed to nonplus him, because he had let his hand drop to his side. 'Two things, Frederick,' Polly had said quietly. 'One, I have my own mind and I intend to use it, and not you or anyone else will tell me different. Two, as you have reminded me constantly over the last months, I am your wife, but that cuts both ways. I expect respect and consideration just as much as you expect it from me. I won't be treated as a doormat or an imbecile when your friends are here or at any time, I just won't. And don't keep calling me young all the time. I'm not young, not here in my head' – she had tapped the side of her skull with a pointed finger – 'and that's partly because of the last thirteen months. Do I make myself clear?' she'd asked with naked bitterness.

Frederick had stared at her, his full lips slightly apart and his eyes narrowed. He was totally taken aback. This was not the reasonable young girl he had proposed to, who had promised him she would try to love him and be a good wife. Neither was it the strained but efficient spouse of daylight hours or the tense young lass who shared his bed each night. Over the last thirteen months a development had been taking place, he'd realised suddenly, and he'd only been aware of it in part. But now Polly's antipathy was glaring out of her eyes, and it was the emotion of a woman, not the slip of the girl he'd married, however much her slender outward appearance gave lie to the fact.

And when he had spluttered and blustered his leave of her – ostensibly to check on his red chestnut, which had had the misfortune to rip a flank that morning – they had both known a new stage of their marriage was beginning. But it was a marriage in which Polly would fight for equality, and there was no going back. And because she had seized equality, rather than having begged for it or coaxed and manoeuvred her way along, Frederick couldn't forgive her.

That had been four years ago.

Now had come the August of 1911 and with it riots that were rocking Britain. Since June, when King George V had been crowned 'King of the United Kingdom of Great Britain and Ireland and of the British Dominions beyond the seas, Defender of the Faith, Emperor of India', a heatwave had steadily been mounting alongside bitter discontent among Britain's workers. British ports had been paralysed by a shipping strike since the second week of June, and in Llanelli, in South Wales, in July nine people had been killed – three by soldiers' bullets – during furious rioting which occurred as a climax to the railway strike which was bringing Britain to its knees. Now it was the middle of August, and fifty thousand troops were on duty as the nationwide strike by stevedores, railwaymen, carters, miners and others caused huge problems for the police, with over two hundred thousand angry workers taking to the streets daily.

Keir Hardie's advice to the strike's leaders – 'The masters show you no mercy. They starve you, they sweat you, they oppress you. Pay them back in their own coin' – had caused fury in Parliament, and few were surprised when the Home Secretary, Winston Churchill, dug his heels in and took an even tougher line against the strikers, saying they were endangering the country's industrial wealth and other men's jobs.

However, the women of Britain's working class were battling with an even more relentless enemy than the government. With temperatures soaring to record-breaking levels, the death rates in the overcrowded tenements in all the big cities were at a new high, with children at most risk. Two and a half thousand children had died in the heatwave in the capital alone, and in Sunderland – especially in the East End, which was a rabbit warren of wretchedness, filth and poverty with unimaginable depths of squalor – there was scarcely a family untouched by the grim reaper. Cholera and typhoid were rearing their ugly heads and causing the overworked medical fraternity to despair, and with the city living on its food reserves and the prices in the shops soaring, some strikers' families were slowly starving.

It was with this last fact in mind that Polly now turned to Emily, who was busy peeling taties in a bowl on the kitchen table, and said, 'Is your mam going to her sister's this afternoon, Emily?'

'Aye, aye, she is, missus.'

'I've got a few things for her.' Polly pointed to a sack beside the door. 'Take them across before she goes, and tell her' – here Polly's blue eyes flashed to Betsy's for a moment – 'tell her to see Croft about your uncle and his lads helping with the harvest next week. The pay won't be much, but it'll be something.'

'Oh, ta, thanks, missus.' Emily's plain little face lit up. Her mam and da were worried sick about her mam's sister and their family, she knew they were. Her uncle and his two eldest lads had been out on strike for ten weeks now, and with the remaining six bairns all being under eleven years old, things were dire. Her mam and da had done what they could, but it was the missus's sacks that had kept her aunt's family going the last month. 'I'll take it across now and tell her, shall I, while the master's riding?'

'Aye, you do that, Emily,' said Polly quietly. Emily was just as aware as Betsy that the matter of the sacks was a sore point between the master and missus, along with other help Polly insisted on giving to the Silksworth strikers. The roof had nearly gone off the farmhouse a couple of times lately.

'How did you get him to agree to having Emily's uncle and the lads for the harvest?' Betsy asked immediately the door had closed behind the kitchen maid, her tone saying quite clearly that wonders never ceased.

'I didn't.' Polly grinned and shrugged her shoulders as she glanced round the huge kitchen, which held all a kitchen should hold. She brushed her hand down the side of one gleaming copper pan that was hanging with its companions on a row of wooden pegs at one side of the black-leaded range. 'But May is beside herself with worry about her sister and the bairns. They're starving, literally starving, so what could I say when she came to see me on the quiet?'

'Oh, lass, lass.' Any formality between the two women had long since been dropped when they were alone, although Betsy was always careful to give Polly her title of missus if Emily or one of the family was present. 'He'll go stark staring barmy if he cottons on.'

'Croft's the one who sets on any casual labourers for the harvest, and I've already seen him. He won't let on.'

Betsy nodded. No, Croft wouldn't say a word. Did the master know how his young wife was regarded among both the inside and outside workers and their families? Likely not. He only saw what he wanted to see, Frederick Weatherburn, and it didn't suit him to acknowledge that although he might have his employees' loyalty up to a point, it was his wife who had their hearts. People weren't daft, and they recognised that the missus went the extra mile – as in the matter of the food sacks for Emily's auntie. Mind, there was one who was constantly pushing Polly's good nature to the limit . . .

Betsy's hands stilled on the butcher's block where she was boning a breast of lamb from the cold meat store at the side of the scullery, and her voice was low when she said, 'What are you goin' to do about Ruth, lass? He was here agen last night an' she's expectin' him to ask Frederick soon, accordin' to what Emily told me on the quiet. She was clearin' out the fire in your mam's bedroom an' she heard the pair of 'em talkin'. They've got it all worked out. He's goin' to come here, that's in their minds, as a manager or somethin' similar.'

'They're mad.' Polly's voice was harsh. 'Frederick would never allow it.'

'Maybe.' Betsy pressed her lips together and narrowed her eyes for a moment before she said, 'But he's wheedled his way in, lass, don't forget that. Who would've thought he'd win your mam over with his blatherin' but he's got her eatin' out of the palm of his hand with his butterin' up an' little presents an' such. An' he's played it crafty with the master an' all. Pretendin' to see everythin' his way now an' actin' as though the master's made him view things different. An' Ruth's forever presentin' his case.'

'She's only interested in him because there's no one else.' Polly's voice was emphatic. 'She can't really like him, not Arnold.'

'Aye, I reckon you're spot-on there, lass, but she's only herself to blame. Young Cecil was clean gone on her, used to disappear up his own backside every time Ruth made an appearance, but your sister wouldn't look the side he was on until it was too late an' he'd taken up with young Mary from East Herrington. I've heard Ruth talk to that lad as though he was muck under her boots, an' soft as clarts as he was about her, she pushed him too far. They're expectin' their first, Cecil an' Mary. Did Emily tell you?'

'Aye.' Polly nodded briefly. She found any talk of babies painful, knowing she was now unlikely to be a mother, with the existing state of affairs between herself and Frederick so dire, but this situation between Arnold and Ruth – ostensibly begun twelve months ago but in reality six months earlier, at Christmas time, when a smiling Arnold had visited the farm with an armful of gifts – was a cause of even greater concern.

Arnold was a hypocrite and a liar and that was the least of it. There was still something dark and menacing staring out of his eyes in the odd unguarded moment, but it seemed to Polly that she was the only member of her family to recognise it. Even her beloved grandfather, on the occasions when Arnold made a visit to his room and sat and talked with the frail old man, seemed pleased to see him and brighter for his company. She didn't understand how they could all be so blind. She wished she could talk to Luke about it. She had thought when he and Katy Chapman had parted company in the spring that Luke might visit the farm a little more, especially as Arnold was coming so often, but if anything, his visits were more infrequent.

A picture of the tall, dark miner came into her mind, and she dwelt on it for a second before pushing it aside sharply. Luke was the brother she had never had, she told herself for the hundredth time, as her heart began to beat a little faster. He looked on her as a sister and she on him as a brother, and that was fine. It was, it was fine and how things should be. She was a married woman and he had never expressed anything other than brotherly affection. They were worlds apart, and these feelings she had . . . She did not go on to explain to herself what the churning feelings embodied but instead turned quickly and walked across to the open kitchen window, leaning out for a moment as she looked up into the startlingly blue sky.

How long could she go on like this? she asked herself silently. In this marriage that wasn't a marriage? And the answer came as it always did – as long as you have to. Till death us do part. She had said that and meant it and that was the end of it. And Frederick had kept to his part of their unspoken agreement to some degree: he provided a roof over their heads and food on their plates for her family, and not grudgingly. No, he was kind to her grandparents and to her mother and Ruth; it was just his wife who saw that other side of him.

She sighed deeply, her eyes on a lark high above as it swooped and glided with the sun on its wings. He hated her, she knew he hated her. He looked at her sometimes as though he wished her dead.

'Not lettin' up, this heat, is it?' Betsy had joined her at the window and now her voice had a gurgle to it as she said, 'Makes folk do funny things when it's as hot as this. Croft told me' – and here the housekeeper's voice dropped even lower – 'he told me that old Parson Casey at Ryhope, him that's always preachin' damnation an' hellfire

198

an' the sins of the flesh, he went for a midnight dip down near Hole Rock as naked as the day he was born. Just unfortunate for the good parson that two of his parishioners were busy courtin' down there an' all. Croft said the parish was rockin' for a week at the picture of the parson in the altogether stumblin' across Biddy McBrodie an' Len from the public house sportin' in the moonlight. An' she's a big girl, Biddy. The parson would have got an eyeful all right.'

'Oh, Betsy.' Polly was shaking with laughter.

'An' accordin' to Croft – an' he got it from the horse's mouth so to speak, bein' on such friendly terms with Len since they were bairns – the parson leapt ten foot in the air an' gave a whinny like a mare before boltin' like the devil himself had stuck his pitchfork where he shouldn't. Croft said Len didn't know which'd given him the more pleasure, Biddy or the parson.'

Betsy's mirth was spilling over now and the two women leaned against each other for long moments before they drew apart, both of them wiping their streaming eyes with their aprons.

What would she do without Betsy? Polly looked into the dear face of this friend who had been tried and tested over the last five years and found to be rock solid. But thank God, aye, thank God indeed that she didn't have to do without her. 'I suppose I'd better go and have a word with Ruth,' said Polly as their smiles faded. 'She should be down here by now anyway, preparing the vegetables for Grandda's broth.'

Betsy nodded. The day Ruth came downstairs to the kitchen after paying her morning call to her mother without being called at least three times would be a miracle, she thought grimly. If ever there was a lazy upstart, that little madam was one. Thought she was the cat's whiskers and the tail an' all, Ruth did. Betsy never ceased to wonder how two sisters could be so different. 'Aye, all right, lass, an' tell her to bring down your mam's breakfast tray, would you? Once I'm finished here I'll be in the dairy; them creampots have been standin' for a week now, so they need churnin'.'

As Betsy bustled back to her work, Polly left the kitchen by the door which led into the passage adjoining the hall, and after mounting the polished wooden staircase, she stopped for a moment and glanced about her. This was a beautiful house, large and well furnished, but she had never felt mistress of it, not deep down. She had visited what remained of her old home a few weeks ago, and it had saddened her to see the ruin it had become. Frederick had decided there was no point in repairing the roof once the extent of the damage had been clear, and as he wanted the forty acres for pasture, the farmhouse had been left to decay. But at least Buttercup had companions in her old age. Polly smiled to herself as she thought of the cow who now – owing to a promise Frederick had made Polly before their marriage – lived in queenly comfort in lush pasture with a host of other bovines and old Bess and Patience.

Once on the wide landing with its deep stone windowsills and leaded windows, Polly walked along to her mother's room, which was between Ruth's and her grandparents'. She could hear voices from within but these stopped immediately she opened the door, and it was clear that the two occupants' conversation had not been for her ears. This was a regular occurrence when Ruth and her mother were together, and it had ceased to bother Polly years ago. Polly looked across to the wide double bed in which her mother was lying and on which Ruth was perched, and her face was expressionless as she said, 'Good morning, Mother.'

'I suppose you've come to take her downstairs.' Hilda's voice was sharp and querulous. 'She's not well, you know, she's had stomach ache this morning.'

'I'm not surprised, given the size of the breakfast she ate,' Polly said pleasantly. 'What was it, Ruth? A bowl of porridge followed by two eggs, sausages and bacon?'

Ruth wasn't fooled by the amiable tone and she slid off the bed after one peevish 'Huh.'

'Bring Mother's tray with you.'

'She's not a servant; let Betsy or that half-witted girl do it.'

'Betsy is busy in the dairy, and even if she wasn't I wouldn't bother her to come and fetch your tray, as you well know,' Polly said steadily, meeting the eyes of the thin-faced woman in the bed. 'And Emily is far from half-witted.'

'She doesn't say boo to a goose.'

'And if she was more outspoken, that would be wrong too.'

'Don't talk to me like that,' Hilda snapped testily. 'Ruth never does.'

Polly didn't bother to answer, merely indicating with a wave of her hand for Ruth – who was now holding her mother's breakfast tray – to precede her out of the room. The tenor of the exchange was the same every morning, it was only the detail which varied.

Once on the landing, with her mother's bedroom door closed, Polly said quietly, 'Just a moment, Ruth.'

'What now?' Ruth flounced round to face her sister, her face set in its perpetual scowl. 'It's not *my* fault if she keeps me in there half the morning.'

'It's not about that.' Polly stared at the young woman in front of her. Ruth was now eighteen years of age and was slightly above middle height. Her hair did not have the rich chestnut tint which Polly's had, but nevertheless the brown curls were thick and shiny and her skin was clear and finely textured. She could have been pretty – she *ought* to have been pretty – and certainly the blue muslin summer

200

dress she was wearing had been chosen with a view to flattering her somewhat voluptuous figure, but the ill-temper which had become a permanent feature dominated her face. 'I just wondered when Arnold is calling next?'

'Why?' It was immediate and aggressive.

'You know why.'

Ruth made no answer, but stood looking at Polly, her face set.

'He's not right for you, Ruth. You must see that. You deserve someone a hundred times better than Arnold.'

'He won't be a miner all his life.'

'I'm not talking about him being a miner,' Polly said sharply. 'There's nothing wrong with that, for goodness' sake. I'm talking about *him*, the man. The last time we had this conversation you promised me you'd think carefully about what you were doing.'

Ruth blinked rapidly, and as her eyes fell away from her sister's she said, 'I did, I have.'

'And?'

'It's all right for you. You're married, no one is going to label you a spinster,' Ruth said bitterly.

'You're eighteen years old, not thirty-eight or even twenty-eight! You've got the rest of your life in front of you.' Polly shook her head, her face softening as she said, 'You're a pretty lass, Ruth. Don't throw your life away on Arnold Blackett.'

Ruth looked at her quickly, and just for a brief moment Polly saw a glimpse of the little sister who had always run to her older sibling with her troubles before their mother had done her best to sour her daughters' relationship. 'But what if no one else asks for me, Polly?'

'They will. I promise you they will. And it would be worse to be married to the wrong man than not married at all.' Then, as Ruth's gaze honed in on her sister's face, Polly forced a bright note into her voice as she realised she might have given too much away. 'Why don't you come into town with me next time I go? You used to do that at one time and we had fun, didn't we, when we used to go to Binns cake shop and restaurant or to Grimshaw's Elephant Tea House?'

'Aye, I know, but Arnold said—'

Ruth stopped abruptly, and as her sister's face turned scarlet Polly said, 'Yes? What did Arnold say?'

Ruth just stared at her, her eyes flickering and her mouth opening once before shutting again. Polly's voice changed tenor as she said again, 'Ruth? What did Arnold say?'

'I . . . I don't know.'

'*Ruth.*'

'He said I hadn't to say anything. He was trying to protect me, warn me in case I heard anything . . .'

201

Ruth's voice trailed away and now she gazed at her sister miserably as Polly said, 'You *will* tell me, Ruth, if we have to stand here all day, and I shall know if you're lying.'

'It's just that there's been some gossip about what happened that day when Da hang— When Da died,' Ruth stuttered. 'Michael leaving like he did, and you . . .'

'And me what?'

'You doing all right for yourself and marrying Frederick and all. Some people seemed to have put two and two together about Michael being our half-brother, and they think you were . . . well, carrying on with him, and then for you to marry your uncle . . .'

'He is not our uncle.' Polly's voice was flat and low. Ruth's words had seemed to freeze her blood. She understood, now, the sly looks and nudges that occurred occasionally in certain shops she frequented when she accompanied Frederick into town on market day. Shops Arnold knew she frequented. He had been saying things about her, wicked, disgusting things. She knew it.

'No, *I* know that,' Ruth agreed quickly, 'but you know what folk are like.'

Aye, she knew what folk were like all right – or one particular man at least. Polly stared at her sister, and then she said, her voice still flat and quiet, 'So that's why you stopped accompanying me into town? Because you were ashamed to be seen with me?'

'No, no.'

Yes, yes. And that was also why Mr and Mrs McCabe from the confectioner's in High Street West always made a point of serving her themselves – to show everyone they were for her. A little glow warmed the ice round Polly's heart. The McCabes had known her since the first time she had accompanied her father into town on market day, and he had treated her to a quarter of stickjaw and two ounces of rhubarb-and-custard sweets from the little shop, which was always redolent with the smell of winter mixtures and aniseed fudge. To this very day, Mrs McCabe continued to slip her a piece of Boy Blue liquorice nougat every time she left.

'You should have told me, Ruth.' And then Polly said, as Ruth continued to stand mute, 'You know Arnold was behind these supposed rumours, don't you? You see that?'

'That's exactly what he said you would say if I told you, which is why I didn't,' Ruth fired back suddenly. 'He knows you don't like him.'

'No, Ruth, I don't.'

'Well, I do!' All the defiance was back, the brief moment of softness gone. 'And you don't like it because he likes me rather than you, admit it. You can't bear for him not to be falling down at your feet. Well,

202

he told me how you tried to make up to him years ago and he wasn't having any of it.'

Polly stared at the red-faced girl in front of her in amazement. 'You can't believe that.'

'I do.' Ruth's chin was out and her eyes were narrowed. 'Well, Arnold is never going to want you because he is mine, do you hear? And he's going to ask me to marry him soon, so what do you think about that?'

Polly's eyes widened before growing darker, and she spoke with a startling crispness as she said, 'I think you would be making the worst mistake of your life, that's what I think, but if you are determined to throw your life away on a man who is a liar and a rogue, that is up to you.'

'He isn't! How dare you say that!'

'Because it is true, and if you weren't such a silly girl you would see if for yourself. He'll make you terribly unhappy, Ruth. He's not capable of anything else.'

'I hate you!'

As Ruth whirled round and made for the stairs, Polly stood looking after her, jumping slightly as her grandmother opened the door to the bedroom she shared with Walter and peered out. 'Trouble?' she asked softly. 'We couldn't help hearing, hinny.'

Polly looked at the old woman and nodded slowly. 'I told her what I think of Arnold. He's not right for her, Gran.'

'Oh, he's not such a bad lad when you get to know him. He's been right good to your grandda, now then. Give the lad a chance, hinny, eh? See how it goes.'

Oh, Arnold had played this so well, she had to give him that! He'd managed to get them all – except Betsy – eating out of the palm of his hand with his soft soap. 'He's dangerous, Gran,' Polly said quietly, 'and cunning with it. Ruth told me about some gossip that's been going around, and it could only be Arnold behind it.'

'Oh, lass, surely not.'

'It's about the day Da died, and – and other things.' She found she couldn't bring herself to repeat what Ruth had said.

'But we knew at the time that there'd be them that wouldn't swallow the tale of an accident,' Alice said softly, after glancing back into the room where Walter was asleep in the big feather bed. 'It doesn't mean Arnold's said anything. Folk jaw, lass, an' there was a fair bit happened in a short time five years ago. Be glad for her, hinny. It's what she wants.'

Was she mad, or was it the rest of the world? Polly asked herself silently. She remembered Arnold's eyes the night before when she had caught him looking at her – they had been black and hard and had bored into her for a second before he'd turned away. No, it wasn't her.

It wasn't. He was working on Ruth, and the end result would be that he would come and live here. She would not let that happen, even if she had to raise hell and fall out with every soul in the farmhouse in the process.

'I'll talk to you later, Gran.' Polly smiled at the old woman as she turned away, but her countenance wasn't so light as she walked down the stairs. Again she found her thoughts turning to the one person she felt would have a real understanding of what Arnold was up to. Perhaps Luke would come soon.

Chapter Sixteen

Luke did not come soon. In fact it was many weeks before he visited Stone Farm, and then it was with a message to say that Eva was very ill and not expected to last the week, and that she was asking for her mother.

It was Polly who answered the door to him one bitterly cold November day – the heat of the baking-hot summer England had both enjoyed and endured being nothing but a distant memory. The last two months had been difficult ones: Alice had been taken ill with acute bronchitis in the middle of September and it had been touch and go for a few weeks in spite of the twenty-four-hour care Polly had given her grandmother. Even now the old woman rarely left her bed and was a shadow of her former self, but since she had moved back into her old room – Ruth had slept with her mother for a few weeks while her grandmother was at her worst so Walter was disturbed as little as possible; Polly resting on a single pallet by the side of the bed – Alice's spirits were higher.

But the extensive nursing and lack of sleep had taken its toll, as Polly's pallor and the deep shadows under her lovely eyes indicated, and Luke's voice was concerned as he said, 'You look tired, lass. Have you been bad or something?'

'Didn't Arnold tell you?'

'Tell me what?'

Polly had stood aside for him to enter as she'd spoken, and now, as he turned to her in the hall, she said, 'Gran's been poorly – bronchitis.'

'No, Arnold didn't tell me,' Luke said flatly.

'She's much better now.' Polly opened the door to the sitting room, and as Luke followed her, the old feeling swept over him with renewed force. It was a palace of a place, this farm, and it had taken Polly as far out of his reach as the man in the moon. She was the wife of a gentleman farmer now; the knowledge twisted his bowels every time he came here, which was why he visited rarely. Oh, he was in no doubt Arnold bowed and scraped to Frederick every time he saw him, which was why his brother had his feet very firmly under the table, but Luke would rather cut his tongue out than do the same. He was a miner, and even if a good proportion of society – Frederick's sort of society, at least – thought he was the scum of the earth, he knew different. The men he worked with were worth twenty – a hundred – times the likes of Frederick Weatherburn.

'Have you heard from your father at all? Is he well?'

Luke brought his thoughts back from the road they were following, but his voice was still tinged with bitterness as he said, 'Aye, he is, although no thanks to the government. They gave him a medal in January and then tell him he's a traitor in July when he's on strike. Now where's the reason in that?'

Polly nodded. When Nathaniel had been involved in the terrible pit disaster at Hutton Colliery near Bolton, where he and Tess had settled, he had apparently been instrumental in rescuing the one sixteen-year-old lad who had survived. Three hundred and fifty men and boys had died in the explosion at the Lancashire pit, and messages of sympathy had flooded in from all round the world for the wives and loved ones of the dead, and the thousand bairns who had lost their fathers. Nathaniel hadn't wanted the silver medal he'd received, but he'd been told refusing it would be an insult to the memory of King Edward VII, who had created the silver and bronze medals for 'heroic miners who endanger their own lives in saving, or endeavouring to save, the lives of others from perils in mines or quarries'. And so he had taken it, reluctantly, but it had given him no pleasure. As he had said to Tess at the time, 'Medals come cheap, lass. I'd far rather see King George doin' somethin' about makin' the owners an' viewers pour some money into safety, but that's as likely as the Pope marryin'.'

'But he's happy?' Polly now asked softly. 'Him and Tess?'

'Aye, they're happy.' Luke smiled at her. Polly was the only person within the family who knew he was in contact with his da. 'They've set up as a married couple and no one knows different, but it looks as if they'll be able to make it legal within the week,' he added soberly.

As he explained the purpose of his call, Polly shook her head slowly. 'Gran can't come, Luke. It's impossible. She's far too ill.'

'Aye, aye, I understand, lass. Arnold didn't say anything, else I wouldn't have come.'

He wouldn't have come. Stupid, *stupid* for it to hurt so much. She searched her mind for something to say, but all she could think of was that he'd said he wouldn't have come.

Luke glanced down on the bowed head and slender shoulders. She was too thin. Beautiful still, even more beautiful, but then he thought that each time he saw her afresh, but now the loveliness had a fragility to it that spoke of exhaustion. And then, as Polly raised her head and said, 'What am I thinking of? You must have a hot drink after coming all this way. There's tea or coffee, or hot ginger if you'd prefer it?' he spoke the words he had promised himself time after time he would never say: 'Are you happy, Polly? With him, Frederick?'

Polly stared at him. How could he ask her a question like that after what he had just said? And then her conscience smote her. He had always looked on her as the little sister he'd never had, she knew that – it was natural he'd be concerned for her. She knew she was looking awful, but she'd only had cat-naps for the last few weeks, and even now she was back in Frederick's bedroom, she wasn't sleeping properly. In fact if anything she'd preferred the straw pallet at the side of her grandmother's bed to the big feather bed she shared with her husband. For three years now there had been a big bolster down the length of the bed, and when she had first placed it there, after a particularly humiliating episode with Frederick when he had blamed her for the fact that he had been unable to make love, she had slept better. But lately her mind had been occupied with the problem of Ruth and Arnold, and – not least – the rapidly failing health of her grandmother, and most days she was awake well before dawn.

'He has been very kind to Gran and Grandda, and my mother and Ruth too.' In fact Frederick and her mother were as thick as thieves.

'That wasn't what I asked.'

Don't do this, Luke. She stared at him mutely.

He would give anything to be free of this desire for her that was with him day and night. He had thought he could assuage it with Katy Chapman, but it had got in the end so the mere sight of the other woman had been a reproach. For months he'd tried to finish it with Katy, after he'd realised he just couldn't bite the bullet and ask the lass to marry him, but she'd played up and things had turned nasty. Three of her brothers had waylaid him up a back alley one night and he'd been off work a week, but at least that had been the end of it. By, he was a fool. He'd had it on a plate with Katy and they'd got on all right, so why, *why*, when push had turned to shove, hadn't he been able to make that final commitment? And then the voice of his mind said – as he looked into Polly's great violet-blue eyes – why ask the road you know? He needed to get away from Sunderland, right away, and if that doctor who had come to Eva last night was right, it wouldn't be long before his obligation to his stepmother was over.

'So?' His heart was pounding against his ribs at the nearness of her, and for the life of him he didn't know why he was persisting with this. 'Are you happy?'

'Yes.' It was short and abrupt, but what else could she say? Polly asked herself painfully. It would do no good to tell him how things really were, and even if she did, Luke could do or say nothing to help. This wasn't like when he had saved her from Arnold in the barn or pulled her out of the river. She had made her bed and she had to lie on it, and she wasn't going to whine or complain about it either. If she could go back five years she would still do exactly the same – even knowing what she now knew about Frederick – because the reason, those two dear old people lying upstairs, hadn't changed. And then, in a bid to change the subject, she said, 'This relationship between Arnold and Ruth, Luke, I don't like it. He's . . . odd, your brother.'

Luke had turned away when she'd first spoken, but now he faced her again, his voice flat as he said, 'He's worse than that, Polly, much worse, but Ruth's nowt but a bit lass. She'll tire of him.'

'I don't know.'

Right at this moment, the last thing he cared about was Arnold and Ruth. 'Look, I need to get back,' he said shortly, 'else I'll miss my shift. I'll explain how things are to Eva.'

'I'll come and see her.' She didn't want to but it was clear no one else would. 'Frederick has business in Bishopwearmouth tomorrow, so I'll ride in with him.'

Polly in Southwick Road? Luke glanced round the sitting room, at the roaring fire in the hearth and the shining furniture, and thought of the state of the house when he had left it that morning. His chin lifted and he said briefly, 'As you like.'

What was the matter with him? As Polly followed him to the front door she was biting her lip. He seemed irritable, angry even. But then Eva *was* his stepmother – the only mother he had ever known – and regardless of what she thought of her aunt, Luke had lived with Eva for as long as he could remember, and had been a better son than many a natural one would have been in similar circumstances. Arnold hadn't been able to move out of Southwick Road quick enough once his leg had healed after the accident at the pit five years ago. It must be horrible for Luke now, knowing Eva was going to die. She touched his arm as they reached the door, and as he turned to look at her she said, 'I'm sorry about Eva. I should have said that sooner.'

'It's all right.'

'And you never had that drink; are you sure you don't want one?' Polly was aware she was gabbling, but she didn't want him to go, and suddenly that was all she could think of. 'Betsy and I normally have a pot of tea about this time to warm us up before we go into the dairy. You could come through to the kitchen if you like.'

He looked at her for a moment, his good-looking, clean-shaven face straight. She could see a tiny cut where he had nicked himself shaving that morning, and for no reason that she could explain, Polly felt her insides begin to tremble. It had been months and months since she had seen him, and right until this second she hadn't realised how much his absence had mattered. 'Do you want me to or are you just being polite?' he asked quietly. 'You must have plenty to do.'

'Masses.' She smiled at him. 'But I'm not being polite. I wouldn't be polite with you.'

208

'Charming.' And he smiled back. 'In that case I'd love a cup of tea and a chat with Betsy.'

Betsy liked Luke as much as she disliked his brother, and when she looked up from her pastry-making, her hands thick with pig's fat and flour, her plump face lit up at the sight of him. Luke was soon ensconced at the kitchen table with a pint mug of tea and a plateful of singing hinnies, hot and fresh from the griddle and thick with butter. 'You get on the other side of them, lad,' she said fondly, bustling about like a mother hen with a lone chick. ''Bout time you called to see us, thought you'd forgotten the way.'

'I've been busy, Betsy,' said Luke through a mouthful of griddle cake.

'Oh, aye?' She glanced at Polly, who was sitting at the table quietly sipping her tea, as she said, 'Busy, he says!' and then, as her gaze returned to Luke, 'So what's kept you so busy you couldn't spare a couple of hours to see old friends? A lass, is it?'

'No, it's not a lass, Betsy.' Luke could feel himself colouring and he took a quick gulp of the hot tea before he said, 'Union business if you want to know, mixed in with a bit of leg-work and such for the Labour Party.'

'The Labour Party?' Betsy winked at Polly over Luke's head. 'By, the lad's into politics in a big way. We might have the next Keir Hardie sittin' in our kitchen, or I should say Ramsay MacDonald now.'

'I'd be proud to be linked with either of them, Betsy, and who knows what the future might hold,' Luke returned with a grin at the plump little housekeeper. 'No one guessed at the beginning of the century that the House of Lords would be forced to give up its claim that it was born to rule and accept the supremacy of the Commons, but it happened in August. Times are changing, and they can't change quick enough for me, I tell you.'

Polly leaned forward, her voice interested. 'Really, Luke? You'd really like to take your interest in politics further?'

She had beautiful eyes. He had never seen another lass with eyes like hers; they drew you, you felt you could swim in them. He blinked to break the spell as he said, in answer to Polly's question, 'There's nothing I'd like better, but it'd take money and influence, lass, and I'm a bit short of both.'

He had been smiling as he spoke, but Polly didn't return the smile and her voice was serious as she said, 'You can make it happen if you want, Keir Hardie did. You've always had a heart for the people and a natural grasp and interest in the unions and politics, and that's more important than anything. Times are only changing because people like you have made them change.'

They looked straight at each other, their gaze holding, as Betsy said from the stove, where she was turning a second batch of singing hinnies cooking on the griddle, 'You can take that as fact, lad; you don't get any butterin' up, not with Polly. Tells you what she thinks, this lass.' It said a lot for Betsy's acceptance of Luke that her manner with her mistress was so relaxed, but this changed in the next moment when the kitchen door opened and Frederick stood framed in the aperture.

Luke was aware of Polly stiffening, although she made no obvious movement. He rose to his feet, forcing his voice to be pleasant as he said, 'Frederick. How are you?' He watched the older man's eyes move from him to Polly and then back again.

'How am I? Same as always.' Frederick was staring at Luke now through narrowed lids. The way they had been looking at each other when he'd opened the door . . . But no, no, it was impossible. They hadn't seen hide nor hair of Luke for months and Polly rarely went into town. He'd have noticed before this if they were carrying on. Nevertheless, his lower jaw was thrust out as he said, 'And what brings you this way in the middle of a working morning? Not on strike again, are you?'

'Eva's dying and she wanted to see Gran.' It was Polly who spoke, and bluntly; her tone making it quite clear how she viewed her husband's rudeness. 'I said I'd call in tomorrow when you go to the bootmaker's.'

'What? Oh. Right, right.' Frederick's hair had begun to recede in the last five years, and now there were one or two strands at the front which stood up from his scalp like threads of wire. It gave him a faintly ridiculous air, and this was accentuated when he swayed once or twice on the heels of his boots and said ponderously, 'I trust my womenfolk are looking after you all right, lad, although the kitchen is no place for a guest.'

'Luke is not a guest. He's family.'

Family be blowed. There was no place in his family for agitators like Luke Blackett. He'd had some interesting chats with Arnold over the last months, and it was clear from what the man said that this brother had done all he could to lead the other into ruination. Because that was what the unions and such were all about. Out to ruin the country and create a state of anarchy. But Arnold had seen the light now; Frederick had set him straight all right. This one, though! Scum of the earth, Luke Blackett, and as arrogant as they came. The manly virility evident in the tall, dark miner was hitting Frederick on the raw, reminding him of his lack of prowess in the bed department and that it was due to his failure as a husband that he would be denied his son and heir. Perversely, he'd found he wanted a son all the more since he'd found he couldn't rise to fathering one.

'I've got to be going.' Luke spoke solely to Polly and she answered him in like, saying, 'I'll walk with you to the lane,' as she rose and reached for her shawl hanging on a wooden peg on the wall.

'Goodbye, Betsy.'

Betsy bobbed her head at Luke as she said, her voice quiet and subdued now, 'I'll give Emily your regards. She's over at the cottages with Croft's wife an' bairns, they've all got the skitters.'

'Goodbye, Frederick.'

Frederick was looking at his wife, and he brought his gaze to the younger man seemingly with some effort before he nodded stiffly. And his voice was stiff too as he said, 'Goodbye, Luke.'

He had guessed. Luke could feel the heat in his neck spreading to his face as he left the kitchen. Frederick had guessed how he felt about Polly; he had seen the realisation in the other man's eyes when he had first come into the kitchen. But what did it matter anyway? Polly was oblivious to it; whether by choice or because she genuinely didn't recognise how he felt, he wasn't sure, but the odds were the same. She was a married woman. Frederick's wife.

The air was cold enough to cut you in two as Luke opened the front door, and it made Polly, just behind him, pull her shawl more tightly round her shoulders. 'Don't come out, not in this.' As a gust of icy wind almost lifted Luke's cap, he turned to Polly. 'I'll perhaps see you tomorrow when you visit Eva.'

She stared at him, and then made herself ask the question that had been at the back of her mind since he had first stated the purpose of his visit. 'Is there any way that Michael could be traced and told about his mother? I feel he ought to know.'

Luke's expression didn't change and his voice was steady and flat as he said, 'That's been taken care of. Apparently Michael informed Dr Henderson as to his whereabouts some years ago with a request that in an emergency he be informed. I only found this out when Henderson called to see Eva yesterday.'

'And the doctor's told him?'

'So I understand.'

Polly's heart was thudding. So Michael was alive and well, although she had always known that deep inside. She would have felt it if it was otherwise, she knew she would. How would she feel if she saw him again? And then she checked herself instantly. The chances of that were very remote. She wouldn't be attending her aunt's funeral, it was better that way for everyone. 'I'll . . . I'll come tomorrow then.'

'Aye, all right. If I'm at work Elsie will likely let you in. Eva's adamant she doesn't want to go into hospital and the doctor said there's no real need as far as he can see, her just having wasted away. She hasn't really eaten in the last five years, not properly. I think she always intended to follow your father. You could say she died the day he did.'

Polly stared at him. That was shocking, but she believed it, having

211

seen how obsessively unbalanced Eva was about her brother that terrible birthday.

'I'm not saying it was right, Polly, so don't get me wrong, but there's been times I've thought there's not many men who get to be loved like Henry was.'

'Luke!' Now she was really shocked. And yet . . . yes, she could see what he meant. She had lived with a man for five years who was incapable of that emotion – either physically or emotionally – and it was a constant fight to believe she wasn't worthless and unattractive and everything else Frederick's rejection of her seemed to say. But she did fight it, and she would continue to do so, because it wasn't her who was the emotional cripple. She'd lost count of how many times she had tried to reach out to Frederick in the very early days of their marriage, before she had understood that there was something missing in him, something basic and essential. So, aye, she could see that to be loved unreservedly and passionately must be a wonderful thing. A precious thing. But not like Eva and her father. Not ever like that.

'I'll let you know . . . when it happens.'

'Thank you.' She didn't want him to go. Oh, how she didn't want him to go. Which was crazy, crazy and wrong. In fact, it was better he went straight away, this second, and she wouldn't walk with him to the lane. A quiver passed over her face but she stood stiff and straight as she watched Luke depart without another word of farewell, and she had shut the door before he was out of sight.

The sky was so low and heavy with the threatened snow that Polly felt it was pressing down just above their heads as the horse and trap clip-clopped its way into Bishopswearmouth the next morning.

Frederick had said little on the ride from the farm, but then that wasn't unusual; he could go for days, weeks, without having a proper conversation with her, although he and her mother always seemed to have plenty to say to each other. Polly glanced at him now out of the corner of her eye. He was dressed smartly as befitted a visit into the town, his fine cloth suit and waistcoat hidden by the thick worsted overcoat and bowler hat, and his feet shod in the best leather boots D. M. Ward of 103 High Street West had been able to make the year before. He was on his way to see about a new pair of riding boots today and she knew he wouldn't stint on the cost. He was vain about what he wore, Frederick, and in the same way he always insisted she was well dressed when she left the farmhouse – wouldn't it reflect on him otherwise?

Polly's long midnight-blue coat was an elegant one, and warm, the shoulder cape edged with fur, as was the matching hat. Her fine woollen gloves, neat boots and leather purse were all equally good quality, and she reflected now, as she brought her eyes forward again, that anyone seeing the pair of them would think they were a prosperous and happily married couple who had every reason to be satisfied with life. Which just showed how deceptive appearances could be.

It was just after midday when Polly alighted from the horse and trap on the Bishopwearmouth end of Wearmouth Bridge. She hadn't demurred when Frederick had suggested dropping her there rather than taking her across the bridge and into North Bridge Street, beyond which, to the left, was Southwick Road. He was being awkward, she knew that, because he hadn't liked Luke calling at Stone Farm the day before, but a brisk fifteen-minute walk to prepare herself for facing her aunt was just what she needed. Frederick had used the excuse that the horse didn't like crossing the bridge for not taking her to her aunt's door, and for the same reason he arranged to meet her where he had dropped her at three o'clock, after he had finished his business and had lunch at his gentlemen's club in Fawcett Street.

Polly stood for a moment watching the horse and trap as it disappeared down Bridge Street towards High Street West, and then with no further ado she turned and walked over the cobbled road with its tramlines to the wide pavement, passing a hawker with his hand-held cart as she did so. He smiled at her, touching his flat cap for a second with one hand, which caused his cart to wobble precariously, and she smiled back before continuing on her way. There were nice people in the world, lots of them, like that tinker man back there, she told herself silently. He had smiled for no reason other than that he wanted to. She had used to think she would never be able to bear living anywhere other than in the country on a farm, but lately she had realised this wasn't so. It was people who mattered more than a place. She'd live on the top of a slack heap with Luke.

The thought, coming from nowhere as it did, caused her to stop stock still so that the young mother behind her, who was pushing a large perambulator containing two wailing infants of indeterminate sex, narrowly missed bumping into her. 'Eee, I'm sorry, lass.' The young woman didn't look old enough to have one child, let alone the two in the baby carriage and the toddler of three or four holding on to the handle. 'They're wantin' their dinner.'

Polly smiled as she said, 'No, it was my fault,' and as she let the harassed quartet pass, the little girl smiled back a shy, sweet look that wrenched Polly's heart. She so wanted a bairn but it seemed impossible, and sometimes the pain was overwhelming. She avoided dwelling on it, but she knew Frederick had been relieved when the bolster had gone into place. Much as he wanted a son and heir, the procuring of one had caused him too much embarrassment and unpleasantness. He was a man who should never have married. That thought was inexorably linked with the one which had caused her to stop in the first place, and now she muttered softly, 'Enough, enough

213

of that,' before continuing to walk on purposefully. This wasn't a time to be thinking about bairns or anything else.

When she reached the corner of Southwick Road, Polly paused for a moment. The noise, which had diminished a little once she had passed over Wearmouth Bridge and reached Monkwearmouth Station, had picked up again, courtesy of Wearmouth Colliery on the one side and, to the right of her, towards Newcastle Road, the Wearmouth foundry, saw mills and goods yard. Beyond them, on the other side of Portobello Lane, was more industry in the form of hemp and wire rope works, iron and steel works, brick works and more foundries, and the overall smell and noise was something the residents of these streets took for granted.

How had her Aunt Eva felt when, as a young bride, Nathaniel had brought her here after the peace and quiet of the farm? For the first time since she had learned of the liaison with her father, Polly felt a rush of sympathy for her aunt. Her father had always said it was his sister who had farming in her blood; Eva must have thought she was being thrown into the bowels of hell. Polly glanced about her one more time and then walked on down Southwick Road.

It wasn't Elsie Appleby or even Luke who opened the door. For a second all Polly could do was stare, open-mouthed, at the tall figure of the young priest in front of her, and then she said on a whisper, 'Michael. *Michael?*'

'Yes, it's me, Polly.' It was Michael's voice coming out of this stranger who looked like him, this man in priest's garb. Still Polly couldn't move. He had grown. He must be as tall as Luke now, although he was still thin and slender in build. And he looked so much like their father. Why had she never noticed it before, when they were young? But then it wasn't unusual for nephews to resemble their uncles, so she wouldn't have thought twice about it, him supposedly being her cousin. But he was her brother. This man standing in front of her was her half-brother, and he was as far removed from the old Michael as it was possible to be. The ache in her heart was threatening to overwhelm her, and then Michael said, 'Come in, Poll, it's freezing out there,' and some of the strangeness vanished.

He reached out his hand and drew her up the step and over the threshold, closing the front door and ushering her in front of him as he said, 'Come into the kitchen, it's warmer in there.'

He was a priest. *A priest.* Polly just couldn't take it in. And her face must have given her away, because Michael said, 'I know this must be something of a shock to you,' as he gestured at his clothing.

'It is.' She stared at him before seating herself in the big padded chair standing to one side of the glowing range which he had indicated with a wave of his hand after he had spoken. 'I didn't know you were

'. . . well, that way inclined.' That sounded ridiculous, and Polly hastily qualified it with, 'What I mean to say is, I knew you were a Catholic, of course, but I wasn't aware your faith meant that much to you – enough to enter the priesthood.'

Michael drew one of the hardbacked chairs from underneath the kitchen table and placed it opposite Polly's on the other side of the range without replying immediately, and it was only after he had pushed the big black kettle further into the glowing coals and then seated himself that he said, his voice quiet, 'It wasn't my first choice, but then you know that.'

'Oh, Michael—'

'No, let me explain.' He cut off her quick response with a raised hand, but then sat looking at her for some seconds more before he said, 'Funnily enough, it was your old lodger, Miss Collins, who set me on this track originally.'

'*Miss Collins?*' She didn't understand any of this. Michael, a priest!

She was more beautiful than the picture he had carried in his mind. Michael had to pull his eyes away from her before the urge to just sit and drink her in became embarrassing for them both, and he rose quickly, saying, 'I'm sorry, what am I thinking of? Take off your coat and hat while I make a pot of tea and then we can talk before you go upstairs to see Mother, or would you rather see her first?'

Mother, not Mam. And his voice was different. Or perhaps it wasn't his voice as such, but his choice of words and the way he articulated them. Polly took a deep breath and said, 'I'll see her later if that's all right,' before standing and divesting herself of her outdoor clothes, then sinking back in the seat she had vacated and sitting watching him mash the tea. She couldn't get over the fact that Michael was only a few feet away from her, but never, in all the times she had imagined meeting him again – and she had imagined it in the darkness of the night with Frederick's snores puncturing the air waves – had she thought it would be like this. 'How . . . how is your mother today?' she asked when the silence became unbearable. 'Is there no chance at all she could pull round?'

Michael shook his head without looking at her. 'She weighs less than nothing, and as I understand it from Dr Henderson, everything is shutting down. It's only a matter of days, if not hours.'

'I'm sorry.' And then, as he turned and handed her a cup of tea before sitting down with one of his own, she said, 'Luke said yesterday that Dr Henderson knew where you were all this time,' and although she tried to keep the hurt out of her voice, a thread came through.

Michael leaned back in his chair. How did you explain to someone like Polly, someone who was intrinsically a fighter and who would move heaven and earth and never admit defeat, that you could be

215

crushed to a point where living was a big black hole in which there was no shaft of light to penetrate the darkness? He had felt like that once; a breakdown, the doctor at the seminary had said. All he had known was that but for Father McTooley and Father Hogarth he would have lost what was left of his mind. And when, slowly, he had begun to get better, he had had to face the fact that he was an essentially weak man – like his father. But in the facing of it some things had clarified, one being the course his life would now take. Father McTooley had once said that men became Catholic priests for all sorts of reasons, but if they thought they were going to escape life they were in for a shock; priests saw more of life than anyone. He'd known what the good father meant, but he didn't agree with him wholly. He had admitted that to his confessor, who hadn't seemed unduly worried.

'Michael?' Or should she call him Father? The thought was like a slap in the face.

'I thought it best there was no contact of any kind, Polly.' His voice was low and steady and revealed nothing of the turmoil he was feeling inside. 'When I left the farm that day I hardly knew what I was saying or doing, and when I met Miss Collins, well, she talked to me. Did you know she was a Catholic too?'

Polly nodded, and he continued, 'She suggested I go and see my priest, but when I said I couldn't, that I had to get right away from Sunderland within the hour or I'd do murder, she gave me a name of someone to go to down south. Someone influential within the Church.' He didn't mention here that he had always believed Miss Collins had an ulterior motive for her magnanimity, namely that she had had plans for Polly herself, and with him out of the way for good it brought them closer to fruition. 'And that was the start of it. I . . . I was ill for a time, very ill, and when I began to get better it became clear what I should do.'

Polly had always felt Miss Collins had known far more than she had let on. She stared into Michael's fine-featured face, which was too beautiful for a man's, and was aware of a core of anger deep inside. It might be irrational – Miss Collins had helped him after all – but surely, if she had had any liking for her at all, the other woman would have told her where Michael had gone.

'I'd always had a fascination with the ceremonial side of the Church.' Michael smiled now, and Polly forced herself to smile back. 'The beauty of the services, the chanting of Latin at the Mass, the smell of incense, the order and purity of it all . . . And after I found out about' – he hesitated a moment – 'about my parentage, I felt filthy, unclean, for a long time.'

'But it wasn't your fault,' said Polly quickly, appalled.

'I know that, the good fathers helped me to understand the mechanics of fallen sinful nature—' He stopped abruptly and then smiled again before saying, 'That sounds very holy, doesn't it? Father McTooley would be proud of me.'

She didn't know what to say. However much she had suffered, he had suffered ten, a hundred times more, and all because of the woman lying upstairs and their father. 'Are . . . are you happy, Michael?' she asked softly.

Happy? That transient emotion wasn't even in the order of things. Peace of mind was what he craved, and that came more frequently now. He had been right to leave Sunderland, though. He looked at her, his eyes veiled. She was still in his mind and his heart, but it was how his body had reacted at the first sight of her that told him he could never come back. That he dared not come back. His eyes roamed over her face and then he drained his cup, forcing his voice into an evenness that was all at odds with his churning insides as he said, 'I'm doing what I was called to do, I believe that, so perhaps fulfilled would be a better description. But of course I am still training, I have a long way to go yet.' And then, recognising the strength of his emotion and the longing that was sweeping over him to throw himself at her feet and clasp her to him, pressing his head between her breasts, he rose to his feet and walked across to the tall cupboard at the side of the range. Help me, God. Dear God, help me . . . And as though in answer to the silent prayer, he heard the back door leading into the scullery open, and a second later Elsie Appleby popped her head round the corner of the kitchen.

'Eee, I'm sorry, Father. I didn't know you had company.' She was holding a steaming plate of tripe and onions and a small crusty loaf. 'I thought you'd be ready for a bite.'

'I am, Mrs Appleby, I am.' Elsie had been in residence when he had arrived at the house the night before, and it had amused him then that her attitude had bordered on the reverential. This was the same Elsie Appleby who had skelped his backside when he was a bairn and she had caught him and Luke in her backyard, messing about with her husband's pigeon cree. They had only been trying to feed the birds a piece of stale bread, but she had acted as though it was the crime of the century and scared them both to death. 'This is my cousin, Mrs Weatherburn, by the way.'

So he knew she was married to Frederick. As Polly nodded at the bustling little woman who was now straightening the kitchen table's oilcloth and setting the plate down with some ceremony, she found herself wondering what Michael had thought to the news.

'Oh, aye, come to see your auntie, have you, lass?' Elsie said sympathetically. ''Tis a cryin' shame, an' her still a young woman.' Elsie was roughly the same age as Eva. She continued, turning to Michael, 'This'll stick to your ribs till tonight, Father, when Luke's home. I've got you both a nice pot pie steamin' for dinner. Do you

217

want me to take your mam a cup of broth afore I go? She normally has one this time of day.'

'Thank you, Mrs Appleby.'

As Elsie lifted the lid of the big kale-pot at the back of the range and ladled a couple of spoonfuls of rabbit broth into a mug, Polly said quickly, 'I'll take it, Mrs Appleby, and leave my cousin to eat his meal in peace.' Suddenly she wanted to get the ordeal of seeing Eva over with.

Elsie, who had had no time for her neighbour in the past but was now already extolling her to sainthood owing to Eva's imminent demise, was only too pleased to relinquish the mug.

Polly went straight to the stairs without glancing Michael's way, although she knew he was looking at her, and as she heard Elsie start fussing about the meal again, she climbed the narrow treads quickly. Once on the small landing she glanced about her. She should have asked Michael which room his mother occupied, but it was too late now. She knocked cautiously on the first door and then opened it carefully.

The narrow iron bed was empty and she realised, with a little jolt to her heart, that this must be Luke's room. Besides the single bed the room held, there was one tall, narrow wardrobe, the doors of which were closed, but the main bulk of the room was taken up with books. Seemingly hundreds of them. They covered an old battered bookcase along one wall and spilled out on to the floor in stacks several feet high.

Polly took a tentative step, and then another into the room, drawn by something stronger than herself. As she studied the bookcase she saw the main content was on the theme of politics, with volumes on the rights of the working man, women's rights and trade unions alongside one another. There were no books of a fictional nature at all, as far as she could see.

Oh, Luke. She stood for some seconds – the mug pressed against her thudding heart – just staring at the books, and the pain in her chest told her something she had been trying to ignore for months, if not years. She loved him. She shut her eyes tightly, but the knowledge was out of her subconscious and into the forefront of her brain. Not as she had loved Michael, as a young, starry-eyed lass with her childhood sweetheart, but as a fully grown woman loves a man.

Her eyes opened and lowered instinctively to the floorboards, as though she could see the man below. She blinked, her heart racing still more. Quite how or when it had happened she wasn't sure, but she knew now that she loved Michael as a sister did a brother. He was dear to her, he would always be dear to her, and she could have wept for him down there, and when she thought of the two happy, trusting bairns they had been and how cruelly the pair of them had

218

been thrust into adulthood, she could weep still. But her tears would be for two distant, misty figures from the past, and the bairns they had been didn't exist any more. They were different people now. How different she hadn't known until she had seen Michael again.

She was still standing gazing downwards, aware of a strong element of relief in the racing confusion of what her mind was trying to absorb, when she heard Elsie call something to Michael and then a moment later the kitchen door bang. The noise galvanised her frozen limbs and she stepped out of the room quickly, shutting the door behind her and walking along the landing to Eva's bedroom.

Her throat felt tight as she knocked gently on the door and she moistened her lips as she turned the handle. It had been five years since she had seen her aunt, and her last memory of Eva was of a big, heavily made, handsome woman, with a force of personality to match her build, weeping hysterically as Frederick had led her from the farmhouse to his horse and trap. The gaunt skeleton in the bed bore no resemblance to a living creature, let alone her aunt, and for a moment all Polly could do was to stare in horror at the sleeping figure. And then it opened its eyes and looked at her, and Polly forced herself to move forwards on legs that felt shaky as she said, 'It's me, Aunt Eva, Polly. I've come to see you as you asked because Gran is ill.'

The eyelids shut for a moment and then rose again, and now the gaze was tight and deep, fixed on her face. The whole bone structure of the skull was visible under the yellow skin, the once thick, vibrant hair sparse and wispy. Polly could hardly believe someone could be so emaciated and still be alive. She wished her aunt would say something, *anything*. And then her wish was granted when the mouth opened and Eva said, 'Polly Farrow, or Weatherburn as you are now. Well, well, well. Come and sit by me, Polly.'

Polly felt herself beginning to sweat with an unknown dread as she approached the bed, partly because the voice was the same as it had ever been and all at odds with the skeletal frame whence it had emerged. But it was her aunt's eyes that were freezing her blood and causing the goose-pimples to prick her skin. Their greenness was so dark as to be black and the power in them was riveting.

'I'm sorry to find you so poorly—'

'Don't give me that.' The tone was low but clear. 'You hate me. You've been wishing me dead for the last five years.'

'That's not true.' Polly hadn't sat down on the straight, hardbacked chair at the side of the bed but had remained standing. Now she offered her aunt the mug of broth, and when it was refused with an irritable gesture from one claw-like hand, she placed it on the little table next to the chair, before repeating, 'That's not true, Aunt Eva.'

'Well, I hate you.' The words were steady and ominous. 'All the trouble you caused, and then you calmly go and marry Frederick

219

Weatherburn not six months later, you dirty little strumpet. I know all about you. Flaunted yourself at all of 'em, I know, but it was Michael who was daft enough to fall for your whoring.'

For a moment Polly could only gape at the figure propped on the pillows. Her aunt was mad. Her granny had always said Eva was mad, and she was right. 'That's not true, Aunt Eva, and you know it.' Compassion for the remains of what once had been a bonny woman moderated Polly's tone, but her stomach was heaving at the nastiness of the confrontation.

'Spoilt you from the day you was born, me mam and da did. There was no one like you and yet they wouldn't give their own daughter the time of day.'

'Aunt Eva—'

'And what are you when all's said and done?' The words were coming deep and guttural now, and they were coated with a bitterness that was tangible. 'A dirty little trollop who's living in clover because she opened her legs for money, that's what. I've always hated me mam and da, for as long as I can remember, but do you know something, Polly Weatherburn? I hate you more, aye, I do, and that's the truth. I wanted to tell me mam that I'll die cursing her, but you'll do even better. Aye, you will.'

'Stop this now, you terrible woman.' Although Polly didn't shout, such was the quality of her voice that it brought Eva's venom to a temporary halt, but she rallied almost immediately.

'Me terrible?' Her eyes were unblinking. 'Well, maybe I am at that, but have you asked yourself who made me that way, eh? Your precious gran and grandda, that's who. An' I'll see 'em in hell, and you an' all.' Eva had raised herself on the pillows with a strength born of hatred, her scrawny neck straining out of her calico nightdress as she shouted at Polly, who had turned and was leaving the room, and even when they heard Michael running up the stairs she still continued to rant on.

Polly passed Michael in the doorway and walked straight down the stairs and into the kitchen, more shaken than she had ever been in all her life. Thank goodness her granny hadn't been well enough to come. That was the first coherent thought when the shock began to recede. And how incredible that a woman like her aunt could have given birth to someone like Michael. That was the second.

It was quiet now upstairs, very quiet, but it was a full minute before Michael came into the kitchen, and his face was very white. 'She's gone into some kind of coma. I need to call the doctor. You'll wait, Polly? You won't leave before I get back?'

The pungent smell of the tripe and onions still sitting on the plate on the table was making Polly feel nauseous, but she nodded quickly. 'Of course not. You go.' She didn't want to stay here with the personification of evil lying upstairs, but there was nothing else she could do.

'I'll be as quick as I can.'

Michael was gone for fifteen minutes, and Polly felt it was the longest fifteen minutes of her life. She busied herself clearing the table and washing the pile of dishes she found in the deep stone sink, before stoking up the fire in the range with more coal and filling the kettle to make a fresh pot of tea for Michael and the doctor. By the time they walked in the door she had stopped shaking and was able to converse quite naturally with Dr Henderson once he came downstairs after examining his patient.

'She won't come out of this coma.' He was quite definite. 'But exactly how long . . . I'm not sure. It could be tonight, or perhaps tomorrow, there's no telling.'

Polly and Michael stared at each other. They both knew Eva had gone into unconsciousness cursing her family, and it was chilling. And then Polly mentally shook herself, offering the doctor and Michael a cup of tea and a shive of Elsie Appleby's seed cake she had found in the pantry.

The doctor didn't stay long, and once he had gone – promising to return in the morning – Polly could see Michael was very upset. And so she stayed talking to him by the fire, and after a little while they found the talking was easier and they could even reminisce about some of the good times from their childhood.

'Why did you marry Frederick, Poll?'

She had just realised three o'clock had come and gone and had jumped up, grabbing her coat and hat, but now she turned to face Michael, the coat limp in her hands. She could prevaricate, give an evasive answer that was no answer at all, but as she looked into the face of this dear brother she knew she owed him the truth. 'There was nothing else I could do if I wanted to keep Gran and Grandda out of the workhouse,' she said quietly. And then she explained it all – the debts, the struggle to keep the family afloat and the final blow on the day of the storm.

Michael listened, and he found it difficult to keep the bitterness out of his voice when he said, 'So he blackmailed you into it.'

'It was my decision, Michael.'

Maybe. Michael looked into the great blue eyes, and then he asked the question Luke had asked the day before. 'Are you happy with him?'

Again she didn't beat about the bush. 'No.' And somehow she found she could talk to him about the true state of affairs between herself and Frederick in a way she could never have done with Luke. Which was strange really, she thought to herself after she had finished telling Michael all of it. 'I must go.' He had listened well, he'd make a good priest. 'I shan't make the bridge where I'm meeting Frederick before half past now.'

He wanted to take her into his arms. He didn't think he had ever wanted anything quite so much, especially after what she had revealed about her husband. Which was why he mustn't touch her. 'Goodbye, Polly.'

'Shall . . . shall I see you again? Will you come back here after . . .'

'I shouldn't think so.' He would want her until the day he died and beyond.

'No.' She nodded slowly and then touched his arm, her manner tentative as she said, 'I don't know if I should say this, but you will always be part of my life, Michael. You're my brother, my only brother, and I love you.' Her left hand unconsciously touched his ring, which she still wore on the third finger of her right hand.

He had noticed it there earlier and it had touched him more than any words could have done, and now it took all his will power to answer quietly, 'And I you, Polly. As my dear sister.'

She smiled at him – a sweet smile – but she didn't reach up to kiss him goodbye, for which he was eternally grateful. And then she was buttoning her coat and adjusting the cape on her shoulders and they were at the front door.

Polly felt the lump in her throat become constricting as she looked into Michael's face. It was probably for the last time, and for a moment she felt she couldn't bear to say goodbye. *She mustn't cry.* He had enough to bear with his mother dying, she told herself silently, forcing herself to say steadily, as a gust of wind nearly took her hat off, 'Don't stand on the doorstep, it's beginning to snow again. Tell Luke I'm sorry I missed him, and that we'd appreciate knowing at the farm when . . . when it happens.'

Michael nodded. 'Luke's on the foreshift today, I thought he would be home before now.' What were they doing talking about Luke and shifts or anything else but what really mattered? Michael asked himself desperately. She was going, and these few hours were going to have to last him a lifetime.

'Goodbye, Michael.' Polly stepped down into the street as she spoke, turning and smiling at him one last time.

'Goodbye, Poll.' He couldn't prolong this, not without spoiling everything and begging her not to go.

Michael shut the door as Polly began walking away, sinking immediately to his knees with a groan that came from the depths of him as he swayed back and forth, his arms crossed against his waist. And it wasn't until he tasted salt on his lips a minute or so later that he even realised the tears were streaming down his face.

Chapter Seventeen

The temperature seemed to have dropped a few degrees since midday, and there were flakes of snow blowing in the wind as Polly hurried along Southwick Road. As she passed the entrance to the Wearmouth Colliery she was aware that there were several groups of miners standing talking and others leaving after their shift, but she didn't look in their direction. She couldn't have coped with seeing Luke right now, besides which – and now she had left Michael, this was a very real worry – she didn't know if Frederick would be waiting for her, the mood he had been in that morning. But he wouldn't leave her to walk home, she reassured herself as she passed the smithy and turned into North Bridge Street. Not even Frederick would do that.

When she reached Bridge Dock she was craning her neck to see over the bridge, the smell of industrial smoke heavy in the cold air. A dredger and a hopper were in the middle of the river, with other smaller vessels fore and aft, but it wasn't until Polly reached the south side of the bridge, near the bottle works at Bishopwearmouth Panns, that she realised there was no horse and trap waiting for her.

How could he! She stood for a moment or two biting her lip as she stared down Bridge Street, and then she nearly jumped out of her skin as a voice just behind her said, 'And what's the lady of the manor doing in this neck of the woods?'

'Arnold.' She stared into the black face in which the mouth and eyes showed in stark contrast to the coal dust. 'You startled me.'

'Been to see Eva?'

His cap was set at a jaunty angle and it matched the tone of his voice, and when Polly said, 'Yes, aye, yes, I have,' he nodded once. 'Aye, I thought so when I saw you pass the colliery gates. I was going there meself once the shift ended, but we had a meeting – union business.'

'Oh, right.'

'You know Luke's the representative now?'

'No, I didn't.'

'Rising star, our Luke. No one can argue the toss like my little brother.'

It wasn't meant to be laudatory, and as his eyes ran all over her Polly forced herself to show no reaction at all, keeping her voice cool and even as she said, 'If you're going to see Eva, haven't you come in the wrong direction?'

Cocky little baggage. She'd got more airs and graces than a duchess. 'Aye, well, I saw you scurrying past and wondered what was what,' Arnold said with elaborate casualness. 'How are you getting back to the farm?'

Polly hesitated just a fraction too long before she said, 'With Frederick. I . . . I'm meeting him.'

'Oh, aye? Where?'

'In Fawcett Street.'

'I'll walk along with you. I want a word with him . . . about Ruth.'

Was he going to ask for her? Polly stared into the mean black eyes as she said quickly, 'I'm going shopping first; besides which, I wouldn't want to delay you. Eva was quite poorly when I left.'

Arnold nodded sagely. There was something going on here, and if he wasn't far wrong she wasn't meeting Frederick at all. Was she meeting someone else, or was it simply that she didn't want to be seen with him? He looked into the beautiful face framed by the soft fur of her hat and felt his body stir. Had them all dangling on a string, Polly did, damn her. And what was she when all was said and done? A bit farmer's daughter, and one who'd been caught sleeping with his own sister. Polly had nothing to be uppity about, not with her heritage. But he'd see his day with her; oh, aye, he would. He'd made himself that promise years ago and put up with that silly halfwit of a sister of hers in order to keep a foot in the door.

He took a step nearer to her, and as he saw the slight recoil she didn't quite manage to hide, his eyes narrowed, but his voice was offhand as he said, 'Right you are, lass. Well, I'm in lodgings round here, so I might as well nip back and change afore I go to see Eva.'

Polly nodded, relieved he wasn't going to be awkward. 'Goodbye, then.' She turned quickly, walking off at a smart pace down Bridge Street, and it wasn't until she reached the intersection with High Street West that she glanced behind her. Arnold was nowhere to be seen, and after searching the pavements for some moments she let out a deep sigh of relief. He had gone. She put her hand to her racing heart and breathed deeply. Now all she had to worry about was getting home before the threatened snow hit. How *could* Frederick have gone without her, and what on earth would he say to the others back at the farmhouse to explain his actions? She would never forgive him for this, never.

There were more fat flakes of snow blowing in the wind now, and as Polly crossed the road into Fawcett Street the sky was low and heavy; the pavements crowded with bustling shoppers anxious to get home to the warm before the weather worsened.

Should she wait for a tram? And then she answered herself almost immediately as one drew away some yards in front of her. No, no, she wouldn't. It would probably be ten minutes or so until the next one, and then it would only take her part of the way home. She was warmly dressed, and a brisk walk wouldn't do her any harm. If she stepped out she could be back at the farm before it was really dark. Having decided what she was going to do, she lifted up her head, pulled her hat more firmly over her ears and set off at a smart rate for the outskirts of the town without looking back. Which was her first mistake.

When Luke had seen Polly hurrying past the colliery yard his first reaction – to call her name – had been quickly checked. He was in his working clothes and as black as the ace of spades, which couldn't have been more of a contrast to Frederick's tweeds and leather boots. She was gone in an instant, but then he noticed Arnold detach himself from a group of the men who were standing about talking after the union meeting and disappear, not in the direction of his old home, as Luke would have expected – Arnold having promised he'd look in on Eva after the shift – but southwards, towards North Bridge Street.

It was instinctual to follow his brother, and when it became obvious that Arnold, in turn, was tailing the slender, blue-coated figure in front of them both, Luke's inherent distrust of his sibling quickened his footsteps, but still he didn't make himself known. He felt slightly ridiculous as the three of them walked on, but then Polly was crossing the bridge and Luke, like Polly, was straining his eyes for Frederick's horse and trap.

And then Polly stopped and he watched Arnold catch her up and the pair of them begin to talk, and he felt even more foolish as he hovered in the middle of the bridge pretending to look at the ships below while he kept an eye on the couple in front of him.

He must look a right Charlie. A three-masted sailing ship was being towed by a tugboat in the distance as he feigned an interest in the river, but within moments Polly and Arnold had parted – Polly walking on down Bridge Street in the direction of Fawcett Street and Arnold turning right into Matloor Street.

Of course – Polly must be meeting Frederick at his gentlemen's club in Fawcett Street. The penny suddenly dropped. Frederick had rammed his damn club down their throats enough on those Sunday afternoons long ago; his membership there, which involved rubbing shoulders with many of the leading lights of the town, was very important to Polly's husband. But where was Arnold going? Luke frowned to himself as he continued to stand on the bridge, a few desultory snowflakes whirling and dancing in the bitterly cold air. His brother had said he was going to come and pay his respects to Eva and have a word with Michael once the shift had finished, and he couldn't be going to his lodgings – Luke knew the room Arnold rented was in a house in Barrington Street, at the back of St Peter's graveyard in Monkwearmouth. Still, it was none of his business. He wasn't his brother's keeper. He'd better get back home; Michael would be wondering what had happened to everyone, and he'd probably had more than enough of his mother by now, and Elsie Appleby oohing and ahhing over him.

Luke smiled to himself as he turned back the way he had come. Elsie had actually genuflected at her first sight of Michael the night before, and he was sure that Eva – as Michael's mother – had immediately achieved a status just a little lower than the Virgin Mary in Elsie's devout Catholic eyes.

They had talked half the night, he and Michael. Luke walked swiftly now, anxious to get home and wash the pit out of his skin and hair. Funny really, but Michael had always been more his brother than Arnold could ever be, even though there was no blood tie between them and in spite of knowing that Michael held Polly's heart. He was glad he had seen him again, although his shock – like Elsie's – had been considerable when he'd first opened the door to a young priest with Michael's face.

He passed Monkwearmouth Station and the row of houses beyond, but it was as he reached the school on the corner and a tumble of children came spilling out that his footsteps slowed. So many raggedy-arsed little nippers, he thought bleakly. When were times going to change? Half of them were bandy-legged with rickets, their stick legs thrust into broken-down boots that were several sizes too large, having been passed down from an older brother or sister. Back-to-back hovels with one living room, one bedroom and a damp, dark cellar for families of fourteen and more was no way to live, and that was what a good number of these bairns would be going home to. Aye, and on their way some of them would be looking for an orange box or wet-fish box that a kind shopkeeper would leave outside to give a family free fuel for a night.

Luke breathed in deeply, the rage which always accompanied the feeling of social injustice he felt at times such as these making his stomach knot.

He was still thinking of the children he'd seen when he reached home, Michael meeting him at the kitchen door. 'Arnold not with you?' Michael asked quietly.

'He'll be here shortly, no doubt.' As Michael mentioned his brother's name Luke felt the same sense of unease he'd felt earlier in the colliery yard, and then he told himself not to be daft. Polly was all right – she was with Frederick. And then, looking at Michael's face, Luke said, 'What is it? Is she worse?'

'Aye, a coma the doctor said, but I can't help feeling it's one of her

226

own making. Polly was here and my mother went for her; I think the bitterness of years was vented on Polly's head,' Michael said soberly. 'You just missed her, she's gone to meet Frederick.'

Luke nodded, thrusting the kettle into the glow of the fire in the range as he said, 'I'll have a quick wash-down and then look in on Eva, although I doubt there's anything anyone can do.'

'There never was, Luke.'

'Aye, you're right there, man.'

They looked at each other for a long moment before Luke turned away.

Once he had filled the tin bath in the scullery and washed the black coal dust out of the pores of his skin and his hair – no easy task with the portion of hard, marble-veined soap – Luke dressed quickly in clean clothes. It was something Nathaniel had always done immediately on returning from the pit, and he and Arnold had followed suit. 'You'll come back mucky but that's no excuse for wallowin' in it like some do,' his father had said to them both on their first days down the pit. 'We're men, not pigs, an' don't you forget it, son.'

After banging his heavy pit clothes against the wall in the backyard to get the thick of the dirt off, Luke cleaned his boots and left the pile to one side of the boiler in the washhouse ready to put on in the morning. They would be cold and slightly damp, but Eva had never allowed any of them to bring their working clothes into the house once they had stripped off, and old habits died hard.

Once back in the kitchen, he accepted the mug of tea Michael handed him, glancing at the clock on the dresser as he said, 'Arnold's taking his time. I saw him take off over the bridge earlier, so I reckon he's got a bit of business in Bishopwearmouth.'

They both knew Arnold's weakness for dabbling in the odd items that fell off the back of a lorry, and he'd got more than one pal who worked at the docks.

'Oh, aye? You didn't see Polly there? She was meeting Frederick at the bridge.'

'At the bridge?' Luke looked up sharply. 'Are you sure?'

Michael nodded. 'She left in something of a hurry, she was late and—'

He found he was talking to thin air. Luke had already left the house at a run, grabbing his coat and cap as he flew out into the street and set off in the direction of Wearmouth Bridge.

Something was wrong, something was very wrong here. He had felt it earlier but ignored his gut instinct, Luke told himself as he half ran, half walked the pavements, which were already covered in a thin white layer of snow.

It was now gone four o'clock, and as Luke reached the bridge the streets were still crowded, but once through the main part of

227

Bishopwearmouth town they began to empty rapidly. Luke passed Mowbray Park and carried on down Burdon Road until he came to the corner of Christ Church, whereupon he turned right towards Tunstall Vale and Tunstall Road. It was the most direct route to Stone Farm and one he had walked many a time, but now his breath was tearing his lungs and he had to stop a moment and take deep pulls of air before again running on.

The light was failing swiftly, but owing to the white blanket settling on the fields and trees it wasn't dark, and Luke's eyes were straining ahead, frantic to catch sight of a blue-coated figure in front of him.

Maybe Arnold *had* gone to see one of his cronies in Bishopwearmouth? No, no, he hadn't. He wasn't sure how he came about his knowledge, but Luke would have bet his life on the fact that Arnold had somehow suspected that Polly had missed Frederick. If indeed she had. No, she had. She had. But pray God she hadn't. By, he wasn't making sense here, not even to himself. The lads at the colliery were forever pulling his leg about how he was so clear and concise about everything; they should hear him now.

If she'd caught a tram part way she could be home by now. Or maybe she would take a horse cab? He might get to the farm and she'd be sitting with the rest of them at her tea or whatever. Still, he could make some excuse about Eva. *Eva.* He groaned inwardly at the realisation that he had never even popped up to see his stepmother, but then dismissed the guilt in the next moment as his anxiety regarding Polly's safety swamped everything. But she *could* be safely home and Arnold could be knocking the door in Southwick Road at this very minute. He could be wrong about all of this. So why didn't he feel that deep inside the core of him?

Stop thinking and concentrate on running. His brain gave the command and he obeyed it, the impetus putting wings on his feet as he ran on through the raw November night.

When Arnold had left Polly he'd walked briskly down Matloor Street for a few yards, but after surreptitiously checking over his shoulder he dived down the street running parallel to Bridge Street and emerged at the junction with High Street West just in time to see Polly cross the road some fifty yards away and continue on along Fawcett Street.

She might be meeting Frederick. He frowned briefly as he crossed the road himself and then hurried on into Fawcett Street, keeping to the opposite side of the road to Polly. But somehow he didn't think so. Adrenalin born of excitement was making his heart pound. Well, he'd soon find out one way or the other, and if she'd got a fancy man somewhere . . . He wetted his lips, his eyes narrowing. He'd have something over her then right enough. By, he'd give his right arm to have her squirming, he would that. Never thought he was good

228

enough, did she? An ordinary working man wasn't good enough for the likes of Polly Weatherburn.

He followed her cautiously, and when Polly walked on down Burdon Road Arnold's brow wrinkled again. Whoever it was she couldn't wait to see him, the brazen hussy. All decked out in her fine togs, but under the fur and linen she was scum, just like her da.

It wasn't until Polly had passed Tunstall Hills Farm that it actually dawned on Arnold what had happened. He'd gone without her! Frederick had gone back without waiting for her. Well, well, well. His bottom lip moved over his top as he narrowed his eyes reflectively. So that was how it was. Mind, he wasn't surprised. All wind and water, Frederick was. It would take a real man to satisfy a tart little piece like Polly, and Frederick didn't have it in him, the soft nowt.

There was only the odd house dotted every few hundred yards along the road now, although the lane was heavily fringed with trees, which Arnold used to his advantage. Polly was still striding out, obviously intent on getting home before dark, and when she came to the fork in the road a third of a mile past Tunstall Hills Farm she took the path which led past the Silksworth Colliery and on to Farrington Hall, beyond which was the village and then the winding path to Stone Farm.

Arnold was sweating heavily now, although it was nothing to do with the pace at which he was walking; rather the realisation that an opportunity had presented itself to him tonight the like of which he might never have again. He was going to have her. For years he had wanted her and tonight he was going to have her. And the way things obviously were with Frederick, she'd probably like it too. Oh, she might squawk a bit, they all squawked when you gave it to them rough, but they liked it too. He knew. Oh, aye, he knew all right. There wasn't much about women he didn't know.

The snowflakes were thicker now, and dodging behind trees as he was, he lost sight of her in front of him for a moment or two. He moved quicker and then had to stop sharply and duck down on his haunches when he saw she had stopped and was talking to two women who looked to be miners' wives from the village. They had a couple of bairns with them and a babe in arms, and after a while he saw Polly open her bag and take something out, pressing it towards the baby before the mother reached out her hand and bobbed her head in thanks.

Obviously crossing a new arrival's palm with silver, Arnold thought to himself. Lady Bountiful to the last. His lips drew back from his teeth in a sneer. Well, she could give him something the night, and he wasn't talking about a silver thrupenny bit neither.

Come on, come on. Twice he thought the women were going to part company, and twice the mother with the baby reached out and took Polly's arm to detain her. What was she yammering on about? And then Polly finally broke away with a wave of her hand and was moving again.

He waited until the two women were out of sight and then he straightened. Anticipation had made him as hard as a rock, and for a second he breathed in the icy cold air, savouring it as his body surged with what was to come, and then he was running after her like a greyhound.

Polly wasn't hurrying the last half a mile or so, she was thinking about the baby. It was such a bonny little thing. She had got to know quite a few of the miners' wives from the village during the summer when the strike was on, when she and Betsy had delivered food parcels and essential supplies, along with fresh milk for the children. Her actions had widened the rift between herself and Frederick, and she had endured many blazing rows when he had accused her of robbing the farm of its profits for the year, but she had stuck to her guns, maintaining starving women and children shouldn't be used in political games to force men back to work. And now Mrs O'Leary had just told her she'd named her new baby daughter Polly.

'She wouldn't be here now if it wasn't for you, lass. Aye, an' that's the truth. 'Twas only your milk an' food kept us goin', an' I'm not soft-soapin', am I, Bridget?'

Bridget had shaken her head.

'An' when our Patrick fell an' sliced his leg open an' it went nasty he'd have bin a goner for sure if you hadn't got the doctor to him, 'cos we hadn't got a brass farthin'. Isn't that right, Bridget?'

Another enthusiastic nod from the compliant Bridget.

'An' it's grateful we are, lass. I've praised God for you times; aye, I have, an' I make no apology for it.'

There had been more of the same and Polly had had to fight not to smile once or twice because the little Irishwoman was a natural comedian, but there was no doubting she had meant every word. Unfortunately she was the sort of woman who could talk the hind leg off a donkey, but owing to the weather and the child buried deep in the folds of her shawl, Mrs O'Leary hadn't tarried too long.

Oh, but the night was beautiful. Polly looked up into the tall trees either side of the lane, their bare branches now feathered with white, and then raised her eyes still further, to the millions of fat snowflakes falling out of a laden sky. Frederick always said snow was one of a farmer's most relentless enemies, and she could understand that, but it *was* amazingly lovely too. The world seemed magical, like a fairyland. She was glad Frederick had gone without her or else she would have missed all this.

She began to hum a hit of a couple of years ago, 'Moonstruck', her

230

thoughts still with the O'Leary baby, who had been fast asleep curled against her mother's warmth, and the tune was still on her lips when something made her turn and see the man almost upon her.

Her high, piercing scream was instinctive and made before she recognised Arnold, but in the moment he reached her she read what was in his face.

Oh God, oh God, help me. It was a whimper deep within but not voiced. Something told her that to display any weakness now would be her downfall. Instead she brought her body up straight, forcing a half-laughing, half-annoyed note into her voice as she said, 'Arnold! For goodness' sake! You scared the life out of me. What is it? Has Eva gone?'

'Eva?' His eyes were hooded in the semi-darkness but the dark light in them was already stripping the clothes from her body. She could feel his lust although he wasn't yet touching her; it was like a live thing, holding its own stench, and it was terrifying. It froze her blood and dried her mouth even as part of her couldn't believe it was happening. 'I don't know nothing about Eva.'

'Then why are you here?' Immediately she said it she realised it was the wrong tack to take, and added quickly, 'Of course, you said you were coming to see Frederick about Ruth. Come up to the farm and have a hot drink.'

'You know I've always wanted you, don't you? I've read it in your eyes when you look at me.' His voice was low and it could have been conversational but for the expression on his face. 'You should have been kind to me years ago, then it wouldn't have been like this.'

'I don't know what you are talking about.' She kept her back straight and her head high. 'You are courting my sister, Arnold.'

'Ruth?' He laughed harshly, his eyes greedy on her body as he looked her up and down with deliberate intent. 'We both know I don't want Ruth.'

Oh, dear God, God, tell me what to do, what to say. If she screamed again it was too far from the farm for anyone to hear; she was alone out here.

In the summer the lane was a green bower with the trees' branches on either side of the road meeting in a leafy arch, and now, like a mockery of the evil below, they were standing under an arc of pure white.

'You've made this happen, you know that, don't you.' It was a statement not requiring an answer. 'I wanted to court you proper years ago, but you'd have none of it. You rubbed me nose in it with Michael, and then to go and marry an old man like Frederick—'

'He's not an old man.' Her voice was stiff, her body was stiff; she dared not relax for a second. 'Forty-six isn't old.'

'It is for a little vixen like you, but then Frederick's got plenty of

231

other attributes, eh? Big farm, money . . . Does all that keep you warm in bed at night, Polly? Does he satisfy you? Eh?' He made a crude gesture at his bulging trousers.

'How dare you talk to me like this.' She had never been so petrified in her life, and her voice wasn't as forceful as she would have liked.

'How dare I?' He was a few inches away from her, so close she could smell the faint odour of the coal dust from his clothes. Melted snow had made thin rivulets of white through the black of his face, giving the strange effect of a painted mask, but there was nothing amused or clownlike about the face staring at her. It was a devil's face. 'And why shouldn't I? What are you, after all? Ruth told me she'd let on about the gossip in town about your goings-on and that you'd blamed me. Right put out about it an' all she was, but you know something, Polly?' The dark eyes watched her, enjoying the moment. 'You were dead right, lass. Oh, aye, you were. Your name's muck in some quarters, I've seen to that. There's folk who wouldn't be surprised at anything you get up to, so don't you go thinking you can open that pretty little mouth and cry rape, 'cos it won't work. Not for you, not for Polly Weatherburn.'

Rape. Oh, oh God, God. Rape. Don't let him. Don't let him touch me.

'You going to fight me, Polly?'

To her horror she saw his hands go to the old frayed belt holding up his trousers.

'I'd like that,' he continued softly as a gust of snow made him blink. 'You don't know how long I've waited for this moment, or maybe you do at that. Me flesh has always wanted you. You've been like an ache I couldn't get rid of.'

'Stop this, Arnold.'

'Stop this, Arnold.' The mockery was cruel, nasty, like a predator that had got hold of its victim and was enjoying playing with it before the kill. 'You can't tell me what to do, Polly. I'm not one of your husband's lackeys. Croft was telling me the last time I was at the farm how things have improved since you married the master. Always paid well, the master did, but since the missus came the perks have got better. As much milk and as many eggs as they want, along with a stone of potatoes a week for each family and a good joint come Sunday. Oh, aye, he was singing your praises right enough. Made me wonder if you've been giving him more than milk and eggs.'

'You're disgusting.'

'Careful, lass. You're in no position to fling insults.'

'You touch me and I'll have the law on you, I swear it.'

'You could try, lass. Aye, you could try. But there's plenty who would be ready to speak out about what they've heard, and the funny thing with rumours is they have a way of becoming fact in people's minds. You ever noticed that, Polly? Led him on, they'd say, and what can you expect after that business with her brother and then marrying her uncle? She's a wrong un, sure as eggs are eggs. And what with her husband and her at odds . . .' At Polly's start of surprise, Arnold smiled slowly. 'Thought I hadn't noticed, eh? I sowed a seed of doubt in Frederick's mind years ago, on your wedding night, and I've dropped the odd hint now and again ever since. You'd get no support from Frederick if you spoke out, so think on.'

'I don't need Frederick's support or anyone else's,' Polly said sharply, her face stony to disguise the fear that was curdling her insides. The snow had settled on Arnold's thick brown hair as they had been talking, and she watched him as he flicked it off but without his eyes leaving her for a second.

'How much do you weigh, Polly?' His tone was contemplative now as he let his eyes wander up and down her again. 'Eight stone, nine, maybe? Now me, I weigh thirteen and I can give you six inches in height. You can't fight me but I don't mind you trying; like I've said I like them with a bit of go in their bellies. We can have it up against a tree so you don't get your nice blue coat mucky, or I'll take you down on the ground, it's all the same to me.'

He moved with a suddenness that took her completely by surprise, as it was meant to, but almost in the same instant her forearm came up and she hit him a hard swipe across his face as she made to run. He caught at her and swung her round so violently her hat went flying off, striking her hard across one cheek with his open hand as he growled, 'Easy or hard, it's all the same to me, Polly, like I said.'

She was kicking and screaming and punching now, but Arnold wasn't just bigger and heavier than her slight frame. His days underground in the pit had made him muscular and formidably strong, and Polly was aware, with a desperation that made her head whirl, that she was hardly making an impact on him.

When his leg came out on the back of her knees and tripped her to the ground she continued to thrash and fight, but then all the breath left her body in a strangled gasp as Arnold's weight descended on her in a great thump, one hand clamping over her mouth and nose so she couldn't breathe and the other raking at her clothes and hoisting her coat and dress and petticoat up over her thighs.

No! No! No! It came from the essence of her.

He was muttering obscenities now, and as she fought to remain conscious, her head vainly trying to move to dislodge the hand cutting off her air and bringing insensibility, and her hands clawing at him frantically, his knee jabbed viciously between her legs, prising her thighs apart.

She could feel a large stone beneath her and it felt as though it was breaking her back, but the sense of asphyxiation was over-riding

233

everything else, and she felt herself dropping into blackness even as she continued to flail and writhe feebly.

She was never sure if she lost consciousness completely, but in the same moment the hand left her face and she gulped painfully for air, Arnold entered her with a thrusting savagery that drove her back so hard against the rock she cried out.

'Aye, that's it, you scream and moan a bit,' he mumbled above her, punctuating his words with driving thrusts as he rammed into her flesh like a steel rod.

The agonising pain in her back and the excruciating force threatening to rip her belly apart was so bad as to be unbearable, but with his hand gone from her nose and mouth Polly found the power to claw at the face above her. She felt her nails rip through skin and heard him shout before he gave her a blow across the side of her head that sent her spinning into oblivion again.

When she came to, the pounding pain was gone and she was aware of cold air and the snow on her lower belly and legs, but she didn't have the strength to move or pull her clothes down. Her whole body was shaking, her legs trembling so violently that it was as if they belonged to someone else.

She could hear the sound of men's voices cursing, and thuds and blows somewhere near her, but it was some moments before she could persuade her dead limbs to move, and then all she could manage was to brush shakily at her clothing until she felt it cover the lower part of her. The effort that had taken threatened to cause her to faint again, but she fought the blackness with all her might, along with the acute sensation of nausea it had produced.

She rolled over on to her stomach and then pulled herself to her knees, glancing over to where Luke and Arnold were locked together, Luke's fingers round Arnold's throat and Arnold's fists battering at his brother's torso. Arnold's knee came up into Luke's groin with enough force to cause Luke to emit a shrill cry, and Luke pushed his brother violently as his hands let go of Arnold's neck and jerked to the bruised flesh between his legs. Arnold stumbled backwards before losing his balance and falling in a sprawl of arms and legs into the long ditch running at the side of the lane.

Luke was on his knees now, groaning horribly and quite unable to move, and as Polly struggled up and stumbled across to him, her one thought was to get him on his feet again before Arnold scrambled out of the ditch. By the time she reached him, Luke was retching, his face as white as the snow about them, and she knelt beside him, shaking his shoulders as she said, 'Luke, Luke, please. Please, before he gets up. Luke, take some deep breaths, *please*.'

'In . . . in the name of . . .' Luke was hunched with his forehead touching the ground. 'Where . . . where is he?'

234

'He fell into the ditch,' Polly said through chattering teeth. 'Please, Luke, get up.'

It was another minute before Luke could comply with that request, and then he looked as though he was going to vomit. He stood, swaying slightly, as he looked towards the side of the road, where it appeared Arnold had knocked himself out, and then he said, 'Are you all right?'

She had the shakes so badly she could barely answer, but when she shut her eyes tightly and shook her head, Luke's voice held a world of grief and anger and regret as he said, 'Oh, Polly, Polly. I'm sorry, lass. Here . . .' He took off his jacket and wrapped it round her shoulders, brushing ineffectually at her wet clothes. 'I'll kill him, I swear it.'

'See . . . see what's happened.' Polly gestured towards the figure in the ditch, one leg – which had got tangled in a tree root – being the only part of Arnold visible. 'Be careful.'

Be careful, she said. Luke looked again at her chalk-white face, her lips blue with cold, and the urge to throttle his brother rose again in a consuming flood. He would have killed him a minute ago, aye, he would, and Arnold had known it – had read the knowledge in his face. He'd seen Arnold's eyes widen when he wouldn't lessen his grip round his neck, seen stark fear come into them. And then he'd pulled the little trick with his knee. But this wasn't over yet, the filthy, dirty, stinking swine. He'd beat him into a pulp.

He didn't have to.

Arnold was quite, quite dead, and when Luke moved the lolling head and saw the extent of the wound caused by the razor-sharp piece of slate which had sliced off the back of his brother's skull, he knew retribution had been swift and final.

'Luke?'

He had told Polly to stay where she was, but when she appeared above him at the side of the road, he said quickly, 'Go back, Polly.'

'What's happened?'

'He hit his head.'

'His head?'

'He's dead, lass.'

Luke had been climbing out of the ditch as he spoke, and when he saw her eyes widen he didn't know what to expect, but it wasn't the words which came out of her mouth as she said woodenly, 'I'm glad. I'm glad he's dead.'

'Polly. Polly, lass—'

'He . . . he . . .' She couldn't go on. Was this Eva's revenge? Had her aunt's curse already begun to work? But no, she didn't believe that. This was Arnold's doing and no one else's.

Luke took Polly gently into his arms, not knowing if she would want him to touch her after what had just occurred, but she leaned against him, still shaking uncontrollably as the flood of tears came in an engulfing torrent.

How long they stood there with the snow falling silently about them Luke didn't know, but a separate part of his mind to the one still reeling with the shock of seeing Polly spread-eagled on the floor with Arnold on top of her, and then the gory mess that had been his brother's head, was thinking, It's taken this, rape and murder, for me to hold her in my arms. Rape. *Rape*. And Arnold dead. He looked over Polly's bent head towards the ditch and felt he wanted to retch again, but that separate part of his mind was now saying, If he had lived he would never have let her alone until his dying day. She'd been an obsession with Arnold, a dark obsession. He had known that for years.

'Luke?' The tears that had been raining down Polly's face were gone, but her great blue eyes were black liquid in the shadows. 'He followed me here on purpose, this was premeditated. And . . . and people would never believe that he died by accident. They'll say you killed him in a fight over me or something, and with all the lies he's told you could go down the line for him.'

'I'll take me chance—'

'No.' Polly pulled away from his arms and he made no attempt to hold on to her. 'Don't you *see*? We can't say anything, we can't.'

'Lass, he forced you.'

'We've got no way of proving that. It's common knowledge the two of you have never got on, and who would believe you just happened along here when he was' – she gulped painfully – 'attacking me? Luke, he's done too good a job in the past, don't you see? You have to see. And anyway . . .' She gulped again, shutting her eyes for a second before she said, 'I don't want people to know he did that to me, not . . . not with him. It can't do any good now he is dead, but if we tell the police they'll likely blame you.' And then she would die. She would really die if Luke was sent down the line over her.

She could see he was wavering, and his tone confirmed this when he said, 'But what'll we do then? Just leave him here?'

'Aye, exactly.' She didn't think she would ever stop shaking again in all her life; the trembling seemed to be coming from a whirlpool of churning deep inside, but somehow her mind was clear. She had to get Luke to understand the danger he was in. 'It was an accident, we both know that. He fell into the ditch himself.'

'I would have killed him, lass, and he knew it. I might not have sliced his head open but I as good as did him in and there's not any part of me that's sorry. He was a wrong un, always was and always would have been, but when I saw him with you tonight—' He couldn't go on.

Polly was frozen, inside and out, and feeling very strange, and her face must have reflected this because Luke said, 'I'm going to carry you, lass. All right?'

'I can walk.'

'Polly—'

'I'd rather, please.' Nevertheless she found she had to lean on Luke's arm when her legs threatened to let her down, and they had only gone a few yards when she said, 'My hat. Look, there.' And then, as the thought occurred to her, 'And my purse, Luke. It's on the ground somewhere.'

Luke found the purse and brought the hat to her and they continued on their way, the snow a thick curtain in the silence of the night. It was taking all of Polly's will to put one foot in front of the other, but mercifully that was stopping her mind from thinking. She didn't want to think, she didn't ever want to think again.

They neither of them said a word until they came to the entrance to the farm road, and then Polly roused herself enough to murmur, 'You'd better go back now, I can manage from here. You mustn't be seen. I can say I fell over with the snow and all.'

'I'm not leaving you here, there's still a good half a mile to go to the farm.'

It was said in such a way that Polly didn't argue, and as they stumbled along in the bitter cold, the wind was chilling without the trees to break its rawness, the sheep either side of the four-foot dry-stone walls huddled together in groups as though seeking comfort from the storm.

When the lights of the farmhouse were clearly visible through the driving snow, Polly stopped. 'This is far enough, Luke,' she said quietly.

He stared at her, his eyes desolate. 'I ought to come in with you; if nothing else to ask why that bast—' He stopped abruptly. 'Why that husband of yours didn't wait for you tonight,' he said tightly. 'How he could leave you to find your own way home is beyond me.'

'It doesn't matter.' Nothing mattered. She wanted to sink into oblivion, to shut out this thing called life that sucked and sucked at the inner self until it was shrivelled and dry. She could feel herself shrinking, diminishing down and down, and she didn't have the strength to fight the feeling. He had entered her. Arnold had entered her. It wasn't to be borne.

'It does matter. Polly, you need help after—'

'I don't want to talk about it.' And then, as he went to say more, she repeated fiercely, '*I don't want to talk about it.*'

'All right, all right.' He was clearly out of his depth and she had it in her to feel sorry for him for a moment.

'Please, Luke, I'll be all right,' she said flatly. 'I just need to . . . to get home.' Home where she could wash herself, scrub at her skin, remove every trace of what had happened from her flesh. She was sticky between her legs and it was from him . . . Oh, dear God, how was she going to be able to bear it? What would she say to them when she first walked in? And Luke, what must he be feeling? He had killed a man tonight and the man was his own brother. She ought to comfort him, say something, but she was glad, *glad* Arnold was dead, so what comfort would that be? She pulled her arm from his, her head whirling. 'I . . . I have to go.'

She hadn't thanked him, but how could she say thank you for killing his brother? The urge to cry was on her again and she knew she mustn't give in to it this time. If she started to cry now, she wouldn't be able to stop. And she had to be in control of herself when she walked in the farmhouse door. Miffed at Frederick, tart and irritated maybe, but clear and controlled in the role she had to play. Luke's life might depend on it.

'Goodbye, Luke.' She touched his arm briefly, and as he looked down into the dark pools of her eyes, the snow a white mantle like a veil on her hat, his Adam's apple worked convulsively but he didn't speak.

And then she turned, smoothing down her wet coat as she stared ahead through the swirling flakes, and putting one foot in front of the other she continued walking down the stony path.

Chapter Eighteen

Luke was halfway home when he first missed his cap. He stood for a moment, his hands twisting together as he tried to decide whether to go back and look for it, but after retracing his footsteps right to the entrance of the farm road and finding nothing, he started for Bishopwearmouth again. A cap was a cap, he'd others, and there was nothing on it to mark it as special in any way. A cap was the least of his problems the night. *Polly, oh, Polly, Polly.* He said her name out loud, his breath misting in a cloud, and his mind continued to reiterate it with every step he took until a sudden picture of Arnold sprawled in the ditch intervened.

He'd killed him, his own brother; shouldn't he be feeling bad? He took a great pull of air that swelled his chest and then let it out in a long hiss. But he wasn't going to play the hypocrite. He remembered one of the priests preaching a sermon on Cain and Abel – Father McAttee, it'd been – and how the one that had killed the other, he couldn't remember if it was Cain or Abel, had been cursed from God from that point on. But that had been an innocent man's blood if he remembered right, and Arnold had been far from innocent. By, if he lived to be a hundred he'd never forget the obscene sight of him when he'd yanked him off her. Oh, Polly, Polly. Why hadn't he made himself known to her when she'd walked past the colliery yard? He could have accompanied her to where she was supposed to be meeting Frederick and then walked her home when it became apparent he hadn't waited for her.

He gulped spittle into his dry mouth, his face screwing up with painful remorse. He hadn't wanted her to see him in his working clothes covered in muck and coal dust. The truth was like a lead weight in his stomach. Well, they said pride went before a fall, but in this case the fall had been taken for him. Damn it. *Damn it.*

He shook his head in the manner of a boxer after a heavy blow. He couldn't believe this had happened; not to Polly, to Arnold, to him. It was the sort of thing you read about in the *Sunderland Echo*, the sort of thing that happened to other people, like the Newcastle train murder the year before. The colliery book-keeper who had been murdered then had been carrying a leather bag containing a small fortune, and the motive for the violence had been plain. Arnold was just an ordinary

239

working man; what would the police make of his death? Murder? An accident? What?

A sudden and grotesque picture of how Arnold's head had looked flashed into Luke's mind, and his limbs became weak, all strength leaving him. He leaned against a tree trunk for support, his eyes searching the swirling white night ahead for the lights of Tunstall Hills Farm. His whole body was shaking now, as if with St Vitus's dance, and he found himself recalling how Polly had shaken in the first minutes he had held her. It was as though she'd been a puppet on jangling wires. How was she going to be able to go on after this, and not even being able to tell anyone? He shouldn't have left her. He should have gone with her to the farm, whatever she said.

His mind continued to rock back and forth with the impact and consequences of what had happened that night, right up until he reached Southwick Road. It was after eight o'clock and four hours since he had left the house at a run, and due to the severe blizzard conditions which now prevailed, the streets had been mercifully deserted for the most part through both Bishopwearmouth and Monkwearmouth. Which made it all the more ironic that he was literally on his own doorstep when a well-remembered, perky voice just behind him said, 'If it isn't the great and mighty Luke Blackett.'

For a moment Luke contemplated just opening the door and walking in without acknowledging Katy, but his racing mind steadied itself and spoke to him with clear reasoning. She was quite capable of banging on the door and demanding to know why he had ignored her if he did that, and he didn't want a scene. 'Hello, Katy.' He turned to face her but he didn't smile, and there was no smile on the hard, pretty face looking him up and down either.

'This is Dennis Pearson.' She was on the arm of a tall, lanky lad who looked to be a good few years younger than Katy; his face still covered with pimples and his narrow shoulders yet to gain the physique of a man. 'He's my lad.' This last was defiant and said quite clearly that she neither wanted nor needed Luke any more.

Luke nodded at the boy, whose bemused expression showed clearly, that he was out of his depth with the volatile Katy.

'What's happened to you, then?'

'What?'

Katy pointed to his coat, and for the first time Luke realised his sleeve was torn and his pocket hanging off. 'Been in a barney?' she asked pertly, her eyes flicking to his bare head.

'No.'

'Huh.' It said quite clearly she didn't believe him, and Luke could have cheerfully wiped the saucy expression off her face with the back of his hand.

240

He shrugged instead, keeping his voice quiet and even as he said, 'It's a might treacherous, in case you hadn't noticed.'

The 'huh' came again, followed by, 'Come on, Dennis. We can have the front room till me mam and da get back from our Sidney's.'

Aye, Luke remembered Wednesday nights well. Katy's mam and da round at their eldest son's place for cards and beer, and him and Katy on the sofa in the front room. He didn't envy the poor devil in front of him. She used sex like a weapon, did Katy, and he hadn't caught on for some time what she was about. The skittish façade she put on was just that – a façade; underneath she was a praying mantis, or perhaps a black widow spider was a better analogy. They were venomous and they devoured their mate. Aye, black widow described Katy Chapman to a tee.

As he opened the front door he heard the lad say, 'Who's that then?' and Katy's reply came loud and clear the second before he banged it to, 'He's nowt.'

Nowt. By, he'd had a lucky escape there, even if in the finishing of it her brothers had tried to break every bone in his body.

He walked into the kitchen feeling drained and empty. His world had exploded and the one person he would have done anything to protect had been hurt beyond measure. And it was down to him. Aye, some of it was down to him. And then he looked at Michael's face as he raised his head, and he knew Eva had gone.

There was something very wrong with Polly. Betsy glanced at her mistress, who was working alongside her in the dairy, straining the milk into the thick white-glazed bowls ready for the next morning, when the cream would be skimmed off and put in the deep creampots. Polly was blaming her demeanour on the fact that she had caught a chill from the soaking she'd received five nights ago, but Betsy didn't altogether believe her. Ever since that night they'd barely had a word out of her, and that wasn't like the lass, well or not.

Betsy slanted another quick glance at Polly. And she wasn't eating; scarcely a bite she'd had in days, and everyone knew you should feed a cold and starve a fever. But she didn't have a cold or a chill. Something had happened that day – she'd bet her life on it. At first she'd thought Polly was going down with the skitters like Croft's wife and bairns, and old Enoch who had the cottage next to Croft and helped with the cows, but it wasn't that.

By, what with Polly, and the weather being so bad, and Emily still tending to Croft's wife and bairns twenty-four hours a day, Betsy didn't know if she was on foot or horseback most of the time. And Madam Ruth needed a hot poker up her backside before she'd lift a finger. Even tending to her own grandparents was too much for that little baggage. She just hoped the old lady continued to hold her own, because the way Polly was at the moment it would be the final straw if anything happened to her beloved gran.

Polly was aware of Betsy's concern but her nerves were frayed to such a pitch she didn't trust herself to talk. Any sympathy from her friend and she might well find herself pouring out what had happened, and she mustn't do that. No one must know, not even Betsy; it was too dangerous for Luke. Her head was constantly muzzy and she felt bone tired, but every time she laid her head on the pillow and closed her eyes, her mind began to replay that walk back from Bishopwearmouth and sleep eluded her.

She wished she could unburden herself to Betsy. She lifted the last bowl on to the wooden shelf fixed on the dairy wall, her movements slow. It wasn't that she didn't trust her, but one word spoken out of place, one slip, and Luke would be— Here her exhausted mind ground to an abrupt halt. She couldn't think of what would happen if anyone found out how Arnold had died, not any more. She had been down that road so often in her head over the last five days, and always with it ending one way – Luke hanging at the end of a rope.

'Why don't you go an' make us a nice cup of tea, lass, an' have a warm by the fire while you're about it?'

Polly turned round to find Betsy's worried eyes tight on her, and she forced a smile as she said lightly, 'It's all right, Betsy, there's life in the old girl yet. It's only a cold I've got.'

If a cold was the trouble, she was an organ-grinder's monkey, Betsy thought grimly. 'Aye, be that as it may, lass, I wouldn't say no to a cup meself. It's bad enough in here on a summer's day, but with the snow up to the windows an' it freezin' hard, I can't think of a worse place right at this minute. I shouldn't think there'll be many folk turn out for your aunt's funeral even in the town.'

Polly nodded her agreement but she didn't speak. She had been in bed – courtesy of her 'chill' – the day after Eva had died, when Michael had braved the atrocious weather and made the journey to the farm to inform her grandparents of their daughter's demise, and so she had heard the news second hand. Apparently Michael had also asked if they knew of Arnold's whereabouts, as they had been unable to find him at his lodgings and he was still unaware his stepmother had passed on. Michael had left saying that no doubt Arnold would call at Southwick Road after his shift at the colliery that afternoon, and moreover he quite understood if – what with the terrible weather and all – no one from the farm was able to attend his mother's funeral. His visit had proved to be one of reconciliation with the old people, for which Polly had been grateful, although according to Ruth their mother had refused to see him. Which didn't surprise either of the girls.

It was just as Betsy had walked through from the dairy to join Polly, who was now sitting at the kitchen table peeling potatoes for the mutton stew they were having for dinner, that Emily burst into the kitchen in a whirl of snow and screams, and brought both women jumping to their feet.

'Missus! Missus! Oh, come quick! Come quick!'

They had found the body. It was Polly's first thought and froze her to the spot.

'What's the matter with you?' Betsy's voice was scathing as she glared at Emily, her hand to her racing heart. 'Scaring us!'

'It's the baby! Oh, missus!'

'The baby?' Relief had made Polly sag for a second, but then she straightened immediately, pushing the kitchen maid into a straight-backed chair as she said, 'Calm down, Emily, and tell us properly. It's Croft's baby? What's wrong with it?'

'It's . . . it's . . .' A fresh wail brought Betsy's hand rising to clip the girl's ear, but Polly stopped her housekeeper, saying again, 'What's wrong with the baby, Emily?'

'It was all right yesterday, but I went to lift it out of the crib this mornin' an' it's dead.'

'Dead?' Polly was pulling her shawl over her shoulders as she spoke. 'Are you sure it's not just sleeping?'

'No, missus, it's stiff an' cold, an' Mrs Croft's worse an' wee Ellen can't sit up.'

'Why didn't you come and tell us things were so bad before this?' Betsy asked crossly. 'You haven't got the sense you were born with, girl.'

'Give her a cup of tea, Betsy. I won't be long.'

Polly left them to it and hurried down to Frederick's labourers' cottages. Croft's was the first in the row of five terraced dwellings, but this end cottage was twice the size of the other four, suiting Croft's superior position as overseer. It boasted two rooms downstairs and one large one above which had been divided into three some years ago, and Mrs Croft always kept the house as clean as a new pin despite her limited resources.

Old Enoch lived in the cottage adjoining Croft's, which, like the other three, consisted of a large kitchen with one room above. He lived there alone, having lost his wife the year before, but two of his married sons occupied the next two cottages, with Emily's parents living in the last. Since Emily's brother had married his Mary he had been working on a farm at East Herrington whilst living with Mary's parents, and Frederick hadn't bothered to replace him, as two of Enoch's grandsons were approaching fourteen and helped on the farm. All the men and lads got on well and Croft was a good overseer, so on the whole it was a happy farm.

But not today. When Polly entered Croft's cottage it held the smell of death. Martha Croft was too exhausted with the constant diarrhoea she had endured over the last week to raise her head from the pillow, and her younger daughter, Ellen, looked as though she was going to follow the baby any minute. The other two children, a boy and a girl, weren't so ill but were still lying wan and listless in their bed.

'They weren't as bad as this yesterday, missus, honest.' Emily had followed her over to the cottage and now stood biting on her nails as she and Polly stared down at the wax-like figure of the baby in his crib. 'In fact Mrs Croft said she was goin' to try an' get up today.'

'How's Enoch?' This wasn't normal diarrhoea and sickness; this was much more serious, Polly felt it in her bones.

'Me da says he was right poorly when he went in this mornin',' Emily whimpered, tears running down her face. 'An' me mam says a couple of the others have it now an' all. An' . . .'

'Yes?'

'I don't feel well, missus.'

Snow or no snow, they had to get the doctor here. She'd been telling Frederick that for the last two or three days, but owing to the huge snow drifts and blocked roads he had kept putting it off – partly, she suspected, because she was insisting on it. Since the night it had started snowing they had barely exchanged a civil word, and she knew he was furious because she had called him a liar in front of the others when he had maintained he had waited for her until past four o'clock and then assumed she had taken a horse cab home. He had known what he was doing that night when he had left her in Bishopwearmouth. It had been in the form of a lesson to bring her to heel, and she would hate him for it until the day she died.

'You go home and go to bed, Emily.' The room was stinking, in fact the whole cottage was stinking, but Polly knew from the amount of time the boiler had been going in the washhouse that the beds had been changed umpteen times a day. Enoch's two daughters-in-law had done nothing but live in there since Croft's family were first taken ill. 'We'll send for the doctor.'

That was the start of the nightmare.

They couldn't get the doctor to the farm until the next day, and only then because Frederick, Emily's father and Enoch's two sons worked until they were ready to drop clearing the road between the farm and the outskirts of Bishopwearmouth. The drifts were high and treacherous, and with Croft now ill, along with Enoch and one of his daughters-in-law and her bairns, the farm was barely ticking over.

It was a while before Polly realised they weren't going to find Arnold's body, for it was effectively buried in a wall of ice and snow which only a consistent thaw would melt. In this, if nothing else, she felt fate was on her side.

When the doctor arrived at the farm he initially examined Martha

Croft, who had been the first to exhibit signs of the bowel upset, and when he found the pink spots on her torso and looked at her stools, he asked if she had visited Newcastle in the last weeks. She hadn't, but she had been to see her brother in Sunderland's East End.

Once downstairs again, the doctor took Frederick and Polly aside in Croft's little sitting room and spoke frankly. 'This is a bad business, Frederick, and it will get worse before it's over. I hold out no hope for the woman or the little girl, although the other two children may pull through. It's typhoid fever, man.'

Frederick went as white as a sheet, and as Polly held on to the back of a chair, the doctor continued, 'There was a spot of it in Newcastle in the autumn but they thought they'd contained it. Then it showed up briefly in Bank Street and round the Quays, but again, after what they learned in the last outbreak at the end of '95, they took measures to keep it enclosed. The last thing we wanted was an epidemic. But I've been to two fresh cases this week – this is the third – although the others are in the East End. But Croft's wife's brother is in the East End and he died two days ago. If I didn't know about that I'd be telling you to boil your water and milk, although you can still do that to be on the safe side. But I doubt your water's infected. Oh, and I didn't tell the lass upstairs about her brother, no need to upset her.'

'Damn slums.' Frederick's colour had come back in an angry red flood. 'People living worse than animals with no drainage and muck up to their doorsteps; my pigs are more particular than some of them.'

'Then your pigs are lucky,' the doctor said sharply. 'The conditions some folk are forced to live in is down to the corporations, Frederick, let's have that plain. I've seen rats the size of cats that have taken chunks out of bairns lying in their beds, so don't tell me the people like it. You were born into comfort and you ought to be down on your knees thanking whatever God you pray to for it. Do you know they're only now talking about getting a water supply into some of those streets round the East End? You see how you fare when you're sharing a tap with ten other households and there's one dry privy and washhouse between the lot of you.'

'A bar of soap doesn't cost much,' Frederick said sulkily.

'Have a bit of sense, man!' And then the doctor moderated his tone as he turned to Polly and said, 'Scour everything, everything, mind, whether it's come into contact with anyone who is showing symptoms or not. Boil all the bedding and whoever carries the buckets of slops to the middens needs to wear a towel round their mouth and nose and wash their hands after. Wash your hands all the time, all of you, do you understand?'

Polly nodded, her eyes wide. For the first time since Arnold had laid his hands on her she wasn't thinking about that night. They could all die, and what if her grandda and gran got it? They had nothing on them to fight the disease, she thought sickly. She had to get back to the farmhouse and start scouring everything like the doctor had said. 'How long before we know who's going to have it and who's not?' she asked faintly.

The doctor shrugged, his face sympathetic. 'Could be days or weeks, that's how this thing is. The weather is for you all, funnily enough. It's worse in hot weather, spreads like wildfire then. You understand I'll have to notify the authorities, Frederick? The farm will be in quarantine until you're clear, and you can't sell any milk or eggs, nothing, for the time being. You understand me?' he asked again, Frederick's face being blank. And as Frederick nodded dazedly, 'I'll be back tomorrow hopefully, weather permitting.'

'Aye, aye, all right.'

'I'll take the child with me.' His voice was sober. 'And if anything similar occurs it would be best to designate a certain area for the bod— For the folk concerned.'

Frederick gaped at the doctor before bringing his mouth shut in a snap, and there was a definite note of pleading in his voice when he mumbled, 'But it's only the weak that don't recover, isn't it? And not everyone gets it.'

'Just do what I have said and you'll be fine.' It was said in professional doctor mode and couldn't have been less reassuring.

Polly left the two men talking and walked back over the banked snow and ice to the farmhouse kitchen, her head spinning. Typhoid, the dreaded word that was a curse in itself. Could her aunt's hatred touch her from the grave? First the attack and now this. But no, no, she didn't, she *wouldn't* believe that. She was innocent of any wrongdoing and this was a natural calamity. She wouldn't let Eva frighten her in death any more than she would have allowed her aunt to dominate her in life.

Betsy was elbow deep in dough at the kitchen table, her round face enquiring, as Polly opened the door. 'Typhoid.' It was succinct but said it all.

Betsy sucked in the air between her teeth and then let it out slowly before she said, 'Aye, well, now we know for sure, eh, lass? We can get on with what needs to be done.'

'There's been one or two cases in the East End, which is where Martha must have caught it. She doesn't know, but her brother's dead.'

They stared at each other for a moment and then Polly said, 'Where's Ruth? She's going to have to help. Emily's worse and her mam's feeling bad. It looks like every cottage is going to be affected.' She didn't say 'And I can't see us escaping it in here,' but it was what they were both thinking.

Ruth was in their mother's room, and for once Hilda wasn't ready

246

with a pointed remark or a jibe when Polly knocked and entered the room, but was lying very still, her eyes wide and frightened and her lips working one over the other. 'Well?'

'It's typhoid.' And as her mother's face blanched, Polly said, 'You are going to have to help, Ruth. Both Enoch's daughter-in-laws are worn out, and we've got to keep the boiler going and the washing done. Come on.'

'Polly, I'm feeling bad.' Ruth's face was as white as a sheet and Polly knew immediately her sister wasn't lying. 'I've been hot and I've got a headache, and . . . and I've been several times already this morning.'

'*Get out of this room!*'

Hilda's voice brought Ruth jumping to her feet from where she had been sitting on the side of the bed, and both the girls stared at the woman in the bed, who was now straining back against the pillows, the sheet and blankets pulled up protectively under her chin.

'Open the window, Polly! Let some air in. How could you come in here knowing you're sick?' Hilda raged at Ruth. 'Get out! Get out this instant!'

'*That's enough.*' It wasn't loud, but the quality of Polly's voice silenced the hysterics. Polly put her arm round Ruth's shaking shoulders and drew her sister to her. 'Let's make one thing very plain, Mother,' she said coldly to the furious woman in the bed. 'If you want any windows opening or if you want to eat, then you get up off your backside and do it yourself from now on. I'm going to be busy and so is everyone else who is still standing.'

She shut the door on streams of abuse, leading Ruth into her bedroom and pulling back the covers as she said quietly, 'Get undressed and get into bed, Ruth. I'll bring you a glass of water shortly, and . . . and don't go into Grandda and Gran's room.'

'Oh, Polly.' Ruth was sobbing unrestrainedly now, the scene with her mother having upset her as much as anything. 'I'm not going to die, am I?'

'Of course you are not going to die,' Polly said firmly. 'Get that idea right out of your head. Now do as I say and try to have a sleep.'

Once outside on the landing, Polly stood for a moment, her eyes shut and her body slumped against the stone wall. What else could happen? she asked herself desperately. In the space of a few days her world had been turned upside down. It was as though a giant hand had thrown everything up into the air and nothing of what she had known remained. Would she care if she died? She opened her eyes and stared towards the window, where she saw it was snowing again. Would she? Only yesterday, when her mind was grappling with the memory of Arnold's body pounding into hers, she might have said

247

no, but now, with the knowledge of death all about them, she knew she wanted to live.

She was alive and Arnold was dead. He couldn't hurt her ever again but he could hurt Luke. She turned to the wall, pressing her hands against it and then resting her forehead on them as she prayed silently, If You're there; if You're really there and all this isn't just a mistake, just folly, with no rhyme or reason to it, then keep Luke safe. Please keep him safe. And help me to forget. Blank that night from my mind, God, or else I feel I might go mad.

Chapter Nineteen

God did not blank the memory of that night from Polly's mind, but neither did she go mad in the days that followed. Indeed, most of the time she found she was too exhausted to think at all.

Martha Croft died the morning after the doctor first called at the farm, and old Enoch followed her two hours later. Amazingly, little Ellen rallied, as did Croft's two other children and Croft himself.

As Polly had predicted, the disease touched each of the cottages. Three days after Enoch's death they lost one of his grandsons, but in the next cottage – where each member of the family was in bed for days – everyone slowly recovered. Emily, who had always looked as though a breath of wind could blow her away, threw off the disease quite rapidly and was able to nurse her mother – a big woman who suffered with arthritis – who died within the week.

In the farmhouse, Polly and Betsy fought first for Ruth's life and then for those of her grandmother and grandfather. They cat-napped in the kitchen, sleeping in their clothes as they worked on and off twenty-four hours a day. Carrying slops down the stairs, changing endless beds covered in liquid filth, spooning boiled water into the invalids along with perfected beef juice, washing the bedding, night-shirts and nightgowns in the boiler, mangling and drying everything – no mean feat in the depths of winter as the rows of linen strung up in the kitchen testified – with their hands becoming so red and swollen with the constant washing that the pain was only relieved temporarily by sticking them in the snow outside until they were numb.

Alice was the first to go, just two days after she had first had the diarrhoea. She died peacefully in her sleep, but the shock was too much for Walter and his resulting heart attack was terribly final.

'No, no, Grandda, no.' From the moment they had been unable to wake Alice, it had been just a few minutes before Walter joined her, and Polly couldn't take it in as she stared down at two of the people she loved best in all the world. Walter had taken his wife's hand in his final contortions and now, as she looked at the two hands joined on the counterpane, Polly heard herself crying, 'Why? Oh, why? It's not fair!' through her bitter tears.

'No one could've done more for 'em, lass.' Betsy had come to join her at the bedside. 'There's many would've put 'em in the workhouse rather than marry a man they didn't love.'

Polly was startled into looking at her. 'You knew?' she hiccuped on a sob.

'I'm not as daft as I look.' It was stoical and would have been funny in any other circumstances.

'Oh, Betsy.'

'They were old, lass, an' worn out as you might say. It was their time.'

'But I don't want them to go.' She stared down into the two dear old faces, which death had made look much younger, smoothing out the lines and wrinkles. 'What will I do without them?' They had always loved her, unreservedly, unconditionally, and it was only now that Polly knew how much she would miss them.

'You'll go on, lass.' Betsy's voice was soft. 'That's your nature.'

'And if I can't?' She was tired. She was so, so tired.

'You don't know the meanin' of the word.'

Polly looked at her friend, a long look. 'You'll help me lay them out? I want them to be clean, nice, when they come for them.'

'Aye, lass. Of course.'

Ruth cried when she was told but Polly stayed with her for some time, holding her sister close and soothing her with kindness. She let Betsy tell their mother.

Over the next three days Polly could see Ruth slipping away from them and she almost lived in her sister's bedroom, forcing her to drink, keeping her clean, sponging her hot forehead and talking to her incessantly. It was on the fourth night after Alice and Walter's deaths – and ten days after Ruth had first got the disease – that some pinkness returned to her face and she was able to sleep most of the night through, with Polly holding her hand as she sat in a chair by the side of her sister's bed.

Through it all Hilda had stayed in her room, emerging only to hurry down to the kitchen for food and drink, which she had whisked back up to the bedroom, and for visits to the midden with her chamber pot, which Polly had insisted her mother empty herself from the first day the typhoid had hit the farmhouse.

'Poll?' It was the morning after Ruth was showing signs of pulling through, and Polly was feeding her sister beef juice as Ruth lay propped against the pillows. 'Thank you.'

'Thank you?' The few hours of uninterrupted sleep in the chair by the bed had made her feel worse, not better, and Polly's voice was drugged with exhaustion as she said, 'What for?'

'For . . . for being my big sister, for loving me.'

'Of course I love you.'

'I don't know why.' Ruth's voice was weak but dogged. 'I've been horrible to you.'

'No you haven't.' And then, as Polly saw Ruth's eyebrows rise, she smiled and said, 'Well, maybe you have sometimes.'

'Oh, Poll, I'm sorry.' Ruth turned her head to the side and bit down hard on her lower lip.

'Don't be daft.' As Polly saw tears squeeze from under Ruth's eyelids she patted her arm, her voice soothing as she said, 'You're feeling low, it's only natural. Give it a couple of days and you'll be more like yourself.'

'I hope not.' It was surprising coming from Ruth. 'I've found I don't like myself very much.'

'Well, it's only you that can do something about that.'

'I know it.' Ruth stared at her, the tears continuing to trickle down her white cheeks, which seemed drawn in to her skull with the effects of the illness. 'I don't want to end up like Mam, Poll. I can feel meself being like her sometimes – most of the time the last few years – and even though I knew how horrible I was being I didn't stop. But I will now, I mean it.'

'Good.' Polly patted her sister's arm again. Ruth's eyelids were already closing and she didn't have the strength of a kitten; sleep was the best medicine at the moment. 'You have a little nap, I'll be back shortly.'

Polly thought about what her sister had said as she walked down the stairs with the tray containing the bowl and towel she had used to wash Ruth's face and hands before she had fed her. Would Ruth try to change once she was feeling better? People said all sorts of things when they were at death's door, and Ruth knew she had nearly died, but once the danger was past and things settled down again, memories were selective. Only time would tell.

For the next few days it seemed as though the farm was in a period of recovery. Ruth slept constantly and barely had the strength to raise herself on her pillows for the beef juice and boiled water and milk Polly insisted her patient swallow every couple of hours, but her sister's cheeks were regaining some colour and the terrible gaunt, sunken look had left her face, and for this Polly was thankful, even as she grieved for her grandparents every minute she was awake. She and Betsy continued to work like horses, but with the danger past they were able to sleep in their own beds for a few hours each night, which both women desperately needed.

Hilda still wouldn't poke her nose out of her bedroom or allow anyone in, scurrying downstairs and then back again like a frightened rabbit when she needed to empty her chamber pot or fetch food. On the fifth day after Ruth's crisis point had passed, Polly knocked on her mother's door, saying, 'There's no need for you to worry any more; the doctor has just gone and he thinks we are over it.'

251

'Huh!' The exclamation was loud and Hilda didn't open her door. 'Fat lot the quacks know. I remember 1895. They said the same then and that was just before the worst bout hit.'

'As you like, Mother. As you like.' She didn't have the time or the inclination to argue with her, Polly thought to herself as she walked downstairs. She couldn't ever remember feeling such a consuming tiredness as was on her now, although she blessed it in a way. When her head touched the pillow at night she was asleep, and slumber meant the gnawing core of hatred at the centre of her being slept too. Hatred against a dead man; hatred against her husband; against the injustice that had made a beast like Arnold so much stronger and physically powerful than a woman; against the disease that had taken her beloved granny and grandda at a time when she most needed to see their dear faces . . .

She forced her mind away from such weakening thoughts as she opened the door to the kitchen, but immediately she saw Betsy's face and Emily sitting at the table, her eyes pink-rimmed, she knew there was further trouble. 'What is it?'

'Me da.' Emily sniffed loudly, rubbing the back of her hand across her nose as she said, 'He's been bad for days an' not told anyone, an' now he's turnin' inside out. I'd better get back to him.'

So her mother had been right after all. Polly stared at the little kitchen maid. It wasn't over yet.

It definitely wasn't over.

Polly had been planning to move into her grandparents' room once the farmhouse returned to normal while she thought about what she was going to do in the immediate future. With her grandparents gone she didn't intend to remain living as Frederick's wife, but the spectre of Arnold's body in its icy tomb seemed to dictate that she had to remain where she was at least until it was found and she knew there were going to be no repercussions involving Luke. The way winter had set in, that could be some months away, but she could just about bear staying if she didn't have to lie next to Frederick each night with just a feather bolster separating her from the man she loathed.

All through the last three weeks Polly and Frederick had exchanged no more than monosyllables, so at three o'clock that afternoon, when she had just lit the oil lamps in the kitchen where she and Betsy were baking a batch of bread, she didn't raise her head from arranging the loaf tins along the fender and covering them with clean cloths as Frederick entered from the hallway.

'I'm bad.'

'What?'

'*Bad.* I've got the skitters.' All Frederick's normal heartiness and patronising manner had been swept away, and the man standing in the doorway looked scared to death.

Polly straightened slowly. She vaguely remembered Frederick using the night closet several times during the night, but such was her exhaustion, she hadn't been sure if she had just dreamed it when she had awoken in the morning to find him sleeping peacefully on the other side of the bolster. Now, as she looked into her husband's face – really looked at him for the first time since the night she had staggered into the house wet through and hurting from Arnold's attack – she thought, He's got it. I can see it in his face.

'What am I going to do?' It was a whimper and could have come from a child rather than a man.

For a moment Polly almost said, 'Why ask me? You couldn't wait an extra few minutes for me and because of that I was attacked and raped and murder was done. Don't ask me what to do because I don't care,' but instead she forced herself to say, and calmly, 'Go to bed, of course.'

'Get the doctor.'

'He will do no more than he has done over the last three weeks and you know it, besides which, he will be here at the end of the week as arranged.'

'*Get the doctor!*'

'Don't shout at me, Frederick.'

It was cold and tight, and for a moment Frederick seemed bereft of speech, but then, possibly because he realised the vulnerable position he was in, he became almost cringing as he said, 'Please, Polly, please. Get the doctor. I have to see him, I do.'

'I'll get Croft to send one of the men in the horse and trap.' It was abrupt. 'You know about Herbert Longhurst?'

'Aye.' Again the whimper. 'I was thinking we'd seen the back of it; he said that, didn't he? The doctor said that.'

'He was wrong.' She stared at him and there was a long pause before he turned on his heel and they heard him mounting the stairs at the end of the hall.

'By, he's fair petrified, lass.'

Like she had been on that snowy road when she stared into the hot eyes of the man who was going to rape her. Polly turned to look at Betsy, and there was something in the younger woman's gaze that silenced any further remarks from the housekeeper.

Dr Braithwaite was not best pleased at being called out to Stone Farm on a bitterly cold night that promised more snow, and he made that plain to his colleague from the gentlemen's club when he said, his tone irritable, 'This could have waited until morning, Frederick. I wouldn't have come but for our friendship. Now, I gather you're worried you have the fever?'

Frederick stared first at the doctor standing by the side of the bed, and then at Polly, who was just inside the bedroom door, and as his eyes slowly returned to the doctor, he said, 'I have it all right, same as Herbert Longhurst. I thought you said we were over the worst?'

The doctor echoed Polly's words as he said shortly, 'I was wrong. Now, you're in the best place, so just stay there. Boiled water or milk, and keep warm. You're a big strong man, Frederick, you'll be all right in time for your Christmas dinner. Now, let's have a look at you.'

The examination completed, during which time Polly had walked across the room to stare out of the window with her back to the bed, Dr Braithwaite said quietly, 'Mrs Weatherburn? You've been scouring everything as I said?'

'Yes, I have, Doctor.'

'And the middens? Have the contents been buried as I suggested?'

Polly turned to look at Frederick; the privies were the men's province.

'Aye.' Frederick nodded. 'Although . . .'

'What? Spit it out, man.'

'Well, the men were tied up with getting the sheep out of the bottom pasture because of the drifts, and you'd said we were over it, so I took the last lot meself to the quarry. The ground's rock hard for digging.'

'But Herbert Longhurst was going down with it,' said Dr Braithwaite sharply.

'Aye, well, I didn't know that, did I? The damn fool never said nowt to no one, not even his own daughter.'

'Did you get any on you?'

'Just a bit on me boots as it went over and a couple of splashes on me breeches. It really needs two to tip it and there was a bit of a wind.' And then Frederick's eyes narrowed. 'Why? Is that how I got it?'

'I told you all that you had to be meticulous where the stools were concerned, as well as everything else. For crying out loud, man!' And then the doctor took a deep breath and his voice was of a soothing quality when he said, 'Come on, Frederick. Don't take on. It'll be all right.'

Only it wasn't.

The doctor called several times over the next ten days, and although he was consistently bright and cheerful with the patient, his face straightened once he was outside the bedroom. Emily's father – partly through his own foolishness of trying to carry on when he was so ill, according to the grim-faced doctor – had died within three days, and a distraught Emily was now sharing Betsy's bed, being unable to face the empty cottage.

On the tenth morning, the doctor took Polly aside once they were downstairs. 'He's not doing too well, I'm afraid,' he said soberly. That was the thing with this disease: it was no respecter of persons, high or low. Inevitably it first broke out in the dismal wilderness of tenemented property in which mean back-to-back houses had little ventilation or light and sanitary conditions were a practical impossibility, but then the thing could spread like wildfire. In the poorer parts of Sunderland and down by the docks in particular, the overcrowding, poverty and

254

consequent ill health made conditions that were ripe for cholera and typhoid, the doctor thought bitterly, and the sailors coming off the boats from foreign parts didn't make his job any easier. It only needed one with an infectious disease and they were off again. But he'd hoped Frederick's farm would get off lighter than it had. And now Frederick himself looked to be sinking . . .

Polly stared at the pleasant-faced man in front of her. Was he saying Frederick was dying? People died of typhoid fever, of course they did, but somehow she had never thought it a possibility with her husband. He was fond of boasting he'd never had a day's illness in his life and had a constitution like a horse, and he'd never known want or hardship either. Good food from a bairn; this lovely home: he'd been cosseted – aye, that was the word all right – cosseted from the day he was born. If little Ellen Croft could fight the disease and win, surely a big robust man like Frederick could? She said as much to the doctor, who shook his head slowly.

'Doesn't always work like that, m'dear, and I don't like this new complication, the vomiting. I'm going to leave you some pepsin and strychnine in tabloid form, and you must keep strictly to the dose, all right?' They were walking to the front door now, and as Polly opened it, Dr Braithwaite looked out on to the swirling snow and leaden sky, and sighed deeply. 'Hasn't let up for a minute, has it,' he murmured. 'I nearly couldn't get through again this morning.'

Polly nodded in reply. She had noticed the doctor had arrived later than was his normal custom when visiting the farm, and that he was on horseback rather than driving his smart horse and trap, and had assumed the roads were bad. The last newspaper the doctor had brought for Frederick had forecast the worst winter for decades.

Betsy joined her at the door as Polly stood watching the doctor walk to his horse, which was tethered in the large cobbled yard beyond the flowerbeds and small stone wall, and as he turned to wave just beyond the wooden gate into the yard and slipped on the cobbles, she said stolidly, 'Arse over head he's gone, everywhere's solid ice.'

They looked at the good doctor scrabbling embarrassedly to his feet, and in spite of the dire circumstances Polly couldn't repress a smile when Betsy added, 'Pity Croft's not long led the bull across to the other barn; I don't think that dung on the back of his nice coat is going to smell too sweet on the ride back.'

'Oh, Betsy.' Polly leaned against the older woman for a moment. Thank God – and she meant that – for Betsy.

'What's wrong, lass? An' I don't mean all this with the fever an' all. There's somethin' else, isn't there? You've not bin right the last month.'

She didn't feel as though she would ever be right again but she knew that would pass. Two brothers and yet they couldn't have been

255

more different, and what she had to keep remembering – and blanking out the rest – was Luke's gentleness and concern, his overwhelming understanding in the aftermath of Arnold's brutality. She remained still for a second more, leaning against Betsy's familiar bulk, and she had to check herself from giving way to the urge to unburden herself. She wanted comfort; she wanted someone to make the last month disappear and for them to be back at the point where Luke had visited the farmhouse and told them Eva was ill. And no one could do that.

'I'm just exhausted, Betsy, and you must be too.'

Betsy nodded. Whatever it was that was weighing Polly down, she didn't want to talk about it, but Betsy had always been of a mind that a trouble shared was a trouble halved. She turned to look into the beautiful face next to her in which the deep blue eyes sat like two jewels in a crown, and her voice was uncharacteristically qentle when she said, 'You know I'm for you, lass? No matter what, I'm for you.'

'I know that, Betsy,' said Polly softly. She straightened, squaring her shoulders and stepping back into the hall before shutting the door. 'I'd better take Frederick some boiled water, it's all he can keep down at the moment.'

'Aye, all right, lass.' You could never tell what went on behind closed doors, but she'd bet her life all this with the lass could be traced back to the man lying upstairs. Had he hit her? Was that it? No, Polly wasn't the type to stand for that. But whatever it was, it was serious.

Polly took Ruth a drink first, and spent a few minutes talking to her sister, who was now gaining ground rapidly and had got up for an hour or two the night before. And it seemed as if Ruth's thoughts had moved along a similar vein to Betsy's, because as Polly rose to leave the room Ruth said quietly, 'What's wrong, Poll? There's something more than Gran and Grandda, isn't there?'

Polly didn't answer for a moment. She and Ruth were getting closer by the day and it really did seem as though the fever had purged Ruth clean of her old ways, but – and awful though it was, considering Ruth was her own sister – she didn't know if she could trust her. And it was Arnold. *Arnold.* Ruth was going to be devastated enough when the body was found without anything more. Her thoughts prompted her to say quietly, 'I'm all right, Ruth, don't worry, but I've been thinking . . . You haven't mentioned Arnold at all. Are you missing him?'

She actually found it repugnant to say the name out loud, and as she watched Ruth's face and the look of surprise that flashed across it she found she was holding her breath.

'Missing him?' Ruth clearly hadn't considered the notion. 'I haven't really thought of him, to be honest, not with being so ill and all. But . . . well, no, not really, Poll. It's . . . well, not like that with him and me, if you know what I mean.'

256

She was stammering and stuttering a bit, and Polly's voice was low as she said, 'I didn't want to embarrass you.'

'I should be missing him, shouldn't I.' It was a statement of fact and made with a note of confusion in her voice. 'If I thought anything of him.'

'Do you? Think anything of him?'

'I don't actually think I like him, Poll.' And now the bewilderment was evident. 'But I haven't faced that until now. He was just so keen on me, that's the thing, but it would have been a terrible mistake, wouldn't it?'

Polly noted the past tense with such relief she had to turn away in case her face betrayed her. You aren't going to break her or me, Arnold, she said fiercely in her mind. We're stronger than you, do you hear me, wherever you are? We're stronger than you. 'I think so, Ruth.'

'I'll tell him.' It was said with resolution. 'The next time I see him I'll tell him. When do you think people will be allowed to call again?'

'Not until the doctor is sure it's safe.' Polly turned at the door to face her. 'There's a notice on the bottom gate in the lane stating we're in quarantine.' Which had sent Frederick into a rage when it was first put up. The thought of her husband prompted her to say, 'I've got to take Frederick this drink, so try and have a nap. You don't want to overdo it.'

'I was going to say you're worse than Mam, but she's never bothered with either of us, even when we were bairns,' Ruth said ruefully. 'I think the only reason she's ever made a fuss of me at times was to try and get at you. It was Gran and Grandda who brought us up, wasn't it? I . . . I miss them, Poll. I wish I could have them back just long enough to say sorry for all the times I was nasty . . .'

'Oh, Ruth, don't cry.' Polly went swiftly to her sister's side, sitting on the edge of the iron bedstead and taking Ruth's shaking body into her arms. Both girls' faces were wet when eventually Polly pulled away, but she could see Ruth had gained some relief from the outpouring of emotion, although the hard angry core where her own heart was was just as heavy for Polly. But it was helping her to get through each day without breaking down, and that was what she needed at the moment, she reminded herself. She had to stay angry; it stopped the desire to lay her head on the pillow and will herself never to wake up, as she'd done in the first few days before the typhoid fever had hit, and it banished the awful feeling of uncleanness that no amount of scrubbing at her skin could take away.

It was true what she'd said to Luke that night on the road – she *was* glad Arnold was dead. She faced the thought head on. He'd paid the ultimate price for what he'd done to her, and she wasn't going to pretend she felt sorry either. If nothing else, knowing he wasn't in the world, sniggering, *gloating* about the rape, made it bearable. Just.

Once outside her sister's room, Polly crossed the shadowed landing, the snow-smeared window letting in little light in spite of it just touching midday, and entered the newer wing of the farmhouse. Since Frederick had been taken ill, Polly had followed through on her earlier decision and moved into her grandparents' old room, ostensibly because of the fever. Since she had done that, she had got into the habit of knocking on the door before she entered her husband's room, but today – her mind being elsewhere – she simply opened the door and walked in, carrying the glass of water.

'What on earth?' Frederick appeared to have fallen out of bed and was scrabbling about on the floor, the big clippy mat at his side of the bed in a heap. 'What are you trying to do?' she asked, quickly placing the glass on the small round table by the side of the bed and helping him to rise.

'I need the closet.'

He was weaker, she knew that, but she didn't think he was so bad he was unable to visit the closet without help. She would have to bring a pallet up tonight and sleep on the horsehair sofa which stood under the big window, even though the smell from the dry closet leading off the room was enough to turn your stomach. She and Betsy between them were cleaning it every couple of hours but still the stench was bad. Or perhaps he'd have to start using a chamber pot?

Frederick did not want to use a chamber pot and he made it into the closet and back to bed without help, although he was a little unsteady on his legs.

Polly straightened the clippy mat whilst he was gone and noticed one of the floorboards it covered had a large chip out of the side of it, which no doubt was the reason for the mat – to prevent splinters in bare feet.

'Here, drink this water.' Once Frederick had pulled the covers over himself she handed him the glass, and then wrinkled her brow when he gazed at it suspiciously.

'What's in it?'

'Water, I told you.'

'I don't believe you.'

'What?'

'You're trying to do me in! I know, I know. I want Hilda to take care of me, we've an understanding, me and her. Where is she?'

'She's in the same place she's been for the last five years,' Polly said drily, 'and if you think she would come and tend to you you don't know her very well. She might consent to swan downstairs and play the gracious invalid in the evenings when everything is normal, but that is the most you will get my mother to do.'

'She'll come if she knows I want her to. She'd do anything for me, Hilda would. She never argues with me like you do.'

'She wouldn't touch you with a bargepole with what you've got,' Polly said flatly. 'Now are you going to drink this water or not?'

258

She left him muttering and talking to himself, and once in the kitchen said to Betsy, 'He's worse, Betsy. I think he's a bit delirious. I'm going to have to sleep in there tonight. Would you help me bring up a straw pallet and some blankets?'

'Aye, lass, aye, but I don't mind a straw pallet meself.' She cast a meaningful look at Emily, who was occupied in jointing a rabbit. The little kitchen maid was inconsolable at the loss of both her parents, and Polly knew Betsy was having her work cut out to maintain sympathy, especially when Emily insisted on talking half the night about times past with her family.

'Thanks, but perhaps when he's getting better?' And he would get better, she couldn't imagine anything else. Frederick was too healthy normally to succumb now.

However, by the next morning it was clear there was a distinct change in him. They had had a dreadful night and she had had to change the bed three times, her stomach heaving until she was sick twice. Was she getting it now? She had sat watching the dawn rise at one point, the light-washed sky a sea of pale pink and mother-of-pearl, and she'd wondered when the nightmare was going to end. There was blood in his stools and in his vomit, and in spite of herself she found she was sorry for him. He was so pathetic, so frightened. Surely the doctor could do something?

Over the next week Polly discovered the doctor was powerless against the slow, insidious creep of death.

'Perforated bowel and other complications,' Dr Braithwaite informed her. 'And the ironic thing, the sad thing,' he continued soberly, 'is that with Frederick being such a big, strong, healthy individual in the normal run of things, he's going more slowly and painfully now. More stamina, you see. A lesser being would have been snuffed out long before this.'

Frederick was delirious most of the time but still in a great deal of pain, and Polly found his suffering had mellowed her feelings towards him. He was dying inch by inch and it was impossible not to feel pity towards him. And he hadn't meant the attack to happen when he had left her so churlishly that night, she told herself as she sponged down his shrinking body. Whatever else, he hadn't meant that, and she wouldn't have wished a rabid dog to die like this.

She was feeling ill herself, especially in the mornings, which she put down to the horrendous night hours when she was lucky if she snatched two or three hours' sleep. Betsy had joined her in Frederick's room on a pallet on the floor, as it took both of them to change the bed, a task which needed to be done incessantly.

It was on December the eighteenth, a Monday, and very early in the morning, when Polly was roused for the umpteenth time by Frederick mumbling her name. He had done this consistently in his delirium, and often when he had soiled himself, but this time, as she leaned over the bed, she felt his eyes were really looking at her. Betsy was fast asleep on her pallet, and Polly, conscious of her friend's exhaustion, whispered softly, 'Frederick? Can you hear me?'

'Polly.'

'Yes, it's Polly.' She felt dazed, weary in mind and body, and her voice reflected this when she said, 'What is it? Do you want a drink?' He didn't appear to be lying in a dirty bed.

'Polly.' His face seemed to have been sucked in but his lips were cracked and swollen despite the goose fat Polly and Betsy smeared on them constantly. 'Polly; sorry, Polly.'

'It's all right, Frederick, it's all right, dear. Go to sleep.'

'No, explain. Explain, Polly.' And then he fell to muttering nonsense again, and she was just going to walk back to her pallet when he clutched out to her, and, once she had taken his hand in her own, mumbled faintly, 'Didn't mean . . . Box yours, Polly. Make it . . . all right.' And then, his face changing, 'Pain . . . bad.'

'I know, dear, I know.' It turned her stomach to see his suffering, and now she did something she would have believed herself incapable of in the first days after Arnold's attack: she sat down on the edge of the bed and cradled his upper body in her arms, stroking his forehead as she said, 'Go to sleep, Frederick, and everything will be all right, I promise.'

'Fri-frightened, Polly. So . . . frightened.'

'There's no need. I'm here and I won't leave you. Do you understand?'

'Box, Polly.'

The box again. 'Aye, yes, the box. Don't worry about the box now, we'll sort it. You sleep and I'll stay with you.'

As his breathing eased a little, Polly leaned back against the wall, still holding Frederick in her arms, and shut her eyes. She could sleep for a week, a month; she'd never felt so tired in all her life.

The next time she awoke it was to the realisation that her arms were numb and her neck was in such an awkward position against the wall she felt as though it was cracking. It was still early morning, but light now, and as she glanced down at Frederick in her arms she thought for a moment he had gone, such was his stillness. But then, after seconds, he took a breath before falling into the long stillness again.

'He's going, lass.' Betsy was sitting on her pallet and she rubbed sleepy eyes as she said, 'I've seen it afore, this breathin'. It won't be long now.'

It wasn't. Within the hour Frederick died, still in Polly's arms and without regaining consciousness. She was a widow.

Chapter Twenty

Polly was sick again the morning after Frederick's passing, and whether it was due to the fact that the punishing regime of the last weeks had eased or that Betsy was with her on this occasion – having brought her an early cup of tea – and something in the other woman's face brought her up sharp, she didn't know. But suddenly she understood. She wasn't ill – this was something far, far worse than the fever. She was expecting a child. Arnold's child.

She raised her head from the big china washing bowl that normally stood on a table under the window with a matching jug, and which Betsy had hastily brought to her when she had begun to heave on sitting up in bed, and such was the look on her face that Betsy said quickly, 'It's natural, lass, it's only natural. A bairn will be some comfort to you.'

Some comfort? The desire to laugh was on her but she knew if she once gave way to it she would go hysterical, and then . . . Then mad perhaps. Who knew? Because certainly if anything was guaranteed to send her over the edge into insanity, this latest development was.

Once a worried Betsy had left the room, Polly lay unmoving in the big feather bed, her eyes staring out of the window directly opposite. She had chosen this room for her grandda and gran because of the view and the low window, knowing her grandda would never leave his bed again. It was a nice outlook in the summer: field upon field of grazing cattle and a low hill in the distance . . . And then her brain clicked out of the stupor it had taken refuge in after the first shock; she had to get rid of it, people did, didn't they? Emily's mother had taken something the year before, according to Betsy, when she'd discovered she was expecting yet another bairn at the ripe old age of forty-five and gone half mad in the process. She'd been ill for weeks, mind, but Polly didn't care how ill she was if she got rid of this . . . this thing, this monster growing inside her. *She couldn't bear it.*

She leapt out of bed and began to pace the room, her eyes wild. She had put the absence of her monthly cycle down to exhaustion and strain; why hadn't she realised before? She must be . . . what? She calculated quickly from the date of her last period. Six weeks pregnant. Six weeks, that wasn't much. You couldn't really call it a baby at six weeks; it would just be like she was taking a laxative like liquorice root or syrup of figs.

She sat down heavily on the bed. Where had Emily's mother got whatever she had used? Somewhere in the town perhaps, or maybe when she'd visited her sister. Would Betsy know?

Betsy didn't know. Furthermore, the housekeeper made it very plain how she viewed such things when Polly took her aside later that morning. 'It's murder, lass, pure an' simple, although there's nothin' pure about it. It nearly did May in when she took that medicine last year, an' I still reckon that's why she took the fever so bad: judgement on her.'

'Oh, don't be so silly, Betsy.' It was a snap and a tight one, and as the housekeeper stared at her in hurt surprise, Polly said, 'I can't have this baby and that's the end of it. If you can't help me I'll have to make my own enquiries, won't I, because I am *not having it.*'

'Granted it's not ideal, but I thought you'd made it up a bit with the master afore he went?'

'It's not as simple as that.'

'Why not?'

Polly turned round, walking out into the washhouse without answering, and began to pummel the clothes in the poss tub that Enoch's daughters-in-law had left soaking, the washing being their job on the farm. The knowledge that Arnold's seed had taken root inside her had brought back images she'd thought she was gaining victory over, and she moaned softly, working the clothes so violently the water washed over the side of the big wooden tub and on to her boots.

'Here, missus, I'll do that. I just left it soakin' while I went to change him.'

Polly turned round to see Lotty, the younger daughter-in-law, standing in the doorway of the washhouse with her twelve-month-old son dangling on her hip. She stared at the child and he stared back at her, his brown eyes enormous and his curly hair drooping over his rounded forehead. He had been clingy since the family had recovered from the typhoid and refused to leave his mother now even for a minute.

'You all right, missus?'

She must look dreadful, given the note in Lotty's voice. Polly forced a smile, dragging her eyes from the child with an effort, as she said, 'So-so, Lotty. So-so.'

'Aye, well, aren't we all.' It was sober. 'Doreen's still half mad at losin' her David like that an' him still just a bairn. It's not so bad when you're older, is it, missus, but it don't seem fair when they're young. All bairns ought to have their fair chance at life. An' there was poor Martha's little un an' all. Just three months, he was.'

The words were hitting Polly with the force of a sledgehammer and it took all her will power to nod and walk out of the washhouse without breaking down. 'All bairns ought to have their fair chance at life.' Oh God, God, how could You do this? How could You let it happen so I have to make this choice?

Polly wrestled with herself for the next few days. Owing to the circumstances, there was to be no grand funeral for Frederick as would have been expected in the normal way of things; just a brief visit to the churchyard, where the parson would say a few words at the open grave before the family and farm workers returned to the farm. Right up until the morning of the funeral, Polly was in a pit of black despair, reliving the horror of the rape over and over and telling herself she couldn't – she just *couldn't* – bear this child for nine months without losing her reason. But every time she decided that a visit to Sunderland's East End was the only option, the vision of a pair of enormous liquid brown eyes would swim into her mind, along with a pair of tiny fat dimpled hands as they had clung to Lotty's buxom hips.

Owing to the fact that Christmas Day fell on a Monday, it was decided to bury Frederick on the Saturday before, the twenty-third, rather than wait until after the festive period.

The clock said twenty minutes past seven when Polly roused herself on the morning of the funeral after another restless night of tossing and turning, and after climbing wearily out of bed she walked across to the window, opening it wide and letting the freezing air into the room. The fields lay before her, clothed in white and beautiful in their starkness, the cattle being in the cow byres for the most part, or in the enclosed field at the back of the farmhouse, owing to the deep snow. Everything looked fresh this morning, and there had been a severe frost the night before which made the snow sparkle like diamond dust. The sun was up, and although it was weak and without warmth, its golden rays touched the silver below and created a brightness that was dazzling. The world was clean, clean and newly washed, and as Polly drank in the pure air in great gulps she felt, for the first time in weeks, that she was clean too.

And it was in that moment she knew she couldn't end the life inside her, because if she did – if she succumbed to what she really wanted to do – she would never feel clean again. Arnold hadn't made her dirty, *he hadn't*, only if she let him. And she wouldn't. She wouldn't let him touch the inner core of herself, the place where her thoughts and her soul were. She was going to fight him and fight the weakness inside herself that tried to make her believe she would never know joy or happiness again. This bright morning was a promise that she would get through this.

She pushed back her mass of hair from her shoulders and took more of the biting air deep into her lungs. Arnold was dead and she was alive; in spite of the typhoid she was alive, and she had never even caught the disease. That said something, didn't it? That was a promise in itself. She had won. *I've won, Arnold. Do you hear me? I have won.*

The funeral was dismal and the only attendees were family, those from the farm Croft could spare, the solicitor – and Luke. Polly's heart leapt out of her breast when she saw him standing to one side of the churchyard entrance. She had asked Dr Braithwaite to get a message to the house in Southwick Road to let them know the present circumstances at the farm, but she hadn't expected Luke would make the journey from Monkwearmouth, not for Frederick.

But it wasn't for Frederick Luke had come.

The ground was so frozen, the gravedigger had had his work cut out, and as the small group of people stood round, Luke found he couldn't take his eyes off the beautiful white face opposite him. She looked ill, fragile. His guts were twisting and turning and it was taking all his control not to leap over the grave and take her in his arms. What had she gone through in the last weeks? He'd nearly gone mad when he'd found access to the farm barred to him. But at least she was free of Frederick now. He had always felt in the heart of him that something was badly wrong with Polly's marriage, and the way Frederick had left her that night, the— He caught at the profanities hovering at the back of his mind, and then in the same breath told himself not to be so damn stupid. What was with this notion that you shouldn't speak ill of the dead? Death didn't change a sinner into a saint or an evil swine into a good man.

'Ashes to ashes, dust to dust . . .'

It was over. Luke made his way immediately to Polly's side – something Hilda's eagle eyes noted – and said without any preamble, 'How are you?'

'I'm . . . I'm all right.' The colour was coming and going in her face, but seeing him here, so big and solid and handsome, was reminding her of so much. His gentleness that night, his protectiveness, the way it had felt to be in his arms . . . But other things too. Her helplessness in the face of Arnold's intent, his brother's body on hers, *in* hers. It was too much. She couldn't cope with this, not now. 'Thank you for coming, but you shouldn't have, not with the snow and all.'

'I wanted to.' She wanted to get away from him, it was coming off her in waves. 'I let Michael know about Frederick but he couldn't get away, not so soon after his mother's death and with Frederick being no relation.'

'Michael?' And then she forced her mind into gear. 'Oh, yes, thank you. Thank you.'

'Arnold didn't see fit to join you then?' Hilda had approached them and her tone was stringent. Since her stepbrother's death everyone at the farm had noticed a startling difference in Polly's mother. It was as though she were the mistress now, not her daughter, Betsy had remarked the previous day to Emily when Hilda had marched into the kitchen and caused mayhem until Polly had arrived on the scene and forced her to retreat. Funny how all of a sudden she'd found the use of her legs, wasn't it? By, they were going to have some do's all right, because Polly wouldn't stand for her mam throwing her weight about. And Ruth now, what had happened to her? All sweetness and light! Betsy had brought her chin down into her neck as she'd nodded conspiratorially at Emily. She didn't have any quarrel with that, mind, of course she didn't, but that wasn't Ruth, was it? That was the thing. All topsy-turvy everything was – backside about tit and never mind the herrings, as her mam used to say.

'Arnold?' Luke's voice was cool. 'No one has seen hide nor hair of him for weeks, so if you see him before I do you can tell him he can forget any more shifts at the colliery. They don't appreciate being let down without a word.'

'What?' Hilda's eyes narrowed like bullets. 'What are you saying? Arnold's missing?'

'I don't know about missing, but like I said, he hasn't turned up for work, and according to his landlady he hasn't been back there for weeks. I've had to bring his things home because she's renting out his room again now.'

'Have you notified the police?'

'Aye.'

'Ruth!' Hilda called to Ruth, who was standing talking to Lotty and Emily. 'Have you heard this?' And as Ruth joined them, 'Tell her, go on. There's something fishy here.'

Ruth listened to Luke but made no comment, and when her mother said irritably, 'Well?' Ruth gave her a long look before she said, 'What do you want me to say? I'm sure he has a good reason for leaving, and no doubt he'll be back soon.'

'You don't think it odd he went without a word to you, girl?'

That 'girl' had stuck in Ruth's craw for years but she'd never realised it till now. She stared into the tight, discontented face of the woman who had borne her – because that was all she had done; she'd certainly never been a mother – and said quietly, 'No, I don't. There was nothing between us; he hadn't asked for me, as you well know.'

'It was just a matter of time.'

'And perhaps he decided the time was right to move on.'

'You can't believe that!' Hilda stared at her younger daughter in exasperation. Arnold had known his place, and he had been so respectful of Frederick and of herself too; she had foreseen herself lording it over him and Ruth for the rest of her life. He had often brought her little gifts: chocolates sometimes, or maybe the *People's Friend* or *The Lady*. He had understood she was a gentlewoman.

'I do.' Ruth's gaze was very level. 'And it suits me just fine.'

'Hmph!' Hilda drew her thin, scraggy body up until she resembled nothing so much as a vicious black crow. 'I can see who you've been listening to,' she hissed quietly with one nasty glance at Polly's white face. 'You're a fool, girl. Always were and always will be.'

'Ruth has been listening to her own mind for once,' Polly said evenly, forcing the words out of her tight throat with some effort. 'And she has never been a fool.'

'Oh, so that's how it is.' Hilda was speaking as though Luke wasn't there. 'How nice and cosy.'

Polly ignored her mother's rudeness, inclining her head towards Luke as she said quietly, 'The doctor has advised it would be unwise for anyone to come to the farm for the next two weeks, until we are sure the disease has burned itself out, but you will be more than welcome then if you would care to call.'

It was a dismissal and Luke recognised it as such, but what he didn't understand was that Polly had reached breaking point. One more word about Arnold – and with the sound in the background of the clods of frozen earth thumping on to Frederick's coffin – and she'd scream, she thought wildly.

Luke nodded, his eyes narrowing and his mouth straight, but he said nothing more as he watched the three women make their way over to Betsy and the others. What had he expected? he asked himself bitterly. It was a wonder she had talked to him at all when you considered his connection with Arnold. Every time she laid eyes on him it would remind her about that night for the rest of her life; he even looked like his brother. Damn it. *Damn it.* But for the fact that it would look bad if he cleared off now, there being no knowing when Arnold's body would be discovered, he'd say to hell with Sunderland right now.

Frederick's solicitor – by nature a nervous, fastidious individual with a pernickety, almost dainty manner that gave him the appearance of a timorous little elf – was sitting on the very edge of the sofa in the sitting room. He had removed neither his overcoat nor his gloves, and as Polly watched him fumble in his briefcase and bring out the large bundle of papers tied with tape, she wanted to say to him, 'It's all right, Mr Johnson, really. You won't catch it if you take off your gloves,' but she remained silent.

By her request both Betsy and Emily were present at the reading of the will. They were sitting with Ruth on the sofa facing Mr Johnson's, and Polly and her mother were seated on two upholstered chairs either side of the roaring fire. Polly fully expected that Frederick would have remembered Betsy in his will; the housekeeper had been part of his life since Frederick was a child and had looked after him very well since his parents had died. And having remembered Betsy, he surely would have put a small bequest in for Emily, just a few pounds possibly.

'Well, now.' Mr Johnson raised his head with one of the quick, bird-like movements that characterised him. 'Mr Weatherburn's will is very straightforward, oh yes, indeed. Very straightforward.' His mild blue eyes flashed round them all and then he lowered his head to his papers again. 'In essence . . .' He hesitated a moment before continuing, 'In essence, Mr Weatherburn has left the farm, this house and the furniture within, and all the land the estate boasts, to . . . his stepsister, Mrs Henry Farrow.' And on the sharp intake of breath from those on the sofa facing him, 'On condition that he has no child from his union with his wife, Mrs Polly Weatherburn. In the case of there being a child, then such individual would inherit everything in Mrs Farrow's place.'

'You old witch!' It was difficult to tell who was the more surprised – the solicitor or Hilda – when Betsy jumped up from the sofa and pointed at Polly's mother with a shaking hand, her face scarlet with outrage. 'You've schemed and connived for this all along, you wicked old biddy! Always artful and calculating from a little lass, you were.'

'*How dare you!*' It was clear Hilda couldn't believe her ears. 'How dare you speak to me like that. You're dismissed! Now, this instant! Get your things and be out of this house before night-fall.'

'Just a moment.' Polly's voice was clear and low, but although she tried very hard she couldn't keep it from shaking. That Frederick had done this, left her penniless and utterly reliant on her mother, was an act of pure spitefulness that was difficult to take in. Had his conscience troubled him at the last? Had it been the will that had been on his mind those last few hours when he had tried to tell her something? Whatever, if it wasn't for this life inside her, this child conceived in lust and fear, she would have been free to walk out of this house with no responsibilities and no ties. 'I am the mistress of this house and I say who stays or goes.'

'I think not.' Hilda was triumphant, her face glowing with satisfaction. She had worked hard for this moment, oh, she had, she had. Always bolstering Frederick's outsize ego, flattering him, listening to his endless discourses on this, that and the other and telling him how wonderful he was. Men were fools – the lot of them were fools. But the years of biting her tongue and taking a back seat had been worth it. *It was all hers.* 'You heard what Mr Johnson said and they were Frederick's wishes, it's all down in black and white, signed and sealed. Isn't that right, Mr Johnson?'

'Well—'

'And you were never a wife to him, not really. Doesn't this will reflect that, Mr Johnson?'

'I don't think—'

'So it is mine, and no court in the land will say different!'

'I'm expecting a child, Mother.'

It was said quietly but it had all the power of an explosion in their midst. For a moment Hilda was absolutely still, and then she seemed to swell with fury before she ground out, 'Never! Never in a hundred years. I know my brother, I know what he's told me. He hasn't touched you in years, so don't you dare say different, girl.'

'I'm no girl, and I am expecting a baby, which will become self-evident in a few months.' Polly was endeavouring to keep calm but it was hard. This woman standing in front of her was her *mother*. There were women all over the country – nice, gentle, normal women – who tried for a baby for years and never fell, and yet this woman in front of her, this unnatural, cold, *horrible* woman, had had two babies almost without trying. Where was the justice in that? 'And while we're on the subject, Frederick is not – was not – your brother,' Polly added coldly. 'In fact, he was no relation to you at all, so even if I wasn't expecting a child, I think you might find you had no case at all in the courts. I was his wife, his *legal* wife.'

'It's not his.' Hilda was speaking through clenched teeth and the look on her face was terrible. 'I know it's not his. You've a fancy man, you little—'

'That's enough.' Mr Johnson was an unlikely champion, but if the truth be known, he had never liked Frederick Weatherburn, and he liked his stepsister less. This little lassie with the poignantly beautiful face had more in her than first met the eye, and he liked her. He couldn't understand how she had come to be married to an arrogant, self-opinionated man like Frederick Weatherburn, but he liked her. 'The terms of the will are most explicit, Mrs Farrow, and as I said, very straightforward. The child Mrs Weatherburn is carrying is the sole beneficiary of its father's estate.'

'*It's not his*. It's not his, is it, girl, and I'll prove it if it's the last thing I do.'

'You shut your lying mouth—'

Betsy's words were cut off by Polly's restraining hand on her arm. Polly didn't speak; she merely stared at her mother with eyes that spoke her disdain and dislike, and as Hilda made a step towards her – Ruth immediately springing up to stand by her sister – she moved not a muscle. There was a single moment when the two women's eyes caught and held – Hilda's cruel and bitter and Polly's unfaltering – and then Hilda turned and swept out of the room, her black linen dress seeming to crackle with the rage that was consuming her.

She would stay at the farm until the child was born. As the door closed behind her mother, Polly knew her course was set. Once the baby was born it would be well looked after by Betsy and its future as Frederick's supposed child would be secure; it wouldn't need her and she couldn't stay. She couldn't love anything that came from Arnold and she wouldn't wish any child to suffer an unnatural mother as she had. She would leave, putting the last years behind her and reaching out for a new life somewhere else. Somewhere far away where the past would have no hold on her.

And Luke? As she felt Ruth's arms about her waist and heard her sister telling her, her voice fierce, that she loved her and was here for her, Polly's heart felt as though it was breaking. Luke would never want her, not now.

And then her own arms went about Ruth, and she felt Betsy and Emily patting her back, their voices joined to Ruth's in support, and she found herself thinking that comfort came at the oddest times and in ways you'd never think of . . .

When Polly awoke the next day, Christmas Eve, the weak rays of a winter sun were slanting in through the window on to the scrubbed floorboards, catching tiny particles of dust in their golden beams. She lay still for some moments, knowing that as soon as she moved the sickness would come. Betsy and Ruth had tried to insist, the night before, that she must have the day in bed – several days in bed – to recover from the exhaustion of looking after everyone the last weeks, but she wouldn't do that. It was nice of them and she appreciated the thought and the concern for herself and the baby, but she knew she wasn't yet sufficiently at peace with herself to be alone for any amount of time.

It would come – she was determined it would come, and that one day she would be able to put the past with its demons behind her for good – but not until after the child was born.

It was the right decision to have the baby, but . . . She twisted restlessly in the bed, her head aching and the sickness rising. She couldn't wait for the next nine months to pass so that she was free of this child growing inside her. It wasn't the baby's fault – it hadn't asked to be born, she knew that – but nevertheless, every day she was pregnant was a day which tied her to the farm and delayed her departure.

Once up and dressed, Polly spent the day with Betsy preparing the hampers for the farm staff, and at five o'clock in the evening she left Ruth and Emily decorating the sitting room with holly her sister had gathered from the hedgerows that afternoon, and walked through to the big stone-flagged kitchen. Hilda had stayed in her room all day, refusing to join in any of the preparations for Christmas and declining to talk to anyone. Polly – along with the rest of the household – didn't

269

mind that. It was when her mother *did* open her mouth that life got unpleasant.

She had popped her head round her mother's bedroom door before going downstairs earlier in the day, looking long and hard at the grim-faced woman lying in the big feather bed. 'Two things, Mother.' Hilda had stared at her but made no response whatsoever. 'If you want to continue to play the invalid I have no objection as long as you stay out of everyone's way and see to the cleaning of your room yourself, and that includes the washing of your bedclothes and so on. Betsy will continue to serve you your food, but that is all. The other thing is that you may have Frederick's suite on the other side of the house if you wish. I have no desire to live in it, and as it is large and can be made into a small sitting room as well as a bedroom, it would perhaps suit you better. I shall continue to sleep in Gran and Grandda's old room.'

Her mother's eyes had widened at the offer and it was clear from Hilda's face that she couldn't understand her daughter's generosity. Polly did not enlighten her mother as to the reasons for her magnanimity. True, Frederick's wing was spacious and luxurious by any standards, with its dressing room and night closet, but to Polly it was a symbol of her married life and she hated it. Also – and here Polly's thoughts had a certain wryness – tucked away on the other side of the house, Hilda was less likely to try and interfere with the rest of the household.

It had been the custom of Frederick's father and a tradition Frederick himself had upheld to give the families on the farm a hamper each Christmas, and this year Polly was adding a gold sovereign for every man, woman and child, despite the fact that she had been surprised how little money was in her husband's bank account. After the solicitor had been paid for his services and the funeral expenses had been taken into account, the amount was meagre for the size and prosperity of the farm at just over two hundred pounds, although Croft had assured her the master had recently invested in some prize cattle as well as new machinery, so it could be that.

Promptly at five o'clock there came a knock at the kitchen door, and Croft and his children, along with Enoch's two sons and their families, filed into the room. The children were all clutching their yule-doos – baby figures made with Christmas dough with their arms folded across and two currants for eyes – which they had made with Lotty earlier, and as Polly's eyes rested on Lotty's youngest, she felt the same pain she had experienced some days earlier as she saw his chubby little hands tight round the dough figure. She remembered past Christmas Eves with her granny and Ruth, when they had savoured the smell of the cooking yule-doos, and then taken them to bed to eat first thing on waking Christmas

270

morning. She had imagined doing the same thing for her bairns one day . . .

Suddenly Polly wanted to cry, and it horrified her, but as she made her little speech of thanks and gave the delighted families their sovereigns and hampers, no one would have guessed from the missus's smiling face the effort it was taking.

And then they had all gone and she let herself sink down on to a kitchen chair, Betsy fussing around her like an old woman and scolding her for doing too much after glancing anxiously at her mistress's drawn white face.

So much change in such a short time . . . Polly let her eyes wander round the warm, sweet-smelling kitchen in which the fire in the brightly shining range dominated the room with its glow. And this was just the beginning. But she would see it through. She squared her slim shoulders and thought again of Lotty's little one before nodding to the thought. Aye, she had to see it through, and then she would have done all she could and she would go.

She would brush the dust of Sunderland off her boots and she would not look back.

271

Part 4 – The Child
1912

Chapter Twenty-one

During the next few months a number of events happened that rocked the country. The terrible loss of life as the *Titanic* – the great ship which was proclaimed the pride of the White Star fleet and unsinkable because of its sixteen watertight compartments – sank within hours of hitting an iceberg shocked the nation. More than fifteen hundred passengers and crew died in the icy waters of the North Atlantic, and as more facts emerged – the overwhelming one being the richer you were, the more chance you had had of surviving – people got angrier and angrier. 'Same the whole world over,' Britain's working class muttered under their breath. 'One law for the rich and one for the poor.'

The big freeze which had taken hold in November continued relentlessly, the temperatures dropping so low in the beleaguered north that two per cent of the population were dying weekly from cold. This was one of the components which fuelled the strikes which paralysed the economy – troops being called in yet again against the coal miners, ostensibly to quell riots. A hundred thousand dockers were talking of strike action, knowing another transport dispute could bring the United Kingdom to a standstill.

And all this against a background of increasing unrest by the nation's women; the cabinet being split down the middle on women's suffrage as it turned more militant, and the police raiding the offices of the Women's Social and Political Union as things turned nasty. With thousands of people attending protest rallies in Ulster against British government proposals to give Ireland Home Rule – folk came in farm carts, traps and charabancs, preceded by drums playing in the rain – the first few months of 1912 were ones of great trial and civil discontent. Indeed, many politicians likened Britain to a powder keg primed and ready to explode.

In Sunderland, especially where the farmers were concerned, the weather had produced the hardest and longest winter anyone could remember. On the more modest farms and smallholdings, where money was scarce and profits nonexistent most of the time, animals were simply dying, and in some cases whole families too. Others chose survival and the workhouse, although that could be termed a living death for many. Snow, sleet, packed ice and then more blizzards, with

275

the occasional slight thaw making conditions ten times worse when it froze again, was the north-east's lot, and it was inexorable.

The winter seemed even more endless to Polly than most, her changing shape making it impossible to get out most of the time in the icy, frozen world about her. By her twenty-second birthday, at the end of April, she was five months pregnant and had felt the baby move inside her. She had been dreading that moment almost as much as she was dreading the time when Arnold's body was discovered, but in the event, although it had felt strange when she had felt the flutters deep in her womb, it had not repulsed her as she had expected. As the weeks had passed she'd found she was managing to detach herself from the fact that the child she was carrying was Arnold's. It had happened gradually, but she welcomed the almost stoical placidity that had come with her increasing waistline. If she had continued to feel as she had done in the first weeks she had realised she was pregnant, she doubted she would have survived nine months of it. The calmness could not last and she knew it, but for the moment she felt as though she were existing in an emotional bubble.

The first major pricking of the bubble came mid afternoon on her birthday. Encouraged by Polly, Croft had visited the Hendon hirings – which were held in a certain street in Hendon each week – after Christmas, with strict orders from his mistress to hire two men with families for the two vacant cottages – Emily having moved in with Betsy permanently. Men who were down on their luck, Polly had emphasised firmly, with families who needed a good home. And he must be fair and explain the farm was only just out of quarantine.

Both the men Croft hired had had to place their bairns in the workhouse whilst they and their wives looked for any work they could get, so their joy at being reunited and in secure work along with being housed and fed had warmed Polly's heart.

She had asked Croft to put a letter through Luke's door before he went to the hirings, a short formal note thanking him again for attending Frederick's funeral and stating that although he was very welcome at the farm they all quite understood that, what with the atrocious weather and all, he would be unable to visit them for some time. She had felt, thinking about it afterwards, that he had felt sorry for her that Saturday before Christmas, and that was why he had made the journey to the churchyard, rather than out of respect for Frederick. And she didn't want him to feel sorry for her – her whole spirit recoiled from it. She wanted . . . Well, what she wanted was impossible and that was the end of it. But his pity was untenable. Hence the note.

After being in a state of restless anxiety for days after Croft had delivered the letter, she had finally come to realise and accept that there was going to be no reply. She had cried in the privacy of her room, bitter hot tears for the unfairness of the circumstances she found

276

herself in and not least the cruelty of fate in causing her to love a man who regarded her as a dear friend, maybe a sister, but nothing more. And then she had dried her eyes, wiped her nose, put any fanciful dreams under lock and key and got on with things.

So she was outwardly calm and composed, and inwardly a mass of jelly, when at half past two in the afternoon on her birthday there was a knock at the front door, and a few moments later Emily put her head round the sitting room door where Polly and Ruth were sitting – Polly patching a couple of sheets which were still too good to use for rags, and Ruth darning some socks for Croft's children. 'It's Mr Luke, missus.' And there he was in the doorway.

Polly's heart was racing and she made herself take a deep breath before she said, 'Luke, what a surprise. Come in,' as Ruth leapt up at the side of her, crying. 'A visitor! We feel as though we've been buried alive for months with this terrible weather. Thank goodness we're nearly into May.'

'Aye, thank goodness.' Luke smiled at Ruth, and he was conscious of thinking for a second, By, she looks a different lass, before he turned his gaze on Polly. And then, as she rose to her feet, there was something in her face – almost a defiance – that brought a puzzled crease to his brow the second before his eyes dropped on her gently rounded stomach. No! It wasn't possible. She couldn't be. He hesitated, his jaw bones moving in and out before he could say, 'Are you both well?'

'We're very well.' Again it was Ruth who answered, her tone gay as she continued, 'Oh, this is lovely, Luke. Have you called to wish Polly a happy birthday?'

He nodded, his colour rising as he quickly pulled a small package from his pocket, saying, 'I'm sorry, I should have given you this at once. Happy birthday, Polly.' He knew he should have stayed away – hadn't she all but told him to in that letter after Christmas – but it had got so he'd felt he was going stark staring barmy and would be fodder for the asylum if he went one more day without setting eyes on her. It wasn't fair of him, no one knew that better than him after what his brother had done to her, but in the end he hadn't been able to help himself. He'd had to come, and her birthday had been the perfect excuse.

'Oh, thank you, thank you, but you shouldn't have. I didn't expect . . .' Polly's voice faded away as she opened the little box and saw the small silver brooch it contained. The tiny bird was delicate, its open wings worked in lacy, threadlike skeins of silver which was quite exquisite.

Luke watched her colour come and go, and his voice was quiet when he said, 'Think of it as flying upwards, Polly, with the sun on its wings and the heavens to soar in; the earth with all its evil and heartache left far below.'

She raised her head and their eyes held as the message behind his words reached her, and then Ruth's voice broke into the moment as her sister said, 'Arnold is not with you, then? Has there been news of him?'

Luke was aware of Polly making an almost imperceptible start of distress, and he spoke quickly now, and loudly, as he said, 'Nothing, I'm afraid, Ruth. I'm sorry.'

'Don't be.' The warm smile Ruth gave him further surprised Luke, and his face reflected this, which caused Polly – in spite of her agitation – to want to smile. This new relationship with Ruth was precious but no longer a surprise to Polly; she knew Ruth had really changed – and so did their mother. As far as Hilda was concerned, Ruth's defection to Polly – which was the way her mother viewed it – was a further nail in Polly's coffin.

'Right.' Luke was clearly out of his depth and both women recognised this. It was Ruth who took pity on the good-looking miner and said, 'You sit down by the fire, Luke, and I'll go and see about a tray of tea for us all. Talk to Polly – you know there's going to be a happy event in August?' as she bustled out of the room.

There was a long silence after Ruth had disappeared, an uncomfortable silence, before Polly said, 'Do sit down, Luke, and I love the brooch. It's beautiful.' And then, when he remained standing, she forced herself to meet his eyes again, and what she saw in them caused her to blush scarlet as she said, 'I'm sorry I didn't tell you about . . . about the baby, but Ruth just assumed you knew.'

'Tell me it isn't what I think.' It was deep and guttural and seemed torn out of him.

'I . . . I don't know what you mean—'

'I can count, Polly.' His face was ashen. 'Tell me it is your husband's child and not . . . his.'

She could lie. She could lie and cover this all up and then they could talk politely about this and that and he would leave not knowing. But she couldn't. She had lied once before to Luke when she had said she was happily married, but now the time for untruth was past. She raised her head proudly, her eyes like blue diamonds and her chestnut hair with its fiery lights glowing like the flames in the fire, and said steadily, 'Frederick and I had not slept together in the sense you mean from the first year of our marriage, Luke. There was nothing left between us; in fact, there never had been anything between us of a romantic nature, to be honest. I married him because there was no other option at the time; the farm was bankrupt and my grandda owed Frederick massive debts. He . . . he would have put them in the workhouse if I hadn't become his wife.'

Luke's face had lost every ounce of its normally ruddy colour and he was staring at her as though he had never seen her before.

278

He thought she was bad, Polly thought wildly. He thought she was bad to marry Frederick just to save her family, to give herself to a man she didn't love. And now he knew she was carrying Arnold's child he was repulsed further. Nevertheless, she forced herself to go on. 'It . . . it wasn't a happy marriage, and when he left me to walk home alone the night of the storm out of a fit of pique and Arnold attacked me—' She drew in a deep, shuddering breath before continuing. 'Well, I decided Frederick could make some poor recompense for his actions when I discovered I was expecting a child, a child his maliciousness had brought into being. His will stated everything was to go to my mother unless there was a child of our marriage, so' – she lifted her chin higher – 'a child there was.'

He was stunned, consumed with the anguish that was causing him to sweat through every pore of his body. And angry, bitter and angry, although he wasn't sure if it was Frederick or Arnold he most desired to vent some of this rage on. But no, that was rubbish, he knew all right. He burned at nights in his own particular hell when he thought of Arnold's hands on her, forcing her. It turned him inside out, and the only relief he got was knowing Arnold was where he couldn't hurt her any more. But he *was* still hurting her. A bairn . . . He mentally bludgeoned himself for his stupidity. Why hadn't he thought something like this might result from Arnold taking her down? But he hadn't. It simply hadn't occurred to him. And all this, *all this* against a background of having lost the one man she'd ever loved, Michael. He felt a sense of awe at the sheer strength of her that seemed to compound the hopelessness of his love.

'So now you know.' She was standing very stiff and straight. 'Do . . . do you despise me?'

'*Despise you?*' It was in the nature of a growl. 'For crying out loud, Polly, how could you think I'd despise you? Admire you, wonder at your strength, marvel at your goodness, be amazed at the extent of your sacrificial love, worship you—'

He hadn't meant the last words to slip out, and as he saw her lovely eyes widen he said quickly, 'Please, Polly, don't be frightened,' and somehow he found himself drawing her down to sit beside him on the sofa as he held her hands gently in his, mindful of what she might be feeling at a man's touch after what had happened to her. He could feel her trembling through the fingers resting in his, and it took all his will power not to draw her soft body into his arms to reassure her. Only he couldn't trust himself, not where Polly was concerned, he warned himself grimly. And the last thing he wanted to do was to cause her further distress.

'Polly.' His voice had a cracked sound, and he cleared his throat before trying again. 'Polly, you're not alone, do you hear me? Oh, I know you've got Betsy and Ruth – do they know about that night?

What really happened?' And after she'd shaken her head, her liquid eyes fixed on his face, he continued, 'I know you've got them, but if at any time you need anything, anything at all, I am here for you. Do you understand me? I don't want you to think—' He cleared his throat again. 'I don't want you to think all men are like Arnold or Frederick. They're not, sweetheart.'

It was the last words, spoken with such gentleness, that caused Polly to moan softly as the tears she had been fighting to contain spilled out of her eyes. He cared for her, she'd read it in his face and she wasn't wrong, she wasn't. But she couldn't tell him how she felt until after the baby was born and she was free to leave her old life and every reminder of it, including his brother's child. And then, if he really wanted her – just her without the farm and all it entailed – the future would be his to declare. It was the only way any relationship between them would have a chance with all that had happened. And there was still Arnold. The roads were almost clear now, and although the snow was still banked high in a few places it would be gone within days. It was better there was no link between them for others to speculate about until all that was finished with.

She had been resting against him as she'd wept, her head buried in his shoulder, but now she pulled away and rose to her feet. She pulled her handkerchief from the belt of her dress and wiped her eyes before saying, her voice low and contained, 'I'm sorry, please forget this happened. I . . . I'm not myself today.'

She was as far out of reach as she had ever been. And he was a fool. Luke's stomach muscles tightened but he merely nodded quietly before rising himself and walking across to the fire, one hand resting on the mantelpiece and his back to the room as he stared down into the flames. And they remained thus until Ruth returned with the tea tray.

So that was the way of it! As Hilda scurried back to her room, she blessed the impulse that had driven her downstairs minutes before. From her vantage point at her window overlooking the front garden she had seen Luke arrive, and had thought to ask him of news of Arnold, but on hearing the low murmur of voices from within the sitting room she had peered through the partly open door to see Polly cradled in Luke's arms.

For some moments she had continued to stare through the thin gap at the woman she hated with an intensity that was second only to the feeling she had had for her husband, before quickly retracing her footsteps before she was discovered.

Now she knew, she *knew* who was the father of Polly's child – Luke Blackett, a low, ignorant, common miner! Hilda's teeth ground together. The unfairness of her situation, the injustice of it, had eaten into her very being these last months – she had felt ill constantly, unable to rest properly or eat – and those two down there were the

280

perpetrators of all her misery, Hilda told herself with self-righteous fury. That *harlot* and the man poor Frederick had always disliked. It had only been the knowledge that her day would come which had enabled her to keep calm in front of them all and pretend she had accepted her lot. God was just, and His justice would prevail – she had known it all along. He wouldn't be mocked, and what was adultery but spitting in the face of the Almighty?

Like father, like daughter. Hilda's thin lips were two straight lines in her bitter face. The pair of them, rotten through and through, and over the last months it had become apparent that Ruth was tainted by the same bad blood. Changed out of all recognition, Ruth had, but before long her younger daughter would see how foolish she'd been to throw her lot in with Polly. Oh, yes. But she had to think about how best to play this.

Hilda reached the door to her quarters, her mind racing. For years she had lived under the shadow of great personal indignity through the heinous crime her husband had committed, which had come to light through that, that *baggage* down there. But for her elder daughter enticing Michael to ask her to marry him, no one would have been any the wiser as to the lad's parentage.

She shut the door behind her, walking across to the large bay window and staring out on to the small front garden and the cobbled farmyard beyond, before turning and surveying the room.

Her stepbrother's enormous feather bed had been removed and a smaller one installed, along with two chairs either side of the horsehair sofa. An ornate walnut writing desk and hardbacked chair occupied the far corner of the room just before the entrance into the dressing room, and a matching bookcase and occasional table took up most of the third wall. It was a pleasant milieu, even charming, but Hilda took no pleasure in her surroundings.

It *all* should have been hers by right, she told herself for the hundredth time as she turned to look out of the window again with dissatisfied eyes. The whole farm and the land and the farmhouse should be hers rather than her occupying this tiny corner of the house as though she was a lodger. Frederick had left it to her, he had, not his wife's flyblow. But now God had placed the weapon of retribution in her hands and she would use it wisely when the time was right. And she'd know when that was.

The clatter of tea things from below and then the sound of Ruth's high laugh floated up through the floorboards, and Hilda's teeth ground together as her eyes narrowed into opaque slits. Oh, aye, she would know all right.

Arnold's body was discovered by a group of Silksworth miners out for a walk the following Sunday, and by Monday afternoon – after the constable had called at the farm and it had been established that yes, they were aware of someone who was missing, and yes, he might well have been on his way to visit the farm – Luke had been called to identify his brother's remains; remains which the cold weather had preserved surprisingly well.

Strange, the police remarked, that two caps were found, one being under the body and the other to the side of it. Was the deceased in the habit of carrying another cap about his person? Not that he knew of, Luke replied, but then his brother had been living in lodgings for some years before the accident, so he couldn't rightly say what he had been about. And did Luke know, the police asked, if anyone had a grudge against his brother? Had there been an argument with anyone in the days before Arnold went missing, anything of that nature? Again, not that he knew of, Luke said stolidly, but then he had seen very little of his brother the last few years. Perhaps it was better to make enquiries among his cronies? And he did know Arnold was prone to doing a spot of . . . business in a certain area in the dockside now and again. That might prove a useful avenue of enquiry.

Hilda was very quiet and subdued for some time after the police-men's visit to the farm, and then one morning at the beginning of June, when Ruth and Emily were busy in the dairy, Polly, sitting at the kitchen table preparing vegetables for dinner and chatting with Betsy, who was dicing meat for some brawn she was making, became aware of a figure standing watching her in the doorway. Betsy had just tipped the small pieces of shin beef into the large pan of cow heel simmering on the range with a meaty bacon bone at the base of it when Polly's voice made her spin round as she said, 'Mother?' in a tone of high surprise.

Both women stared at Hilda. Not only was she out of bed and downstairs at the unheard-of time of nine o'clock, but she was fully dressed with her hat and coat on. To their knowledge Hilda had only left the farm once since Polly had brought the family to live there, and that had been for her stepbrother's funeral.

'It's the first Monday in the month,' Hilda said shortly in reply to Polly's amazed face. 'Market day. I thought I would go in to town with Croft; I presume he's driving in as usual?'

Polly nodded. 'Yes, he is.'

She was totally taken aback and it showed, and now Hilda smiled thinly as she said, 'I thought the change would do me good. It's time I got out a little.'

Believe that, believe anything! Betsy surveyed Hilda with narrowed eyes. The old biddy was up to something for sure. There had never been any love lost between the two women, but since the reading of the will, when Betsy had spoken her mind all too plainly, Hilda for the most part pretended the housekeeper didn't exist. This troubled

282

Betsy not at all, but she didn't like this latest development. She said as much to Polly once the two women had watched Hilda – sitting as stiff as a board – drive off beside Croft in the horse and cart.

Polly nodded her agreement. The last weeks had been worrying ones, and if she had followed the dictates of her body she would have stayed in bed this morning. The child had been lying awkwardly for the last few days and she was finding she had to visit the privy more frequently, added to which an ache in her back felt like a giant fist pressing inwards and the feeling of nausea reminiscent of the first weeks of pregnancy had returned. But she couldn't have lain in bed, she just couldn't. Since they'd found Arnold all her hard-won stoicism had evaporated and she had Luke on her mind night and day.

Why hadn't she noticed he had lost his cap that night? she had asked herself a thousand times since the constable had pointed out that this might not be a straightforward accident after all. Only to answer silently in the next breath, You weren't in a state to notice anything, that's why. And they couldn't prove it was Luke's, or anyone else's if it came to it . . . could they?

Half a mile or so away Croft, after one or two fruitless attempts, had given up trying to make conversation with the 'old witch' – as Hilda was referred to privately by the farm workers – and the journey into Bishopwearmouth was conducted in silence.

After the relentless ice and snow of the long winter, spring had decided to arrive with spectacular gusto some weeks previously, and on this mild, early June day the sun had brought to birth the scents of myriad wild flowers and rapidly growing vegetation in the rich earthy air.

It was all quite lost on Hilda, however. Polly's mother was blind and deaf to everything but the desire to prove what she knew in her heart to be true: that Luke Blackett was the father of her daughter's baby and that somehow Arnold had found out about their affair and been murdered for it. Whether to keep him quiet or in an argument over Polly Hilda wasn't sure – she knew full well Arnold had always desired her elder daughter and that courting Ruth had been a ruse to gain access to the farm, but the situation had amused her, especially because it was clear that Polly loathed the man and didn't like having him in her home. It had given Hilda great satisfaction to encourage Arnold all she could.

However, suspicion and conjecture wasn't enough, even though according to the police their enquiries at the colliery and Arnold's lodgings indicted that Arnold had gone missing the very same night Frederick had arrived home without Polly and her daughter had stumbled in later, wet through and covered in mud, supposedly from a fall. A fall! Polly had obviously avoided meeting Frederick

283

on purpose so she could be with Luke, and it was clear Arnold had either followed them or arranged to meet them to discuss what he knew. He might even have been blackmailing them. Hilda's eyes narrowed thoughtfully. Whatever, she was going to dig and dig until she found out something – anything – to confirm she was on the right track. Someone, somewhere knew something or had seen something. She would use Arnold's relationship with Ruth as her excuse; what was more natural than a concerned mother trying to find out what had happened to her dear daughter's betrothed in order to bring her daughter a little peace of mind in these dreadful circumstances? Yes, that was the tack she would take.

Once in the town Hilda told Croft she would be taking a horse cab home because she was going to be late; there was an old friend she was going to see. Croft could relay that message to Mrs Weatherburn and tell her not to expect her at any specific time.

Hilda now began to work methodically through the list she had made. She visited Arnold's old lodgings first but got no joy there; neither did she gain any information in the colliery office or in the shops round Arnold's lodgings and then later Southwick Road. By tea time she was tired and discouraged and ready to give up. She had spoken to the neighbours at both Arnold's lodgings and the house in Southwick Road, and although she had had several cups of tea and conversations about everything from Mr Asquith's refusal to accept the unions' demand for a minimum wage for miners to the dreadful price of bread at tuppence a loaf – neither of which interested Hilda in the slightest – she had learned nothing of interest.

She had actually decided she could do nothing more that day, after being embroiled in a fruitless conversation with an old lady for nigh on half an hour at the top end of Southwick Road, and was making her way down the street whilst keeping a weather eye out for Luke – the last thing she needed was to see him – when a lighted window in the house but one to the Blacketts' made her hesitate. There had been no one at home earlier when she had knocked at that door, and as she was passing . . . A pretty, fluffy-haired lass answered the door, her dark eyes in striking contrast to her fair curls. She listened with interest as Hilda began to explain the reason for her call, and then she stretched out her arm and pulled her inside.

Twenty minutes later the door opened and Hilda emerged on to the street again, but now her eyes were bright and her face was flushed. Her stepbrother had always quoted a saying when he was at his most pompous, one that had grated on her unbearably after she had heard it the first ten times, but now it came into her mind and she found herself saying it out loud as she hurried towards Thomas Street to see about a horse cab. 'The mills of God grind slowly but they grind exceedingly fair.' *Oh, yes.* She stopped for a moment, lifting her face to the evening air, which was warm and moist, and putting her hand to her heart, which was racing alarmingly. She must calm down. She took several deep breaths to compose herself. What if she really did have a weak heart? But no, no, it was the excitement, that was all. She was as fit as a fiddle and she intended to live a long and enjoyable life as the rightful mistress of Stone Farm.

She smiled to herself, smoothing down her coat and adjusting her neat felt hat with gloved hands. Thought you'd cheat me, did you, Polly my girl? Well, think again, Aye, think again. This isn't over yet by a long chalk.

Chapter Twenty-two

It was another full week before Hilda went into town again with Croft on market day. Polly, under protest, had spent the intervening days in bed, due to the doctor diagnosing a nasty kidney infection after Betsy, worried about her mistress's condition, called him out. The icebag on her back and the chloroform ointment, along with the gallons of boiled water Betsy made her drink with the medicine the doctor had prescribed, did the trick, but Polly was still pale and tired when Hilda arrived back at the farmhouse after her second outing.

Polly was sitting on one of the sofas in the sitting room with her feet up, and as she glanced at Hilda, who was standing in the doorway looking at her with an odd expression on her face, she said politely, 'Did you have an enjoyable time, Mother?' keeping any apprehension out of her voice. Like Betsy, she didn't trust the reason for these sudden excursions after years of self-imposed incarceration.

'Wonderful.' It was high and animated. 'Just wonderful.'

'Good.'

They stared at each other, but Hilda didn't break the silence for some seconds, and then she said, 'You shouldn't have prevented me inheriting what was rightfully mine, girl. You know that, don't you?'

'Mother, we've had this conversation before. As Frederick's wife, most folk would agree I should have been the main beneficiary of his will anyway, but certainly in view of his wishes concerning the child you have no cause for complaint. And I've told you I will be more than happy to give you an allowance.'

'An allowance! Huh!' Hilda now stretched her neck and, her tone changing into one of thin bitterness, said tightly, 'I am going to my room but I would like you to remember this conversation, Polly.'

'I'll remember it, Mother.' And it was Hilda who looked away first, turning and flouncing from the room as she muttered something indiscernible under her breath.

Once she was alone Polly leaned back against the cushions of the sofa with a deep sigh. How was it, with her father having been such an easy-going, sensitive soul, that he had been ensnared by two of the most unnatural women in the world? Unnatural in different ways admittedly, but unnatural all the same. But then she knew the answer

287

to that, she told herself silently. It was her father's inherent weakness that both of them, in their own ways, had fastened on to.

And then she shook her head irritably, annoyed with herself. Why was she wasting time thinking of her father now? She ought to be trying to determine what her mother was about, because she *was* up to something, for sure. Polly eased her position on the sofa, resting her hand on the raised dome of her stomach for a moment. The doctor had said that either she had an excess of water or the baby was a large one, and that in either case the confinement could well be early. She hoped that would be the case, oh, she did. Since they had found Arnold's body, this pregnancy had suddenly become intolerable.

And then, as the evening drew on, her mind returned to the problem of her mother, worrying at it like a dog with a bone, and she could find no peace of mind.

Very early on the morning of the twelfth of June, two days after Hilda's second trip into Bishopwearmouth, Luke was awakened from a deep sleep by the sound of banging on the front door. An hour later he was sitting in a police cell, his head spinning with the speed at which his world had fallen apart. They knew. Somehow they knew. He glanced round the small, dank cell, his hands clasped in front of him and hanging loosely between his knees.

Had he been right to play it as he had? He rubbed his hand across his sweaty face. He had told the police he remembered little of that night beyond the fact that his mother – and he'd stressed the fact Eva was the only mother he had known – had died. Grief did strange things to the memory. How could he recall what time he'd got home or what had happened that evening when faced with the devastating loss of the woman he had chosen to care for and love? It had all turned into a terrible blur. Yes, there had been someone else present. Her natural son, Michael. Where could they contact him? He wasn't sure. He'd never been given notice of his whereabouts. He omitted to mention Dr Henderson. But Michael was a priest. A Roman Catholic priest.

They would trace Michael, of course, and he would tell them what he knew: that Luke Blackett had entered the house after a union meeting in the afternoon and then left fairly rapidly some time later, to return home after more than three hours. Where had Luke been? He would tell them what Luke had said later that evening – that there had been a crisis of some kind with the family of one of the men with whom Luke worked. And what was the name of this man? Michael would not have an answer to that question.

And then they would come back to Luke and he would say . . . what? Luke swallowed deeply, shutting his eyes for a second. Nothing. He would say nothing. There was no way Polly was being dragged into this. He hadn't been able to protect her that night but he would protect her now. He straightened for a moment, stretching his back, and then resumed his bent position as he stared at the dirty stone-flagged floor.

At ten o'clock that same morning, two grim-faced policemen had just left the farmhouse and Polly was facing her mother in the sitting room, Ruth sitting in shocked silence beside her.

'This "acting on information received" regarding Luke's arrest is something to do with you, isn't it?' Polly accused harshly. 'Along with the questions about Luke and me. Don't bother to deny it.'

'I wouldn't dream of denying it.' Hilda was exuding self-satisfaction. 'It's as clear as the nose on your face that Luke is responsible for his brother's death, and there's a witness to prove it! What do you think about that?'

'I don't believe it.' This was from Ruth, and now Hilda turned on her younger daughter as she mimicked nastily, 'I don't believe it! Well, don't believe was made to believe, girl. Luke was observed coming home late the night Arnold disappeared, the night his stepmother died, incidentally.' This last was accompanied by a pointed glance at Polly. 'His clothes were torn, his cap was gone, and it was clear as far as Katy and her young man could ascertain that he'd been in a fight. The police aren't fools, girl, and they are more than capable of putting two and two together.'

'And making ten by the sound of it.' Polly's voice was icy, but inside she felt as though she was melting with fear for Luke. 'I gather you're referring to Katy Chapman? Do the police know she vowed to get even with Luke when he finished his association with her?'

'And of course you'd know all about that!' Hilda had thrown all caution to the wind and her cards were very clearly on the table. 'You're the reason Luke did away with his brother; it's your conscience Arnold's blood's on.' Hilda turned to the open-mouthed Ruth as she said, 'Been carrying on with Luke for years she has, the harlot! Ask her, ask her who's the father of the brat she's carrying. It's not my stepbrother, that's for sure, and it'll be proved so. It'll be proved, all right.'

'You evil woman.' It was clear Hilda thought Polly was going to strike her as she backed away from her daughter, but Polly merely came to a halt in front of her mother, her lips drawn back from her teeth and her blue eyes narrowed. Her heart was thumping against her ribs but it was anger – not fear – which was driving her as she said again, 'You evil, evil woman. You've lain in that bed up there for years pretending to be ill, and then the last few weeks you've been plotting and scheming like an obscene great spider trying to enmesh victims in your web. Well, you're wrong, do you hear? Wrong! And I'm going to go to the police

289

station and reiterate all I've just said to those two policemen. Luke's innocent.'

'And you think they would take any notice of you?' Hilda had recovered her poise and now her neck was craning forward like a crow preparing to peck. 'Think again! Not after what I told them.'

Polly made no response for a moment, and then her voice was flat, the anger gone, as she said, 'All my life I've waited for a word of love from you. I used to cry myself to sleep at nights when I was a bairn and wonder why the one person in all the world who should love me didn't. But no more. I'm free of you at last. I don't need or want anything from you any more.'

And as Hilda looked into her daughter's great blue eyes she saw something was missing from the depths of them: a need, a want, that she had never fully acknowledged or understood but which had always been there, and such is the potential for oscillation in the human spirit that for a moment she felt bereft at the passing of it. And then she drew herself up, her eyes narrowing as she said, 'And you are no daughter of mine, not after the way you have so lowered yourself as to become involved with that . . . that creature that Frederick disliked so much.'

'That's the best thing you have said to me in years.' Polly turned and left the room, but once in the hall she put her fist to her mouth and bit down hard on it, her concern for Luke overwhelming. She flew along the hall to the kitchen as swiftly as her increased bulk would allow, explaining the reason for the policemen's visit to the two in the kitchen and instructing Emily to go and tell Croft to get the horse and trap ready.

She could hear raised voices from the sitting room, where her mother and Ruth were, and she had only been a moment or two in her room, pulling on her thin summer coat and straw bonnet, when Ruth followed her into the bedroom, shutting the door behind her. 'Polly?' Ruth's face was straight, her eyes enormous. 'Mam is right in as much as something happened that night Aunt Eva died, isn't she? Do you know anything about Arnold's death?'

Polly looked at her sister. The truth could smash this new relationship – which she had thought right up to a second ago was firm and solid but which suddenly felt horribly fragile – into a million pieces and put a rope round Luke's neck, but if she didn't tell her now, if she prevaricated or lied, Ruth would sense it and this thing would always be a great wedge between them. She loved her sister, she had always loved her – even when Ruth had been at her worst – but trusting her with this was something else. And then she looked into the worried little face in front of her which had grown so much more pretty over the last months since the expression of discontent had been erased, and the baby sister who had always looked to her for security and love was there. Ruth needed to be trusted, and more than that *know* she was trusted, Polly realised with a jolt of guilty surprise. Ruth's need was evident in her face. 'Yes.' It was simple, but Ruth would never know how hard that one word had been. 'Do you want to hear about it? It . . . it isn't pleasant.'

Ruth made no answer beyond a nervous nod, and Polly swallowed deeply before she could begin. She told her sister all of it, starting from the moment she left the house in Southwick Road to the time she entered the farmhouse, and at the end of it Ruth's eyes fell to the mound of her stomach and she said very flatly, 'It's his, isn't it? Arnold's.'

Polly nodded.

'How can you bear to have it?'

'I couldn't not,' Polly said quietly. 'It's not responsible for what its father did, but . . . I shan't stay after it's born, Ruth. I couldn't love it and it wouldn't be fair. As far as the world is concerned it's Frederick's child, whatever Mother might think, she can't prove it is not Frederick's. It can live here with you all and be provided for, but I intend to make my life somewhere else. It's the only way I can cope.'

'Oh, Poll.' Ruth's head had dropped but now she raised it, her eyes wet as she said fiercely, 'I'm glad he's dead, he didn't deserve to live,' and as Polly's arms went round her the two women held each other tightly for long moments and the ache in Polly's heart was eased a little.

'What are you going to do?' As they drew apart, Ruth's voice was soft, her tone sympathetic.

Polly had been thinking while they had embraced. If she went to the police station it actually might do more harm than good. Her mother had woven her web well and compromised Polly's relationship with Luke very adeptly in the law's eyes. They wouldn't believe anything she said in Luke's defence; moreover, it might confirm the suspicions her mother had induced if she went flying to see him as soon as she heard he had been arrested. But he needed someone to speak for him, someone the police would trust. 'I'm going to see Dr Henderson,' she said quietly. 'He knows where Michael is and I need to see him before the police talk to him.'

'Dr Henderson?'

'And when he has given me Michael's whereabouts I'm going to see Michael and tell him everything and ask him to give Luke an alibi for that night. If it comes down to a priest's word against Katy Chapman's, there'll be no contest.'

'But . . .'

'Yes?' Polly regarded her sister's perplexed face very steadily.

'If you tell Michael everything he'll know Luke *did* do it. I know

291

it was self-defence and he was protecting you,' Ruth added hastily, 'but it would still be lying, wouldn't it, if he said Luke was with him all the time?'

Polly's gaze didn't falter as she said, 'Aye, it would.'

'Oh, Polly.'

Ruth insisted on accompanying Polly into town – an action firmly backed by a deeply concerned Betsy, who couldn't understand why her very pregnant mistress suddenly had to take off like a bat out of hell – as Betsy put it. 'I know it's awful, lass, but there's nowt you can say to change them coppers' minds,' she said worriedly, 'an' it'll help no one if you end up havin' the bairn on the road somewhere.'

'I have no intention of having the bairn for another couple of months, Betsy,' Polly said firmly. 'And I have to go, all right?'

'Well, I'll be wastin' me breath if I say any more, I suppose.'

'You suppose right.'

'By, I hope if I'm ever locked away you'll do the same for me,' Betsy said with a resigned note in her voice.

'You can count on it.'

They arrived in Barclay Street in Monkwearmouth, where the good doctor had his premises, just in time to find him eating his dinner, and when Polly explained that she had to let her cousin know about his half-brother's arrest quickly because Michael had some information which would help to prove Luke's innocence, she had no trouble in persuading Dr Henderson to give her the address of Michael's whereabouts.

'Consett?' She stared at him in surprise. 'But that's only twenty-five miles or so from here, isn't it?' Somehow she had expected Michael to have gone much further, but this meant she could actually go and see him today.

Dr Henderson nodded. 'Large thriving community in Consett these days,' he said as he showed the women to the door. 'As the ironworks have grown so has the town, and they've excellent local amenities and a steelworks that's the envy of Newcastle and Sunderland. Nice town hall, and the infirmary in Parliament Street is run by a friend of mine. Room for twenty in-patients.' His tone suggested the two women should be suitably overawed. 'There's a good few churches, so I understand, but of course you'll be wanting the Roman Catholic one near the school in Thomas Street. Michael has done all right for himself being appointed to a church in Consett as part of his training.'

Once outside in the hot June air, which carried the smell of the hops and yeast from Monkwearmouth Brewery down on the waterfront, Polly and Ruth stared at each other for a moment. 'We're going to Consett now, aren't we.'

292

It was a statement, not a question, but Polly answered it anyway as she said, 'It won't take long in the horse and trap.'

It didn't, and the ride was not unpleasant once they got out of Bishopwearmouth and on to the country lanes. When they arrived in Consett the first thing the women noticed was the red dust from the ironworks, which gave a pink tinge to seemingly everything, and the enormous slag heaps far in the distance to the west of the town.

Ruth was holding the reins as they drove into Consett, Polly sitting quietly at the side of her with her hands folded on her rounded belly and her straw hat pulled down well on to her forehead, but in spite of her air of propriety, inside she was in turmoil. What if Michael refused to help her? As Ruth had pointed out, she was in effect asking him to lie for her – him, a priest. But he was still Michael under his priest's garb, her inner voice told her stoutly. And when she explained the circumstances . . . The baby moved suddenly, as though in protest at what she was about to do, and she felt her heart begin to beat wildly. This had to work, he had to help her. *He had to.*

'You want to see Father Blackett?'

The priest was old, grey-haired, but his face was not unkind as he stared at her, and when Polly said in a rush, 'I told your housekeeper, I'm his cousin,' he nodded slowly. 'There's . . . family problems, with his brother – his half-brother,' she continued stumblingly. 'My sister and I have come Sunderland.'

'And she is where?'

'Waiting outside. The horse . . . the horse gets nervous when he is left alone.'

The father nodded understandingly. When his housekeeper had said a young woman was asking for Father Blackett he had thought she was another of these shameless young things who had all but thrown themselves at his associate since he'd arrived in Consett. May the good Lord forgive him for the carnality of his thoughts. Father Benson's eyes rested briefly on Polly's stomach again as he said, 'Father Blackett is at the school, he's something of a favourite with the bairns.'

His smile made it easier to say, 'Would it be all right if I went there to see him? I won't keep him long.'

'Of course, Mrs . . . ?'

'Weatherburn. Polly Weatherburn.' She could see the good father didn't understand how a woman in her condition came to be asking for his colleague when by rights it should be her husband who had made the journey, and now she looked him straight in the eye when she said, 'He might have mentioned me? My husband died just after his mother passed away.'

The priest's face stretched a little and his voice was grave when he said, 'I'm sorry, Mrs Weatherburn. Sometimes this earthly valley in which the good Lord has called us to walk can be very dark. Would you like me to accompany you to the school?'

There was nothing she would like less, but she couldn't very well say so. She forced herself to say politely, 'Thank you, but I don't want to put you to any trouble.'

What a nice bonny young woman, and how tragic that her husband would not share in the joy of their little one. The priest's voice was hearty when he said, 'No trouble, child. No trouble at all.'

The school was a stone's throw away, and Ruth stayed outside the priest's house whilst he led Polly into the building, which smelt of carbolic soap and something fusty which she couldn't quite place. 'Wait here a moment.' They were in the stone-flagged corridor and he tapped on the first door before opening it, putting his head round and stepping inside. A moment or two later Michael was there in front of her, and such was Polly's relief that she grabbed at his hands and was quite unable to speak.

'Polly, what is it?' asked Michael urgently. He had hardly been able to believe his ears when Father Benson had said she was here. And then, as he took in her changed shape, which the full summer coat was unable to hide, he felt a rushing in his ears and his heart began to thud hard. Polly had told him she hadn't been Frederick's wife in the true sense of the word for years, but here she was expecting a child. Had they had a reconciliation before her husband had died and determined to try and make a go of their marriage? If so, it would make Frederick's passing all the more lamentable, Michael told himself forcefully, aiming to quell the feeling which had taken hold of him and which was insisting that Polly had betrayed him in some obscure way. He stared at her, and as he looked deep into the beautiful face under the straw bonnet it was only in that moment that he acknowledged the comfort he had drawn from knowing she was unhappy in her marriage. Which made him what? Michael asked himself. Not the man he had thought himself to be for a start. And certainly not the priest God desired.

'Michael . . .' Polly was holding on to him as though she were drowning. 'Oh, Michael. Something . . . something terrible has happened. Luke's in prison, he was arrested late last night.'

'*What?*' She felt his hands jerk in hers. 'Whatever for?'

'For Arnold's murder. My mother's angry because of the baby and she found Katy Chapman who said she'd seen Luke and—'

'Polly, Polly.' He drew her against him briefly. 'Shush now, shush. Calm down and tell me all of it from the beginning, all right? We'll sit in the yard in the sunshine, and don't worry, dear. Luke hasn't done anything wrong, I'm sure of it.' And then, as he saw the expression on her face his words had wrought, he said, his voice very low, 'Polly?'

294

Once in the tiny yard, they sat on the long wooden bench which stretched all down one wall, and Polly told him. She related everything, and in the telling revealed much more than the actual words to the tall, thin man watching her so intently. And when she had finished, Michael took her in his arms once more, his touch comforting as a brother's would have been because he knew that was how she viewed him, and his voice throaty as he said, 'You did right to come and tell me, Polly.' She had taken off her bonnet as they had talked, and her hair was very soft and smelt of apples and corn and summer days. For a moment the pain in his heart was so strong he was a young lad of sixteen again, back on that country lane with his world having fallen down about his ears and in front of him a black abyss in which nothing existed but the horror of living.

And then she said, 'I knew you would help me,' and he opened his eyes over her head and stared across the school yard, and his voice was soft when he said, 'Of course I'll help you.' He let her go, standing swiftly and pulling her to her feet as he continued, 'Don't worry any more; go home now with Ruth and rest. Betsy was right, you shouldn't be jolting about in the horse and trap.'

Father Benson wasn't altogether surprised when his young associate asked for leave to go and pray in the church rather than continue with the afternoon lessons. He had seen the look in Michael's eyes when he had told him who was waiting in the corridor, and he hadn't got to sixty-five years of age without knowing a great deal about human nature and all its turns and twists.

The church was quiet and deserted when Michael entered it, sunlight glancing through the stained-glass windows over the chancel and sending beams of light on to the marble floor below. He stood quite still for a moment before the altar and then genuflected and passed through to the priests' private quarters, where he glanced about him almost vaguely. *Help me, Lord.* The room was small, holding nothing more than a table and two chairs, a bookcase and two easy chairs either side of the small fireplace, and as Michael fell first to his knees, and then stretched out with his face pressed against the floorboards and his arms and legs spread-eagled, he almost reached either end of it.

All Luke had done was to defend Polly against a man who had been vile and base; a man who had taken her against her will and given her a bairn in the process. It couldn't be right for a good man – and Luke *was* a good man – to go down the line for something he hadn't intended to happen when he was protecting the innocent, it couldn't. And Polly loved him. Here his thoughts jangled for a time, whirling through his head as he brought reason to bear on the devastation he had felt when he had read the truth in Polly's eyes. She loved Luke. He reiterated it in his mind over and over until the sick emptiness began to be replaced by acceptance. For Michael knew she still loved him too – aye, as a brother maybe, but it was love which had glowed in her eyes as she had looked at him. And if he had been there on that winter night and come across what Luke had come across, he would have wanted to kill Arnold. He twisted on the floor, but it was inescapable. Priest or no, he would have had murder in his heart right enough. Dear God, *dear God* . . .

Luke was his brother. Perhaps not by blood, but in every other way that mattered. It'd been Luke who had stuck up for him in the playground when the other bairns had bullied him for being so small and slight; Luke who'd wiped his snotty nose and told him he was worth ten of Cyril Bramwell and Philip MacKay and he could knock them into a cocked hat if he'd had the chance to take them one at a time, although they had both known that was sheer bull; Luke who'd got between him and his mother time and time again when her hand had come to clip his ear for some small misdemeanour. She had never struck Luke or Arnold, always him – and hard. So hard he'd been deaf in one ear for a while. And with Arnold . . . By, he doubted he'd be here now if Luke hadn't protected him from Arnold. Arnold had always been a perverted, sick individual with a desire to hurt and destroy.

How long he was on the floor Michael didn't know, but when he finally rose to his feet his heart was at peace with his God. The law would take Luke's life if the real facts came to light because the law looked only at the facts, not at the heart. When Rahab the prostitute had sheltered the spies sent against her country, God had looked at her heart and spared her and her loved ones. Moses had killed the Egyptian and God had been merciful to him, the same as He had to Jacob, the father of the twelve tribes of Israel, who obtained his brother Esau's birthright and blessing. Pray God, *pray God* that on Judgment Day, when Michael stood before the Throne of Grace and looked into the Lord's eyes, He would look at his heart on this matter. And only God really knew the heart of the men and women He had created in His image. Michael was content to leave his eternal judgement in the hands of the One who had died for him at Calvary.

'Well, I don't mind telling you, Father, we did wonder a bit at this lass, this Katy Chapman, coming forward like she did. Mind, her young man backed her up, so we had to go with it, you understand?'

'I'm sure no malice was intended on the young woman's part,' Michael said soothingly to the two policemen facing him across the interview room at the police station in West Wear Street in Sunderland's East End the next morning. 'It's easy to muddle up one night with another when some time has gone by.'

'Aye, maybe, but we've since heard reports they were thick at one time, the lass and your brother, and she took umbrage when he wasn't keen on getting wed. You know, Father, a woman scorned and all that?

But if you're sure Luke was with you from when he got home from his shift that night, that settles it, and you should know – it being the night your mam passed away. Not likely to forget that night, are you? I understand Luke was in a terrible state, but then he hasn't seen death like you, Father.'

'Quite.'

The policeman, a good Catholic, nodded reverently. Women were the very devil, and shouldn't he know? His Mabel could play him up something rotten if she didn't get her own way. And the bonny ones were the worst. Oh, aye, they were that. Have you disappearing up your own backside, they could, if you weren't careful. Mind, the old un, the mother of the lass the two brothers were supposed to have argued about, was a tartar in her own right. Came in here breathing fire and damnation with the Chapman lass, she had. More there than met the eye, he'd be bound. Maybe the priest knew the reason for that.

The priest did, and having outlined the contents of Frederick's will, the two policemen relaxed back in their chairs, the older one whistling through his teeth before saying, 'I'm not surprised, I thought there was something fishy about all this, like I said. Money is the root of all evil, isn't that what the good book says, Father?'

'Actually, it says the *love* of money is the root of all evil,' Michael said gently, rising as he spoke.

'Aye, you're right, Father. Subtle difference there, eh? Subtle difference sure enough. Well, I think we're satisfied your brother is free to leave, so perhaps you'd like to be the one to tell him, eh? Seeing as you've come all this way to put the matter straight?'

'That's very kind of you, Inspector.' Funnily enough, he didn't want to see Luke right at this moment, or perhaps it wasn't so strange after all. With the benefit of hindsight he could now see that it wasn't only himself and Arnold who had wanted Polly. A hundred little incidents, buried in his subconscious but now as clear as crystal, bore evidence to the fact that Luke loved her. And Polly loved him, although whether Luke was aware of that was another question. Whatever, these were the two people he loved best in the world and he could do one last thing for them now. As the Inspector had just said, he could put the matter straight.

It was another ten minutes before Michael walked out into the sunshine and across to the horse and trap in which Father Benson was sitting waiting for him. 'All done here, Father?' Father Benson did not comment on his young colleague's wet eyes.

It was a full minute before Michael answered, and then it was with an air of finality that he said, 'Aye, Father. I'm all done here.' He had said his goodbyes and he was at peace. This chapter of his life was closed for good, and he would not look back again.

Chapter Twenty-three

Luke was approaching the farmhouse within an hour of leaving the police station, and as Polly glanced up from where she was sitting in the small front garden shelling peas, she thought for a moment she must be dreaming. And then the tin bowl had fallen off her lap and she was out of the garden and across the farmyard just as he reached the end of the stony path, careless of her shape and anything else but the fact that he was here, he was free.

'Luke! Luke!' She had felt as cumbersome as a hippopotamus the last weeks, but now it was though she was skimming the ground, and as he opened his arms to her she went into them without a thought of decorum or the unseemliness of a woman in her condition being whisked off her feet and held against the chest of a man who was not her husband.

'Polly, oh, Polly. My love, my love.' Luke's voice was almost incoherent and for long moments they just held each other tight, before Polly raised her head and saw the look in his eyes. Nothing could have stopped the kiss that followed, and it answered the last of Luke's lingering doubts as to the validity of what Michael had told him more effectively than any words could have done.

'Why didn't you tell me?' Luke's voice was soft as he placed her on her feet, his arms still about her. 'The last months I've felt like I've been going insane thinking you would never care for me. You *do* care for me?' he added swiftly, and at her radiant 'Oh so much, so much,' he shut his eyes tight for one second before opening them and saying, 'Last night I was in a prison cell thinking I might as well be dead, and today . . .'

'I couldn't tell you, not until—' She shook her head, her burnished curls falling in disarray across her forehead. 'You know.'

'Polly, the baby doesn't make any difference, not to me,' Luke said softly. 'Don't you know how much I love you?'

'I'm leaving it, Luke, once it's born. I'm leaving everything.' She had to tell him, now, quickly, before he said anything more. And then if he still wanted her – just her with nothing to her name but the clothes on her back . . . 'I'm letting Ruth and Betsy bring the child up and it will inherit the farm. I don't want to stay here a second longer than I have to, I hate it now. I can't explain . . .'

299

'You don't have to.' His voice was so tender, everything she could have hoped for. 'With ten children or none, rich or poor, in sickness and in health I want you, Polly Farrow. And you'll always be Polly Farrow to me, until you become Mrs Luke Blackett, of course. And we're not waiting two or three years to get wed to please folk either, I don't care what they think.'

Marriage. For a second, just a second, the images of Frederick and Arnold were there in her mind's eye, and then she brushed the shadows away determinedly. It would be different with Luke, this thing that most men set such great store by. She had never been taken in love before. Nevertheless, she swayed slightly, and immediately Luke said, 'Come on, come back to the house and sit down. This has all been too much for you, I shouldn't have gone on like that.'

They met Ruth in the doorway to the farmhouse, and Polly had just cried excitedly, 'Oh, Ruth, isn't it wonderful! He's free!' when there was a high-pitched 'No!' from the top of the stairs that momentarily froze everyone, and then her mother was racing down the treads like a mad woman. And it was as a mad woman that Hilda attacked her daughter, leaping on her with such ferocity that the impact bore Polly to the ground, where she landed heavily on her back, her mother's weight knocking the breath out of her as Hilda thudded down on her belly, crying, 'You! You! You've got him off, haven't you!' amid curses that could have come from a hard-boiled docker rather than the gentlewoman Hilda purported to be.

In the resulting mêlée, Polly was aware of Luke hauling Hilda off her by the hair and slinging her aside amid screams and shouts from all and sundry, and then Betsy's horrified face was bending over her, saying, 'Lass, oh, lass,' over and over again. She was still saying it when the first pain hit moments later.

It was thirty long hours before Polly's daughter was born, on a sultry Saturday evening, and the hard labour was only made bearable for Polly by the thought that she would soon be free to start a new life with Luke. He had been waiting outside her room throughout, once he had returned from Bishopwearmouth with the midwife. Betsy and Ruth had stayed with Polly every moment; sponging her down, encouraging her, urging her on, and both of the women secretly fearing two lives would be lost. The baby was tiny, and exhausted though she was, Polly had seen the buxom midwife shake her head at Betsy when the first weak mew of a cry was heard.

Well, wouldn't that be for the best in one way? Polly asked herself wearily, watching as Betsy wrapped the baby in a blanket. This child wasn't going to have an easy life if it lived, not living here with Hilda, even though materially it would want for nothing. And then Betsy – without asking – placed the tiny bundle in Polly's arms, and she looked down into the miniature face, and fell in love. As quickly and as simply as that. Her daughter looked sleepily up at her and then yawned daintily, and Polly felt such a welling-up of love and emotion that the warmth of it melted the last of the ice from round her heart and trickled into the back of her eyes, spilling out on to her cheeks.

When Ruth went to take the baby from her, Polly shook her head, unable to speak, and she still continued to weep when Ruth brought Luke into the room. He simply held mother and child close as he sat on the bed, aware that something deep inside Polly which had been damaged and torn and buried had been brought into the light and was now able to heal fully at last. He touched the baby's face lightly, grateful that the tiny girl-child was the image of her lovely mother, and when minute fingers fastened on his thumb he felt something stir in his own heart for this tiny, helpless scrap of humanity.

'I want to keep her.' It was a whisper. 'I want to keep her, Luke, but not here. I want a fresh start for the three of us.'

There was a question in the words and Luke answered it with 'Whatever you want, my love.' He'd been so scared as the hours had dragged by that he was going to lose her, that in the bringing forth of the child which had been forced upon her Polly would lose her life. He had been knotted up with sick anxiety and frustration – and, aye, and hate, he acknowledged silently – but now, as he looked down into the tiny face, a great weight was lifted off his heart. He could love this innocent life, love her as his own daughter. The biological side of things was nothing, any animal could procreate. What was important was what happened after the birth process, and he would make sure everything which happened was good. He hugged Polly and the child closer as he whispered, 'The moon, the stars, just name what you want and I'll get it for you. I promise.'

Polly gave a little gurgle of laughter, nestling against the hard, strong bulk of him, and almost in the same moment Hilda's voice came from the doorway, saying, 'And you say that bairn isn't his!'

'Get out of here, Mam.' Ruth had appeared behind Hilda, Betsy at the side of her. 'You've done enough damage.'

'Wait a minute.' Luke rose from the bed, ignoring Polly's urgent 'Please, Luke, leave it. She's not worth it.' He walked slowly up to Hilda, thrusting his face close to hers as his narrowed eyes raked her defiant face. 'Polly's baby *is* mine, but not in the way your cesspit of a mind thinks,' he said quietly. 'In every way that really counts the bairn's mine because of my love for the exceptional lady who's her mother. And that's what sticks in your craw, isn't it – that Polly is special, special and loved, whereas you are a dried-up stick of a woman who's never been any good to anyone.'

'How dare you!' As Hilda's hand rose, Luke made no attempt to avoid the slap she delivered across his face, but when she went to repeat it, he said quietly, 'I wouldn't if I were you. I owe you that one for telling you the truth you've tried to avoid for years, but although I've never raised my hand to a woman in my life, I'd be prepared to make an exception with you.'

'You! You . . . low, ignorant, coarse individual!' Hilda was spluttering. 'I'll see my day with you, with the pair of you! You see if I don't!' And then, to her utter outrage, she found herself being frogmarched out of the bedroom by an indignant Ruth and Betsy, who were determined that Polly and Luke should have a minute or two alone.

Luke walked back to the bed, holding Polly close again until Ruth and Betsy came bustling in and shooed him out. Polly caught at his hand as he left, her voice soft as she said, 'Come back soon.' All this with her mother had upset her more than she'd have expected.

'Try and keep me away.'

'Aye, well, she won't be movin' out of that bed for three weeks an' more,' Betsy said stolidly as she flapped at Luke's departing back. 'The midwife says complete rest for at least that long.' The midwife had also said it would be a miracle if the bairn pulled through, but then she didn't know their Polly, Betsy told herself silently. And the wee babby herself might be tiny, but the way she'd pulled at her mam's breast soon after birth, she had all of Polly's will power and then some.

'What are you going to call her?' Luke turned in the doorway and looked across at mother and baby as the thought occurred to him. And then he smiled, inclining his head in understanding as Polly said simply, 'Alice.'

Over the next few days, as Polly began to slowly recover her strength, Ruth was never far from her. Her sister was utterly besotted with her tiny niece, possibly because little Alice seemed determined to have a shot at the perfect infant award – sleeping, waking and feeding on cue, and rarely crying. Although alert when awake, the baby was also very peaceful, something Polly found quite amazing in view of the traumatic pregnancy.

Ruth had got upset when Polly had confided her new plans for the baby, which meant her niece would be taken away from the farm. 'But can't you stay here?' she had begged tearfully. 'Luke would be happy wherever you're happy.'

'I wouldn't *be* happy here, Ruth.'

'And you don't want to sell the farm? It *is* yours, Poll. It would mean Luke would never have to go down the pit again and you could buy a nice house—'

'Ruth, face facts.' Polly had cut her sister off before she could continue further. 'The terms of the will state that Alice inherits everything, not me. This place will be held in trust for her until she is older, and that is fine – I don't want it and I couldn't bear to live here, but this way my mother can't throw her weight about and dismiss Betsy or anyone else who crosses her. Everyone's jobs are safe and Croft will carry on managing everything as he has done in the past, with monthly reports to me wherever I live. The bank balance is already rising rapidly, so there'll be no shortage of cash for you and everyone else.'

'I don't care about that. It will just be so awful without you and Alice.'

'But you know how Luke and I are going to be placed,' Polly said gently. 'There'll be little money for anything with what Luke earns. I shall take an allowance from the farm profits for Alice's education and so on, but that's all.'

'But Polly, that's daft, it is really. You said that at the end Frederick was trying to tell you something. It could have been about the will.'

'And it might not. There was all that about a box, but the will was with the solicitor, now wasn't it?'

'Oh, Polly!'

That conversation had been on the afternoon following the day Alice was born, and exactly seven days later, early in the morning of Sunday the twenty-third of June, Polly awoke from a long, involved dream with her heart thudding and her mind crystal clear. Why had she never understood before? she asked herself dazedly. How could she not have realised what Frederick was trying to tell her? But she had been sick in body and mind at the time, just coping one moment to another had been all she could manage, and once he had died and she had found out she was with child everything else had got put to one side.

She climbed carefully out of bed and was almost to the door of her room when she turned back and lifted Alice from her wicker crib. Somehow, with her mother in the mood she had been in since the birth of the child, she didn't want Alice out of her sight. Was she saying she thought her mother would harm her own granddaughter? she asked herself as she padded silently across to the door. She didn't know and she didn't really want to think about it; she just knew she had to keep the baby with her at all times until she was out of this place. And that couldn't come soon enough for her.

Ruth was lying on top of the covers on her bed in her lawn nightdress, one arm flung across her face. She was sleeping peacefully until Polly gently touched her arm, whereupon her sister gave an almighty start that frightened them both. 'Polly?' Ruth peered at her in the burgeoning light, sitting up in bed with one hand to her racing heart. 'What are you doing out of bed? You know what the midwife said.' And then, as a thought occurred to her, 'Is Alice all right?' she asked urgently.

303

'Aye, yes, and keep your voice down or you'll wake her and she'll start bawling. I just want to talk to you.'

'*Now?*' Ruth's tone made it clear how she viewed the early-morning visit. 'Polly, you shouldn't be up. The midwife said—'

'Fiddle the midwife.' Polly sat down on the coverlet with Alice cradled in her arms. 'Look, it's just come to me – don't ask me why – but I think I know what Frederick was trying to say when he was dying. I came in one day unexpectedly and thought he'd fallen out of bed, but I think he was trying to get to the box he spoke of. The rug by the side of the bed was moved and there was a broken floorboard; I think it's under there, the box.'

'Oh, Poll.' Ruth's voice was soft now, with a touch of deference in its quietness. 'You think he'd got a bit put away?'

'He didn't like banks. He told me that before we were married. Only money you could see in your hand meant anything, he said, and land, and bricks and mortar. And there was hardly anything in his bank account, you know that, and just in the last months it's doubled. He only ever banked a fraction of the profits, Ruth. I'm sure of it.'

'What are we going to do?'

'Get Mother out of that room and have a look,' Polly said grimly. 'Now, today.'

'You don't think she's found it?'

The same thought had occurred to Polly and it made her feel sick. 'I hope not, but there's only one way to find out.' The blood was singing through Polly's veins and she felt so excited she didn't know how to contain herself. 'Look, we're going to need Betsy's help, so go and have a word with her and Emily now. Tell her to say she noticed one of the cats in Mother's room and she thinks it's infested with fleas, and she'll strip the bed and scrub the floorboards – something like that. With this hot weather it needs to be done straightaway, before the room's alive. You know what Mother is like over fleas and bed bugs and the like.'

'All right.' Ruth was out of bed in a twinkling, returning a few minutes later as Polly was feeding her daughter. 'It's all arranged,' she said with a high, nervous giggle. 'Oh, Poll.'

Betsy had no trouble at all in persuading Hilda out of the suite of rooms and down to the sitting room once she'd mentioned the dreaded word 'infestation'. Since the typhoid, Hilda had become positively paranoid about cleanliness – insisting all water and milk was boiled, washing her hands umpteen times a day and taking all matters of a sanitary nature to excess.

Once the sitting room door had closed behind her mother and Emily was posted as lookout at the top of the landing, Ruth went into Polly's room, where her sister was lying in bed, the bassinet to the side of it.

Polly's cheeks were flushed with their first real colour since the exhausting confinement, and as Ruth nodded across at the bright blue eyes, Polly slid quickly out of bed, gathering Alice to her a moment later. The three hours which had elapsed since the women had made their plans had seemed like three days, but now the moment was here, Polly was suddenly scared to death. What if she was wrong? What if Frederick hadn't been trying to let her know about some secret hoard he'd hidden away? He had always insisted that while the farm made little actual profit it enabled family and workers alike to live very well, and that was enough, but she didn't believe that any more, not after the steady profit of the last months. No, she was right about the box, she knew she was. Pray God her mother hadn't found it first.

They flitted across the landing and into the extended part of the house like will o' the wisps, to find that Betsy had already stripped the bed and hung the mattress out of the window. 'Just in case she comes back for anythin',' Betsy whispered as Ruth closed the door behind them. Polly's legs were shaking and she sat on one of the easy chairs Betsy drew forward for her before pulling the heavy, thick rug to one side. They all stared down at the innocuous floorboards, the one with the great chip out of it riveting their gaze.

'By, lass, I don't mind tellin' you I've had the skitters since Ruth come in an' woke us up this mornin',' Betsy murmured softly, 'but it all fits, you know. Croft's said many a time on the quiet he reckons the master's got a bit salted away. He's not as daft as he looks, Croft.'

'Go on, Betsy. Try and lift it up,' Polly said quietly, hugging the sleeping baby against her swollen breasts. Alice was due for a feed, and in spite of the fact that Polly was still bleeding quite heavily and felt incredibly tired, she was producing an abundance of milk, which Alice took with relish. 'But quietly, mind,' she warned. 'Mother's got ears like cuddy-lugs.'

The floorboard took a little prising, but then it was up, and the three women peered into the hole. There it was, a large tin box – too large to extract through the space.

'Perhaps the other floorboards lift away now?' Polly whispered softly. They did, and then Betsy and Ruth between them heaved the box on to the bedroom floor. Polly handed Alice to Ruth, then knelt down on the floor and reached out a hand to lift the lid of the box. There were numerous little cloth bags inside, all secured with string, perhaps two dozen or more, along with some documents tied with faded ribbon. Polly opened one and then tipped the shining contents into her lap. Some fifty or so gold sovereigns clinked a sound that was sweeter than any music.

'Eee, lass, lass.' Betsy's round eyes nearly popped out of her head. 'The crafty old so-an'-so; who'd have thought it?'

'Oh, Polly, you were right, you were right.' Ruth's body had gone limp; only her arms remained fixed round the tiniest member of the quartet, who was blissfully unaware of the drama being enacted in front of her.

Polly herself said nothing, just stared at the rows and rows of neat little bags as her heart thudded and reverberated against her ribcage. There was a fortune here, a small fortune. Years and years and years of careful saving, possibly begun by Frederick's father before him. And he had wanted her to have it at the end, he had. She was his legal wife, and although when she had married him she hadn't thought about inheriting his wealth, the farm would have been hers but for her mother's scheming.

She picked up the bundle of documents and untied them. There were his father's two marriage certificates and what looked a couple of Sunday school awards for Frederick, along with three documents relating to the purchase of land as the farm had grown. One was in Frederick's father's time, another related to the old Nicholson property Frederick had acquired, and the third – the third was an independent summary of what her grandfather's farm had been worth when Frederick had taken it over. And it was more, much more, than Frederick had led them to believe.

Polly sat back on her heels, stunned. He had cheated them, Frederick had cheated her grandparents out of their rightful due. Her grandda and gran could have sold the farm and had plenty of money to pay off their debts and buy a little house somewhere, perhaps with a garden where they could have kept a goat and a few chickens. Who had he bribed to keep quiet? And how could he? How could he have done that to two old people who had never wished him a day's harm in their lives?

'What is it, lass? What's the matter?' As Betsy's anxious voice penetrated her stupor, Polly silently took Alice from Ruth. She passed her sister the document, and then, as Ruth scanned the written page, explained to both of the women what it meant.

'The mean old blighter!' Betsy's head wagged with indignation. 'But I wouldn't put anythin' past him now, lass. All this money up here an' all any of the workers got at Christmas was a few bits of groceries. They improved once you come, I can tell you! By, you live an' learn, you do straight.'

Aye, you lived and learned all right. Polly thought back again to the horror of her wedding night, the brutality and degradation she'd suffered and the misery that had unfolded from that time. Of the numerous slurs and insults she'd endured in this house, and the constant fight she had engaged in to hold her head up high and not be browbeaten either by circumstances or by her husband and her mother. And Arnold, the vicious lies he had spread about her, the stain he had attempted to smear on her reputation – him, the lowest, the most base of individuals. Oh, you lived and learned all right.

306

She breathed in deeply, her head rising and her deep blue eyes looking round the room as she exhaled. But the cruel and the depraved and the liars didn't always win. She thought of Luke, how he had been the night before when he had visited the farm, and the sweet, tender and wonderful things he had said to her, things she would carry in her heart to her dying day. And she glanced down at her precious daughter, at the blessing which had been so unexpected and was now so treasured. And then her gaze took in Ruth and Betsy, their faces concerned for her because of their love. Real love. She was so rich. Forget this box and all it held; she had been rich beyond measure before this.

'Can you carry the box into my room?' she asked Betsy and Ruth. 'I'll check with Emily that the coast is clear first.'

'Eee, don't you worry, lass, I'll take it,' Betsy said as Ruth went to help her. 'Weighs nowt more than half a sack of spuds or a basket of wet washin' fresh from the mangle.'

There was only dappled sunlight on the landing besides Emily, and once they were all ensconced in Polly's room, and Polly was sitting feeding Alice, Betsy pushed the box under the bed and Ruth covered it with a blanket just to be sure, although it was not visible to anyone standing in the room.

'I'll go an' finish in your mam's room, lass, an' then I'll be back,' Betsy said. 'Don't want her nosin' about before we're straight. Come on, Emily.'

'And I'll go down and make a cup of tea for us all for when you've finished,' Ruth put in swiftly. 'I'll bring it up here with that seed cake you made yesterday, Betsy, and we'll have a little celebration.'

They all beamed at her as they filed out, and Polly beamed back. Aye, she was rich all right, and she wanted Alice to grow up surrounded by all this love, and why not? Aye, why not indeed? she thought as Alice continued to suckle and the vista beyond the window was bathed in mellow golden sunlight. She could make this money work for them, for them all. Luke could leave the pit for good, and it would enable him to follow the desire of his heart and get involved in local politics to begin with. He could educate himself further, do whatever was necessary, and then . . . who knew? The sky was the limit. Money opened doors. It wasn't right maybe, but that was the way of the world, and the social reforms that Luke and others were already working and fighting for might come to pass all the quicker.

She and Luke could buy a nice house, a big house, but not just for themselves. Ruth could live with them, Betsy and Emily too, and she and the three other women could run the place as a boarding house to begin with – she had had practice enough back on her grandda's farm. And then, once Luke was established and if things turned out well, they could maybe think about taking in non-paying guests – a sort of halfway house for needy or destitute families, perhaps? There was a need, a desperate need for such places. She didn't quite know how the mechanics of such an operation would work, but all that could be sorted out later – for the moment, it was enough that it could happen. And it could, oh, it could.

A few minutes later the others came bustling back and Polly reflected that her mother couldn't fail to be suspicious of the glow on their faces if she saw them. All three women were positively bursting with excitement.

'You know what this means, don't you?' Polly said once they were drinking tea and eating cake. 'We're all free of the farm and the past – we can make our own life, all of us, if we want to.'

'I'm not with you, lass,' Betsy said bemusedly.

'Oh yes you are, Betsy.' And now Polly's face was alight too. 'You're with me all right, the same as Ruth and Emily are. If you want to you can leave here, and soon, as quickly as I can arrange things.'

'Have you gone doolally, lass?'

'Probably, but it feels wonderful!'

'Polly, what exactly are you saying?' Ruth asked softly.

She quickly outlined her thoughts to them, and as their mouths dropped open, one by one, it was truly comical. 'We can set the boarding house up as a business between us all,' Polly said eagerly, 'and we'll have it stated in writing legally by Mr Johnson. Then any profits – as well as the hard work and worry a business entails – can be shared by us all.'

'I don't know what to say, lass.' Betsy looked to be near tears, and then she dug Emily in the ribs as she added, her voice stronger, 'An' stop your blubbin', you! You oughta be down on your knees thankin' God for today, not bawlin' your eyes out.'

'Do you think Luke will agree to you sharing with us?' Ruth asked quietly.

'Oh, yes.'

'He might not. He might think you're being far too generous.'

'Not Luke,' Polly said positively. 'He's the only man I know who has always put his money where his mouth is. He's a man for the people, Ruth, that's the only way I can explain it. He'll make a difference, I know he will, and I wouldn't be surprised if he's a Member of Parliament one day. Times are changing, and fast; you ought to hear him talk the last few nights. He's . . . he's wonderful.'

'When are you going to tell him?'

'Now, today. I want you to help me get Alice dressed and ready for a drive, and I'm going to pack enough to tide us over until I can get everything I need picked up.' And to the chorus of protest that immediately ensued, Polly added, 'I can't stay here another day,' in a tone of voice that quietened the others.

308

'But, lass, you're not well enough,' said Betsy soberly.

'Ruth will come with me.' Polly stretched out her hand to her sister, and as Ruth clasped it, Polly said, 'We'll stay in town somewhere, we're not exactly short of cash,' and they both laughed with the shrillness of nervous excitement. 'And then once everything is ready, we'll send for you and Emily.'

'But you shouldn't be out of bed for another two weeks!'

'I don't think I've ever done what I was told to do, Betsy, just what I felt I had to,' Polly said with a big grin. 'And I need to do this. I . . . I have to get away from my mother.' And here the smile faded. 'She means Alice harm, I can feel it in my bones.'

Betsy would have liked to reassure Polly she was merely in the grip of a first rush of fiercely protective maternal love, but in all honesty she could not. Hilda had all the natural motherly instincts of a spitting cobra, and was the reason Betsy herself had slept with one ear cocked since the little one had been born. She would never forget the wild exultation on Hilda's face when Polly had gone into premature labour, or the almost insane rage when she had discovered the child was alive. Her own granddaughter! She felt a little shiver slither down her spine. Perhaps it *was* best Polly left today, even though she was still middling.

When Emily went to find Croft in order that the horse and cart – the trap not being large enough to accommodate both women and the luggage they would take – could be harnessed, she found he was dealing with one of the large beasts down in the far field, and so it was into the afternoon before they were ready. Hilda had been back in her own quarters since mid morning, and whilst the house was quiet, Betsy had helped Ruth pack a large trunk with the women's clothing and night attire – the contents of the tin box now secure under several pairs of Ruth's calico drawers and petticoats – along with a small portmanteau holding items for Alice.

It was just touching three o'clock when Polly, feeling a little shaky but determined to leave, began to descend the staircase, Ruth a step or so behind her with Alice in her arms, and Betsy and Emily carrying the trunk between them with the portmanteau tucked under Betsy's other arm.

Polly had just reached the foot of the stairs when the door of the sitting room opened and Hilda stood framed on the threshold. Polly heard her sister gasp, but she herself was not surprised. This confrontation had had to come; whether by accident or when Hilda had seen them leave from her vantage point in the rooms overlooking the front garden and farmyard.

'Aha! I knew something was going on.' Hilda advanced on Polly, one arm pointing in a theatrical gesture. 'Those two' – here she waved a disparaging hand at Betsy and Emily – 'are as transparent as glass.'

'They clearly haven't got your gift of duplicity, Mother.' As Polly faced this woman who had, in one way or another, been the bane of her life ever since she could remember, she felt none of the turmoil normally associated with a head-to-head encounter with her mother. Hilda's vindictiveness regarding Luke, her desire to incriminate him, had finally cut the emotional umbilical cord, and it had happened that day Polly had discovered her mother's scheming to have Luke arrested. There was nothing left any more.

'And what does that mean?'

'You knew your stepbrother cheated my grandparents out of what was rightfully theirs, didn't you?' Polly said steadily. And as her mother's face betrayed her guilt, Polly added quietly, 'I pray to God there is no part of you in me. I'm leaving, Mother, and Ruth is coming with me. You can call this your home for as long as you live, and I hope playing the mistress brings you pleasure, because that is the only pleasure you will know. There will be no children or grandchildren to alleviate your isolation, no one to love you. Perhaps I ought to feel sorry for you, but in all truthfulness I don't.'

'You're leaving?' Her mother's eyes had opened wide. Whatever she had been expecting, it clearly wasn't this latest development. 'But . . . the farm . . .'

'Croft will take care of the running of the farm; he's been doing it for years anyway whilst Frederick played the gentleman at his club and with his hunt cronies.'

'Croft!' It was a snort. 'You're mad, girl! Croft's not capable—'

'Croft is extremely capable,' Polly interrupted evenly, 'and I shall be sending a tutor to the farm every week for the foreseeable future to teach him the elementaries regarding accounts and such. Frederick believed in keeping his workers illiterate where he could; I do not. Croft knows his letters but he needs further instruction, and I intend to see that he – and any of the others who wish to avail themselves of the opportunity – receive it. Croft will report to me on a monthly basis until Alice reaches the age of twenty-one and is able to decide whether she wishes to run the farm herself or sell it. Should anything happen to me before then, Ruth will assume responsibility.'

'You can't do this!'

'Oh yes I can, Mother.' Hilda was now poised in the doorway as though she was going to fly at her again, but strangely Polly knew no fear or even apprehension. This was a bitter, cruel-natured woman and she was never going to let her intimidate her again. 'The profits from the farm will be ploughed back into improving conditions, by the way, the first stage of that being new accommodation for Croft and the others.'

The glare Hilda was levelling at her daughter should have killed Polly on the spot, and Polly was aware of the three women behind

310

her moving protectively round her in a little cluster as her mother hissed, 'And they say whoring doesn't pay! By, you could teach some of them sorts down by the dockside a thing or two. You're scum, girl, scum – like your father before you. And I shall pray to God that He'll bring you to an end like Henry's, dangling on the end of a rope with your eyes bulging and your tongue hanging out. You and your flyblow with you.'

As Betsy went to spring towards Hilda, Polly stopped her with the flat of her hand without taking her eyes off the contorted face of the woman in front of her. 'My daughter and I will live long and contented lives with the man I love,' she said, unable to keep the slight tremor her mother's venom had produced out of her voice, although her head was high and her back was straight. 'And we'll be surrounded by family and friends.'

'In a miner's cottage? Huh!' Hilda ground out through clenched teeth. 'More fool you. You'll soon be tired of him, girl.'

'Goodbye, Mother.' She would never set foot in this place again. Let Alice do what she wanted with it when she was of an age to come into her inheritance, but she would never come back to Stone Farm, Polly thought, as she turned and walked out of the front door, Ruth just behind her and Betsy and Emily making up the rear.

Croft was waiting at the entrance to the farmyard, and he came hurrying up to them, helping her over the cobbles and up into the seat at the front of the cart before he did the same with Ruth and Alice, and then placed the trunk and portmanteau in the back of it.

'It will just be a few weeks till I find the right place.' Polly was bending down to Betsy, who had tears rolling down her face now. 'And then we'll all be together for good.'

'God bless you, lass. God bless you.'

And then the horse was trotting off and Polly straightened in the seat, breathing deeply of the clean summer air as she smiled at Ruth. *She had done it.* She was leaving. Going to a new life, a new beginning.

And then she saw him. Walking down the stony path towards them. A tall, dark figure with his cloth jacket slung over his shoulder and his shirt sleeves rolled up in the brilliant sunshine.

'Luke . . .' His name was a whisper on the soft summer breeze, and then, more strongly, 'Luke, oh, Luke.'

She told Croft to stop the horse and was down from the seat before he could help her, and then she was running and stumbling, and Luke – after one short moment of surprise – was running towards her too, his face expressing concern.

Down the stony path she flew, her heart singing, and as she got nearer, the concern on his face was replaced by anticipation as he saw her glowing countenance. She ran straight into his arms and he lifted her off her feet for a second before saying, 'What is it? What's

311

happened? I was on the early shift today so I thought I'd surprise you,' before he kissed her, careless of the onlookers in the cart.

'I've got so much to tell you, but I was coming to you,' she said breathlessly as he raised his face from hers, her straw bonnet hanging on the back of her neck by its ribbons round her chin and her russet hair tumbling about her pink cheeks. 'Me and Alice and Ruth, and later there'll be Betsy and Emily too.'

He blinked and then laughed, his head going back as he said, 'Never one to do things by halves, not my Polly Farrow! Not my love.'

'You don't mind?'

'Mind?' He looked down into her azure eyes, stroking back the curls from her forehead as he said, 'Sweetheart, I'd take the whole world on if it meant I'd have you too. We'll manage, my love. Somehow we'll manage.'

She thought of the little bags lying secure in their hidey-hole in the trunk. They wouldn't have to manage, but that explanation could come later. For now it was enough that he had come for her, that he loved her, that she was his.

'There's not another like you in the whole wide world, you know that, don't you?' Luke whispered lovingly. 'But are you sure you want to do this today, so soon after having Alice? Are you sure you don't want to stay at home a few days more?'

She felt his strong arms around her, her hands resting on the sun-warmed rough cloth of his shirt, through which she could feel the steady beat of his heart, and the past with all its demons melted away. She raised her face to his, her mouth seeking his lips as she whispered, 'I *am* home.'